IN THE GRAVEYARD

"No, Steve! Get off him!"

I turned my attention away only an instant to see Cat at the top of the bank, baby-white hair wild in the wind. It was only an instant, but when I looked back, Nicholas was gone. There was still something between my straddled legs, something beneath my grasping hands, but it wasn't Nicholas. It wasn't even human.

The light was not good, all shadow and shades of moss and earth tones. The thing beneath me was reptilian, canine, obscenely anthropoid—a combination of species so grossly mutated, one to the other, that my brain refused to comprehend the atrocity, the abnormality, the utter impossibility of what I was seeing.

Michael C. Norton

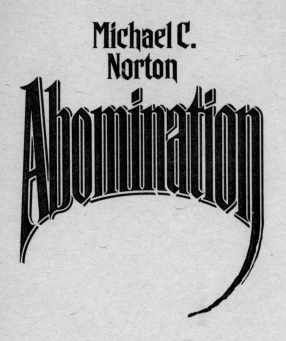

Abomination

LEISURE BOOKS ✥ NEW YORK CITY

A LEISURE BOOK

Published by

Dorchester Publishing Co., Inc.
6 East 39th Street
New York, NY 10016

Printed in the United States of America

Evil exists in the world, and things supernatural do happen. Obsession is the root of all things evil. Obsession—and therefore, by definition, evil—has haunted my life. This is my story.

1

I was born in 1947, the autumn of the year. The Big One, WW II, was over, the Bomb a reality—just ask the wretched survivors of Nagasaki and Hiroshima. Ask the crew of the Enola Gay. The Bomb was not a reality to me, a child in the Heartland of Mid-America. Reality, what it is, has always eluded me. I preferred fantasy.

It was a golden time, the time of my youth. A time when prosperity became possible even for small farming communities like Greenriver, Michigan. The few small factories were retooling from war materiel on Uncle Sam's post-war bucks—bucks that stopped with Harry S. Truman, started in the Treasury Building, went through innumerable give-away committees, and drifted across the land freely, like leaflets dumped from a plane.

Certain Greenriver families had grown fat during the war with government contracts, and after the war with plant retooling allowances and grain subsidies, they grew fatter. There were plenty of jobs for Greenriver natives, but there was nothing special about the little town to draw in newcomers and spur population growth. We baby-boomer kids were the only area of increase in Greenriver's demographics.

Greenriver's main street was roughly three blocks of stores flanked by gas stations on both ends of town. Entering from the south, on the road that came up arrow-straight from Indiana five miles away, visitors were forced right through Greenriver's business district in order to cross the river's roughly north-to-south flow at that particular bend. The bridge over the Green River, the muddy brown sluggish water flow for which the town was named, was a WPA concrete construction with a low archway over its western end. Inscribed on the arch in modified Old English script was the town's name, in case anyone who lived there ever forgot. It certainly wasn't there to wow the tourist trade. Greenriver was on the beaten path to nowhere.

Main Street—that's what it was called—was east of the bridge, the first of the gas stations on the right, the city power plant and water tower on the left. The VFW built a pretty little meeting hall up on the hill to the right, above the Super Par station in early '46.

There were some houses, both left and right, the lumber yard smelling of sweet pine pitch by the railroad tracks, and the tiny depot, also a WPA project. Then visitors to our little burg would be in the downtown district. In a place the size of Greenriver, the terms downtown and uptown were interchangeable. Just one more reason we small town folk sound like such hicks in the big city when we open our mouths.

Beyond the depot, at the beginnings of downtown, a white Sinclair station stood on the right, the Greenriver Gazette building on the left. The Carnegie library was on the next short block, kitty-corner across from the two-story Monkey Wards. The Wards and J.C. Penney both had high ceilings and a mezzanine floor where kids could stand, heads pressed between bannister uprights staring out over the merchandise and people below, fighting the urge to spit, while their moms tried on the latest middle class fashions.

On down the street crouched a few one-storey stores: a Western Auto smelling of new tires and factory-oiled tools, and a McClellan's five and ten, whose smells were myriad. There was the rather musty smell of the store itself—old, with slightly bowing wooden tongue-and-groove floors and the oily smell of freshly roasted nuts from the Kars display and the rich odor of the bins of Brach's chocolate stars, peanut clusters, and bridge mix. The clerks all seemed to be mummified old ladies who never died. When I was a tot, they frightened the hell out of me with their stoop-shouldered walk and funereal purple-black dresses trimmed with yellowed lace. I never met anyone from my generation who knew these ladies' names or where they lived or had acquaintance with anyone related to them.

Greenriver had one movie theatre, the Strand, though once in a while older residents would speak of the Roxy, a smaller theatre that used to be where Vito's Sweet Shop now stood.

Main Street ran up to a town circle, a small green area with a white peak-roofed gazebo surrounded by pansy beds, then shot out of town, arrow-straight, to the north. There were Walgreen's and Rexall drug stores near the town circle. In the first you could get the thickest chocolate shakes in the world, and in the latter you could enjoy bone-chilling air conditioning on Michigan's muggy hot July and August days, sipping a Coke with mounds of crushed ice from a glass making sweat rings on tables topped with heavy cool black slabs of real Italian marble.

A Shell station and a Phillips 66 station would bid the visitor farewell on that gray band of road that knifed between the endless fields of summer corn immediately beyond the gas stations' black-tropped drives.

We Daltons—Ed and Blanche, my parents, big brother Brian and me, Steve—lived on Harrison Street —south on Harrison off Main, a turn at the Sinclair station and down three maple-shaded blocks to the big square frame house painted Dutch blue. The railroad tracks ran about one hundred yards from our back door, and the white finger of the grain elevator was just the other side of the tracks. Some of my earliest memories are of those endlessly long freight trains clackety-clacking past our back yard. I remember the engines looked immense, like fierce yoked beasts waiting for a chance to break free and jump those tracks. My mother always said

7

when the fast ones flew by at night that some time one would come through too fast, jump the rails and come plowing right through our house, killing us all in our beds. You have to wonder some times why the hell parents say things like that in front of little kids. I had visions of the black screaming diesel hulks pointed surely as a hunter's shot at our house, wheels cutting trenches in the lawn, through the flower beds heavy with night moisture, howling that mournful call to death as they slammed through the wood of our house and claimed our lives.

Our house was a good strong one, but being wood frame, lathe and plaster it had almost no insulation. Air was the great insulator when it had been built. In the summer we roasted, sleeping with our heads literally hanging out screened windows, counting cicadae thrums until hypnotized into sleep despite the heat—and in winter we froze. Dad would stoke hell out of the old coal furnace, last thing at night and first thing in the morning.

Winter mornings would find Mom busy over breakfast in the kitchen, standing beside the gas stove because the oven was on and its door open to help heat the room. Brian and I would huddle together over the big kitchen register, a shared blanket over our shoulders like waifs out of Dickens. The pipes would vibrate under our feet as Dad stoked hell out of the furnace below, cussing the fire, trying to stretch the supply of coal and still keep his family warm.

Life seemed so simple for Brian and myself as kids in Greenriver. We were well-fed and cared for, and found it difficult to even remotely understand when our parents muttered at each other about food bills or buying bituminous coal instead of anthricite, because the softer coal was cheaper. General Eisenhower had become president and all was right with the world, as far as we could see. We had our friends—well, Brian had his and I had mine, since he was six years older. Our days all seemed filled with the heady luxury of youth combined with time.

My best friends were Billy and Catherine Charlene St. Charles. I met them quite by accident one day, when I was eight going on thirty. I had an active imagination, and my favorite thing to imagine was that I was Richard Diamond, as portrayed by David Janssen on TV. I had my Bulldog cap gun—two molded pieces of white metal bolted together, the material so brittle and the alloy so cheap that if you dropped the gun on concrete, you became the instant owner of two guns.

My penchant for detective drama, I suppose, made me assume the attitude of cynical superiority of the urban sophisticate, though in reality I remained the naive small town boy I had been born. It was true then, and it's true even now.

That fateful high summer day when I first met Billy and Catherine Charlene St. Charles, my superior attitude was to earn me both my first black eye and my two closest friends for the next few years of my life. And more. So much more.

I was standing in front of our house on Harrison Street, a candy cigarette dangling from my lips, the cardboard pack of Kools spelled with a "C" in my shirt pocket. I had the Bulldog cap pistol in my pants pocket. I imagined a jauntily angled pork-pie hat on my head and was trying desperately to think of my Western Flyer bicycle as a shiny new '55 Cadillac convertible. Billy St. Charles wheeled up on a black English three-speed, his younger sister behind him on a weaving rusty girl's twenty-inch with bent and broken spokes protruding like porcupine spines in all directions out from her wheels.

"Hey," Billy shouted, using his caliper brakes to halt the snazzy bike on a dime before me. "What you got in your mouth, kid?"

It's obvious, I thought, it's a cigarette. I never thought of them as candy. Would David Janssen suck a candy cigarette?

"Move along, sonny," I said in my best whisky-voiced Richard Diamond tone.

9

Billy's face clouded over. It was a phenomenon I would come to recognize as something genetic with all the St. Charles family.

"Hey, squirt, don't get smart. Smoking ain't good for you, ya know." He sniggered to himself. He was a lot bigger than me. I was a pretty scrawny kid at eight, and he was big—husky bordering on chunky—for ten. The girl straddled the center of her bike, feet planted wide apart, watching the unfolding scene like a thriller movie, her pink full-lipped mouth open in a slack "O" of riveted interest.

As I looked from one to the other, it never struck me they were brother and sister. There was no family resemblance whatsoever. He was big, as I have noted, and edging into fat, with long rather greasy-looking brownish-red hair. His face was an average face for a boy of ten—nothing to draw particular attention to him in a crowd, other than a million freckles that dotted his face and arms like brown ink spatters.

The girl was short for her age (which, with the intuitive sense of the very young, I pegged immediately as near my own but a tad younger), small-boned but sturdy-looking. She had smooth creamy white skin, like French vanilla ice cream, and a wild wind-tossed mane of wispy hair, the color of pure white summer clouds framing her small and angelic face. Her lips were candy-pink and full, the upper one tipped up a bit in the center, looking babyish. Her nose was upturned and small with delicate almost transparent nostrils. Her eyes were enormous and shone like China-blue enamel out from copious featherings of sun-bleached long eyelashes. I felt an unaccountable stirring when I looked at her.

I pulled out the Bulldog pistol, playing my role to the maximum. "Ya bother me, sonny. Be a good boy and move along," I said, out of the corner of my mouth. The candy cigarette dangling from the other corner flapped as I talked. I spun the pistol on my finger, cocked my head to the side and gave him my best squint-eyed stare. Richard Diamond could not have done better.

Billy St. Charles laughed. He got off his shiny black English three-speed, put down the kickstand with a slow assured movement, walked over to me and broke my candy cigarette in half while it was still in my mouth. Next, he relieved me of my cap pistol and tossed it over his shoulder like a wad of paper for the trash. I watched as it hit the sidewalk and split in two. He fished into my shirt pocket and caught the pack of candy cigarettes.

"Thanks, skinny. I'll take these. Like I say, smokin' is bad for ya. 'Sides, you're way too young." That said, he pushed me so I staggered back, fell, and sat down hard on my rump. Then he slowly, purposefully got back on his three-speed and pedaled away laughing.

His sister, white clouds of hair wisping in the gentle summer breeze that seemed suddenly heavy and oppressive to me, walked her bike up to me.

"Jeez, I'm sorry," she mumbled in a constricted little voice. "My brother can be sort of a bully sometimes."

"Bully?" I said from my perspective on the ground. "He's an A-hole!" I had heard brother Brian use that term when talking to his friends. Brian was fifteen and he knew what such terms meant. I didn't. I only knew it meant something awful.

Apparently Catherine Charlene St. Charles knew, also. Without saying a word, one of her tiny balled-up fists round-housed right into my eye.

"I'm sorry Billy took your candy, but you don't go callin' him no A-hole," she said, and pedaled off, bike fenders clanking like battle armor.

I was sitting there on the cool shaded grass, both hands pressed hard over the injured eye, trying my damnedest not to cry, when I heard the easily recognizable guffaws of laughter coming from my brother Brian's upstairs bedroom window.

"Hey, champ," he laughed, pressing his crew cut head against the window screen, making the mesh bow out, "I saw it all. You sure gave them what for."

"You shut up, Bry. I'll get 'em . . . I'll get back at 'em!" It occurred to me that I might have some trouble

11

there because I had no idea who they were. I had never seen either of them before in my life. But Brian would know. I'd have to swallow my tough-guy pride and ask him.

"Uh . . . do you know where they live?"

"Sure, killer. Everybody does. That's Billy and Catherine St. Charles. They live over on Willow . . . by the cemetery." He let out a passable imitation of a Boris Karloff evil laugh. The name rang a bell with me. Of course Brian would know all about them. He dated their older sister Jennifer off and on.

I probably wasn't supposed to know that Brian went out with Jennifer St. Charles, because Mom said he wasn't supposed to go out with her. Mom said that at fifteen, which both Brian and Jennifer were, children should still be children and not start worrying about such foolishness as dating. Besides, I once heard her say to Dad that Jennifer St. Charles was nothing but poor trash and probably just as big a floozy as her mother. I knew no more what a floozy was than I did an A-hole, but I figured they meant pretty much the same thing. At least, I surmised, they were both nasty things to call people. In a small town, as far as the older generation is concerned, children are what their parents are perceived to be.

I sat there on the cool grass of our front lawn on Harrison Street, Brian's laughter stinging in my ears, tears burning my eyes, and vowed to get even.

The following day, I got up early and headed out on my bike, shunning even my usual breakfast of Sugar Jets. I wasn't supposed to cross Poplar Street—my mother saw it as a bustling thoroughfare—but I had to get to the cemetery.

Going to the cemetery didn't bother me. I knew cemeteries were supposed to be scary places for little kids, and for that reason alone, I did not fear them. Inforced individualism was a resolve I adopted early on.

There was a cooling morning summer breeze wafting

12

across dew-heavy grass when I hid my bike behind a huge granite gravestone with the name Moorehead on it. I remember the smell of the air—a heady odor of cleanliness that made the lungs expand to take in as much as possible at one breath.

I didn't have a firm plan in mind. I only knew I had to get even at the boy named Billy for his theft and at the girl named Catherine for her surprise sucker-punch. I told myself if I had ever had an inkling she was going to deck me, I could have dodged, avoiding the shiner that lit up my left eye like purple neon.

Moving up like a commando scoping out the enemy pillbox, I worked toward the house on the edge of the cemetery. It was a modest Cape Cod in its better days, whenever that may have been, and just a few degrees on the good side of being an absolute dump on that day, when first I saw it. Shake shingles dripped off the roof like rain, and a blood red paint peeled from its wooden skin, showing black weathered wood beneath. Back steps were missing entirely, and when I angled around to the front, the wrought iron railing by the front steps hung limply to one side like a broken arm. Windows were cracked ruined eyes, hooded by cheap water-stained shades and chintzy dime store curtains. My blood chilled a bit as a chance slant of light and shadow made me think—just for a moment—that the house lived, saw and breathed with the rasping inhalations of a dying consumptive. Thankfully such lines of thought were quickly forgotten when I saw the plumpish bully boy and his cloud-haired sister crash out onto the porch, laughing and tickling at each other, the fragile old wooden screen door blam-blam-blamming behind them.

I was angry all over again, seeing them. I couldn't hear their words from where I stood, artfully concealed in the vegetation, but I could see an abrupt change in the girl's mood. Her face became serious as she adopted a listening attitude. Then she bent toward her brother, her mouth forming a few terse words, and they were both off the porch, leaping the steps entirely, heading off in opposite directions. Some logical sense told me I should follow the boy, but I ignored it and skulked off after the girl.

I had gone no more than ten steps down the hedge-row when something heavy sacked me from behind. I went down like an ill-balanced bag of potatoes, spat dirt out of my mouth and looked up at the dirty tennis-shoed bare legs of the girl.

She was standing straddle-legged before me, hands balled into fists resting imperiously on her hips.

"You here for another black eye, or what?" she asked.

I tried to suck wind for a suitably snotty retort, but the weight on my back that I realized must be her brother would not allow my lungs such luxury. I must have begun to turn blue in the face, because she looked at me rather strangely and told her brother to let me up.

"Aw, okay," he said, and suddenly I could breathe again.

"You stole my cigarettes," I said, trying not to cry. He shrugged, while she twisted up her face but remained as mute as her brother.

"You broke my gun," I said, scrambling to my feet, rubbing at my eyes then.

"Billy's sorry," she said.

"Am not," he said defiantly.

"Y . . . you hit me," I said, no longer able to keep the tears, traitorous though they were to my self-image, from rolling down my dirt-caked cheeks.

Her eyes, those enormous China-blue eyes, went all sad like a puppy's.

"Don't cry. I'm awful sorry . . . Jeez, Billy, he's crying."

"Aw, yeah . . . so what?"

"So that's awful. What you did made him cry."

"I can't help it if he's a crybaby."

"Am not!" I maintained through my tears. "You're just a . . . a . . . bully."

"Don't call my brother names, now," the girl warned. "I'm sorry he was bad to you, but if you call

14

him names, I'll slug you again. I promise. Right or wrong, he's my brother and you're not."

"Jeez," the boy named Billy said. "I can slug him myself." He seemed offended that his sister was having all the fun lately in the slugging-strange-kids category.

"You owe me a new gun and a new pack of candy cigarettes," I maintained loudly, choking back the tears and getting mad again, too mad to be frightened by the two to one odds.

"Billy will get you new ones," the girl promised.

"Like fun," he said belligerantly.

"Oh, yes you will. It was wrong. You made him cry." She turned back to me, a sort of soft motherly look in her beautiful hypnotic eyes. "You go back home, boy. Later today, Billy and I will come to your house with what we owe you. We know where you live. Go on home now."

For reasons I will never know, I obeyed, without further words of exchange. I did keep looking back to see if they were laughing at me, though. Failing so miserably at my mission of revenge, I almost felt I had the ridicule coming. They weren't laughing. Billy looked disgusted but resigned, picking bits of greenery from a yew bush; his sister stared after me, the China-blue eyes burning like bits of the sky torn down and set afire and watching me until I was out of sight.

I went back home to wait.

That was a mistake.

Mother saw the black eye for the first time. The day before it hadn't discolored so badly and I had successfully hidden it from her at supper.

When she saw it, I knew what she would say before she said it. It was a familiar lecture for me.

"Fighting? Fighting, Steven? Fighting is abomination before the Lord." Then she would stop, cocking her head to one side, letting her golden blonde hair fall softly so it grazed her shoulders. She would look me in the eye and say, "What is fighting, Steven Dalton?"

"Abomination before the Lord," I would dutifully

repeat. It would do no good. What came next was inevitable.

"Perhaps the Reverend Miles can help you remember."

"No, Mom," I would say. "I'll remember, really." I would have dropped to my knees and pleaded with her, if there had ever been a chance, but there never was. Mother was not openly fanatical about religion, but she held great stock in the Reverend Stoney Miles' ability to lay Satan and Sin to rest. And he did it all through the black-and-white reality of our TV screen.

"You sit in front of that television, young man, while I get your lunch ready. You listen to what the Reverend has to say."

I switched on the old Crosley TV with a trembling hand. My eyes would always shoot to her, to estimate the chance of a reprieve. There was never one forthcoming. I would sit on the sofa as the picture tube warmed up and images became distinct.

The voice was always there first, rattling the TV's little speaker with the intensity of the wrath of the Almighty who spoke through Reverend Stoney, who spoke thorugh our TV.

My mother would then leave the room, satisfied that I would accept the Reverend's words with the open willing heart of the repentant sinner.

She was wrong. She was leaving me alone with a voice and a man, coming at me from the TV screen, that chilled the center of my bones, freezing marrow, and letting my blood turn white. Reverend Stoney Miles knew Sin, knew Satan, and knew the Abomination. The Reverend spoke in capital letters and lived in capital letters. He was raw power—the voice, the sword and the retribution of the Lord. He said so himself.

His voice boomed from the speaker:

" . . . and I sayeth onto YOU, it is A-BOMB-ination to the Lord!" There came a lot of dead air—Reverend Miles' dramatic pause. The Crosley's picture tube was still blank.

"Friends . . ." his voice became as smooth as whipped

ice cream, "some practitioners of so-called religion would have you believe that God Almighty has given onto us free will. And Reverend Stoney Miles says there is no such thing as free will. You've heard me say that very thing many, many times before. And I say it again today." There was another batch of dead air big enough to drive a truck through. This time, though, there was a picture—a round head with black Brylcreamed hair and the indulgent smile of the understanding father looking out over his many troubled, erring children.

"So you ask me, Stoney, how can the big time so-called religious leaders say God hath given us a free will, and you, Stoney, say there is no such thing as free will. Well, friends, the solution is simple. MOST of us are born unto God. We are God's children. Oh, we have little sins, and yes, even a little sin is a thing of pain to our Lord. But if we repent our little sins, the Lord will forgive us them. MOST of us never have to worry about a free will choice between God and Satan. We are born onto him. We repent our sins. We go to our reward when we die.

"So you say onto me, Reverend Stoney, if this is true, why do I need YOU, Reverend Stoney, to save me? Reverend Stoney says, that in the eyes of God, MOST of us are already saved!

"Oh, but you need me, children. You need me to save you from the Others. MOST of us are born onto God. MOST of us are saved in the eyes of our Lord, but the OTHERS, the OTHERS, my friends . . . they are born onto Satan. Yes! Those who lie, those who cheat, those who steal, drink, smoke, fight. Those who play cards for money, those who lust after the FLESH of others . . . those who are OB-Sessed with the FLESH of others, and yes! those OB-Sessed with the pleasure of their OWN flesh . . . they are BORN onto Satan, and are A-BOMB-ination! Yes! And I can save YOU from these OTHERS, who would desTROY us, would TAKE our Lord's Garden from US, and turn it into SOD-dum and Go-MOR-rah!"

"You're lunch is ready, Steven, did you learn anything?" Mother had switched off the Crosley, but I sat there, still staring at the little white dot as it grew smaller and smaller, my fingers digging into the cushions of the couch.

"Y . . . yes, Mother," I managed. I was terrified. I knew why she made me watch Reverend Stoney. It was a warning to me. I was not one of those born unto God —I was one of the Others. She knew it, I knew it, and worst of all, Reverend Stoney knew it.

After lunch, I sat on our screened-in front porch watching the summer world through the micro-grids of the screening. When I did this, everything took on an otherworldly dimension. Sometimes I would do it so long that I would frighten myself, thinking I had forgotten how to get back to my familiar reality. I had just reached this point when I saw movement approaching the porch.

The screen gave a look of reptilian scale to the white-haired girl's skin. It was an unsettling image, and I shook my head to dispell the fantasy. Only opening the screen door and admitting her alleviated it.

"C'mon, Billy," she called. Her brother skulked sulkily up the steps, hands jammed deep in jean pockets. "Give."

"Jeez, alright!" he growled. Out of his pocket came a pack of candy cigarettes. "Here," he said, thrusting them into my hands.

His sister waited. Then she said, "C'mon, Billy, give."

"Oh, horseshit," he moaned. Out of his back jeans pocket he pulled a nickle-plated exact replica of a snub-nosed detective .38. It was one of those expensive cap guns made by the Nichols Company in Texas—the kind with bullets in the chambers that you took apart, put special caps in and loaded like a real gun. I had drooled over them in the dime stores but had never dreamed I would own one.

"Tell him," the girl said, tossing her cloud of white hair.

"This is for you. For the one I broke."

"And . . . ?" she prodded.

"And I'm sorry, okay?" he said it to her, not me.

"I can't take this," I said. "It's . . . it's . . ."

"It's okay, is what it is," he said. Once the gun was actually in my hands and the chance of him keeping it for himself was remote, his surly attitude softened. "You're welcome to it. It's only right."

"It's . . . great," I said. "Wanna play detective? I like to be Richard Diamond," I said, practically stroking the gun like a nervous animal I wished to tame and make my own.

"If I can be the bad guy," he said and smiled. I notice even his lips seemed to have freckles.

"Who can I be?" the girl asked, almost pouting. Her full lips made it an easy attitude for her.

"You can be the telephone girl," I said excitedly.

"Do I look like her?" she asked, warming to the suggestion. "Is she pretty?"

"Heck," I said, "I don't know. They never show nothin' but her legs . . ." Her face clouded over, just as I had seen her brother's do the day before.

"Hey, but she must be," I said hastily. "They always show her legs, and her legs are real pretty."

Her face brightened slowly, her full lips parting to show her slightly too-large front teeth, in a totally beguiling smile. I think I first fell in love at that precise instant.

"What's the telephone girl's name," she asked softly, halfway between coy and embarrassed.

"Sam," I said. "Her name is Sam."

"And I'll be the gangland boss. My name's . . . Spider Callihan." The freckled boy's voice startled me, since I was busy being lost in those enormous China-blue eyes of hers. "I'll run home and get my gun." And he was gone before another word could be uttered, leaving me with his sister, the first member of the opposite sex to attract and frighten me.

"Does your brother always do like you tell him?" It was a pointless question since I really didn't care if he did or didn't. I was merely looking for conversation that would cover my lack of sophistication, would keep me from succumbing to the feeling of vertigo that threatened to topple me to the ground if she pressed any nearer to me.

"Not always," she responded blithely. "But Mom says I have to watch out for the boys, 'cause Jenny won't. Jenny's my big sister," she said proudly.

"I know."

"How do you know?" She cocked her head like an inquisitive puppy.

"My brother Brian goes on dates an' stuff with her."

"Your brother is Brian Dalton?"

"Yeah." It was my turn to sound proud. I don't know why. Brian always treated me like a member of the Unclean Caste. It must be an anomaly of siblings. You can hate them privately, but publicly, they're the greatest—just like this girl had defended her brother by punching me in the eye.

"Jenny thinks he's really neat . . . but I don't get it. I think he's a schmo."

I felt my anger rise, then quickly die. There was no malice in her pretty blue eyes. It was a cool assessment, and one, in essence, I shared. I sided with this stranger against blood. That should have been my first hint that this relationship would lead to nothing good.

"Yeah, I guess. So, you have aother brother?"

Several expressions danced across her face—pain, anger, fear, panic. She settled on a smile under eyes that held no pleasure or humor.

"Yes. His name is Nicholas. Show me your back yard." And she was off, running with grace uncommon to eight year olds, and I followed her, wondering what was going on.

Her brother came back with a gun for each of them. I noticed they were much cheaper toys than the one they had presented to me. Billy's was even taped to hold the barrel up. It didn't seem to bother them, but I felt embarrassed.

We played gangster-detective games of our own

devising. One of us would say, "let's do this,' or 'you say this and I'll say that,' as children will, writing scripts for their play as they go along. Unlike other kids I had played with, their imaginations matched my own in richness and their total immersion in their character roles was thrilling. The world of grown-ups dissolved for several hours that summer day. It ended only with my mother's familiar call: "Time to come in, Steven. The street lights are on."

"Coming," I hollered from the sidewalk in front of Draper's house, three lots away from home. Violet dusk crept thickly about us, turning the hanging bowers of maple leaves ominous with ebony shadows of night-terrors under each bush and around each corner.

The air thickened, too, making breathing difficult, especially after our hours of exertion.

"You really gotta go?" Billy asked.

"Yeah, I guess," I said.

"Tomorrow?" was all Catherine said.

"Yes," I enthused. I hadn't dared believe we could repeat the day we had just experienced.

"Tomorrow," Billy said decisively. "Our place, okay?"

"Sure," I said, then thought of playing into the twilight next to the cemetery. A little shudder began at the base of my skull, traversed my spine and shook itself off my tailbone. "Sure . . . why not?" I asked them and myself simultaneously.

That night in my bed, hanging my head out the window, face pressed to the sagging screen to catch the exciting night breeze, I could see the spot on the side-walk under the low maple branches where we had said good-bye. I imagined I still saw her standing there—small, elfin-lean, with her wild cloud of snowy white hair ruffling in the breeze like the coat of some wild animal. Even in the dark, her China-blue eyes glowed up at me as I lay in my bed. Her candy-pink lips parted slightly, and I was no longer safe there, in my bed, not even under the protection of covers.

Is it possible for an eight year old boy to be obsessed by a member of the opposite sex? I don't know how common it is, or if a psychiatrist would make some federal case out of it. All I know is—I was. The next day could not come fast enough for me.

I couldn't ask my mother's permission to spend the entire day into the evening away from home, because I knew the answer would be no. I was aware I would be punished. I knew the rules and broke them willingly—to be with her.

I found the two of them climbing a gnarled, twisting oak tree, deep in the cemetery, far from any disapproving adults.

"C'mon up," Billy urged. His sister sat far out on a swaying limb, giggling with the excitement of her daring. I scrambled quickly up to where Billy straddled a limb.

"C'mon out here," Catherine gestured to me wildly, nearly losing her grip on the limb.

"It's too small for me. I'll break it."

"C'mon . . . don't be chicken," she teased, smiling.

"Don't go out there," Billy said.

"I won't. She's crazy."

"Yeah, I know." He crossed his eyes, lolled his tongue out of the side of his mouth, and made circles at his temple with his index finger.

She overheard and pouted briefly. Then she laughed and leaned toward me, crooking her finger in a come-hither gesture.

"C'mon, Steve . . . I want you to be with me."

Some nascent chemical stirred in my body, overriding reason, and I began to crawl along the swaying limb.

"Jeez, don't," Billy exclaimed and grabbed for me, but he was too late. I was captivated, like a bird by the cobra's swaying dance.

I was within touching distance of her, when her grip slipped, the limb jerked, and she flew off into blue sky. The ground came up quickly, and she landed with a sickening thud.

Billy and I scrambled down the tree, expecting to have to run for a doctor or an ambulance.

Our fear-blanched faces turned from the base of the tree to see her standing there, brushing twigs from her dirt-stained white shorts.

"Mom's gonna whip me," she said, picking at bits of leaves in her hair.

"Are you okay?" Billy asked, amazed.

She looked at him like he was insane.

"Of course I am, dopey."

"That's thirty-forty feet up," I said, pointing to the still swaying oak limb, fantastically high above us.

She shrugged. "I'm fine."

"Jeez, did ya land on yer feet? Like a cat or somethin'?" Billy laughed.

"We ought to call her Cat," I said. "She must have nine lives." She smiled at me, and she had her new name. Cat!

I stayed with them late that day.

I finally recognized the necessity of leaving when the gravestone shadows melted into solid black on the ground around us.

"I gotta go," I announced. Billy's face looked almost demonical in the deepening violet shadows, and Cat's face shone angelic, hair haloing her perfect baby features.

"No . . . please," she pleaded, tugging at my shirt sleeve.

"Yeah, it's early yet," Billy echoed.

"No, it's not. I'm gonna get skinned." Actually, the punishment I knew was coming was far worse than a simple medieval flaying of flesh.

"Tomorrow, then," Cat pouted, saying the words as a command.

"I'll try."

"See ya," Billy called, already running off into the confused shadows of tombstones and night.

Unexpectedly, Cat pulled herself up to me and brushed her soft full lips against my cheek.

"Bye," she murmured, and was gone, lost there in the

23

cricket-throbbing night the same way as her brother.

"And where have you been, young man?" Her arms were folded across her stomach, her eyes burning in her sallow face. Every moment or so she would unfold her arms to allow a thin blue-veined hand to roughly push a maverick strand of blonde hair off her forehead, only to have it descend again after she had refolded her arms.

"I . . . I was playing at a friend's house and didn't know what time it was," I responded meekly.

"What kind of friends would have a mother that would let you stay out after dark?"

What mother? I thought. I never saw a mother. And dark? What if Mom knew it had been the utter dark of the town cemetery? I did not enlighten her.

"Tomorrow morning, young man, you will listen to the Reverend preach all morning. As for now, you will go to bed without your supper. And there'll be no good-night kiss from me." Her thin lips all but disappeared, so compressed were they with anger. It was with great relief I skirted by her and ran up the stairs to bed. Her eyes always seemed to stab at me when she was angry.

Sleep did not come easily that night, even though a gentle summer rain began about midnight, cooling the old house and inviting slumber. Cat—Catherine Charlene St. Charles—haunted my every thought. And when at last sleep came, only one dream played again and again through my mind: Cat's soft full lips brushing and burning the flesh of my cheek.

Morning came, fresh and washed by the rain. I went to the bathroom, washed my face and dressed in jeans and a T-shirt.

Downstairs, Mother waited with folded arms and the same expression of disgust, anger and firm resolve lining her face. Curiously, it was at that moment I first thought how pretty she must have been, years ago, before she had allowed life's burdens to weigh so heavily upon her.

"Well, young man, it's about time you were getting

24

up. No breakfast for you, until you have listened to the Reverend." The light wood finish of the Crosley gleamed with new polish, and the set was already warmed up. A hard metal stool sat before it. "Have a seat, young man," she said sternly. I complied. She left the room.

" . . . talk this morning of lust," Reverend Stoney Miles intoned. "There are women in this world . . . YOU know the kind I mean . . . women who shake the very foundations of religion when they walk down the streets of our cities, shaking obscene portions of their anaATomy. You DO know what I mean, don't you, friends? They are painted women in tight dresses and high heeled shoes—not worried about home and family, not concerned with the raising up of children, as is God's decree for the women of the world. No! These women seek only personal PLEasure, PERsonal GRAT-ification, and worse! They are the DEVil's tools, and seek to lay RIGHTeous men LOW! Oh, yes!"

The Reverend's face lost its anger and sagged like a basset hound's, filled with pain and remorse at the very thought of what he was about to say.

"And friends . . . these women . . . these women are SOMEone's daughters. Oh, yes! And they may be the daughters of RIGHTeous, GOD-fearing people. But the lust is strong in them, the devil is strong in them, and the demons are upon them!" Reverend Stoney Miles wiped his brow with a handkerchief so white it made the studio cameras broadcast a strobing effect to all the black-and-white TV's tuned into his morning prayer service. "SOMEtimes, the devil comes to them in the innocence of their youth. Yes, sometimes even at the moment of their birth. Old Lucifer KNOWS, friends: old SCRATCH knows which ones will be the most BEAUTiful, knows which ones will TEAR at the souls of RIGHTeous men with their sheer BEAUTy alone. He picks them, marks them as his own, and puts the burning unGODly lust into them. BEWARE, I say onto you! They are the desTRUCTion of our pure and true A-MERican morality."

Reverend Stoney Miles went on in the same vein for what seemed hours—especially to me, sitting there on that hard metal stool, my stomach churning from lack of food and my mind burning with thoughts of Cat and of my unGODly lust for her. In my mind, at that precise moment, there was no doubt—Cat was the tool of old Scratch, and I was lost to her demoniac wiles. Reverend Stoney never did say what his friends out in TV land could do if they were already snared by these succubi. He only railed on and on about the evil of it all, the unGODliness of it all.

Before my mother came and released me from my punishment and led me to a breakfast of eggs and toast, I learned many new linguistic terms—Whores of Babylon, sluts, fornicators, adulterers, Sinful Sisters of Sodom and Giggling Girls of Gomorrah, and many, many more. The Reverend was on a roll. Amazing what the Standards and Practices Board would let air in the name of religion. I owe all my early sexual awareness to the Reverend Stoney Miles. I also owe to him, with peripheral aid from my mother and Greenriver in general, the indelible sense that sex must be dirty to be good. Instead of turning me away from those women in tight dresses and high heeled shoes, the good Reverend had peaked my nascent sexual curiosity. Oh, Mother, oh Reverend: what did you do to me that sunny dew-drenched mud-puddled summer morning in 1954 America?

Not a day passed after that when I did not see Cat for some span of time. I would violate any and every rule or restriction laid down by my mother to do so. Obsession, yes! I had lost—no, had relinquished—all control of my destiny.

2

I was eleven years old and sprouting a few blond silky hairs on my chin and cheeks, hairs that I counted endlessly in the medicine cabinet mirror amid smells of my dad's Old Spice and the antiseptic sharpness of his half-used stiptic pencil. Jerry Lee Lewis ranted "Breathless" on the black bakelite Motorola sitting atop the terry-covered tank of the toilet. Brian would call through the door:

"Steve! What the devil are you doing?"

Older brothers, I would think to myself, and continue counting. Thirteen. Thirteen long downy blond hairs. Beard hairs. When I was old, maybe twenty, I'd have a beard like Steve Reeves had in 'Hercules Unchained.' And muscles like him, too.

"Steve, what in the name of . . ."

"Brian!" Mother would call out. "Leave your brother to his business." The Coasters sang out of the Motorola's speaker: "Yakety-Yak."

I would hear the click of Mother's shoes in the hardwood maple-floored hall.

"But Mom, I got a date . . ."

"You *have* a date." She would pause, waiting.

"I have a date," Brian would mutter dutifully. He knew she would wait forever, if need be, for him to use correct English.

"With whom?"

"Jennifer."

"Jennifer?"

"Yeah. Jennifer St. Charles."

There would be a long silence. I would become so interested in the conversation outside the bathroom door, I'd forget to admire my beard. Mother didn't like

Jennifer. She had grown quite a reputation, based on Greenriver's general disapproval of her mother.

"What kind of a date?"

"Aw, Mom, the usual. Just a date. A movie. Cokes and fries at the candy shop."

"Vito LaRosa's candy shop?"

I could sense Brian squirming on the other side of the thick bathroom door. Mom didn't like Vito's. Vito's had a reputation, too. It had tall dark booths where teenagers could hide puppy love indiscretions, mysterious trysts to most people my age—or my Mother's age. Having an eighteen year old brother, though, I knew the routine: Brian would meet Jennifer St. Charles in a dark back booth at Vito's. They would sit on the same bench in the booth. The high backs would hide them from unwanted stares. They would get two orders of Vito's limp greasy fries, but only one giant Coke with two straws. Jennifer would feed the fries to Brian, each one dripping watery catsup. After a few, she would tease him, making his mouth follow the flacid dangling French fry as she pulled it away.

They would giggle and touch cheeks as they sucked Coke up through their translucent paper straws. Finally, Jennifer would put one end of a long fry in her mouth and wait, eyes flashing. Brian would put the other end in his mouth and they would work toward each other.

All this game-playing would take about thirty minutes. But it would end in a kiss. Leaving the fries and most of the giant Coke, they would hurry to the darkness of the movie theater down the street.

I knew all this, because I had often studied the pattern from a booth across the way in Vito's. I counted on Brian. I relied on Jennifer. I would sit with Jennifer's sister, my Cat, and wait. When Brian and Jennifer hurried to the sanctuary of the dark movie theater, Cat and I would move into their booth and devour the fries and remaining Coke, the spoils of our vigil.

"Just go away, and I'm sure Steven will be right out," Mother would say, and I could hear the edge in her voice. Brian was too old to be told again to stay away from Jennifer St. Charles and Vito's. He was graduating in a month.

Brian would shuffle away muttering unintelligible things. I knew Mother hung at the door of the bathroom, and I always knew what was next.

"Steven," she would say softly, "do I need to call your father?"

"No, ma'am. I'm just doing my business. Almost done."

"You'd better be. I don't want any dirtiness going on in there."

And I knew what she meant by dirtiness. The image of the night five years earlier when Brian had left the bathroom door unlocked was vivid in my mind. It played itself again for me, like a technicolor movie short:

Six year old Steven sees the crack of light around the bathroom door and pushed it open just as Mother is walking down the hall. Twelve year old Brian is seated on the stool, a black and white magazine on the floor before him. His eyes are glazed and his hand is moving furiously in his lap.

Mother nearly screams so only dogs can hear her: "Brian Dalton!"

Brian's eyes whip up from the magazine, but he can't stop his hand. Something spurts and splatters onto the pictures of the magazine on the floor. Brian is standing up, pants around his ankles, and there is something malformed about the place where his legs come together that his trembling hands can't hide. Mother pushes six year old Steven out of the room and slams the door. Steven hears the sound of flesh striking flesh again and again. Mother's head emerges from the crack of the bathroom door. "Edward. Edward Dalton! Come up here right now!" Father (Edward Dalton) takes the stairs three at a time and sprints the long hall to Steven's side, even as the bathroom door slams again.

"What's going on, little pal?" he says, pausing near little Steven.

"Brian's got a picture book of pretty ladies in there, and Mom's awful mad."

"Oh, shit," says Edward Dalton. Steven has never heard Father curse before. It isn't until later that Steven discovers the magazine, the center of Brian's fall from grace, belongs to Edward Dalton, and should have been residing in the bottom of Father's sock drawer.

The words "dirty and obscene" come up a lot in the days that follow, but in Steven's presence, there is only grim-faced silence from everyone. End of movie short.

I took over surreptitious proprietorship of those secreted picture books a few years later, after Brian discovered real girls. I remained locked in 2-D fantasies while Brian tried his luck in 3-D.

I repeated the beard hair counting weekly, and almost the same exact scenario would play outside the bathroom door. The words varied a little, but not much.

The mini-theatrics that took place that particular May Saturday evening were much the same as all the others, but I remember it vividly now because that evening was the beginning of the events that brought me to where I am today.

I flushed the toilet as noisily as possible, rattling the handle so it would not overflow. I slapped some of Dad's Old Spice on my cheeks and opened the door.

Brian appeared at the jamb as though teleported there.

"About time, squirt!" He shouldered past me and slammed the door, nearly catching my butt as I exited. His calling me squirt was sort of a required brother-thing—in truth, I was only half a head shorter than him. In a few more years, I would be calling him shorty. But not to his face.

I put on a clean T-shirt and my least faded jeans. I

had reached a point in my incipient manhood where looking neat to go uptown was important to me.

I had no doubt as I clumped down the stairs in my sneaks that Cat would be waiting at our usual appointed meeting place in the alley behind the Sinclair station. She would have been watching Jennifer's preparations of rouge, powder and pink lipstick, and would know.

I hit the ground floor with a particularly loud clump, and Dad rattled his papers down to his lap and gave me an appraising look, one eyebrow raised in scrutiny.

"That a clean T-shirt, pal?" He had stopped calling me little pal years before.

"Uh . . . yeah." I remember kicking at the edge of the carpet where it overlapped the maple boards that Mom kept shining like ship's hardware. A great place to break a neck.

Dad rattled his papers a bit more. "Now, I know young Brian has a date, and he's getting all spiffed up. Say, you don't have a date, do you?" He was smiling. I knew he was smiling, even though I couldn't look at his face. I felt my cheeks get hot.

"No. No date. Just goin' to see Billy."

"The St. Charles boy?"

"Yeah. Him."

"Doesn't Bill have a sister about your age?"

"Yeah. Catherine Charlene. She's only ten."

"Uh huh." He paused, and I knew he was grinning like a Cheshire. I still couldn't look at him, but I knew. "You usually get all spiffy, clean shirt and all, for Bill?"

"No . . . I mean, yes . . . I mean . . . aw, Dad, I'm just gonna hang around awhile."

"Uh huh. Nice warm night for it. A nice spring night." He rattled the papers up again, as if to resume reading, done with me. "Be home by eight, okay?"

"Sure, Dad." I felt the release like ecstasy. I headed for the door.

"Oh, and Steve, say hi to little Catherine for me, okay?"

I ran out the door, hearing him chuckling and rattling the papers behind me as the screen door bam-bam-bammed.

Since that long ago day at the cemetery when she fell from the oak, we—Billy and I—continued to call her Cat. Sometimes, the Cat. She moved with feline grace and cheetah speed. She could do anything a boy could do, some things better because of her agility, speed and small perfectly proportioned frame.

I saw her behind the Sinclair station potting pebbles into old water-filled paint cans. The late red sun set fire to her wild wispy hair, still white-blond like a baby's. She was dressed identically to me in sneakers, jeans and T-shirt, but her T-shirt had bumps distorting the soft lines of the shirt front.

"Hey, Cat," I whisper-yelled.

She wheeled like a panther, a smile showing front teeth a trifle too large, a bit too prominent. The full candy-colored lips and enormous China-blue eyes made her look younger than ten.

"Hey, Steverino." Only Cat and her brother Billy could get away with that. If other kids tried, they ended up without a tooth or sporting a black eye. Only Cat and Billy called me that knowing I idolized Steve Allen and so called me Steverino out of respect. It was an honor being associated with my idol by my two best friends. At age eleven, my great ambition was to be as funny as Steve Allen and make people laugh. Problem was, I had no idea how to go about it.

I playfully punched her arm, and she pretended it hurt like the devil, pretended to be on the verge of tears, then smacked me back hard enough to raise a bruise.

"Jeez, Cat. Take it easy!"

"Whatsa matter, Steverino, can't take what you dish out?" She laughed. Then she struck a vulnerable coyly feminine pose and fluttered her lashes. "I'm only a poor widdle girl, you know." She laughed again, and sprinted off to the corner of Main and Harrison. I stood still, having been startled in that instant by how adult and beguiling she had looked. I stood startled, experiencing strange emotions I could not fathom.

"C'mon, slowpoke. We've gotta get to Vito's before the lovebirds. 'Else they'll see us!" She was off again, carelessly zig-zagging the traffic as she sprinted across Main Street.

I followed.

Billy was on the steps of the Carnegie Library as we passed.

"Hey, Steverino. Hey, Cat."

"Hey, yourself, Billy-boy Billy-boy," Cat sing-songed.

"Careful, Catherine Charlene," Billy whined the name she hated back at her, "a little respect for your elders and betters." He leaped the four steps to the sidewalk. "You two goin' to Vito's?"

"Yeah. What are you up to?" I asked.

He pulled a magazine-sized something out of his back pocket. It was barely better than newsprint quality.

"Got this for you from Jenny's drawer," he said and handed it to me. I unrolled the thing to see fantastically proportioned women, some artist's fantasies, dressed in provocative lingerie. The masthead said 'Frederick's of Hollywood.'

"Thought you'd dig that," Billy laughed. "Jenny orders brassieres and stuff from that."

"Let me see," Cat said, pushing in close as I thumbed slowly through this realm I never suspected existed. I looked at all those pushed in and up and out padded pointed bosoms, fishnetted legs and high, high, highest spiked heeled feet, and thought of Reverend Stoney Miles. God! Was I brainwashed?

"Wow . . ." was all Cat said.

I rolled up the catalog and stuffed it quickly into my rear pocket.

"I guess I may as well go with you to Vito's," Billy said, inviting himself to partake of the booty which was rightfully Cat's and mine alone. "I was watchin' Nicholas for Mom, but the little turd gave me the slip."

"Watch your mouth, Billy-boy. I'll tell Mom you called Nicholas a turd."

"He is a turd, Cathy-Charlie, and watch your own damned mouth. Hey, Steverino, mind if I come with ya?"

I was shocked. Bill was older than me, and he had never deferred to me in that manner before.

"I don't care . . . Cat?"

"He's being awful rude, and besides, there won't be enough French fries for everybody."

"Sure there will," I said knowingly. "You shoulda seen Brian. He's hot to trot tonight."

Billy laughed like a donkey braying. "You bet. Jenny too. You shoulda seen all the eye-gook and crap she put on. Hell, she musta changed clothes five times, all the while sputtering and swearing. She musta had on three or four different ones of them bra-things like in the Frederick's book, all the time shoving her chest out, lookin' in the mirror and cussin' . . . really worked up, man."

I noticed how uncomfortable Cat was becoming and wondered why.

"Well, yeah, sure. Come on, Billy. Okay, Cat? There oughta be enough for all three of us."

We moved on down the street as the red ball of sun slipped behind the treeline of the horizon completely, pausing a second to make black leafy silhouettes of the maples, elms and oaks. The moon was up already in the East.

We took our station in Vito's, giggling and joking, trying to go unnoticed by Vito's busy waitresses. If they saw us, they would make us order something or leave.

"Shut up, shut up!" Cat hissed. "Here comes the lovebirds."

Brian and Jenny came in holding hands, strolling unconsciously in step. Brian placed their order suavely with the waitress at the soda fountain, and gestured with the practice of a sophisticate to their usual both in the back, parallel to ours. The three of us shrank into the depths of the booth as they approached.

34

They sat down, snuggled close, each obviously dying for the other, but each waiting on the ritual.

Jerry Lee's "Great Balls of Fire" faded and the Wurlitzer's mechanisms sought out, seized, and slapped another seven-inch disk on the turntable. Phil Spector and friends, A.K.A. the Teddy Bears, crooned out "To Know Him is to Love Him." Brian and Jenny's eyes were like big moony saucers as they gazed at one another.

The waitress brought the giant Coke and the two orders of fries. We watched intently, as Jennifer dipped a long fry in catsup and teased Brian's moronically gasping mouth with it. Catsup dribbled down his chin, but he captured the prize. Even from across the room, I saw Jenny's eyes flash. Her red tongue came from between pink lips and licked the smear of catsup from Brian's chin. His mouth opened again, and her tongue flicked inside.

"Jesus, how gross," Billy moaned.

"Shut up, shut up!" Cat hissed. She was squirming next to me in the booth like she had to go to the bathroom or something.

We were riveted, unable to look away, as Jenny and Brian locked in an embrace of passion in the dark wooden booth across the way. Time seemed suspended. It was hot, the air unbreathable.

They broke, finally, panting for breath. Brian grabbed her hand and dragged her from the booth.

"C'mon," Billy whispered, his voice gruff. I thought he meant to the fries and Coke, the booty, but no—he had Cat by the arm, dragging her just as Brian had taken Jennifer.

I followed.

Billy took us around the corner, running at full-tilt, Cat in tow, me running after, too confused to form words with my mouth.

We were in the alley behind the theater. Billy fiddled with the heavy fire door, and we were in.

The early movie was on. We were behind the screen, and the speakers boomed out music and dialogue next to us. Through the back of the transluscent screen, I could see Brigitte Bardot, pouty lips and wild hair. In the reflected glow, I could see Cat next to me, thin arms still manacled in Billy's gripping hand, looking like a much younger version of the child-woman on the screen. We were all breathing heavily, from exertion, excitement and frightened nervous tension.

"C'mon," Billy whispered again, the urgency in his voice scaring me even more.

We came around the heavy velvet curtains that stank of dust and rancid popcorn butter, down the steps and into the small orchestra area.

"There!" he hissed, triumphant.

I could see nothing, blinded by the dark and the single shaft of dusty light from the projection room, high and away.

"Billy," Cat said, "Billy, what . . ."

"I want to see. Shut up. C'mon!"

He took us up the aisle and pushed us into seats—me first into the row, then Cat, then Billy. We craned our heads around at Billy's cue, and behind us, two rows back, sat Brian and Jenny. I was in awe. I could not believe their fevered contortions. This was my brother? This was Cat and Billy's sister? I was embarrassed. I felt guilty watching, but nonetheless, I watched on, because I felt something else. There was a tightness in my chest, a crawling in my groin. I was panting like a dog. I was aware of Cat's hand on my leg, fingers digging in.

Jennifer's blouse was open, and Brian's hand punished her swollen breasts as her mouth attacked his mouth, his face, his throat, like a ravaging wild beast.

"Go for it!" Billy's whisper startled me so badly I jumped. It also took my attention away from the couple enough so I noticed a movement in the row behind them.

A light flashed on over their heads, and a small piping voice screamed with fiendish glee.

"Lookit! Lookit here, everybody."

Brian jumped up. In the spotlight his pants were open. Jenny struggled to cover herself and at the same

36

time close Brian's gaping pants. Brian's arm flailed at the light, his curses louder than the crescendoing titters and exclamations throughout the theatre.

The light moved, wobbled.

"Nicholas!" Cat shouted.

It was their little brother, Nicholas, with a flashlight. He screamed impishly, giggling and chanting as he ran.

"Jenny is a whore, Jenny is a whore. Whatcha doin' in his pants, Jenny?"

The house lights went up, and the hulking theater manager was suddenly there by Brian and Jenny.

"Let's get out of here!" I said, running down the aisle toward the screen where Bardot pouted in nothing but a towel. I didn't know if Cat and Billy were behind me or not. I didn't care. I didn't care if I saw either of them again. My face was hot with fear and embarrassment. I could still feel Cat's fingers on my thigh, and it was difficult for me to run.

The fire door clanged open, and the chill of the spring night hit me full force. The damp air carved holes in my lungs and my heart pounded, thudding in my chest.

Billy caught up, Cat by his side.

"Hey, Steverino," he said softly. The two years difference in our ages was showing—he at thirteen, me at eleven. I knew, even though I didn't want to see him right then, I'd go wherever he said and do as I was told.

"Where to?"

"Down to the park."

"It's late. I gotta go home."

"No you don't. That theater manager probably has your old man and my mother down there already to pick up Jenny and Brian. Our folks won't have time to worry about where we are."

The park had a natural amphitheater in its center, landscaped with benches of concrete, steps of flagstone slabs, and tall Douglas firs.

We were reclining in the dampening grass halfway down the slope.

"They're gonna be in real hot water." I could see Billy shake his head in the light of the moon.

37

"Our mom won't care about Jenny. She'll just be mad she had to leave home to pick her up."

Cat was pulling up tufts of grass and tossing them carelessly aside. The earthy smell wafted up to me on the gentle spring breeze.

"My mom will insist they get married, or something," I said.

"Aw, c'mon," Cat said, tossing a tuft of grass on my pants.

"No, really. Jeez, they were both half undressed."

"Yeah," Billy laughed. "I couldn't believe it! When ol' Nick hit 'em with the light . . ."

"I'm gonna kill him when I catch him!" Cat slammed the palms of both hands against the earth.

"Aw, he was just screwin' around . . ."

"No, Billy. He's . . . evil. The little bastard!"

"Catherine Charlene! You watch your mouth!"

"I mean it, Billy."

"Calm down." Bill reached over and tickled his sister under the chin until her frown transposed to a giggling smile.

There was silence for a moment.

"What I couldn't believe was when she kept puttin' her tongue in his mouth. God! Yuck!"

"Oh, Billy. It's just a French kiss."

"What do you know about French kisses?" Billy was shocked.

"Jenny taught me. People in love aren't afraid to do anything with each other. She says the sexier the stuff you do with each other, the more it proves your love."

"I still say it has to be awful. Slimy!" Billy made wretching noises, while I sat there watching the exchange, still numb and confused.

"Not slimy," Cat maintained, grabbing my face. "Look! I'll show ya." When she was sure Billy was watching, she kissed me, her tongue moving between my lips.

I felt lightheaded. I reached for her, to press the kiss, but she was done.

38

"See?" she said to Billy, as if I were an inanimate object. "Not awful."

"That doesn't show me anything, sis."

"What do you mean, Billy-boy?" she teased.

"I mean show me. Do it to me."

She scrunched up her face for a moment, moonlight making a frosty nimbus of her hair around her face and shoulders.

"Okay," she shrugged, "what the heck?"

She did to Billy what she had done to me, except it lasted a lot longer. At least, it seemed so to me. It lasted an eternity. It ended with them giggling and rolling on the night grass.

I stood. I ran. Down the slope, across the natural amphitheater and up the other side, legs pumping, breath ragged.

"Hey!" Billy yelled. "Hey, Steverino! Whatsa matter? You jealous! Just 'cause I'm kissin' your girl? Hey!"

"Shut up, shut up, shut up!" I heard Cat yell at her brother.

The night closed in, dark and deep, the moon taking refuge behind clouds. It would rain.

Lightning without audible thunder was flashing miles away by the time I reached the door to our house.

I opened the screen as quietly as possible. I caught the words from the semi-darkened living room as I entered and knew I had nothing to fear, even though I was an hour and a half late. Billy had been right. They were too busy with Brian to worry about me.

" . . . a tart just like her mother, totally without morals!" Mother was saying, the bitterness a razor blade in her voice.

"Now, Blanche, I think Brian was as much to blame . . ."

"It wouldn't have happened with the Whittaker girl. Or the Tobias girl. Only with that harlot!"

" . . . is as much to blame, and he accepts that responsibility, don't you, Brian?"

" . . . just like her mother. It's hereditary. The apple

39

doesn't fall far from the tree!"

"Blanche, I think . . ."

"Edward Dalton, I don't care what you think! What this boy needs is a father who takes his job seriously and is willing to put his foot down!"

"Blanche, what are you talking about?"

"I want you to tell this boy, and your other son too, that no one in this family is to have anything to do with any St. Charles ever again. As long as I'm alive, I won't stand for it, do you hear?"

"Blanche . . ."

I went to bed.

I thought of Mother's words. I saw Reverend Stoney Miles' stern fatherly face in my mind, heard his fiery words in my brain, and knew his words were Mother's words. I thought of Jenny and Brian. I thought of Brigitte Bardot, enormous on the theater screen looking out at Jenny and Brian's shame. I thought of the Bardot in miniature next to me in that steaming theater, next to me on the hill at the park, thought of her kiss, thought of her kissing her brother then—then and maybe not only then.

The rain came, finally, drowning out the voices below and the oozing thoughts in my head that linked harlot, tramp, and slut to Jenny St. Charles, her mother, and to my beloved Cat.

The rain came pattering softly at first, on my window and the roof overhead. Then it grew stronger, the thunder rolling and the lightning flashing. It was washing away something old, comfortable and friendly, making way for something unfamiliar, serious and unsafe.

I didn't see Billy or Catherine Charlene anymore that month. My father reluctantly put his foot down. My mother made sure by paying a personal visit to the St. Charles house and speaking directly to Mrs. St. Charles.

Brian changed radically. He spoke to no one. As the end of May came, the school notified Mom and Dad that Brian refused to take his final exams. They had no choice but to give him failing marks. Fortunately, his term averages were so high, even failing finals, he managed to graduate.

Brian did not show up on June fifth for the graduation ceremonies. He did not show up for his birthday party the next day, either. Father did some minor investigation around town and discovered Brian had joined the army. He was eighteen and gone. Simple as that.

Mother became more bitter. I looked at her and saw more gray in her blonde hair.

Father was smoking more, chain-smoking sometimes, and smiled even less than before.

And yet, I have called these the golden times, and looking back, I know that even amid my confusion and adolescent groping, no time in life could ever be so simple and so free. Things were about to happen in my young life that would alter me forever—things my parents would never suspect or understand.

Summer had arrived, and school was out. I had nothing worse to drag me down than mowing and watering the lawn and sweeping out the garage.

Mom had taken a job as a cashier at the Sears store— just for something to do, she said. That meant from nine to five daily, I was free from her analyzing, cold, criticizing eyes.

I took advantage of the freedom immediately, the first Monday after school was out. I combed my hair, put on a gingham sport shirt, a pair of new Levi's and walked to Willow Street.

Waiting near the spirea bushes, swatting away drone bees, a trickle of sweat made its way down my spine in the heat of the Michigan morning.

The trickle turned to a frozen stream when she stepped out of the darkness of the screen porch.

"Just out!" She hollered back at the house. She pulled sunglasses down over those China-blue eyes and pouted with her candy-pink lips. They pouted with a natural sensual beauty that even then made nascent enzymes and hormones in my body stir, made flesh respond on its

41

own. Next month was her birthday, and she too would be eleven. I would turn twelve in September. At that moment my pre-teen lusting stirred realization—she was my one true love, my destiny. My body wanted me to possess her, but my confused mind had only dim knowledge of what that entailed.

"Cat," I breathed, meaning to call out. "Catherine Charlene," I whispered, taking care to stay behind the cover of the sheltering spirea.

I wanted to see her, talk to her, but curiously, I also wished I could stay hidden forever, watching her, my presence undetected, possessing her in fantasy only.

"Lookit," came the shrill giggling voice, "lookit, Steverino! Whatcha doin', Steverino . . . pissin' in our bushes?" It was Nicholas St. Charles. I turned, struck out at his grinning round pie of a face, but missed. I ran. I cut into the cemetery that backed the St. Charles house and stumbled through the jumble of headstones, blindly seeking escape.

I should have known I could not elude The Cat.

She called out my name, again and again, pain in her voice. I heard the sound of it getting closer. I felt her near to me, pacing me, as though there were a magnetic field between us, repelling even as it attracted. I wouldn't stop, I couldn't.

Then my legs went out from under me, and I crashed to the ground, barely missing the sharp corner of a marble tombstone with my head.

The Cat had tackled me.

She rolled me over and clambered up me, like a squirrel on a fallen tree. She flung aside the green-lensed sunglasses, and her big eyes let tears irrigate her rosy cheeks. We lay panting from the chase on the sun-dappled ground, robins singing sweetly in the maples, and oaks, the smell of fertile earth strong and good in our nostrils.

"Oh, Steve, I've missed seeing you so bad . . ."

I said nothing. I could say nothing. I could not tell her the perimeters of the anguish I had experienced. I could not define them to myself. I felt odd and

42

confused, even more confused than during her absence from my life—here, now, with her sprawled atop my body.

Words seemed to fail her also, so she kissed me—hard, on the mouth. I struggled to push her away, thinking only of that night in the park and the repulsion I felt watching her kiss her brother as she had kissed me. Then some stronger emotion overtook me and I returned the kiss and thought only of Brian and Jenny in the theater.

Without knowing what I was doing or why, I mimicked Brian and my hand went under Cat's T-shirt. The small bumps under cloth felt large in my hand, my fingers tingling with pleasure at the swelling softness. And an urgent firmness grew in the center of the flesh I fondled.

Cat made a noise in her throat, an animal sound, and broke off the kiss.

"Oh, I knew you loved me, Steve. When I saw Brian and Jenny in the movie that night, I knew it was the same for us." She renewed the kiss, her lips hot, salty with her tears. Her small hand slid into the top of my jeans and opened them, her hot mouth sliding—and wild weird fascinating things happened, things I never thought possible. Suddenly a new world opened to me, as eerily frightening as it was ecstatic.

Later we were sitting on a low crypt marked Loring. I was seated with my legs dangling off, sneakers kicking against the nameplate. She sat in an uncharacteristically feminine pose, legs drawn under her, leaning towards me on one arm, the other draped gracefully in her lap. She was not diminished in her femininity, though I knew she would never be tomboyish again. She was more. She was completed by our found love.

I, on the other hand, was more fragmented than ever by it. It seemed as if what we had done was something only Cat had wanted, had known about. In truth, I had been led like a blind man—no, a poor brain-damaged idiot, unknowing and ignorant even of my own ignorance.

43

And Cat—what of her? What did she feel? And how did she know what to do? I assumed her knowledge of such things was as sketchy as my own. All I knew were rumors and street-talk innuendoes. All I could think of at that moment, much as I hated myself for it, was that slanderous rhetoric my Mother had spouted on the night of Brian's fall from grace with Jennifer. But surely Cat wasn't like that. She was only ten years old!

"Steve, whatsa matter?"

"Nothing . . . I don't know."

"Are you nervous or something about what we did?"

"Cat, you're just a child . . . a baby . . ."

She was hurt. The beautiful pout came so easily.

"I am not, Steve Dalton. I'm a woman. I have been for a whole year. Mom says so."

"What do you mean . . . a woman?"

"I mean I . . . well, I bleed . . . every month, you know?"

I didn't know. Rumors . . . innuendoes . . . .

She stretched over and kissed my mouth. I returned the kiss.

"It's like Jenny said, you know, about men and women. When they're in love, you know, romantic and . . ."

Suddenly we were pelted by stinging pebbles.

"Cat an' Stevie sittin' in a tree, k-i-s-s-i-n-g!" A rain of more pebbles.

"Hey!" I shouted, scanning gravestones and bushes.

"Nicholas, you little bastard!" It was a woman's fury on Cat's clouded face—at least, that's how it looked to me then, how I remember it now.

"Shouldn't be kissin', shouldn't mess around, I saw 'em screwin' down on the ground." The piping maniac voice continued, but I still couldn't see where he was.

"Nicholas! God damn you!" Cat hissed.

Bigger pebbles. Ones that left bruises.

"Did it in the graveyard, where the corpses sleep, Cat screws the corpses, six feet deep."

I saw him. He was in the lower branches of a nearby oak, off to the left. I was off the crypt in an instant. He

44

dropped from the tree and ran. I lost sight of him behind a mausoleum.

The cemetery rambled from there down to a branch of Green River through the twisted oaks and stunted drowned-out elms. I saw him again scrabbling down the bank toward the rivulet.

He was quick. His short eight-year-old legs did not misstep, but my longer legs allowed me to bound down the bank, taking vast stretches of distance with each stride.

I had him at the water. If he had jumped it, I might have missed him, but for some reason he paused, turning to run beside the water rather than crossing it.

I grabbed his collar and hurled him down. I was straddling him.

"Take it back, Nicholas. Take it all back and apologize to your sister, now!" I snarled in his face. There was no fear in his eyes. In fact, he seemed to be trying hard to stifle a giggle.

"No, Steve! Get off of him!"

I turned my attention away only an instant to see Cat at the top of the bank, baby-white hair wild in the wind, back-lit by the sun. It was only an instant, but when I looked back, Nicholas was gone. There was still something between my straddled legs, something beneath my grasping hands, but it wasn't Nicholas. It wasn't even human.

The light was not good, all shadow and shades of moss and earth tones. The thing beneath me was reptilian, canine, obscenely anthropoid—a combination of species so grossly mutated, one to the other, that my brain refused to comprehend the atrocity, the abnormality, the utter impossibility of what I was seeing.

It threw me back, its strength incredible for its small size. I fell back, striking my head on a piece of crumbled tombstone time had sent tumbling down the embankment. I raised up enough to see it slither-hop-run up the near bank, upstream ten yards from where Cat stood. My head dropped back and a film covered my eyes as I saw Cat sliding down the muddy incline to me. The darkness turned black as I fought the image of that monstrosity, that abomination from my mind, fought the memory of the feel of its greasy puffy mutating flesh under my hands.

There was damp coolness on my face. Reality swirled back, my eyes refusing to focus. I could see blues, green, a cloud of wispy white. I closed my eyes, swallowed the seeming dry lump of mud in my throat and ran a dry swollen tongue over my lips.

When I opened my eyes again, I managed to focus on Cat's worried face. She was wiping river water onto my face with a soaked corner of her T-shirt.

"Are you okay, Steve?"

"Abomination!" I cried out. In my daze, I remembered Reverend Stoney Miles' words. The Abomination was Nicholas, not me. Not me after all.

"Yeah, yeah, I'm okay," I said. Her brother was a monstrosity, and I was telling her I was okay. "I'm fine."

"Then I'll go. I . . . I can't ever see you anymore. Goodbye, Steve. I love you, I guess, but you've seen . . . you know."

"No, Cat . . . don't go . . ." I tried to raise up, but the world swam again. She was up the bank and gone.

That night, I sat on the porch and listened to the crickets and cicadae. Usually a peaceful summer evening song for me, they were about to make me scream. Every nerve in my body sat upright and precariously balanced, dominoes ready for one little shove.

"Didn't eat much supper. Fact, you didn't eat any."

Dad's voice nearly caused my body to catapult off the wide porch railing.

"Little nervous? What's troubling you, son?"

"N . . . nothing, Dad."

He sat down on the glider, which creaked a welcome to his familiar weight. I could see his face dimly in the light of the street lamp halfway up the block. His hairline was receding, but it was still black-brown. There was the beginning of frost in his eyebrows and moustache. Only his eyes looked ancient. The blue of the irises was all washed out, as though the years were a river leeching them of their vibrancy. I was born on his birthday. I was exactly thirty years younger than Dad—a span of time so incomprehensible to me, it might easily have been a millennium. I could not even imagine myself someday being forty-one.

"Steve, I feel . . . well, I feel we should talk more."

"What do you want to talk about, Dad?"

He pulled his pipe from one back pocket, his leather pouch from the other. He filled the pipe and the cherry wood smell filled the summer air with its comfortable familiarity. Old Spice and Cherry Blend tobacco equaled the essence of my Father in my olfactory memory, then and now.

"I want to talk about what's on your mind, what's bothering you."

"But there's nothing . . ."

He didn't raise his voice—my father never raised his voice to me—but there was an edge. I thought it was anger. I learned with what he said next that it was desperation.

"I feel I made a mistake with Brian, not talking to him enough. I don't want to make the same mistake with you, Steve. I just don't want to lose you, too."

It was one of those moments in growing up when a door opens and we must step through it. The night hung heavy around us. I feared my Father's authority, though he had always been kind, if uncommunicative. Now he was asking and opening the door. I ignored fear and stepped through.

"You should talk with me."

"That's what I want, son."

"No, you said 'talk to me.' You said you didn't 'talk to' Brian enough."

He relit the pipe. The light from the match made the knot of care on his brow stand out in stark relief.

47

"I see," he said quietly almost below the incessant drone of the cicadae. "I see the distinction. Here you've become a man, too, without my noticing."

"Dad, I . . ."

"Yes, Steve?"

Given the things that had happened to me that day, he had picked the wrong time to talk. I could speak to no one about those things except Cat, and she, it appeared, was lost to me.

"I can't talk about the things that are bothering me."

"You aren't in trouble, are you? If you are, I'd like to try to help."

"Thanks. No, I don't think I'm in trouble. It's just . . . weird stuff." How accurate that was, he would never know.

One corner of his mouth smiled. I'm sure he thought I was worried about sandlot baseball, the flat tire on my bike, or missing Twilight Zone on Friday nights. He had no idea that his son, at the ripe old age of eleven, had copulated, had wild carnal knowledge of an unsettlingly sensuous girl even younger, and had discovered moments later that her brother was Abomination. Did Dad know of Abomination? Or was it the exclusive knowledge of Blanche and Steven Dalton, Reverend Stoney Miles and the entire St. Charles family?

"Okay. Okay, Steve. But when you're ready, I'll try to be ready. To talk *with* you."

I nodded and went back to staring at the gentle rustling of the maple leaves in the summer breeze. The low hiss the leaves made was barely audible under the drone of the cicadae and the rhythmic chirrup of the crickets, but I knew it was really voices—voices telling me of the straining desire for Cat, the obsession for her growing inside my young body, churning at my guts. Obsessive lust was a new sensation, frightening enough by itself, without the wild chaotic thoughts of her brother.

I didn't see Cat or Billy or even the Abomination, Nicholas, for the rest of the summer—odd in a town the

48

size of Greenriver. I did occasionally see Jennifer St. Charles. The college men, home to work in their father's businesses for exorbitant wages over the summer, were her constant escorts down the evening streets of the town. Though she was only seventeen, she dressed and acted much older—too much older, the whole town thought. They all knew of the theater incident. My mother, in a concerted effort to exonerate Brian from all guilt, had spread the story of Jennifer's harlotry far and wide. They all knew, and they all whispered of it incessantly. Jennifer apparently saw no difference in hanging with sheep or lambs, and so matched her actions to her reputation.

One night after standing in the spirea outside the St. Charles place for nearly two hours with no sign of Cat or Billy—or Nicholas, thank God—the need to know exploded within me. When Jennifer exited the shiny new '58 Thunderbird with a flourish of slapped away grasping hands and giggles, I made up my mind to confront her.

The car roared away, and I slipped out of the darkness and the spirea.

"What are you doing there, Steve Dalton?" The merriment of her face was replaced by the clouded-over look I had seen so often on the faces of Billy and Cat.

"I . . . Jennifer, I was wondering . . ."

"You've got a lot of nerve coming around here, after what your old bitch mother has done to me in this town. God! If I could only get away . . ." Her sentence drifted off, and her eyes looked after the departed Thunderbird, then up at the stars in the blue velvet night.

"I'm sorry about my mother. I know Brian . . ."

"Don't you mention his name to me! That bastard! Running off when things got rough. And not one word to me! Not before he left, or since. Billy heard somebody say he was going to Germany. You know what that means? The army gives him two weeks furlough before he goes. Do you think I'll see him? Not a chance! He doesn't care a damn for me. Never did. He just wanted to get in my pants!"

"Jennifer. I . . . I just want to know about Cat . . ."

"And you, you little perverted snot! You're no better than that conniving brother of yours! Cat told me! Yes she did! And I told Mother. That's why they're all away for the summer. It's all your fault. Mom was so furious she wanted you sent to reform school, but I told her not to ruin Catherine Charlene's life the way your mother has ruined mine. Besides, little Cathy said she did it to you, not the other way around. Not that I believe that for a minute. I know how the male mind works! Anyway, they're all at Aunt Delilah's in Detroit. They won't be back 'til fall, and if Mom has any sense, she won't come back to this pig hole at all. Now get out of my sight and don't you ever, ever come sneakin' around here again!"

She was crying as she shoved me aside and stormed up the rickety steps to the porch, through the sagging screen door and into the blackness of the St. Charles house.

So that was it. I was denied Cat because of what we'd done. What she'd done. It was her fault, damn it. She even admitted it to her family. I didn't even know how. Maybe Mom was right about the St. Charles women.

3

I was fifteen when I again came into direct contact with members of the St. Charles family. It was 1963, and much had happened in my life during the past four years. I had been taken over by the magic of rock and roll. The forced viewings of Reverend Stoney Miles' sermons had continued as my mother's chief means of punishment, and rock and roll was tied tightly to the good reverend's view of sin, lust, loose painted women in sky-high heels and the Abomination. Nevertheless—or perhaps because of his sermons—Chuck Berry, Little Richard, Jerry Lee Lewis and the Everly Brothers dominated my life. I had a cheap Japanese transistor radio that made their music sound like homogenized noise in the key of E. I traded my bike and all my hoarded allowance money for a Gibson Firebird guitar and a Fender Bassman amp, both of which needed a lot of work. I rewired the pick-ups on the guitar, and patched the amp's paper-cone speaker with rubber cement. I sounded like a B-52 with engine trouble, but I learned the chords quickly and picked up lead riffs from old Les Paul records my father collected but never listened to himself, since they made my mother nervous.

I smoked Benson and Hedges Deluxe cigarettes, a definite status choice, because they came in a gilt-lettered black and brown box. I was the only kid in school who would pay thirty-five cents a box for status. I didn't even belong to a clique or social group that demanded I impress anyone.

I had been shaving four times a week for two years and had learned the use of Dad's stiptic pencil. Though my needs were more frequent than his, we still shared the same one that had been in the medicine cabinet when I was eleven. I figured the stiptic pencil business was not a field with high growth potential.

I wore my light brown hair in a style known then by different names, depending on your barber. It was called a coconut, a buzz cut, a Princeton. I just called it a haircut. Hair was not as important to young males in 1963 as it would be in 1964.

I was arrested for shoplifting a carton of cigarettes. Why do teenagers think store clerks won't notice a long stiff rectangular shape up a coat sleeve? "I'm too smart, they won't catch me"? Or, in my case, "who gives a damn if they do?" It just made me angry at the inconvenience of all the stupid questions like: "Why did you do it?" Or my mother's: "Don't you know smoking's bad for you?" Good old Mom, a master of getting at the heart of the matter. Thank God they didn't catch me the week before when I lifted a sixty-nine cent bottle of Michigan Cask Vin Rose from the corner market.

Mom acted like I had become a commie or something. Dad just looked hurt. I knew he was thinking: "Son, I thought you agreed to talk *with* me." I couldn't say a thing in my defense. I didn't really want to. I didn't care.

" . . . stealing! We're not rich, Lord knows, but I've always told you, if you want something, ask, and we'll try to afford it. I thought we told you. Didn't we tell you? I told you and told you." That was the first time I thought my mother's voice sounded shrill. It was the first time I decided she sounded crazy, the way she kept on an on, talking, on and on, like she would never stop. I saw, for the first time, my father, in his silence, sitting there shaking his head, praying to himself that she would just please-God shut up.

I wasn't proud of being a thief, but I wasn't particularly shamed by it, either. I really didn't care what my peers or Greenriver society in general thought of my morals. I just didn't care. There had been nothing to care about since Cat escaped from my life.

What I grew to care about was my band. Music had brought me new best friends to take the place vacated by the members of the St. Charles family. I don't mean vacated; I mean abandoned. That's how I felt— abandoned.

The drummer was Todd. Todd the Bod, the girls called him, and he loved it. He was 6'1", curly blonde hair and a V-shaped body with biceps as big as the homecoming queen's thighs. His eyes were as blue as mountain water, and his teeth could blind you when he flashed his trademark Raintree grin. Todd Raintree wasn't big on brains, but it didn't matter. He had more rhythm than it was righteous for a white boy to have. It was a good thing, because Geoffrey Prang, who was black, had almost no sense of rhythm. Another myth blown. Geoffie played bass for us, and Todd helped him with the syncopation of the riffs I taught him. Geoffie was smart as any fifteen year old could be. He simply wasn't cool. Being from the only black family in Greenriver, his people had spent so much time trying to be white, trying to fit in, trying to stay unnoticed and unnoticable, that poor Geoffie had no idea how to be natural, how to be black. He was handsome, but it would do him no good in Greenriver. The only girls he ever talked to were his sisters. He wasn't afraid of white girls; his father was afraid of them for him. Geoffie just didn't understand.

Our keyboard player did. Paulie Gibbs was from Georgia, a transfer student. He didn't hate blacks, since his family was upper-class genteel Southerners. He was merely uncomfortable in the company of more than one of them at a time. Geoffie didn't mind. It was just one more thing in this world he didn't understand. The band needed Paulie, and that was good enough for Geoffie. Paulie made his little Fender Rhodes electric piano sound like Jerry Lee himself had set in.

We played the people I liked—Chuck Berry, the Everlys, Little Richard, Jerry Lee. The places we performed were restricted to the nearly defunct skating rink and the school Youth Center. We played regularly, Friday and Saturday nights, and cleared about fifty dollars a week apiece—damned good money for high school boys in 1963. We even had "uniforms"—red blazers, grey pegged slacks, black Italian pointed-toed shoes, white shirts with black silk ascots. We were sharp. Even though it wasn't necessary to get gigs— there were only three other rock bands in or around Greenriver—we were damned good.

It was the first week in June in 1963, and we had lucked into a beautiful job. Todd's older sister went to college in Haines City, a quiet little town thirty miles west of Detroit and one hundred miles east of Greenriver. She was having a birthday bash, put on by her sorority sisters, and she asked them to hire our band. They were going to pay us one thousand dollars for the gig, plus traveling expenses. We could not believe our good fortune—two hundred fifty apiece for one night's work, plus the excitement of earning the money playing in a college town.

Todd was almost seventeen, and in honor of our getting such a fabulous gig, Todd's old man, on a whim, bought his son a shiny red 1963 snub-nosed Ford Econoline van to haul our equipment.

The last day of school was Friday. I blew off all the exams. It didn't worry me—nothing about school worried me. No matter how little I did, I'd wind up with my usual assortment of A's, B's, and C's. Strong in literature and communications, just passable in science and math. The clock in old Miss Jenkins' Biology classroom finally crept up on three o'clock, and the brass bell above it exploded with its ear-shattering ring. I was out of my seat and out the door before it stopped.

I saw Todd running up the hall toward me from the shop class, massive shoulders hunched, blond head low, face pulled wide in his most joyous grin.

"Damn!" was all he said, and slapped my back solidly.

Geoffie was at the entrance door, grinning almost as much as Todd.

"Tomorrow," he said. "Tomorrow morning."

Then Paulie sprinted up from around the corner of the building. We watched him vault the granite lion beside the steps as we burst out the doors.

"It's damn near time, ol' sons!"

"Let's go, right now, and load up the van," Todd said, slapping backs all around.

We sprinted the ten blocks to Todd's house. The Econoline sat in the drive shining like a big apple in the golden sun.

It only took us five minutes to pack Todd's drums behind the bench seat in the van's rear. Then we piled in, roaring down the streets to the Gibbs place. Kendall Gibbs, Paulie's father, had been recruited up from Atlanta to be top executive for Greenriver's largest business, the Greenriver Furniture Company. The

Gibbs family had purchased and renovated the Van Wylen mansion, an old rambling Victorian edifice, constructed by Greenriver's founding family in the 1800s when the town was just a bare patch of ground in dense woods by the slow moving brownish-green water.

The drive snaked around behind the mansion. Mrs. Gibbs was sunning in a white wrought iron lawn chaise, wearing a floral print bit of chiffon that clung and flowed over the youthful voluptuousness of her body. She was only sixteen years older than Paulie.

We waited in the van while Paulie told whatever lie was necessary to his gorgeous mother, then hauled his equipment out of the house and tossed it in the back of the van.

My house was next. No one would be home. I would leave a note.

The maples made a low green tunnel over Harrison Street. The red van brushed them aside as we entered the driveway to my house.

"The mics and P.A. amp are in the garage, guys. My guitar and amp are upstairs. I'll get 'em. Back in a minute." I opened the side door and jumped out. The porch door slam-slam-slammed behind me, the summer tattoo of old wooden screen doors all across the Midwest.

The drapes were drawn in the living room. It was dark, a single ray of gold shafting between the heavy material and spotlighting the floating dust.

My father sat on the sofa, slumped forward, head down, hands dangling to the floor. His body jerked upright at the sound of my entrance. He seemed to wipe at his face in the darkened room.

" 'Lo, son. Home so soon?"

"School's been out over an hour. You're the one who's not supposed to be home now."

"Yes. Well . . . just lucky today, I guess." There was a strange quality to his voice. Almost eerie.

"Well, anyway. The group and I just wanted to get the van loaded."

"Ah, yes." He wiped at his face again. "The big band

55

job in Haines City. Well, let me wish you luck, son. All the best luck in the world." His voice quaivered, then he broke down. He hid his face in his big hands.

I went to him, sat beside him, and put my arm around him. It felt strange to touch him like that, to feel his shoulders shake with his sobs.

"Dad . . . what is it? What's the matter?"

"Oh, son!" he wailed. The sound of his voice, the pain tearing at his vocal cords, sent ice water down my spine. "So many things. Your mother . . . Brian . . . you and me . . . mostly just me. God, son, what a failure I am!"

"Dad . . . Dad, you're not, why . . ."

"Oh, yes. Yes I am. I've failed your mother, Brian, you . . . all of you. In so many ways, I . . ."

"Dad, stop this. You can't . . . I mean . . ."

He sighed deeply, stopped the uncontrolled sobbing. He was more frightening to me in his silence.

"I've . . . lost . . . my job, son."

I had no idea what to say. Adults—fathers—always had jobs. My father, at any rate, had always had a job. The same job. For eighteen years my father had worked for the Greenriver Furniture Company, Customer Service Department. It was the way of things.

"Were you fired?"

"Yes. Oh, they said something about restructuring . . . combining departments . . . said I was laid off. Funny way to put it. Destroyed would be the way to put it. God, Steve, I'm forty-five. Forty-five. Where am I going to go to find a job in this town?"

"You could move."

"No. Your mother is permanently rooted in this town. I think her feet are set in the sidewalk somewhere, dried and set right in the concrete, you know?" He tried to laugh. The resultant croaking sound was a dismal failure.

"No . . . no, I'm afraid not. All those years . . . I was good. I mean, I was a good company man. All those years . . . passed over for promotions and raises. I kept on, though, plugging away. What did it get me? What,

I ask you? Laid off! Laid off, f'Christsake, two years shy of a pension. I have nothing!"

"Dad, calm down . . ."

"I asked him, I asked the bastard, you know, to cut the bullshit. Know what he said?"

"Dad, please . . ." He was up now, striding about the room plucking at his sweat-soiled white shirt, at his tie.

"He said I wasn't dynamic enough. Dynamic enough, can you imagine? I said, what the hell is that supposed to mean? And he says, I'm a drone. A God-damned drone!"

"Dad!" I stood up, reached out my hands. I thought if I could only stop his insane stiding about, I might be able to stop everything. Maybe if I held him in my arms, I could hold on to my old safe reality.

"No room in the company for drones, son!"

"Jesus, Dad! You . . . you've got to stop this! Mom will be home . . ."

"Eighteen years!"

I ran. Up the stairs, into my room. I couldn't . . . I could do nothing for him. Hell, I didn't even know the man.

I had to think. I grabbed my band outfit from the closet—the blazer, shirt, pants, the shoes. Some other things, I didn't know what. I balled all the clothing in my arms, grabbed up the guitar and the top to the Fender Bassman. I'd make a second trip for the speaker box.

Downstairs, my father was seated again on the sofa.

"Uh . . . change of plans, Dad. We're, uh, going to Haines City tonight. I . . . ah . . ."

I crashed out the door. The guys had loaded the P.A. equipment.

"Listen, we've gotta go up tonight."

"What?" Geoffie pushed his hornrims back up his nose so hard I thought he'd bruise himself.

"Great! I can dig it!" Todd grinned.

"Shut up, all of you!" I silenced Paulie before he could add his opinion. "I mean it. We have to go tonight. My dad . . . we've got to go tonight, that's all."

57

"Wait a minute, I can't . . ."

"I'll talk to your mother, Geoffie. Don't worry. It'll be okay. I'll be right back." I went into the house again, moving past Father as though he were just another piece of fading furniture.

I got the speaker box to my amp and bumped and banged it down the stairs and out the door.

"This is crazy." The van was speeding back to Geoffie Prang's house. "Where will we stay?" Paulie shook his head as he spoke, his blond curls dancing across his forehead.

"No sweat. My sister will find us a place."

"Where, old son? She lives in a sorority house."

"Trust me."

Mrs. Prang was a pretty woman, her skin the color of cinnamon. She was plumping with the years, but her face was almost childlike.

I don't know to this day what I said to her. I remember smiling a lot, and her smiling back. All I could think about was my father, sitting in that darkened living room, with dust dancing in slow motion in a single shaft of sun.

It was a quarter past seven when we rolled down the long hill into Haines City. We made the turn at the street with the sign that said Haines City College in big green and white lettering.

"Where's your sister's sorority house?"

"On Superior Street. Just a few blocks . . . down toward the river."

"Is that part of Green River?"

"Naw, Geoffie. Green River flows west into Lake Michigan. This is the Huron. Flows into . . . well, Lake Erie, I guess." Todd turned a corner sharply. We were headed downhill again.

"I thought it flowed into a drainage ditch south of Detroit," Paulie laughed.

"Same difference," I said.

"This is it." Todd wheeled the van into a dirt lot behind a three-storey Tudor building. Too big for a

58

house, it had to have been originally built for the purpose it still served. It was old, the ivy almost a foot thick in places.

There were easily twenty cars in the dirt lot, ranging from a shiny new Mercedes to a fenderless VW bug with more rust than paint.

"You can't park there," the angry female voice called from somewhere above. "This is a private lot. Go on, move, or I'll call a tow truck."

She was hanging out a third story gabled window, a towel wrapped about her hair. Todd got out of the van.

"But in your case, it's open parking, sweetheart. Don't you move an inch! I'll be right down!"

Todd turned back to us mere mortals in the van and grinned.

Her hair was still in the towel, and she was dressed in tight jeans, sandals and a paint-smeared sweatshirt.

"What Greek legend did you drop out of?" she said to Todd, ignoring the stares of the rest of us, like dogs drooling over prime rib just out of reach.

"I'm Todd Raintree. Do you know my sister Ginger?"

"You're Ginger's little brother?" She ran a hand over his arm. "What do you do on weekends? Bench-press half-ton trucks? Your arms are like telephone poles, swear t'God!"

"We're the band for my sister's party tomorrow . . ."

"What?" She was running her hand across his pectorals. "Oh. Of course you are. But that's tomorrow. What are you doing here tonight? Not that I have any objections, mind."

"We . . . that is . . ."

"Hungry? C'mon in. I'll get the house mother to scare up some mystery meat or something. I'm Candi Jones, by the way. Remember that name, Hercules. At some point tonight you'll want to know it so you can beg for mercy, swear t'God!" She tucked her hand under his belt buckle and began pulling Todd toward the house.

"What about the guys?"

"What guys?"

"The other guys. In the band. They're in the truck."

"Oh. Well, bring them in, too, I guess."

The house mother was a portly woman in her fifties with wild grey hair, a stern set to her mouth, a strong chin, but with kind brown Old Country eyes.

"So where can we put them up, Maudie?"

"Don't you call me that, you smart-mouthed brat. And you know very well they can't sleep here. We'll lose the sorority charter." Maud slammed the breaded veal, mashed potatoes, gravy and broccoli before each of us. When Candi Jones reached for a sprig of Todd's broccoli, Maud slapped her hand smartly with a wooden spoon.

"Dammit, Maudie, that hurt!" Candi sucked her knuckles. "We can't make 'em sleep in that van, can we?"

"Well . . ." Maud's eyes seemed to melt like warm chocolate.

Todd swallowed a big mouthful of the veal. "I thought maybe Ginger would know of some guys with an apartment or something."

The gorgeous college girl named Candi Jones toweled her long red hair and snickered. "You just bet she does!"

"Candice!"

"Well, she does, Maudie."

Todd just grinned and wolfed more veal.

"Todd! What the hell are you doing here?" Ginger Raintree had come into the big kitchen with two other girls. Ginger was a big girl, big and blonde like Todd. Broad shouldered and big-busted, she was well-muscled and proportioned like an athlete, which she was. Ginger was a P.E. major. If her personality hadn't been as open and genial as Todd's, she would have been intimidating.

The girls with Ginger looked like midgets by comparison. One was an oriental—tiny, small-boned and fragile as Ming pottery, with straight glistening black hair down to her butt. Ginger introduced her as Kamii. The other girl, with hazel-nut brown hair hanging over her gold-flecked eye-glassed green eyes and a slender boyish body slouched like a question mark against the

60

door jamb, was Donna-somebody. I missed the last name. She was intimidating with her unblinking direct stare and frowning countenance.

"Well, listen, Todd, the Theta Chi's can find some room for you guys. I'll give 'em a call. The other girls will show you where to stash your equipment and junk."

Kamii zeroed in wordlessly on Geoffie with an ingratiating smile. I could see Geoffie's Adam's apple bobbing even from across the table as he swallowed hard. Ginger went with Paulie and Todd out to the van with Candi drooling and stalking after them. That left me with Maud, who was clearing the table in a bustling no-nonsense manner, and the sulky intimidating girl, still slouching in the doorway.

"So you want to listen to some music?" Her voice was harsh, with strident tones that made the question seem an accusation.

"Sure. Why not?"

"Why, indeed, not? Come on."

"I'll tell you what I told Candice. These boys all have to be out of this house by ten." Maud clanked heavy institutional china in the sink for emphasis.

"Not to worry, Mrs. Polaczak."

"I'm Steve Dalton," I said, as I followed her through the house's maze of hall, stairs and floors.

"From?"

"Er . . . Greenriver."

"What, if I may be so bold, is a Greenriver?"

"Greenriver, Michigan. A little hole-in-the-wall town. Ginger's from there, too. She's Todd's sister."

"Right. All you guys from Greenbottom?"

"River. Yes, we are."

"Here's my room."

We were on the top floor of the Tudor house. Her room had one of the gabled windows that faced the street. It was small, about nine feet square, with a ceiling that slanted down to the floor, making the room a right triangle. There were grubby clothes littered about the unmade bed and the floor, an accoustic guitar with more broken strings than whole, and books and crumpled legal pad sheets adding to the general debris. In the corner on the wall by the door stood a rather expensive-looking stereo. There were pictures and posters of people I didn't recognize all over the walls.

"You a folkie?"

"A what?" I said, eyeing the shambles and looking for a place to sit.

"A folkie. Do you like folk music?"

"I don't know . . . guess I haven't heard too much."

"Guess you haven't heard any. Well, I'll change that in a minute."

"This," she said, handling an album like a holy relic, "is Muddy Waters. This ambrosia for the ears is categorized as folk-blues. This cut is called 'Mannish Boy.' " She sat the record on the turntable and placed the tone arm carefully in the groove. Then she cranked up the volume. The speakers hissed for a second, then exploded with bass, drums, and Muddy Waters' funky slide guitar.

I was transported. I was speechless.

"This is Josh White. Song's called 'Strange Fruit.' "

Clear ringing acoustic guitar notes, a voice at once sweet and rough. Enthralling. She followed that cut with 'Empty Bed Blues.' Then came a Leadbelly album. Cisco Houston. Big Bill Broonzey. Woody Guthrie. Pete Seeger.

"Enough, enough!" I yelled. I could no longer sit on the littered bed. "Where can I get these records? Where?"

For the first time, Donna smiled. "Ann Arbor." She looked at her watch. "Stores are open to nine. We can still make it, no sweat."

"Damn! I don't have much money . . ."

"I'll front you. This is too important. I feel like Annie Sullivan to your Helen Keller. Let's go."

We went back through the maze, only this time it was all down instead of up. The van was gone, and there was no trace of any of the others. I assumed Ginger was finding places for the other guys to bed down.

Donna made for her car, which turned out to be the fenderless rust-encrusted VW bug. It had been yellow, I guessed, at one far distant time. The seats were ripped and the windshield was cracked on the passenger side, a circle with radiating arms like a glass etching of a spider web.

The engine sounded sick, as the car jerked and rattled out of the parking lot and into the road. Night had come, and the cross-eyed headlights of the VW scanned the trees above the bushes along the street, but not the road before us. I thanked God the streets were well lit.

I guessed Ann Arbor was about ten miles, though we never really left one city and entered the other. There was constant civilization—K-marts, shopping centers, gas stations—all along the way.

"Haines City is still small-town. It's like it never recovered from the fact that the University of Michigan is in Ann Arbor just down the road. Only one movie theatre, and almost no businesses to cater to the college crowd. We all go to Ann Arbor for everything—clothes, food, culture—like tonight. You can't buy any decent records in Haines City."

The place was called Alfie's, and there was bin after bin of records of all sorts. Donna led me to those marked "Folk, Blues, and Folk-Blues," and hand-picked a selection of fifteen albums.

"These," she said smuggly, as she paid the tab in wrinkled currency from the depths of her tight jeans pockets, "will change your entire life. They may even change the course of history in Greenwater."

"River. But listen, I don't know when I'll pay you back . . ."

"Don't bother. Listen, you're a musician. Any musician, especially any guitarist who doesn't have roots in this kind of stuff," she tapped the albums with an almost nail-less index finger, "ain't never gonna amount to a hill of shit. Call it my contribution to the future of American music. Come on, let's go back to the house and listen to these. You don't have much time to learn how to play this stuff before tomorrow night."

"But . . ."

"No buts, Steven. Your future, the future of music, lies in these black vinyl electronic impressions."

She dragged me quickly back to the VW, and we rattled and coughed our way back through the night streets to Haines City, back to the sprawling Tudor home of Sigma Alpha Tau.

Inside she hopped up the stairs to her piquant pig sty, with me following. The door closed and the music blared. I got the gospel of the genesis of popular American music from Donna. I also discovered she was an anthropology major who liked nothing better than referring to Haines City as her field work and Sigma Alpha Tau as her focus of ethnographic study. It was fascinating, and all beyond my grasp.

After some length of time that allowed us to each consume a pack of my cigarettes, I felt the need to interrupt Donna's nonstop enthusiastic dissertation.

"I have to tell you I don't understand a word."

"You wanna fuck, or not?"

"That's plain enough. Is this charity?"

"Call it missionary work. Like missionaries, I will be violating the first directive of the field-working anthropologist by exposing my customs, mores and ritualistic practices to the unspoiled subject."

"You're gonna have to expose more than that." I laughed and unbuttoned my shirt. Donna laughed, too, and reached over the rubble on the bed to unsnap my jeans.

A June morning in Michigan is a blessed thing. The sun is golden, the sky is blue with whisps of high white clouds, if any clouds there be, the grass and maple leaves are vibrant green, and the dew on the grass tips is heavy, making the air clean and fresh to the smell. The air is often still crisp in the hour following complete sunrise, and it exhilarates even the plodders of this world.

I dressed without awakening Donna, who was actually snoring.

Gathering my albums under my arm, I made my halting way through the castle maze past the silent rooms of the slumbering maidens, past the fuming wild-haired dragon fumbling about in the fortress kitchen, and out the door to the condensation-drenched red van.

I popped the rear door, and Todd grinned up at me, wiping sleep from his eyes.

"Hey, Steve. What's up?" he whispered.

"Me, Todd. Just wanted to drop these off." I indicated the records under my arm. "Then you can go back to sleep. I'm gonna take a walk."

"Sleep? Hell, man, I ain't slept all night. I'll come with ya.'"

As he dragged his wide V-shaped body out of the truck, off from under the jumble of blankets, I could see he was trying to extricate himself from the grasping limbs of Candi Jones.

Todd was standing next to me in the golden morning light, wholly naked and unabashed. He dug around the redheaded girl's nude body until he had located shoes, T-shirt and jeans.

"Je-sus- It's nippy this mornin', ain't it?" he said, hopping into his tight jeans.

"Yeah, 'specially if you're in your birthday suit."

"Got a point. Wonder when Paulie and Geoffie are gonna roll out."

"Did Ginger find them a place at the fraternity she was talking about?"

Todd grinned. "Hardly. Seems we were quite a novelty to these college ladies. I guess you made out okay, huh?"

"I guess. You certainly did."

Todd glanced back at Candi's slumbering form wrapped in the blankets and quickly latched the van's rear door. "Yeah, that's no lie. Think I surprised her a little, though. I sure didn't beg for mercy, like she said I would. I can tell you that!"

"Did she?"

"Almost, buddy, almost." He slapped my back. "Where we walkin' to?"

"Damned if I know. I'm out of cigarettes. Let's start by finding a place to buy more."

We walked. The air was warming as the sun rose higher in the blue.

"So . . . where did Geoffie end up? You know, Mrs. Prang said . . . well, she said the damnedest thing to me. She said I was responsible for Geoffie."

"Then you in trouble, boy! That is, unless Mrs. Prang considers chink girls A-OK."

"What'ya mean?"

"What do you think I mean? Geoffie bedded down with that Kamii girl."

"No!"

"Yeah! Old virgin-britches himself."

"All night?"

"All night."

"Damn!" I kicked a puff ball in the grass. It exploded, sending its yellow-white dust all over the toe of my sneaker. "Todd, can you believe any of this? I mean, why should these girls want . . . us?"

Todd just grinned when I looked at him.

"Well, okay, I can see why they'd all want a crack at you. What'd she call you? Hercules?"

Todd laughed.

"But Geoffie? Me?"

"Hey, don't put yourself down. You're a good lookin' cat. And don't put Geoffie down, either. You know what they say about Negro guys."

"Yeah, I know. But that's all bull."

"Is it?"

"Sure it is . . . at least, I think."

"Anyway, there's a lot goin' on up here, all the girls are . . . I don't know . . . Candi kept talking about 'The Movement'—freedom marches, equal rights, a lot of weird shit. She kept talkin' about freedom . . . bein' free to do whatever anybody wanted to do . . . about government, about laws, life . . . about sex."

"Wow!"

"Yeah, I know. Not much like the girls in Greenriver."

"There's a store over there. Let's get my cigarettes."

The bell over the door tinkled, and we walked out of the sun into the dark cool shop. It was a little store, all self-service, with a cash register by the door. There was a single clerk bending down behind the counter, where the cigarettes were. Todd wandered to the back of the store, looking around.

"Do you have Benson and Hedges Deluxe?"

The clerk stood up.

I'm sure my jaw dropped.

"You!" the clerk said, as surprised as I was.

"J . . . Jenny? Jenny St. Charles?"

"As if you didn't know. What are you doing here?"

"My band . . . that is, I have a rock'n'roll band . . . we're playing up here . . . a party . . . Ginger Raintree's birthday . . . our drummer's her brother . . ."

"Ginger Raintree? You're playing at her party tonight?" A strange smile of acceptance played about her mouth. She had lost much of the girlish cuteness from her face. I did a quick math in my head. She must have been twenty-one or so, and she looked hardened. "Fate. You can't fight it, can you? I know Ginger. I'm going to her party. If you hadn't wandered in here I would have seen you tonight, anyway." She laughed, but there was no mirth in it.

"I just wanted cigarettes . . ."

"What are you? Sixteen?"

"Fifteen. I'll be sixteen in September."

"It's illegal to sell cigarettes to minors, you know. But what the hell, huh? I mean, we small town folk have to stick together. What brand?"

I told her again.

"Here. A carton on the store. Here, take it." She shoved the box at me.

"I don't want to get you into trouble . . ."

"Trouble? Trouble with who? I own this store. Me and the bank. Surprised? Surprised the town bad girl of good old Greenriver is a shopowner?"

"No, I . . ." I didn't know what to say in the face of her anger.

She gave another short laugh and shook her head.

"Never mind. I've even forgotten why I hate you. Oh, yes. One reason was your brother. You looked a bit like him when I saw you last. Don't anymore." She reached across the counter and brushed the front shock of hair up off my forehead. "You're taller than Brian was . . . better looking, too." Her hand fluttered slightly in midair, then she hid it with the other one behind the counter. "Have you . . . did you ever hear from him? Brian, I mean."

"No. We never did."

"I'm sorry." She seemed to mean it. Did she blame herself for my family's loss of Brian?

"Well. See you tonight, I guess."

"How's . . ." How is Cat, I wanted to shout; where's Cat, I wanted to scream. "Yeah, I guess so. Todd . . . you ready?" He was prowling the store's recesses.

"Yeah. I'm hungry, but I don't see anything I want."

"Thanks again for the cigarettes." I waved the carton at her as we made our way out the door. Todd grinned and winked at her as the little bell above the door tinkled.

"Don't mention it. We have to stick together, remember?"

The door closed behind us. The day had become hot.

"You know her?"

"Yeah. She's from Greenriver. Jennifer St. Charles."

"Bill St. Charles' sister?"

"Yeah. You know Bill?"

Todd shrugged. "We were on the wrestling team together before I dropped out. Mean bastard. Used to try to kill me. I mean it. All us guys who were bigger. Like he had to prove something."

"Yeah. That's Bill."

"Hey, did you ever know that weird little brother of his?"

My blood chilled in my veins.

"Nicholas." I tried to keep my voice level.

"Yeah. I guess. Jesus, I remember . . . I was just a kid, eleven or twelve, I don't know . . . but I remember I

68

caught the little bastard teasing a puppy. I mean, teasing it to hurt it, you know? I yelled at him to stop, and he didn't even look at me. Then he did something I couldn't see, and the pup started squealing. Well, I ran over and grabbed him, you know, and the dog was just laying there. I thought the kid had killed it or something, so I whipped him around and he spit at me and laughed.

"I'm not proud of it, you know, I was twice his size, but I smacked him good, in the face. The little bastard laughed again." Todd's steps slowed. I looked at him. His head was low, his brow furrowed.

"Then, you know, his eyes . . . his eyes, Steve, they went all weird. And . . . and the skin on his arms, where I was holdin' him got all . . . slimy. I let go of him and he ran off laughing like a loon." Todd stopped talking, swallowed hard, looked about at the beautiful day and his grin returned. "But the dog, the puppy, you know? I picked it up and it licked my face. I took it home. That puppy grew up to be Shep. You know, my dog Shep?"

"Yeah. Shep's a great dog." Seeing Jenny and hearing Todd's grim story about Nicholas dredged up a lot of unpleasant, even frightening thoughts and memories from what I thought were healed-over wounds in my brain. Though the June sun made the colors of the day brilliant, everything had become grey charcoal sketches for me.

Back at the sorority house, Geoffie was sitting on the stone and concrete steps grinning one of Todd's broad grins. The reason sat beside him. Kamii, brushing her butt-length glistening black hair, was smiling, coy and knowing. Her eyes never left Geoffie even as we approached.

"Hi, Geoffie," I called. He nodded sagely in my direction, grinning, grinning, grinning. "Had breakfast?" More grins.

"Mrs. Polaczak has oatmeal," Kamii giggled.

Todd swallowed an imaginary lump. "Think I'll pass. Not that hungry. I'll never be that hungry. You, Steve?"

"Mmmm? No. Guess I'll pass, too." My brain felt as

though it had become a patch of primordial ooze. I have never lacked intelligence, but I always have had trouble sorting things out in my head. It always seemed to be a quagmire of fifty thoughts, one sinking, one rising, five others flippering through the ooze. At that moment there were memories of Cat—good and bad. There were thoughts of Jenny and Brian. There was the confusion and sadness brought on by my father's pain. And there were the nagging fearful rememberances of what I thought I had seen Nicholas St. Charles become that day in the cemetery. I had no room in my mind for what tunes the band would play that night, let along whether or not I was hungry enough to eat oatmeal.

"Hey, Geoffie, where's Paulie?"

Geoffie couldn't interrupt his grin to answer Todd's question.

Kamii, it seemed, had become his self-appointed mouthpiece.

"I think," she tilted her head, childlike, an oriental princess unused to answering questions put forth by the coolie class, "he spent the night with Ginger." No tact or compassion for a sixteen year old muscle-bound brother about the college girl Paulie had bedded.

"What?" It was the first time since I had known Todd that there was no trace of a grin, no twinkle in his eye. "Whadya mean, spent the night . . . !"

"Cool it, Todd, Paulie probably . . ."

"None of your smooth-talkin' shit, Steve. You know Paulie." He spun back to face Kamii, oriental princess, unruffled by his peon emotionalism. "Where? Tell me where."

"Todd, don't . . ."

"Shut up, Steve. Christ! My sister . . ."

"Nobody forced her, Todd, she's . . ."

"She's on the second floor. Room at the end, to the right." I glared at Kamii. She showed no emotion whatsoever. She didn't seem to realize that someone as big as Todd could make eggroll stuffing out of Paulie with one hand behind his back. Or maybe she did.

"Todd, please . . ." I said, but he was gone. Into the sorority house, and gone.

"Damn it! Why did you have to tell him that?"

The oriental princess almost frowned, then shrugged. She couldn't be bothered.

"And you! Geoffie. Stop that stupid grinning! Don't you realize what's going on?"

Geoffie sobered up immediately. Then Kamii's tiny hand touched his knee, and I lost him again.

It was up to me. I certainly didn't want to insert myself in this thing between Todd and Paulie, but if I didn't do something, only three of us would be going back to Greenriver in Todd's van. Paulie could be mailed back in a business envelope.

I didn't have to follow Kamii's directions. All I had to do was follow the crashing and the sound of Todd's bellowing voice.

The room was golden brown. The morning sun, filtered through the drawn curtains, made the rumpled bed look like desert terrain. Ginger lay in the bed, knees drawn up under the sheet making enormous sand dunes. Her firm athlete's breasts were a high crested ridge below her sheet-clutching hands and blank face. She was the Sphinx in the desert of the bed.

Paulie was hopping about in his jockey shorts, hands raised in an expression both placating and defensive, should Todd decide to throw a punch with one of his tightly balled fists.

"What the hell, Paulie," Todd was bellowing, "my God-damn sister, f'Christsake!"

"Listen, Todd, I didn't . . . I mean, it wasn't . . ."

"I oughta kill ya! Kill ya, d'ya hear?"

"You aren't going to do anything except apologize for breaking into my room, and then apologize for being such an ass to your friend. Then you're going to get out." Ginger's voice was calm and level—an older sister's voice, the voice of reason.

Todd didn't give a damn about reason.

"Get dressed. My sister shouldn't have to watch me beat you shitless."

71

"Todd! Stop it. Get out, now!" No longer the voice or an older sister. More master to bad dog.

"I will. But not 'til this little Southern sonofabitch comes with me. I wanna kick his butt down the God-damned stairs."

"Todd, what's with you? If anything, you ought to be mad at me. Christ, he didn't force me. He didn't seduce me. I don't need your protection. In case you've forgotten, you're here for my birthday party. I'm turning twenty-one, remember?"

"Doesn't make any difference. And maybe I am . . . more mad at you than him. But it don't matter. This is a thing between Paulie and me. He had no right . . ."

"Oh, Christ, grow up, Todd! You'd think he'd spent the night with you, violated you."

"If Mom and Dad knew, they'd . . ."

"Don't you throw them up to me here, Todd Rain-tree! I'm here at college, turning twenty-one, paying my own God-damned way, and you, you're sixteen years old, wet behind the ears in Greenriver mid-America fantasy land, and they buy you a brand new van just because you're a boy, you're the little man . . . oh, just get the hell out of my room!" She turned her face away. The inscrutable Sphinx visage was gone. In its place, the dramatic mask of tragedy, lit by the dusky gold of the feeble sun through drawn curtains.

Paulie had stopped dancing about, his hands hung limp at his sides. He looked from Todd to Ginger, then his eyes fell on me. His expression said "I've been an absolute idiot, Steve. Make Todd understand I'm sorry. Better yet, make it so none of this ever happened."

I couldn't. It was just one more scene encapsulated in memory, one more thing to flounder and flipper through the ooze of my brain.

Todd pushed past me, shoving me hard against the door jamb. I saw the hint of tears in his eyes.

Paulie searched out his clothes on the floor and clumsily put them on, looking neither at me nor Ginger.

She was on her side now, fetal, in pain. Her body trembled under the gold-lit sheet with her silent crying.

I found Todd in the dirt and gravel parking lot behind the sorority, kicking at the big rocks more than half-embedded in the tan earth. Geoffie stood by, the grin gone, eyes confused behind his serious hornrims.

"What's wrong? What's happening?" Geoffie whispered to me.

"Paulie, Ginger."

"I don't know . . . oh!" Geoffie was getting quicker. The night before must have opened all sorts of new neuron links in his brain. "And Todd's mad. What about tonight, Steve? Can we get the two of them to forget it?"

"I don't think anybody's ever going to forget it."

"Oh, damn! Just when the band's getting started!" I was shocked. I had never heard Geoffie Prang swear. Fine guardian angel I was. He was picking up all sorts of nasty habits under my protection.

"Hey, Geoffie, let's leave Todd alone. C'mon up to Donna's room and bring your bass. There's some records I want you to hear. I'll get my guitar.

Paulie was on the stairs on the way up to Donna's room.

"Steve, I'm sorry. I feel so damned stupid . . ."

"Shut up, Paulie, c'mon upstairs. Geoffie and I are going to listen to some records and see if we can work some new stuff up for tonight. Just shut up and c'mon." He followed Geoffie and me up the stairs.

We sat, the three of us, in that semi-dark pig-sty of a room the rest of the day. Maud Polaczak sent up bologna sandwishes and milk with one of the girls. The room was filled with the sounds of Muddy Waters, Willie Dixon, Howlin' Wolf and Sonny Boy Williamson. I riffed along with the records on my guitar, while Geoffie thumped almost silently on his solid-body Ampeg. His fingers moved as they never had before. He was getting it. Paulie flexed his fingers and hummed. He had perfect pitch and didn't need a keyboard to work it out on. It was all there in his head.

The surprise came about midafternoon. The door opened, and in walked Todd, a storm cloud still sitting on his brow. He was a different person, a stranger without the old omnipresent grin.

Not a word passed. He simply sat down on the floor amid the rubble, across from where Paulie was on the bed.

The beat in the music thudding out of the speakers was irresistible. It would have made a dead man tap his foot. But Todd, a drummer, sat like a man of marble, a tormented grotesque from some Gothic cathedral.

It promised to be a long night.

The party was to start at eight. Some of the girls took Ginger to Ann Arbor to a beauty parlor, in a concerted attempt to soften her rugged lady-jock beauty into accepible 1963 femininity. Others decorated the large downstairs lounge with crepe paper and a gay banner proclaiming "Happy Birthday Ginger."

We sat up our equipment on the small raised platform in silence. Excitement lay, barely contained, just below the surface in all of us—all of us except Todd. He was an automaton, setting up his drums, checking the reach to his cymbals, tuning his snare, adjusting and readjusting the tension on his bass drum pedal. It was looking at him that stifled our excitement and kept grim expressions on all of our faces.

"Let's run a few things down," I suggested. "Okay, Todd?" He only nodded, using his drum key on his floor tom.

"R . . . right," Geoffie stammered. "Let's try that Mannish Boy song."

"Key of E-flat?" Paulie asked, hazarding a furtive glance at Todd.

"Right. Hard, slow four-beat. Put in a B-seventh bridge, and come up heavy on it."

"H . . . how about like triplets?" Geoffie asked, the question meant for Todd, but Geoffie knew Todd wouldn't answer.

"Yeah," I said. "Even emphasis, though. Okay, Todd?" He nodded again. It seemed the frowning nod was to replace the vanished grin as his stock expression.

"Okay then. One, two, three . . ."

I was amazed. It was fantastic. I cranked up the volume of my guitar, and the split speaker in my amp fuzzed out the chords. Geoffrie thumbed the E-string on his bass and Paulie put in low chords hammered out in triplets. Below it all, Todd thudded out a strong back-beat that wrenched at my guts.

I riffled out leads, combinations of Chuck Berry and Muddy Waters. I couldn't help smiling crazily to myself.

We ran down five other songs, all low-down blues. It was easy to learn—beautiful raw poetry.

"It's almost eight. Shouldn't we get dressed?" Geoffie asked.

"Dressed?" Todd's voice startled us all. He hadn't spoken since his outburst to Paulie in Ginger's room.

"Y . . . yeah. Our band outfits." Geoffie was sweating.

"You can't dress up in those pansy-assed outfits and play music like this. Besides, I don't feel like it. Those uniforms always made me feel like a monkey in a silk suit."

"Todd's right," Paulie said. "We can't wear those . . ."

"Shut up. You guys can do what you want. I'm wearing my jeans, that's all."

"C'mon, Todd. It's your sister's birthday. She's over in Ann Arbor buying a new dress, getting a new hair style. We can't play at her party looking like farm boys."

"To hell with my sister." He said and threw his drumsticks to the floor. He stalked out of the big room, his steps echoing, his movements making the twisted crepe paper flutter.

"What are we going to do?" Geoffie asked me.

"Whatever you like," I said. "I don't give a damn."

They started arriving at seven forty-five. Young college and fraternity men in button-down Oxford cloth shirts with locker loops, pegged slacks, penny loafers without socks, and short, neat, the man-who-reads-Playboy hair. Young college women in tight-bodiced

75

dresses with full short skirts flounced out with creno-
lins, flat-heeled shoes, teased and sprayed bubble
hairdos crowned with tiny bows. Some adventurous
types wore second-skin sheaths, stiletto heels, high
beehive hairdos, French twists, and eyes starkly lined in
black. I thought of Reverend Miles, the dumb sonofabitch. He didn't know beauty when he saw it. Those
girls were straight out of my fantasies. But then,
perhaps I was one of those the good Reverend spoke of
—a lost soul, Abomination, reveling in women who
chose artificial beauty to lead men to sin.

At seven fifty-five, the other faction entered. Donna,
in shapeless sweatshirt, dirty jeans and sandals led the
parade. All the others, men and women, were similarly
attired—the females without make-up, hair combed
and clean but unstyled; the males with uncombed short
hair, a few attempting rather scraggly beards and
succeeding.

It was as if someone had drawn a line down the
middle of the large room—frats to one side, bohemians
to the other.

Candi Jones, of the smart set, approached us. Todd
ignored her probing intimate gaze. The rest of us
drooled.

"Do you guys . . . I mean, can you play 'Happy
Birthday'? They're about to bring Ginger in."

"Sure," I said, tuning my guitar for the thirty-fifth
time. "C'mon guys. Slow four. Give it a blues feel.
Imagine Elmore James doing it."

"Yeah!" Paulie exclaimed. "Let's get it!"

We played the most performed song in American
music, only we played it our way, our new way.

Ginger entered. I remembered her in her female jock
outfit of shorts, sweatshirt, and simple pulled-back
ponytail. I remembered her in the bed, the golden
desert bed, making sand dunes out of the sheets. I had
never seen her as she appeared that night.

Her dress was a blue taffeta sheath, tight, revealing
the taut flatness and well-developed swells of her
woman's body. In her pointed-toed stiletto pumps she

towered over most of the males in the room. Her blond hair was piled high in swirls and folds, accented with a multitude of tiny blue bows that matched her dress. She was smiling a slightly embarrassed smile that added pretty roses to her cheeks.

She came down the line of demarcation between the two factions, and the groups merged about her, laughing, oohing and remarking on her beauty. Apparently none of them had ever seen her in a dress either.

We broke from "Happy Birthday" right into Chuck Berry's "Blue Feeling." People from both groups stared at us pointedly. Geoffie and Paulie flanked me in full band uniform, Todd and I were in T-shirts and jeans. They stared, then they began to dance.

They liked it when we did the Everly Brother's "Crying in the Rain" with a heavy back-beat. They liked it when we did Little Richard's "Rip It Up." They loved it when we did "Mannish Boy." When we did Howlin' Wolf's "Evil Is Goin' On," I thought they'd scream the house down. By the time we got to our first break, they were all standing, crowding about the stage.

They had never heard music like we played that night. We had never heard music like that. The combination of Everly Brothers' harmony, Chuck Berry side-beats, the metallic buzz of my blown speaker, and the blues infusion of the electric piano chords, thudding bass, fat-back drums and Muddy Waters guitar leads were wholly new.

In five years, some of it would be called psychedelic rock, some of it folk-rock, some of it blues-rock. In ten years, some of it would be categorized heavy metal. In twenty years, it would be New Wave. In 1963, there was probably no other band in America playing any of it.

We couldn't leave the stage for all the words of praise the slaps on the back, the job offers for keggers, grassers, even weddings.

Then I saw someone who made me forget the heady

excitement of instant adulation and shoved my way off the stage.

Cat!

It was her. I knew it instinctively, though the person standing there in the doorway bore little resemblance to the girl I had known four years previously.

Her baby-white hair was in a shoulder-length bouffant with a small black leather bow above the bangs sheltering her enormous China-blue eyes. Her pale complexion was made moon-pale by make-up, paler still by the lack of rouge and the application of light pink-almost-white lipstick to her full pouting lips.

She wore black flat-heeled shoes, lace-figured hose, a straight-skirted black velvet jumper that hugged her hips and cut away below her breasts. A ruffled white silk blouse emphasized her ripe jutting bustline.

I kept shoving people out of my way, pushing endlessly, drinking in the vision of her with my eyes. The room seemed abnormally elongated and crowded with more bodies between me and Cat than resided in the entire state of Michigan.

She saw me. Color rose in the moon-pale cheeks. She smiled, then her face attempted to frown. She was beautiful even doing that. Her eyes shot to either side of her.

It was only then I realized she was not alone.

To her left was Jenny St. Charles, taller, visibly older than Cat, attractive with her long chestnut hair, but almost invisible next to her luminous sister.

To Cat's right stood a tall gangly boy. Even though I was only fifteen and the person I saw was half a head taller than me, I called him a boy in my mind. Though tall, all knees and elbows, his face was that—I knew no other way to describe it to myself—of an infant. It was a round pie-face, almost doughy like new bread. Dark little eyes, a pug nose and a tiny wet-pink mouth completed the impression. I stared at the face of a baby impaled on a tall body. I stared, I realized, at Nicholas St. Charles.

Finally, I broke through the wall of people. Jenny

78

stepped between me and Cat, one more obstacle. Her face was set and hard, though masked with a false smile.

"Catherine insisted on coming. I blame myself for letting it slip that you were here."

"Cat . . . " I called over Jenny's shoulder. Jenny restrained me with a hand on my arm, clutching so tightly that it trembled.

"I warn you," even the pretend smile was suddenly gone, "if you cause her any pain, any grief . . ."

I jerked my arm free and traveled the two long steps to Cat.

"Cat . . . I . . ." No more words would come.

"Steve. How are you?" Her eyes skittered about, not looking at me, not wanting to look at Jenny or the mutant being that was her thirteen year old brother. "Can you . . . do you have the time to step outside?"

"Sure . . . sure, c'mon."

Jenny made a move toward us, but Nicholas made no move at all. He simply licked his odd baby-pink lips and smiled at me.

I motioned Cat to the hallway, afraid to touch her. She turned and flowed into the hall, a river of grace. I followed.

She led me through the maze of halls to the front of the building. It was like breaking through some cosmic barrier into another dimension, so different was the confining leaden air of the sorority house from the cool free black of the June night.

I watched as she turned her face up to the night sky. I could not believe I was with her, next to her again.

"Cat, I can't begin to say the things . . ."

She put a finger on my lips. Her hand hesitated, cool fingers traced lines down my cheek, then the hand dropped to her side. I couldn't tell her of the undying lust, of the aching erections in the night, of the sweating dreams every night since last I had seen her, dreams I denied in my conscious mind until that very moment.

"Steve . . . me too. You're all I've thought about—four long years . . ."

"I never thought . . . we were only eleven years old . . ."

"Some things, some people are just meant to be. Meant to be together, I mean."

I fumbled, lit a cigarette. She took it from my lips and smoked, throwing back her head as she exhaled at the night clouds.

I lit another cigarette for myself.

She hid her face from me behind the hand holding the cigarette. I thought she was about to cry.

She composed herself in an instant and took another deep drag on the cigarette.

"But even if it was meant to be, it can't be." She gave a little laugh. "Here I am, living with my aunt in Detroit, and you're still back there, still in Greenriver. I miss it, you know. I miss Greenriver terribly." She threw away the cigarette and it glowed like an eye on the sidewalk.

"How can you miss a hick town like Greenriver?"

"You don't know, you can't know until you've lived someplace like Detroit."

"Isn't it exciting? I mean, big city life?"

"Oh, yes. Frightening, too. So much tension, so many awful things going on."

"Yeah," I flicked away my cigarette and lit another. She took it from my lips, puffed, put it back in my lips, her eyes locked on mine. "But the tension, that's part of it, part of the excitement. A person can mold and grow mushrooms on their body in Greenriver." I could taste her on the cigarette. I passed it back to her.

"There are more opportunities. I'm taking dance in high school."

"Oh, yeah?"

"Yes. It's a private high school. For the arts. I take regular classes, plus music, plus dance. It's really great."

"Sounds like it."

"You don't need it. What you guys were doing tonight is really new. So different. So . . . fantastic!"

"I don't know what to say. You're embarrassing me."

Then she tilted her head slightly, and her lips touched mine. Her hands slid up around my neck. "I need you," was all she said, and we kissed.

Not even sex with Donna could approach the ecstatic delight of Cat's mouth on mine.

Then, reluctantly, she pushed me away.

"I was foolish to come here, foolish to see you again. It will only make us both hurt more to be apart now." She motioned for a cigarette and held my hand in hers as I lit it. "It can never be, Steve. I'm so sorry."

"But it can. We both graduate in two years . . . just two years."

"Things will never be right for us. There are reasons . . . things I could never explain to anyone."

"Cat . . ." I pulled the cigarette from her mouth and flung it away. I pulled her to me roughly and kissed her with a passion that could never be sated.

I felt the hand on my shoulder, like long tentacles. The fingers that were not fingers gouged into my flesh, and I winced with pain. I turned to stare into that impossible pie of a face that belonged to Nicholas St. Charles.

"Time to go, sister dear." The voice was as chilling as the face and the iron grip of the tentacle fingers. I knew he was no more than thirteen, yet his voice was an octave below mine. It was eerie; it was demonic. The singsong sardonic tone was pitched in bass notes from that ugly baby face.

I looked back at Cat. Her moon-pale cheeks blanched in a mask of death white.

"Y . . . yes, Nicholas." She was afraid of him— deathly afraid!

"Say goodbye, Steverino," the bass voice singsonged.

"Cat . . ." I tried to break free of the grip on my shoulder, but the long spider-fingered hand would not relent.

"Goodbye, Steve." Her voice trembled, tears rolling down the death-mask cheeks, and she fled into the night.

The thing that was her brother released my shoulder, laughed like a maniac, and loped off after her.

81

better believe I care! Uninvolved? This God-damned was possible to cry the night before.

I could do nothing but stand and stare. I touched fingers to my mouth, where her lips had pressed. I could still feel the heavenly heat of them.

The second set, the music helped. It made me forget, at least while the notes rang in my ears.

Midnight came and went. Then one, then two. Most of the others were gone, only the sorority members and their dates remained.

Donna was with one of the bearded set. Geoffie was with Kamii. Paulie was drunk, passed out on a couch. Todd was tearing down his drums, intent and scowling.

Jenny St. Charles was still there, talking and drinking Stroh's from the bottle. When I took off my guitar, I felt like a gunfighter putting up his pistols for good. There was something strangely final about it.

I walked like a zombie out into the depths of the night. Suddenly, everything came rushing up out of my quagmire mind, bombarding my consciousness all at once. My father, my brother and Jenny, Cat—Nicholas, the Abomination. I slouched against the van, sliding down its cold surface to sit on the rear bumper.

I cried. I cried for the first time in years. I cried the rest of the night, tears of pain and confusion and self-pity, tears meant to make it all better—but they didn't, they didn't at all.

Despite the depth of my depression, the sun rose. I felt it on my face and opened my eyes. The gold that should have warmed only blinded and pushed my mind further into hiding. I wanted darkness, eternal darkness.

A shadow blocked the sun, and I was grateful for even the minimal darkness. Then a voice, a grating bass voice, sent ice shooting through the blood vessels in my brain.

"Morning, Steverino. You look like cow shit. And that's good, 'cause that's just what you are."

I knew it was Nicholas. Why he was there or what he wanted of me, I couldn't guess. I didn't want to know. I only wanted to be left alone. He told me why and what anyway.

"I hate your guts, Steverino. You know what I am."

I shook my head. I couldn't see him, back-lit by the rising sun. Just as well. I didn't want to see him. I was afraid of what my eyes might behold.

"Yeah. You know what I am. You don't want to admit it. Your stupid little pea-brain doesn't want to admit it, but you know, and that's why I hate your guts. And you know what, Steverino? I'm gonna kill you. Someday. You wait for it. You watch for it. You worry about it. Someday, when you least expect it, I'll get you. Just like Candid-fucking-Camera." The laugh was hideous, like metal scraping concrete in staccato bursts. Then he was gone. The sun beat on my eyes again, and he was gone—a bad dream, an illusion.

I don't know what feelings were uppermost in my mind when I scrambled to my feet in the early morning sun, dusting off my jeans and smoothing my rumpled T-shirt with shaking hands, but I suspect it was a churning homogenization of every emotion known to humans.

I heard footsteps approaching and squinted into the sun, afraid of—perhaps resigned to—Nicholas returning. It was Todd.

"Here," he said and tossed a ring of keys at me. "Drop the van off at my folks. I'm staying here with Ginger for the summer. We got a lot to work out."

"Wha . . . whaddya mean? What about the band? The new stuff, it's hot . . ."

"Fuck the band." He said it softly, without anger. He said it all, though. Fuck the band. What difference did any of it make?

"Right. How about Geoffie and Paulie? Are they staying, too?"

"Don't be stupid. They don't have sisters up here. But Kamii is driving Geoffie back to Greenriver. Paulie . . . I don't know where that sonofawhore is. What does it matter?"

"What," I shook my head, "indeed."

"Hey. A lot has happened. I can't sort it out."

"And that makes you unique? Jesus Christ, Raintree, your sister screwing Paulie is like tea with the parson compared to what's going on in my life . . ."

"Oh, sure, Steve. Tell me. Tell me all about it. You're the most laid back uninvolved uncaring sonofa . . ."

"Whaddya mean, uncaring? God-damn! I care. You better believe I care! Uninvolved? This God-damned band wouldn't exist without me. Laid back? Jesus, Joseph and Mary. Until you found out your sister could fuck, you were a grinning idiot! Shit, you almost drooled you were so laid back."

I'll never know what was harder—the metal of the van door that clanged against my head as I flew back, or the cast-iron fist on the end of Todd's arm that sent me flying to the truck. All I knew for sure when I picked myself up off the ground was that both face and rear skull hurt like hell, and there was red stuff all over my previously white T-shirt.

Normally, logic would have told me not to do what I did next. But then, logic should have kept me from saying those things to him in the first place.

Logic was not part of my make up that day. I looked at Todd Raintree through the lashes of my closing eye, looked at that two hundred twenty pounds of compressed beef, and hit him. Square in the jaw.

And unlike the cliche of the big musclebound guy with the jaw of glass, Todd's head jerked back with the force of my punch, rolled, and came up with the old familiar grin.

"It took guts to do that. And if it was anybody but you, Steve, I'd fuckin' kill ya." Grin. "Let's just drop it. I'll see ya in the fall." He turned and began to walk away. He turned back. "And hey! Don't smash up my van on the way home, okay?"

I hoped to Christ and God Almighty that my right hand wasn't broken. "Can you do me a favor? Bring my guitar and amp out. I wanna leave. I don't want to go back inside."

"You got it." Grin.

I couldn't believe it, but it seemed to be true. Allowing Todd to bust my face in and making his face shatter my hand let the old Todd Raintree reemerge from his self-imposed ugliness of spirit.

Paulie came out, dragging the folded up Fender Rhodes bumping down the steps. I winced with every crash. I knew what those damned electric pianos cost.

"Paulie! Your piano . . ."

"Who gives two shits in a shoebox? It's all over, isn't it?" He slammed open the rear door to the van and threw the instrument in. Solid state did not mean indestructible. I knew at least half of the piano's tones would never sound again.

Todd came out with my guitar case and amp. Only Todd could handle the top and bottom of the Fender Bassman and a guitar case all at the same time. His old perpetual grin wavered only a bit at the sight of Paulie.

He gently set guitar and amp inside the van. "I'll get the P.A. and sound equipment."

"Don't bother. Keep it. Pawn it. Whatever."

"What? You're kidding, right, Steve?"

"No, Todd. Consider it yours. Like Paulie said, it's over. I guess I knew it last night. It was too good to be true. Hell, maybe it was a dream."

"It was no dream." Paulie bummed a cigarette. "But it is over, ol' son. If you don't mind, I think I'll take a bus back." He glanced at Todd, his expression saying he'd be damned if he'd ride back to Greenriver with Todd Raintree.

"Don't sweat it. I'm not going back. Geoffie's goin' back with Kamii in her car. It's just you and Steve." Then Todd did a very uncharacteristic thing. He clapped a hand on my shoulder, shook my hand and riveted me with his clear blue eyes that brimmed with tears, his mouth a grim line.

"Steve . . . I'm really sorry. Since this band thing started . . . hell, you've been my best friend. My Goddamned best friend. I know how much the band meant to you . . . still means to you, but . . . well, try to understand." Then a tear escaped down his cheek. "I only

85

hope, when I come back in September, you know, that we can still be best friends. I love you, Steve, love you like a brother." He relinquished my hand and nearly ran back into the sorority house.

The morning air was thick and unbreathable then, and there was a lump of rock in my throat. My own tear ducts betrayed me, though I thought I had cried all it was possible to cry the night before.

Paulie slapped my back, refusing to look at my face. He slammed the van door.

"Come on, Steve. That's about it. All she wrote." He got in the passenger side, and I climbed, tear-blinded, into the driver's seat.

The little six engine purred between us under the black metal housing. I wiped at my face with the front of my T-shirt.

"Got a cigarette?" Paulie's voice sounded funny, but I dared not look at him, dared not force him to see my tears. The Code could not be violated.

"Sure." I tossed him the pack. "Light one for me, too."

I was shocked to feel how much his hand shook as he handed me the cigarette.

"Paulie . . . " I committed the high treason of the Male Code, I looked right at him, and damned if he wasn't crying, too.

"No, Steve. Shit! It's all my fault! Shit! Oh, it was good what we played last night, wasn't it? Good? Hell, it was fantastic! And I blew it, blew it all just to ball an older woman!"

"Paulie, you didn't . . ."

"Yeah, you're right. I didn't. Todd did. Well, indirectly. You know what started it? That God-damned hot-pants Candi Jones started it when she saw Todd, when we first drove up. The girls, y'see, at Candi's eggin' 'em on, had a little ol' game, like a football pool, y'know, to see which one of 'em could be the first to ball the high school guys from the hick town!"

"What? You mean . . ."

86

"I mean nothin' but, ol' son! Ginger told me this morning. All this shit because Candi Jones wanted to latch onto Todd the Bod's muscular meat, and the other girls bet her they could get one of the rest of us before she de-pantsed Mr. Raintree."

The red Ford van climbed the hill up to U.S. 12, leaving Haines City nestled, unknowing, uncaring in its snug little river valley—snug in its little-big town college self-assurance and its scorn of teenaged boys from a little farming community called Greenriver.

"You had better drive, Paulie. Todd would probably crap, but I don't think I'm steady enough. Besides, you know I don't have a license yet . . . guess Todd forgot."

"Yeah, okay. Why don't you put on Geoffie's spare T-shirt his momma made him bring. It's in the back there, someplace. I won't ask what happened to your nose and eye."

I pulled to the shoulder, and we switched places as a few cars and a few errant semis whipped past. It was still too early on a Sunday for there to be much traffic.

Paulie drove too fast, but I didn't care. I sat slumped in the passenger bucket, watching the summer scenery slide by—smoking, thinking, trying not to think.

"It's a crock of shit, isn't it, Paulie?"

He nearly swerved off the road. The drone of the little engine, the emptiness of the highway, had lulled him; my voice had the effect of an alarm clock to a sleeper lost in a deep dream of warmth and sameness.

"Whaddya mean?"

"Life. A crock. Of shit."

"Man, I don't know. It's all screwed up, but, like, if you go so far as to say it's all shit, with no chance of getting better, well then, I guess you have to kill yourself or something."

"Exactly."

I closed my eyes. Below the self-pity, below the confusion, below the hurting ache for things I could not have and things I could not change and people I could not understand, I felt a pulsing indefinable something that told me not to go home. I slept, trying not to think about it, but at the same time being constantly drawn down to that unknown something.

When I awoke, it was early afternoon. The sunny Sunday morning had turned to an overcast storm-threatening grey. Big drops bombarded the windshield sporadically, then the clouds ripped open and the van swayed under the weight of the deluge.

"Better turn on the radio, Paulie. Looks like tornado weather."

"Hmmm? Yeah." He flicked on the radio and fumbled the tuner to find a weather report. I lit him a cigarette, passed it to him and took over the radio dial. I dialed through stations playing "Walk Right In," "Walk Like a Man," and "Our Day Will Come." I tuned past snatches of Andy Williams, Dodie Stevens and Bobby Vinton. Finally, I got the Coldwater station. We were about ten-fifteen miles east of Coldwater, I guessed.

" . . . heavy showers, thunderstorms and a good chance of tornadoes. There are unconfirmed reports of one touching down south of Kalamazoo near Portager Lake, but that is unconfirmed. Stay tuned for . . ."

I clicked it off.

"We better step on it or find someplace to hole up," I said.

"I vote for steppin' on it. Momma hates this kinda shit, and my Daddy's outta town."

I nodded, settled back, lit another cigarette, crumpled the empty box and let it fall to the floor-boards. I didn't want to think about how the van swayed in the growing wind, how it fish-tailed on the curves as Paulie goosed the accelerator.

Somehow, we made it to Greenriver. The little town looked deserted. All the sane people were backed into southwest corners of their basements with candles, flashlights and transistor radios. The maples along the streets rattled angry leaves, and branches too big to move swayed in the gusting wind. The rain was being splashed down from enormous buckets in the sky and sometimes went past the windshield from side to side instead of up to down.

Paulie stomped the brakes in the circular drive in front of his parent's house, and the rear end of the van skidded us in a half-circle. He slammed it into park and leaped out into the rain. The wind knocked him on his ass. He was drenched in half an instant. His eyes were big and empty, like a night creature startled by lights.

He gulped rainwater, trying to speak. I jumped into the driver's seat and slammed the door. As I slid and swerved down the drive, I saw him crash through the open front door of his house, straight into his mother's arms.

Branches were coming down about me, not just dead wood, but living branches of maple and elm, leaves fluttering like helpless birds sadistically tied to perches.

I pulled in to the Raintree drive and leaped out. I had to tell them the van was back, then I would run like hell to get home.

The door opened before I reached the steps.

"The van is . . ." I screamed against the wind and rain.

"Come in," Mr. Raintree said, gesturing hard with his arm, as if by sheer force the gesture would drag me in and save me from the wind's pull.

" . . . got to go home. I . . ."

"No. No, you can't. Come on in here!"

The wind ripped at the aluminim screen door. Mr. Raintree scrabbled at it with a beefy hand and made the pulling gestures at me again with the free arm.

I went in. Water drizzled off me onto the linoleum of the foyer. There were warm comforting smells of Sunday dinner—fried chicken and gravy. There would be whipped potatoes with yellow butter swimming and shelled corn with kernels big as peanuts.

I wiped the rainwater from my eyes and looked at Mr. Raintree, a big man, once muscular, now fat and pot-bellied. He wore his pants below the pot, and his T-shirt, dazzling white, gaped above the pot to show his hairy belly. His face and balding head was florid, his eyes sad and darting. Something was wrong.

"Todd stayed in Haines City. It's okay. He . . ."

"I know, I know. He called hours ago." He laid one of the beefy hands on my shoulder gently, as though touching a fragile bit of crystal he thought might shatter.

"Son, there's no easy way, no easy way at all . . ." His hand—that big, beefy paw—trembled on my shoulder.

"Son," he began again, "your father . . . he's dead, son."

"No . . . what? No . . . can't be . . . he was just . . ."

"It's true, Steven. Car accident. Hit a tree out on Airport Road. The curves, those God-damned curves . . . I guess he died instantly. No pain, son, Chief Barnes said . . ."

"Mom. I've got to get . . . she's not strong, you know, not since Brian left . . . not right, she hasn't been really okay since . . ."

"She's with her sister, over in White Pigeon. Under a doctor's care. Come on in and sit down. It's you we have to . . ."

"When? God! Jesus Christ, when did it happen?"

"Early morning. 'Bout five a.m., near as anybody can figure."

"Why didn't somebody call? Why didn't somebody tell me? Jesus Christ, don't I have a right . . ."

"You were already on the road when we knew. When Todd called. There was no way . . ."

"I don't believe it. What was he doing on Airport Road at five in the morning?"

"Nobody knows that, son. There's no way to answer the whys in this. I told the doc the missus and I would see to you. Your ma's in no shape, and your aunt's got her hands full. You can stay up in Todd's room. Come on in the living room now. I'll get some towels and, well, Todd's clothes won't fit you . . . maybe his pajamas and robe. Okay?"

I stumbled into the living room, trailing rivulets of rain water. I sat on a vinyl chair, not wanting to get the sofa wet. I remember thinking: how stupid! Dad's dead

90

and I'm worried about the Raintrees' sofa.

I dried myself with the towels, stripped down right there in the Raintree's living room and put on Todd's comically large pajamas and robe, while Mr. Raintree watched, hands on his hips and brow furrowed.

I sat down, hands folded in my lap. I had forgotten to dry the vinyl chair, and the back of the robe and pajamas were immediately damp.

"Hungry?"

"I think I'll just . . . lie down, if I could."

"Why sure, sure, anything you want. Todd's room is to the left at the top of the stairs. Bathroom's right next door."

I got up, walked like a zombie in my bare feet, the pajama cuffs flapping in rolls around my ankles. I ascended the stairs.

"You want anything, just holler." Mr. Raintree called up after me. "Steve?"

I turned at the top of the stairs. His head was bald and shiny from above.

"Steve . . . I'm sorry as hell. I really am."

"I know. Thank you." I went into Todd's room and shut the door.

There were shelves of wrestling and weight lifting trophies, framed black and white photos of Todd and teams of other musclebound guys I recognized in various gym outfits. They were all smiling, grinning like Todd, their hands folded self-consciously over their crotches.

Baseball gloves, bats, balls and cleated shoes for various sports littered the floor. The bed was made like a military bunk. I had to fight the blankets to get them untucked.

The sheets were clean and cool. The pajamas rode up to my knees as I slid in, so I stood again and took them off. The sheets felt even better on my naked body.

Sleep descended like a hammer. Dreams came like ravening creatures of the night.

My father, in the depths of his despair, as I had left him in our living room, appeared in the dream. He was pleading with me, asking my help. I reached for him, but he was ever too distant.

At length, his image blurred, faded, and blessed oblivion came.

The next dream image was of Cat. Again she was in my arms. Again I felt the soft heat, her mouth on mine, her breasts firm against me. She breathed fire into my mouth, life into my passive body.

Then her arms seemed to be crushing me. As the passionate kiss ended, I opened my eyes to stare into the wild crazed eyes of Nicholas! His gangling arms tightened and my breath whooshed from my lungs. I could not draw another.

His words came, in that nightmare bass voice, a voice that should have echoed only in chambers of the dead or the pit of Hell.

"It was me, buddy, little Steverino. I killed your old man. He was always a worthless insect of a man. You know it. I know it. Now he's dead, and I did it. I killed him. Just like I'm gonna kill you. You're as worthless as your old man."

I struggled in the dream and in the bed, there in the Raintree house, as the wind and rain walked with crashing thunder and blinding lightning outside. I could not free myself from the crushing grasp of the Abomination.

I awoke. I was sitting on the floor staring goggle-eyed into the darkness, bathed in sweat, legs tangled in sheets, and—not breathing.

I forced air in, a conscious effort to activate the involuntary functioning of lungs, trachea muscles, diaphragm. It ripped the interior of my chest like acid.

Trembling, falling in the tangle of sheets, I finally found the wall and the light switch. The thing I saw in the mirror over Todd's dresser was hollow-eyed, a rictus of horror freezing the face muscles. The rib cage of the thing was contracted, sunken, and blue with bruises. The thing in the mirror was me.

It was night. The storm still raged outside. Wind

lashed rain against the windows, rattled the panes, popped caulking and rattled the panes.

I knew it was all true. The dream. It was true. The aching ugly blue marks on my ribs proved it all. Nicholas had been there. Nihcolas had somehow murdered my father, just as surely as he would murder me. He was evil, he was Abomination, and he would kill me.

I passed the rest of the night sitting on the edge of Todd's bed, naked, lights on, hoping, praying Nicholas St. Charles would not return to take me before dawn. I did not want to die in the dark of night, when the Abomination could take my soul to the pits of Hell without a living being to see.

Dawn finally did come, and I yanked the sheets about me when the knock came at the bedroom door.

It was Mrs. Raintree.

"The mister went by your house. Your momma left him a . . . I mean, we have a key . . . and he brought you some clothes. I have breakfast cooking. How you like your eggs?"

"Not . . . hungry," I managed to say.

"Now my husband was right about not getting run down. You have to eat. Scrambled okay?"

I nodded. She laid the clothes on a straight-backed chair next to the door.

I dressed, I went to the bathroom and washed my worn, hollow-eyed face. I went downstairs and ate.

When I had consumed most of the enormous breakfast at Mrs. Raintree's constant urging, I spoke.

"I want to go home, Mrs. Raintree."

"Oh, no. I don't think so."

"Yes, I have to. I can't impose and take advantage of your hospitality." The words sounded alien and phony in my mouth. "I'll be fine. I am fine. Thank you for all you and Mr. Raintree have done. Really." I wiped my mouth on the napkin and folded it next to my plate. "I'm going to leave my amplifier in Todd's van if that's all right. I'll just take my guitar."

93

"Of course, it's fine. I do wish you'd reconsider, I do wish you'd stay. The mister will be upset."

"I need . . . to be alone, Mrs. Raintree."

"I understand. Do you have any money?"

"No."

"Then here. Just a minute." She disappeared into the kitchen. I stood up, but could not follow her into that room she obviously considered her personal domain.

She came back in a few seconds and pressed a batch of neatly stacked bills in my hand. I quickly counted it.

"Mrs. Raintree, I can't. There's over a hundred dollars here!"

"Don't be silly. I have more." She chuckled. "It's my rainy day fund." Her pleasant face sobered. "Your rainy day is here. You take it. You need more, I have more."

"Mrs. Raintree, how can I ever . . . it's a loan, okay? Just a loan."

"If it makes you feel better."

I nodded, pocketed the money, and went out the front door.

Early morning dew stood on the points of the grass blades and beaded on the roof of Todd's van.

I opened the rear door and got splattered with the moisture collected along the black rubber molding. I pulled my guitar case out. I saw the fifteen record albums stashed by the wheel well. I gathered them up and took them along.

Partly sunny, weathermen called that type of day. In Michigan, that means some places could be under dark threatening clouds all day. Greenriver was one of those places.

The maples were black-barked, like charcoal drawings by an angry artist. The leaves were still; no wind moved among them. Walking under the sheltering leaves, I felt I was the only living thing in motion as I made my way to my house. Cars would pass, tires hissing on the wet pavement and splashing in the puddles, but they were mechanical things, cold metal things that might or might not have living things trapped in their innards.

The house was more empty than any house should ever be. Had the furniture been gone, the carpets removed, light bulbs and fixtures ripped out, the structure could not have been more barren.

I set the guitar and albums down. I dialed the phone.

"Hello?"

"Aunt Jane? This is Steven."

"Oh, my goodness, Steven. Are you all right?"

"I'm okay."

"Are those people . . . what's their name? Are they taking care of you?"

"The Raintrees. They took good care of me. I'm home now."

"Oh, no, Steven. You can't stay alone."

"I'm fine. I'll be fine."

"No . . . if you're sure . . ."

"I'm sure. How's Mom?"

The pause was a bit too long for me to believe the sudden cheerful lift in Aunt Jane's voice.

"Oh, she's doing wonderfully. Really she is. Of course, the doctor is sedating her, but she's doing just fine."

"When can she come home?"

The pause was even longer.

"Well, the doctor hasn't said. That's why I think you ought to not stay alone."

"It could be a long time?"

"Well, Steven . . ."

"I'll talk to you later, okay, Aunt Jane? 'Bye."

I hung up the phone before she could say anything else.

My father was dead.

My older brother hadn't been heard from since he joined the Army four years previously.

I was the man of the family.

I knew what that meant. Small town enculturation had told me all my life.

Breadwinner. The one who brings home the bacon. Head of the household. Decision-maker. Prime-mover.

Other than making the money that brought the food

95

and paid the bills, my father had filled no other facets of the job description while he lived. Mother, through argument and prolonged insistence and protracted stubbornness, had managed everything else.

But she was "sedated," as Aunt Jane put it. What I feared was that she was over the edge. Crazy.

She had had a good start after the incident with Brian and Jennifer St. Charles. With father dead, I feared she'd gone all the way.

It would probably be necessary for me to take charge. So I did.

I hitchhiked the twelve miles to Aunt Jane's house in White Pigeon. It took about an hour.

White Pigeon was a wide spot in the road. At least, that's how it seemed. All the businesses were on five blocks of U.S. 12. The major crossroad was further west. There were no important roads going north-south off of U.S. 12, so the impression was two-dimensional— a town that went side to side but not front to back. Driving through, one could believe that even the houses and businesses along both sides of U.S. 12 were pasteboard false fronts. To the passer-by, White Pigeon was a town without depth.

I knew it had depth. Aunt Jane's house was two blocks south of U.S. 12.

I stood on the porch of the white frame house with the kelly green shutters and rang a bell that was so loud from where I stood, it must have rattled china inside the house.

"Why, Steven!"

I had taken Aunt Jane by surprise. She was mother's older sister, probably ten to fifteen years older. She wore her grey hair in a puffed bouffant that would have looked more appropriate on a teenage girl at a prom. She had it done every week at Dodie's Cut 'n' Curl next to White Pigeon's IGA. Mother once whispered that Aunt Jane probably slept sitting up so she wouldn't have to try to comb the hairdo between trips to the beauty salon. Other than the somewhat incongruous hair style

96

she affected, Aunt Jane was not unattractive. Especially for her age. She hung out in bars, her favorite being the Dew Drop Inn on 131 south of Three Rivers, and according to Mother, "did all right." Aunt Jane's husband had been dead a dozen years. He tried to pull some jammed ears out of the John Deere cornpicker without shutting it off. It pulled his arm in. Unlike the many one-armed farmers who lived to tell the tale of the unreliable nature of machinery ("I done it a hunert times, an' never got so much as a scratch"), Uncle Delbert lay in the field, arm severed, clogging the picker that droned on like a too-full blender, and bled to death.

"Where's Mom?"

"Why, she's in bed. Sedated. I told you . . ."

"I want to see her."

"Now, Steven, it will do no good . . ."

"She's crazy, isn't she?"

"Steven! Steven Dalton!"

"I know it's true. Tell me the truth. I'm not a baby anymore."

She looked at me as if I were on fire, and she didn't know if she could slap me for being so inconsiderate or call out the fire engines. Then she nodded.

"You're right. You're not. Not a baby anymore. Truth is . . ." She finally let her eyes unlock from mine. She glanced over at the kelly green porch swing hanging from rusty chains. "Let's sit."

We moved to the porch swing and I pulled out my cigarettes. She bummed one without a word. I lit them both.

"Truth is, it's too soon to tell. The doctor said things like shock, emotional trauma, unstable, and a lot more. What it all boils down to is, yes, I think the doc's gonna wanna put her away somewhere. Least for awhile."

"I see." I puffed on the cigarette and tried to seem old.

"I've already called your family's insurance man, and there's no worry about the cost. Of caring for your mom as long as need be, I mean. Seems Ed, your dad . . . I mean, well, he had a whole shit-house full of life insurance. And on top of it, the insurance man said it was double indemnity. I'm not sure what that means, but it boils down to twice as much money because Ed was killed accidentally." She flicked away her half-finished cigarette. It almost made it out to the street. "How do you smoke those things?" She patted my knee. "Wish to Christ Delbert had been as thoughtful. Least the damn house is paid for. Mmmm! So's yours. I called the Greenriver bank, too. Ed had a rider on the mortgage. They'll be sending the title to your house by registered mail by the end of the week." She was staring at me again. I was just listening to the squeal of the rusty swing chains as we moved ever so slightly, back and forth.

"But damn it, Steven, you're upset and I'm babbling about insurance and mortgages."

"I'm okay. I'm fine. I'll be fine." I got another cigarette out, then remembered the one dangling from my lips. I put the cigarette carefully back into the silver foil of the box.

"I'd have you stay here with me, but Laurel's here and with your mom . . ."

"No. I'll go back home. I just wanted the truth. I'm not a baby anymore."

"No, not you're not. I'm sorry, Steven."

"I'll just go home." I got up from the swing and walked off the porch.

"Wait. How'd you get here?"

"Hitched. The family car . . . Dad . . . well . . ."

"Let me get Laurel to drive you."

"No, I'll be . . ."

"Fine. I know, but I insist. Laurel!"

Laurel appeared in answer to Aunt Jane's bellow in the dimness behind the screen. She was Aunt Jane's only daughter, my cousin. A blowsy blonde with wild curls of brassy hair framing a plump pretty face covered with amateurishly applied make-up, she was almost a stranger to me. She was nearly twice my age, single, and hung out with motorcycle types. Stepping into the grey day she wore flat shoes, pegged greasy Levi's on her plump legs and her full hips, and a tight T-shirt with holes and a Harley insignia stretched wildly out of shape across her giant bosom.

"Laurel, run Steven back to Greenriver for me."

"Sure, Ma. C'mon, Stevie. Car's out back." She beckoned with a pudgy finger and a sardonic smile as she flounced past me down the steps.

We rounded the porch to the side of the house, Laurel in the lead, me following dumbly, watching her fat butt roll and jiggle in the tight jeans.

"I'll phone you, Steven," Aunt Jane called after us. "If you need anything, call me. Day or night."

The car was a '57 Chevy sedan, gleaming black with polished chrome and white trim on the sweep of the fins. The interior was custom tuck 'n' roll red leather. The door slammed with the solidity of a Wells Fargo safe. The engine roared deep-throated through glass-pack dual mufflers.

Laurel peeled out of the drive like an Indy pace car.

"Like my wheels?"

"Nice."

"My old man customized it, keeps it cherry. Wanna drink? There's Jack Daniels under the seat."

"No . . ."

"You look like you could fuckin' use a drink."

"I'm fine."

"Shit, what a bitch. I 'member when my dad croaked. A real bitch. It'll be okay, Stevie."

"I know. I'm fine."

She was staring at me more than she watched the road. I wished she would watch the road. We were doing ninety.

"You got balls, y'know? Shit! What are you, sixteen, seventeen?"

"Fifteen. Sixteen in September."

"Christ a'mighty! Fifteen. Shit!"

"Yeah."

"Listen . . . I know you like hardly know me, an' I know I'm like the fuckin' family black sheep or some kinda shit, but . . . what I mean is, you got balls and I think I like you."

"Thanks."

"Don't mention it. Hey. You like cycles? Ever been on a hill climb?"

"No, I've never . . ."

"Damn, you oughta come with me and my old man sometime. Shit, there's all kinds of young poon for you at a climb." She laughed a lewd laugh and slapped my thigh.

Laurel went on about cycles, hill climbs and young poon all the rest of the way to Greenriver. I suspected I made her very nervous. I also suspected she was reliving the loss of her own father through me. She wanted to say things her tough greaser-image persona would not allow her to say.

I was numb—or didn't care. I couldn't decide. At least I thought so until, with my directions, we zoomed into the driveway and screeched to a halt.

She turned to me, dampness on her cheeks beneath the shadow of her false eyelashes.

"Damn it, kid, I know it hurts like a motherfucker. You don't know what way's up. I wish I could do somethin'."

It all went to hell. I cried like a child with a favorite toy shattered to bits.

"There," she said and pulled my head against her yielding breasts. "There, there." I sat in the car a long time wetting the Harley insignia on her bosom with my tears.

The day never cleared, and with evening the wind returned, not cyclonic like the day before, but strong, constant, and intense, sighing in the trees.

I hadn't eaten, I couldn't. I wished I could sleep, go to sleep and not waken, but I feared the dreams that might come. I couldn't go in the living room—that's where I last saw him, where he pleaded and begged for my compassion and understanding, and I cut him cold and walked out. So I sat on the porch and smoked until

I had a headache from no food and too much nicotine.

I can't say how many days passed, how many nights without sleep. I know I spent little time in the house unless it was in my own room, the sanctuary of my childhood.

I never did see my mother before they took her to someplace in Kalamazoo. For the best, Aunt Jane said, and she'll be fine.

Unexpectedly, the high points in those faceless summer days after my father's death were the frequent visits of my cousin, Laurel Willer.

The title to the house arrived, as my Aunt Jane predicted, and I signed for it. Our postman, Mr. Fair, a bandy-legged old geezer dwarfed by his worn leather mail pouch, solemnly scrutinized my signature and offered his sympathy to the family. He told me what a fine upstanding citizen Mr. Ed Dalton had been. I thanked him.

At some point I had to go to court. I don't know who decided it was necessary, and the proceedings are blurry even now in my mind. It was informal—social worker, the doctor who had ministered to Mother in White Pigeon, Aunt Jane, a decrepit old man who was Aunt Jane's lawyer, and a craggy-faced old judge. We met in the judge's chambers in the county courthouse at Centerville.

Boiled down, Aunt Jane said, Mother was to be hospitalized for some time and was judged unfit to serve as guardian to me, as so diagnosed by the doctor. Effective immediately, until the location of my older brother, Aunt Jane would serve as legal guardian. I would live with her.

Aunt Jane was a pragmatic. She didn't mind watching out for me, but she really didn't want a fifteen year old under her roof. That suited me, because I didn't want to live and go to school in White Pigeon. As we left the courthouse, we struck a bargain. I would live at home, and call her daily to report how I was, how I felt, how things were in general. She would administer the trust set up from Dad's insurance benefits and pay all the bills for mother's hospitalization, all house bills such as utilities for my parents' house, and send me a food and clothing allowance of fifty dollars a week. She would tell all concerned authorities she had moved in with me in Greenriver.

Geoffie called once. Paulie, a couple of times. Mr. Raintree dropped off my amp. All the conversations revolved around the death of my father and the lock-up of my mother, spattered with I'm sorrys, how-are-you-doing-reallys, and I'm fines.

4

It was July 4th. Dogs all over town barked or cringed under beds as illegal fireworks exploded throughout the day. The sun had dropped to the horizon, but the 100-plus degree air still hung heavy over Greenriver.

I was in my usual spot, rain or shine, night or day— sitting on the front porch swing, feet propped on the broad rail, occupied with my usual pastime of chain-smoking.

Other than the occasional M-80 burst or lady-finger crackle that hushed the early crickets and locusts for brief seconds, the streets were becoming silent.

Suddenly, my colorless, thoughtless reverie was shattered by the thunder of a powerful engine growling through gears, unhampered by unconventional mufflers. Laurel's gleaming black Chevy, itself a creature of the night, exploded into sight and careened into the drive.

She vaulted out of the car and strolled toward the porch.

High-heeled and studded black boots came up to her knees; skin-tight black leather pants hugged her thighs and hips. She wore a black motorcycle jacket with zippers everywhere. It was belted tight at the waist, but open all the way up from there showing the powder-white flesh of her plump belly and bountiful breasts. A black leather Harley cap sat rakishly on her wild tangled mane of brassy hair.

She stopped in front of me, slightly below my perspective on the high porch, straddle-legged, fists on hips, head cocked. Her familiar lewd smile played on her lips.

"Awright, you sorry sonofabitch! Enough of this drag-ass bullshit. You know, you look like hell!"

"Thanks, Laurel."

"No, I mean it. Ma asked me to come see how you were gettin' on and I said to myself, I know how he's gettin' on, he's drag-ass fucked up. Well, enough, Steve."

"Hey. I appreciate your concern, but I'm okay. Really."

"Bullshit! Looked in a mirror lately? Your eyes are so sunken, they practically come out the back of your head. You're losin' weight. You look sick. Hell, I let you go any longer, and your dick will probably stop workin'."

"You're a real poet."

"Look, don't give me any crap, or I'll drag your draggy ass offa that porch."

"Yeah? I'd like to see that." I chuckled. I thought it was pretty funny. It was the first thing I'd thought was funny in over a month.

Her high-heels clicked on the porch steps. One of her pudgy hands grabbed my collar, and the other reached down my back and latched onto my belt. Then I was airborn—right through the screen door and down to the ground. I rolled over and gazed up at her, stunned.

"Anything else you'd like to see, smart-ass?"

She came down off the porch, pulled me by the hand until I was standing, and steered me to the car.

I sat meekly in the passenger side of the front seat, as she hung on the door, leaning in, breasts bulging at me like flesh-colored volleyballs.

"Didja learn not to mess with Mama Laurel?"

I nodded.

"You gonna put yourself in my hands tonight? Do what I say?"

I nodded again.

"I swear, we're gonna have a good time!"

First, she stopped at the party store and bought a cold case of Colt 45. She put a cold can, popped and ready to go, in my crotch. She peeled out of the dirt drive at the party store, and by the time we hit the stop light, she had drained her first one and was reaching back over the seat for another.

"Drink up. I could drink this whole case myself, but I don't wanna get ripped. This is your night."

I dutifully guzzled at the cold malt liquor.

We tooled Greenriver's main street five or six times, back and forth, turning at the A & W root beer stand at the west end of town, reversing in the Buy-Low supermarket at the east end.

"So . . . you wanna do anything?" she asked.

"Like what?"

"I dunno, whatever turns on your lights."

"There's only one thing that does that. Used to be two, but my band broke up."

"Yeah. yeah. So what's the other thing?"

"Nothing we can do in Greenriver."

"That's probably the truth! Tell me anyway."

"There's this girl . . ."

"Hey. No kidding?"

"There used to be this girl . . . no, that's not right, either. Aw, shit! She lived someplace up by Detroit now, anyway. What's the point?"

"No problem. Old Chevy's full of gas. We got all the time in the world. I'll drive ya to Detroit."

"There is a problem. I don't know where she lives."

"Jesus Keerist! You are a mess, ain't ya?"

"It's worse than that." I was getting pretty drunk. I had never talked about Cat and Nicholas to anyone. "Even if I did know where she lived, I couldn't go there. Her brother said he was going to kill me."

"Big sucker, huh? How old is he?"

"Thirteen."

"What?" She nearly ran the car over the curb.

"Yep. Thirteen. But he's a big thirteen. And he can . . . change."

"Whaddya mean?"

"Know where the cemetery is?"

"Yeah. Used to go there to drink when I was underage. The old man I had then was from Greenriver. Worked at the grey iron foundry."

"Drive over there."

We drove over there. The black Chevy purred through the narrow twists and turns of the unlit cemetery lanes. We drove through the old part.

"Right there, right down there by the creek. I saw him change into something. I doubt if even God knows that."

"Whaddya mean, change?"

"Mutate. The little kid—he was eight then— changed into something with scales, claws . . . a tail."

"You on somethin'? Sometimes my old man does pills and shit, and he sees things."

"No. I saw it. I saw him change." I smacked the flat of my hand hard against the dash.

"Okay, okay. I believe ya," she said. "So this is the brother of the girl you're hot for?"

"Yeah. One of her brothers."

"Did this girl ever change into anything?"

"Yeah," I said, the image of Cat beautiful in my mind. "Yeah. She changed into a gorgeous woman."

"Blonde, brunette?"

"Blonde. Hair the color of clouds in summer."

"Big tits?"

I looked at her sharply. In the greenish light from the dash, I saw her lewd smile.

"Yeah."

"You like blondes with big tits, huh?" She stuck her hand unerringly into my crotch.

I jumped away as best I could.

"Yeah, I do. But don't do that. It's incest or something, isn't it? First cousins?"

"Hell, I ain't gonna have your babies or nothin'." She pulled her hand back—reluctantly, I thought.

"She used to live there."

We had rounded the back side of the cemetery, and I could see the St. Charles house silhouetted in the street lamp glow.

Laurel braked the car to a quick stop, and I nearly hit the windshield.

"You're kidding, right?"

"No. She lived there. Her mom and older brother still do."

"Oh, shit, this is too damned scarry!"

"What?"

Laurel turned off the ignition key, and the engine growled to a halt. Only crickets interrupted the heavy night silence around us there in the cemetery.

"I don't go in much for ghost stories and that kinda shit, but if ever I knew of a spooky place, that house is it."

I took two Colt 45's from the case in the back, handing one to Laurel. She guzzled it to empty in about eight seconds. I watched the rivulets of malt liquor run down her chin, dripping into the cleavage between her breasts. She didn't need my encouragement to go on. She needed to tell somebody—somebody who would believe.

"I told you I used to come here to drink when I was underage. Sixteen, seventeen. Nothin' else to do. I was here one night, pretty well crocked. My old man was supposed to be with me but he copped out. I was sittin' on that stone thing over there." She pointed off into the darkness.

"That crypt over there?"

"Yeah, whatever ya call it. I was sittin' there with a

fifth of Cactus Jack, about halfway through it.

"The first thing I noticed was a stink. I mean a real bad stink, like meat left out in the sun for a week mixed with the smell of human shit. I tell ya, it damn near knocked me over.

"Then I started hearing the noises. Sounds like a woman screaming. Not just scared-screaming, but pain-screaming, like she was gettin' cut up or something'.

"The woman's scream goes on and on, then I heard this . . . this bellow like a bull bein' castrated, and suddenly the woman's scream is just like loud cryin'.

"There's a lot of bangin' and crashin', a man cussin' loud, somethin' about goin' back, hollerin' for somethin' to go back. Then there was a noise like a . . . well, like an explosion in reverse, y'know, like in those funny TV shows when they blow up a building and then show the film backwards so the tumbled down building stands up again.

"The wind got all calm, I remember. The air was still as death and clammy, too. There wasn't a sound. No fuckin' crickets or nothin'.

"Then the man screams somethin' about what are you doin' here, and he screams the name Catherine again and again. And the woman stops cryin' and screams leave my baby alone."

She paused to grab another Colt .45.

My blood had stopped flowing; I was sure of it. I was cold sober. I grabbed another malt liquor and chugged down half of it.

"All I heard then was like a baby cryin'. Cryin' hard like she was real scared."

She drank the rest of the Colt. I could see even in the dark that she was shaking, sweating heavily.

"You're sure the man said the name Catherine?"

"Positive. I'll never forget anything that happened that night."

"Well, that sure is interesting. You see Catherine St. Charles is the name of the girl I was telling you about."

"Jesus, Joseph and Mary! I'd give my left tit to know what went on that night." She lit a Camel, offering me

107

one, which I declined. "Maybe we could ask your girl. How old you figure she was then?"

"When did it all happen?"

"I'm thirty now, I was seventeen then. Musta been 1950. In late June."

I nodded, the realization coming slowly, making me want to retch.

"Cat would have been two. About the time Nicholas was born."

"The brother? The one who wants to kill you?"

"Yeah, timing's just about right. Just about exactly when Nicholas would have been born."

She flicked the glowing cigarette butt out the open window. "Yeah," she said, exhaling a vast quantity of smoke. "Born or maybe conceived."

I opened the car door just in time to save the Chevy's tuck'n'roll from being splattered with vomit.

Later, at home alone, feeling relief from having unburdened myself to Laurel, confiding in someone at last, I foolishly allowed sleep to come.

And with it came Nicholas.

In the dream, we were in the cemetery. It was summer. The day was lovely, peaceful, an azure sky.

The gravestones themselves seemed to have life. They shimmered in the dappled sunlight, their shapes indefinite and mutable. The trickling creek in the old section was a fast-flowing, wide river. On the bank opposite from where I stood, Nicholas St. Charles reclined, a sickly smile on his puffy pie-face, his lanky malformed limbs arranged in a deceptively relaxed attitude.

When he saw me, he stood, as if in slow motion.

I thought to myself that this is a dream, only a dream, but even knowing that, I was terrified. If he had been a fantastic creature with two venom-drooling sawtooth mouthed heads, dragon scales and condor talons, he could not have been more horrifying. The mere fact that he was supposedly human—human but not quite— made him infinitely more a monster.

108

He laughed the laugh that sounded like metal scraping pavement, and stretched out those long arms, fingers flexing, as if he could reach me, even across that broad expanse of rushing water.

I laughed a humorless laugh of fear.

"You can't get me, not across water. I know that. I'm safe. I'm safe."

Then I was in the air. I felt the sensation of flying as an actuality. The water below me gurgled and ran over rock, grass, root of tree.

And I was beside him, side by side with the Abomination.

"I killed your father and made your mother crazy," he singsonged like a child. I remembered he was thirteen. "I can kill your aunt and cousin, too. Be careful, Steverino. Be careful."

"Why do you want to punish me?"

"Because you know. Because you told your pig cousin. Because she told you! Because now you know even more than you did before."

"I don't know anything! Not for sure. Don't hurt anyone else."

"That's my job." The metal-scraping laugh again.

"You're not real! You can't be real. This is a dream, and you can't be real."

"Wanna bet, Steverino? I can show you how real I am. I live in dreams."

"Then you can't be real when I'm awake."

"Yes I can. I can do whatever I want. Be whatever I want. Hurt whoever I want."

"But why? Why?"

"Because that's why I'm here."

"I'll stop you."

That grim grating laugh was his response.

"No. I will. I'll stop you so you can't hurt anyone ever again."

"I hurt your daddy, hurt your mommy. I'll hurt you when I want to." He was petulant in his glee.

"Go ahead. Do it to me. But don't hurt . . ."

"Catherine? Catherine Charlene? Little Cat? Your

pussy-Cat?" I had heard that before . . . Laurel!

"You won't . . . you can't! She's your sister!"

"I can do anything I want to my sister. She's my sister. Mine! Not yours. I can even do dirty stuff to her . . . just like you did."

"No!"

"I saw you, saw you do it. I can do it too!" The laugh —deep and abrasive—and all the while gamboling about like he did in the cemetery, that day he saw, the day I saw. . . .

I lunged at him.

Those long arms snapped up and tentacle fingers wrapped around my throat. He lifted me so my feet dangled above the ground.

Air was gone. The river rushed on, the gravestones danced, the leaves in the trees hissed, the azure sky and puffy white clouds, swirled like a whirlpool all about me.

"I'll give you something to prove how real I am." I heard this dimly as unconsciousness swirled and danced like the clouds and sky.

He still held me with one horrible hand. I felt the nails of the other rake my chest. I felt blood trickle down my belly. Then nothing.

The sun came brightly through my bedroom window, and I awoke from the deathlike sleep. I felt a tightness on the flesh of my chest and stomach as I stirred, and looking down, saw the dried brown-red blood. I looked at the sheets. They were covered with it.

Washing off the clotted blood in the bathroom, I saw the five long gashes on the body of the boy quickly becoming an old man reflected in the mirror on the bathroom door.

The marks were each about two inches apart and ran straight like roads from collarbone to navel.

I was nauseous, my head reeling. Was it a dream? How could I be marked from an occurrence in a dream? If not a dream, where lay reality? Could I have done this thing to myself?

I hid the sign of the Abomination under a clean

T-shirt and dressed for the day, hoping that my actions were not of a dream, not in a dream, that I was embarking on a new day of reality after a too vivid nightmare.

Downstairs, I was turning toward the kitchen to find breakfast when the front door opened.

"Laurel, I . . ." I expected Laurel, because I knew she had a key. It wasn't Laurel. It was a stranger in an army dress uniform.

"Hey, squirt, you've really grown." The stranger tossed his duffel across the room where it thudded before the sofa. I read "Dalton, B.N., M. Sgt."

This thin, crewcut man, half a head shorter than me, was no stranger. He was my brother. Brian was home.

"Brian . . . ? What are you doing here?"

"Not much of a welcome, after four years." He tossed the cap he held in his hand onto the coffee table.

"I mean, how . . ."

" . . . did they find me? Hell, it's not hard. Uncle Sam always knows where his G.I.'s are. I guess Aunt Jane had her lawyer make some calls. Stated the case to my C.O., and here I am. Three months hardship leave."

"There's no hardship. Dad's insurance . . ."

"Hardship doesn't always mean lack of funds to the Army. I'm here to find a permanent guardian for you, somebody to watch out for you for the next couple of years."

"I've got Aunt Jane, cousin Laurel."

"C'mon, Steve. Give me a break. A barfly and a cycle slut? Hardly suitable guardians. I've already seen Aunt Jane, and she admitted she was letting you live here alone."

"I'm okay."

"I bet. I would've loved to be on my own at fifteen. What is it, squirt? A party every night? Where's the empty beer bottles? Where's the cheerleading squad's discarded panties?"

I wasn't impressed with what Brian had become. Thinking about it then, I guessed Brian wasn't all that different. I had never really liked him much. The

111

uniform placed something else between us. It made him even more superior, at least in his own mind.

"I was just going to fix myself some breakfast. Want some?"

"Hell, no. It's after ten a.m., kid. I had breakfast four hours ago. See? That's what I mean. You need some discipline."

"Like the Army?"

"It's not bad . . . not bad at all. Four years overseas and I'm a master sergeant. Another two years or so, I'll be a lieutenant, and I never even graduated high school. Not some college ROTC second lieutenant, but up through the ranks."

He opened his tunic buttons and plopped down in Dad's overstuffed recliner, spit-shined Army brogans gleaming darkly as he flipped the chair back, crossing his legs at the ankles.

I sat on the couch, careful not to disturb the duffel bag.

"So what's the plan, Brian, to give my life some discipline?" Even I bridled at the weight of the sarcasm in my voice.

"Look, kid, I flew over from Berlin to get you set straight. I sure didn't come here to get loaded down with a batch of bullshit from a snot-nosed fifteen year old."

"I can appreciate your point of view. I'm not much in the mood for bullshit, either."

He slammed the chair into the upright position, leaning toward me threateningly.

"You watch your mouth, boy. When you're talking to me, you're talking to . . ."

" . . . my superior officer? The local shining representative of the Army's finest? Shit, Brian, you're still just my brother. Like Dad used to say, a monkey in a silk suit is still a monkey in a silk suit." I opened a new box of Benson and Hedges laying on the coffee table. I lit up and blew a smoke ring in his direction. "And speaking of Dad, thanks for your condolences."

He leaned back, a sardonic smile twisting his mouth and making it ugly.

"You're really something, aren't you? A real smart-ass . . ."

"I'm not, Brian . . ."

"Yeah, you are. A smart-assed kid. Think you're pretty grown up, don't you?"

"Sometimes these days, I feel real old, yeah."

"You don't have a clue, Sherlock. Let me tell you, if the Army took young shits like you, I'd toss you in so fast . . ."

"No thanks, Brian. If the Army makes men like you, I want no part of it. You know, I realized just a few minutes ago that I never really liked you much, but at least I used to look up to you, respect you. I guess it was just because you were older. Believe me, since Dad died, I have grown up. I won't be fooled again into respecting someone just because of position or age, or anything else so flimsy." I blew another smoke ring—a big fat, puffy one. It drifted over to Brian. He snatched it out of the air as if it were an enemy grenade.

"Maybe I ought to wise you up. You talk as though some tragic twist of fate took our beloved father from us. Wake up, kid. I got the story. They sacked the old fart, and spineless wimp that he was, he ran the car up a tree. He would have rather bought the farm than face the old lady with the news."

I was off the couch and on top of him before he could defend himself. I bloodied his nose, cut his lip and closed one eye before he reacted, but when he did, I was on the other side of the room suddenly, cracking plaster and lathe with my body, then sliding down the wall to sit like a broken puppet on the carpet. He was standing over me, legs set in a firm stance, fists balled into murderous iron maces. I looked up at him, standing as he was like a prize fighter over his downed opponent, awaiting the order from the ref to go to a neutral corner, and wished he would beat the shit out of me. Then I knew I would be able to hate him one hundred percent, and have it over and done. It would also exorcise my feelings of guilt over not seeing or caring about Mother. I wondered if he had said what he did about our father, acted the way he did, because of pain and guilt of his own over Dad's death.

Later I would learn I was wrong. Brian was just an uncaring shit.

5

Brian's arrival did put discipline into my life, but not because of anything directly attributable to his actions. His presence just made me want to get out and away from the house as much as possible.

It was timely, because I was scheduled to begin the mandatory driver's training program within the week.

Every other day—Monday, Wednesday and Friday —I would rise early and pile into a spanking new Buick Elektra, donated by the local G.M. dealer, with another guy, two girls and Coach Billy Doakes. To this day, I don't know what qualifications Coach Doakes had to teach Driver Ed, other than the fact he was a basketball coach with nothing else to do with his summer.

The Driver Ed days were pretty uneventful—no major accidents, no major insights. Coach Billy "Deacon" Doakes was boring as a bologna sandwich.

Four weeks later, I had successfully avoided Brian for most of my waking hours, had enjoyed the respite of dreamless sleep, and had made four new friends. All of us—Debbie, Jim, Michelle and myself—had survived Deacon Doakes' Driver Ed course and all had our highly coveted learner's permits. Debbie's older sister Deanna Frankwiler had just graduated high school, but seemed only slightly less hair brained than her sibling. She was willing to be the licensed driver whose presence was necessary for the four of us to practice our driving.

Jim Harper had begun his driving experience at the age of eleven, when he stole his neighbor's car for what he presumed would be a joy ride to California. He made it as far as White Pigeon before a state bull had the presence of mind to wonder what such a short person was doing in such a big car and stopped him. Jim had about two months probation for that one and since then had been in minor trouble almost constantly.

He wasn't a bad kid, and he wasn't malicious. He got in trouble for pranks and his constant pursuit of thrills and good times. He had become the master of the deadpan. He had big brown eyes matching his dark hair and a thin face. Because of his many scrapes, he had acquired the knack of looking pitiful, doleful of eye, with a hint of a God-I'm-sorry smile. It worked so well on adults, he used it to get laughs with his peers.

Debbie was petite, vivacious in a kewpie-doll-cute way, with a complexion of cream and greenish eyes, big and blinking behind stylish Cadillac-wing eye glasses.

Deanna was red-headed like her sister, but not as pretty. She was taller and more gangly than Debbie. Her eyes seemed dull behind severe black-framed glasses. She saw herself as the unattractive Frankwiler girl, and so became it. It would have saddened me to think of her as the constant fifth wheel of our group had it not been for the fact she seemed to come out of her shell when with us, experiencing life's excitements somewhat vicariously. We were her excuse for doing things, for going places she would never attempt alone.

Michelle "Boobs" Bailey, as she was nicknamed, was smart but giggly. She wore her black hair in a short bubble style, her blouses and sweaters ridiculously snug.

Though she blushed when the boys called her Boobs

Bailey, she did everything she could to emphasize her overripe proportions. She enjoyed playing the tease. Her carefree attitude toward life was exactly what I needed at that particular point in my life. Being near her kept Cat and all the dark things associated with her from my mind. At least that's what I thought at the outset.

The four of us had been misfits together in Driver's Ed—the 1963 group unlucky enough to draw Deacon Doakes as an instructor, the fifteen year olds unlicensed to drive in a culture where cars ruled and in the state that built them all. It was a firm bond of deprivation between us. Deanna's importance to us, wrong or right, was based on her already owning a car.

We were counting down the days to school opening, all of us reluctant to see summer end, Deanna more than any of us. The rest of us would still be together, though stifled by the requirements of being back in school. Deanna had graduated. When September came, she was off to Berkley to begin her undergraduate college career. She was going to be an anthropologist. She would have to learn to exist, mousy and undynamic as she was, in a world of strangers.

"California!" I would say to her. "And you don't want to go?"

"It's not that I don't want to go. I mean I want to get on with my life, get my degrees. It's just that I'll miss all of you so awfully."

There was never anything to be said to that.

One fateful day, as we cruised the countryside, Deanna stopped, suggesting we get a Coke. "C'mon," she said. "I'll buy."

"I don't feel like a Coke. Think I'll stay here," I said.

Michelle stared into my eyes a minute, then breathed, "I think I'll just stay here, too."

"They must have something very private and personal to say to one another," Jim deadpanned. "We should respect their plaintive plea for privacy."

"Oh, Jim!" Debbie said and slapped his shoulder.

"I'm serious. People need time alone to talk things

116

out. Quiet moments to reflect . . ." Debbie and Deanna dragged him away as he continued to spout nonsense.

Michelle giggled, looking after them, then gazed into my eyes again. Her breathing quickened, doing marvelous things to the front of the tight top she wore.

"Would you . . . kiss me, Steven?" The sexual tension between us was magnet and steel. I gladly obliged.

"You kiss better than any guy I've ever known," she sighed.

"What do I say to something like that?"

"Nothing. Just do it some more." She opened her mouth and we kissed. I put my hand on her breast, the first time I had ever attempted it. Michelle took my hand away, and I was destroyed—then she shoved it under her yielding jersey.

The kiss escalated rapidly, and soon we were stretched out on the rear seat, four hands groping, bodies rocking with passion, mouths hungry and locked onto each other.

She broke from the kiss, out of breath.

"I want you, Steven. I really do."

"I want it, too." I doubted she noticed the distinction in our differing use of pronouns. I knew why I said what I did and I was relieved she missed it.

"We can't here."

"I know."

"Where? Where can we go?"

"I don't know. My brother is home, so we can't go there."

She was planting hot kisses all over my cheeks, my forehead, my throat, where she would linger and suck longingly at my jugular.

"I'm not teasing, Steven, I don't want to tease you. I've never felt this way before." She bit my ear lobe, snaked her tongue into the hollow of my ear and whispered, "I've never done this before, any of this, with any boy. You're the first. I want you. You make me crazy hot. Steven, I love you!" She bit the hard muscle in my neck until stars of pain danced before my eyes.

I was excited. I wanted her, but those last three

117

words nearly paralyzed me. It would be so easy to lie, to just say the words, but I couldn't.

"We'd better stop. There's nowhere to go and the others will be back in a minute. C'mon. Sit up, Michelle. You'd better fix your hair."

I helped her sit upright. Her eyes were searching mine and there was a tiny furrow between her brows. She was too confused to be angry.

"All right. Okay . . . you're right. Won't do any good to get worked up . . . God, I wish there was some-place . . ."

She pulled an odd little instrument out of her clutch purse and ministered to her ruined hairdo, trying to see in the rear view mirror. She checked her mascara and reapplied white-pink lipstick to her passion-reddened lips. She pressed her palms repeatedly to her cheeks as if trying to eliminate the heat and the blush of our encounter in the back seat.

"I'm okay now. Maybe we ought to go inside. A cold drink might help me calm down." Michelle smiled at me, but there was still confusion in her eyes. She couldn't decide if I had rejected her advances or was simply being logical about our plight. Either way, I must have been as much an enigma to her as I sometimes was to myself.

Deanna had stopped at the Glass House, a service area restaurant on the Indiana Toll Road, where there were access drives for the employees of the plazas. Local people went there to eat on occasion because they were open all night, because they were halfway in ambiance between Greenriver's grills and hamburger stands and the posh expensive restaurants in Kalamazoo, Elkhart, and South Bend.

We were nearly to the door before Michelle spoke.

"We could do it in the woods, sometime, I wouldn't mind."

I pictured Michelle, with her perfect hair, perfect make-up, tidy, immaculate Bobbie Brooks separates, rutting in the dead leaves, damp moss and brambles of some local woods, sweating and thrashing beneath me in the heat of passion. It was surely only fantasy on my part even to be able to picture such a scene, and surely honest desperation on her part to suggest such a possibility.

"We'd still need a car. Kimble's woods is closest to town, and that's still five miles. Besides, it would be pretty messy out in the open like that."

She was pouting as I opened the door for her. Then she turned to me, halfway in, eyes glowing.

"I know! The park!"

"Police patrol there at night . . . we'd be caught . . ."

"Then the cemetery! Oh, Steven, no one would bother us in the cemetery."

I froze where I stood. I couldn't move or speak, as images I didn't want to recall came to mind.

"No. Absolutely not," I said at last, swallowing a hard lump in my throat. I pushed her gently but firmly through the doorway, guiding her into the restaurant by the elbow.

"If I didn't know better, I'd think you didn't want to." She tried a coy pout, but her confusion at my attitude made it fail.

"I want to, Michelle. I just want it to be right. Your first time . . ."

She kissed my cheek lightly. She was blushing again.

"Oh, Steven. You really are wonderful." She walked a few steps, then turned to me again.

"Will it be your first time?"

"No." I hadn't meant to say it with such force. It was almost as if I had struck her face. Again, it would have been so easy to lie, to say yes. Intead, I told the truth, said the words that would hurt her most, cause confrontation.

"Another girl? D . . . do I know her?"

"I don't want to talk about it, Michelle. Please understand."

"Oh, I do." She obviously didn't, and it didn't really matter to me if she did.

We were at the table where the others sat. I was never so glad for multiple companionship as at that moment.

"See? I told you," Jim Harper nodded morosely, "they only needed a little time alone to talk. Feeling better now, aren't you, Michelle? Got it all . . . off your chest?"

Debbie slapped his shoulder hard. Deanna pretended to count the ceiling tiles. Michelle's cheeks were aflame. She slid into the booth without a word, eyes locked on the salt shaker.

"Knock it off, Jim," I growled.

"Right you are, Steven old man. None of my business."

The waitress came over, and I ordered Cokes and fries for Michelle and myself. Small talk was exchanged until we left, but the tension hung in the air between Michelle and me like animal musk.

All the way back to Greenriver, some ten miles of twisting country lanes, Michelle sat as far from me as the width of the Falcon's back seat would allow. She attempted gaiety, laughter, small talk and jokes, but no one in the car was fooled.

Back in Greenriver, she asked to be dropped first, claiming she had developed a headache. I asked Deanna to let me off uptown at Vito's. Harper got out with me.

As the car pulled away, Jim put his hand on my shoulder.

"Don't get too involved with a girl who has headaches, Steve old man. That can lead to a woman who has headaches."

I frowned at him. His sober face broke into a smile.

"Hey, I'm only joking." Then he became serious. I had never seen Jim's face assume a truly serious expression before. It was pitiful. He didn't know how to carry it off.

"Steve, if my joking caused any trouble . . ."

"Well, it sure didn't help out."

"I'm really sorry."

"Oh, don't be. Michelle wants to get in deep and I don't right now. That's all."

"Yeah. Debbie's the same, but in a different way. It's been over a month now and she barely lets me kiss her good-night. You'd think a kiss meant a lifelong commitment. At least you're making out."

We stood there on the street watching the lazy summer traffic drift by. Cars with seemingly nowhere to go and in no hurry to get there made shushing sounds with their tires on the hot pavement.

I avoided the group for a couple of days, not that Michelle Bailey would forget about trying to work out a sexual tryst. I wanted that with her, but I hoped she would have a change of heart and no longer consider love a prerequisite.

My birthday came on September first. Brian was still at the house, and we still weren't speaking.

Jim Harper called in the morning around ten, inviting me to a combination birthday and only-eight-days-'til-school-starts party. I accepted and asked where and when.

"Great. Nine o'clock at Michelle's."

"I'll be there."

Brian was in his army fatigues, just starting the third beer of his first six-pack of the day.

"What was that all about?"

"What was what all about?"

"Always the smart-ass, huh, squirt? On the phone."

"A friend. Inviting me to a birthday party tonight."

"Birthday party, huh? Whose?"

"Mine."

"Your birthday?"

"Yeah. Sixteen. Laurel's driving over tomorrow so I can borrow her car to take my driving test and get my license."

"Well, happy birthday, squirt."

"Stop calling me that. It worked when I was eleven, but now you're just too damned short . . . in a lot of ways."

"Don't get belligerent, kid, or I'll show you height don't mean shit."

"Dry up, Brian. When are you going back to the Army?"

"You really don't appreciate what I'm doin' for you, do you, squirt?"

"What you're doing for me? For me? You call drinkin' four six-packs a day, bitchin' at me whenever I'm home and threatening to kick my ass every five minutes doing something for me?"

"Why you little . . ."

"Don't push it, Brian. You don't have to prove to me what a big tough guy you are. Why don't you just head on out, fly back to Berlin or wherever it was. Stop making both our lives miserable."

"I've gotta take care of you. You're my kid brother. Not right for a fifteen year old . . ."

" . . . sixteen. I was getting along just fine until you came home. You know, I missed you . . . your running off like that. I felt sorry for you. I thought you got a raw deal."

He spilled beer on himself, his eyes looking at me glazed and cruel.

The black stain of beer on his fatigue shirt looked like fresh wet blood, I thought. "I figured you'd do two years in the Army, save your money, and come back to Jenny . . . come back for her." The stain spread over his chest, down his stomach. "Well, I saw Jenny. She said you didn't write. You didn't even say goodbye when you left town. Then I knew what a shit you really were. Then I remembered what a shit you'd always been. Now I know you'll always be a shit. An older shit, a drunken shit, a shit in a green Uncle Sam monkey suit."

First he threw the half-full beer can at me, then he screamed like a maniac and jumped on me. Wild as he was I could probably have taken him, even with his Army hand-to-hand combat training, but I didn't even try.

He beat at me and kicked me, screaming and crying for probably fifteen minutes. Then he broke down entirely, collapsing in a sodden, simpering heap, the blood from my face covering his hands. I had been right. I couldn't tell the blood stains from the beer stains on his fatigues.

I eased myself up. It was painful, but I made it to an upright position and went up the stairs to my room. I didn't look in the mirror to see how bad the damage was. I changed out of the tatters of my bloody T-shirt and jeans and put on tan cords and a short-sleeved oxford button-down. I wiped at my face with the T-shirt. It had even more blood on it when I was finished.

Brian was still on the living room floor, crying, when I went out the door. I thought of Dad. I walked.

It didn't take long to walk all over Greenriver. I spent time staring into the river on the southside of town. I sat in the gazebo in the town square. I walked to the outskirts of town and threw stones into the sewage tanks at the sanitary plant. I stayed as far away from the park and cemetery as I could.

The day passed. I watched the sun travel across the sky, east to west. I noted its drop, degrees down the invisible scale from summer's zenith, starting its slow death march to winter's nadir.

I would miss the green of summer. It never stayed long enough. But Autumn's gold and winter's barren blue-white made the green all that much sweeter the next summer.

I couldn't help wondering how old people must feel, thinking each winter might be their last, the green of summer never coming to them again. And it would be winter that took them—oh, yes!

The sun hid itself behind trees in the west, leaving oranges and lavenders above the darkening green. Night bled down like spilled ink from above—or blood, night blood, spilled in the fabric of the sky. I walked.

I found myself in front of Michelle's house, a rambling brick ranch in the same neighborhood as Paulie Gibbs' house.

123

I rang the door bell. The door opened, and Michelle stood there, staring.

Jim Harper came from behind her.

"So, it's the birthday boy at long last. Nothing like a grand entrance, eh, old man . . . Jesus Christ! What happened to you? What does the other guy look like? Or the train? Whichever it was."

"L . . . look, would you all leave, please?" Michelle took my arms like I was an invalid and led me past the people.

The room was bright. Crepe paper streamers festooned the lights, the chandelier over the table and the ten-foot-long sign on the far wall that said "Happy Birthday Steve." An enormous white cake sat on the coffee table before the sofa. It said "Best Wishes Steven."

Everyone had stopped talking. They were all staring at me, as if I were a leper, one of the unclean, complete with bell and sign around my neck.

Deanna and Debbie were there, along with Jim and about fifteen other people I recognized dimly from school, most of them strangers to me, blurred faces from last year's yearbook photos.

Jim Harper rounded them all up like cattle.

"C'mon guys, you heard the lady of the house. Party's over. This warrior needs the medical attention of the lady fair. C'mon. Move!"

They all filed out, without a word. Jim stopped at the door.

"Hey. Maybe you better think about taking him to the hospital, Boobs. He looks pretty rocky to me."

"I'll take care of him."

"Yeah. Well . . . if you need help, call me. Okay?"

"Sure."

"G'night, then."

"Good-night, Jim, and thanks."

He closed the door. Without a word, she led me through the maze of halls and rooms, into a bedroom of pink and white that must have been hers. She laid me on the satin coverlet on the canopy bed. She disappeared, then came back with a damp pink towel. She folded it expertly and placed it gently on my forehead.

Then she undressed.

"Your parents . . ." I mumbled.

"Gone." That was all she said. She undressed me. The love she made to me was so gentle, so tender, that it was more like a healing by a mystic.

When finally she slept, I rose from the bed. In the bathroom, I turned on the lights. The harsh fluorescents showed me the damage to my face and naked body that had so shocked the party guests and caused Michelle's gentle ministrations. I was like something returned from the grave—or at best, something ready for the mortician's smooth hands and sharp piercing tools.

Back in the bedroom, I found my clothes and put them on. I turned on the small ruffle-shaded lamp on her vanity and found some pink note paper and a pen.

"Thanks," I wrote, and "You were right." I knew what those word would mean to her, but I didn't know how I felt about it.

It was a night for notes and sneaking bastards.

When I got home, the house was dark. Brian's note was in the middle of the kitchen table.

"I didn't want to screw things up," it read. "I wanted to help. Seems I don't know how. I'll send Aunt Jane and the court a wire from Germany. They probably will let it ride like it was before I came home. I do miss Dad. I'm sorry about Mom. I'm sorry about everything. That's me, one sorry sonofabitch. Good-bye, Brian."

I went to bed.

The dreams came back right on schedule.

They mostly consisted of Nicholas, the Abomination, pointing and laughing at me. Me protesting, not able to awaken, not able to escape the dream, escape Nicholas, get him out of my head. It was so infantile in nature, yet perhaps all the more terrifying, because the childish dream stirred nameless childish horrors.

I didn't answer the phone or the knocks on the door. I didn't need to part the curtains or look out to know it was Michelle, always Michelle.

6

The ninth of September came, and I went back to school.

Michelle was waiting on the school's front steps, standing like a tainted virgin sacrifice between the stone lions. When she saw me, she ran to me and kissed my cheek. She was bubbling over with happiness. I was to pay for my cryptic note, left in the night.

"I was so worried about you. I couldn't get you on the phone, and there was nobody at home at your house." She threaded her arm through the crook of my elbow. "Are your hurts all better?"

"Pretty much."

"What happened anyway?"

"My brother and I had a little difference of opinion."

"My God! Your brother did that to you? That bastard!"

"Please, Michelle. He couldn't help it. I know that now. He's needed to strike out at someone in my family for years now."

"But Steven, you were really beat up."

"It's all right, I tell you."

"Still . . . nobody can hurt my sweet baby." She pooched out her lower lip in a mock pout, then laughed.

"What's your first class?" she asked, with the fluidity of thought only a teenager could accomplish.

"Poli Sci with Parkhurst."

"The new guy. That's my first class, too. Oh, isn't this heaven? I wonder what other classes we have together."

"We can compare schedules in Parkhurt's class." I slid my arm about her tiny waist.

"We can compare more than that next month," she whispered. "My father is going to buy me a car for my birthday. No more worry about where."

"Great," I said. I didn't know why I didn't tell her Brian was gone, that we could screw our brains out at my house if we wanted. We were at the classroom.

"Where do you want to sit? Up front, where we can be studious, or in the back, where we can pass dirty notes?"

"How about in the middle," I said, "then we can pass studiously dirty notes."

Michelle laughed. I loved her laugh. It came free and easily. I was glad I could make her laugh.

Parkhurst was young, probably about twenty-eight. He was tall, thin, with a shock of sandy hair that loved to fall over his brow and piercing blue eyes. He favored cord sport jackets with leather-patched elbows, primary colored shirts and narrow knit ties.

"All right, guys. Settle in." He sat on the front edge of his desk. "Pick your spots. I don't hold with seating charts. The school requires me to take roll, but I think that's an insult to both you and me. I hope to make this class interesting enough so you won't want to cut it. If I fail, then I deserve an empty room."

There was a general rumble of disbelief.

"Now. This is a Junior-level class. It's called American Political Systems. I'll start out by confessing I'm a card-carrying Kennedy Democrat. I believe John Kennedy is the best thing that ever happened to this country's presidency."

More rumbles, more disbelief.

"I know, I know. Dangerous talk in this marvelously Republican hamlet. But I'll stir the murky waters 'til I see the feathers and smell the hot tar. I want to teach you to think, to question, not merely grow up to vote Republican because your parents do. If you vote for the fogeys who follow the elephant, do it because you've considered the alternative."

"You mean the guys who run with the jackasses," an anonymous male voice from the rear of the room offered. The classroom roared with laughter. Parkhurst laughed the loudest.

"Now you've got the idea. There are some very

humorous things about politics and the political process in general. Most people take it much too seriously. The system stinks sometimes, but if it occasionally puts men like Kennedy in power, it can't be all bad.

"Now let me tell you a few things about our president . . ."

The entire class, even the joker in the rear, was enthralled. Parkhurst spoke of Kennedy's charisma, but the president had nothing on Parkhurst. I had no idea just how much charisma Parkhurst possessed, not on that first day of class, nor did I suspect for a moment how it would affect my life.

Michelle and I had one other class together, Arts and Crafts, and Study Hall right after lunch. It became a great arrangement. Eight o'clock we were together in Mr. Parkhurst's class for an hour of political enlightenment. At nine, I had Lit while Michelle had Home Economics, a must for all females in 1963, if not a requirement of the curriculum.

Ten o'clock found me in speech class, Communication Arts, actually, while Michelle spent the hour in Gym class.

Eleven o'clock, we were back together in Mr. Henry's art class. Twelve was lunch; one was Study Hall.

At two o'clock we went our separate ways again. I was in Chemistry, Michelle in Typing, another given for female students. At three Michelle had her Lit class, and I went to World History.

The beauty of the Art-lunch-Study Hall arrangement was that Mr. Henry would give us both passes to be out of his class, then there was lunch when we were free to do as we pleased, and then Study Hall which we could skip. That meant we could be together for three hours straight, away from the school.

The first time we took advantage of it was the first full week of school. It was also the last time.

The day was warm and sunny, with a cool breeze dancing in the maple leaves. The only hint of approaching autumn was in my mind. I sensed it there, waiting. In two weeks the wind would be much colder, the maple leaves would lose their lush green, and in three weeks the sugar maples would turn. Oaks would have leaves of hammered bronze overnight, and the elms would be pale yellow. But the anticipation was within me, that particular September day.

As we walked, I noticed Michelle unconsciously paced her stride so we moved in step, harmoniously. I passed my arm around her narrow waist and pulled her close.

"So, where we goin'?"

"We can go to my house. It's about a twenty minute walk. If we skip study hall, that gives us almost two and a half hours alone together."

In her bedroom, we made a laughing game of undressing one another. She dusted her nude body with powder bearing that potent Shalimar fragrance which so excited my senses. I knew where I had first scented it, but I pushed that thought from my mind.

I took her in my arms, crushing her breasts against me. Her soft lips parted, her tongue spearing into my mouth. We collapsed on the bed, her legs opening, graceful wings rising into the sky.

After the first time, she strolled about the room, smiling to herself. She opened a drawer and extracted long white silk gloves.

"Apple Festival Princess, last fall," she said, grinning. She made a show of putting them on, touching her full upper lips with the tip of her saucy tongue, all the time watching me through lowered lashes. Her little act had the desired effect: I rose to the occasion. She knelt over me and feather-touched my body from head to toe with the silken gloves.

After nearly forty minutes of her teasing touch and rationed kisses, I grabbed her hovering head and forced her to me. She laughed and brought me rapidly to ecstasy.

Still laughing, she fell next to me, wiping at the droplets that had fallen all over both of us.

I got up and perused the drawers of her dresser and vanity. I held up various items of clothing, making different faces at her, all of which she found immensely funny.

Finally in the closet, amid her winter things, I uncovered a white rabbit-fur muff.

I brandished it like a madman with a bomb, a club, or some other death-dealing device. She giggled so hard she couldn't catch her breath.

Leaping onto the bed next to her, I pinned her wrists together above her head with one hand, and worked the muff over her breasts, her stomach, her thighs.

In a few moments, she was moaning softly. A few minutes more and she was pleading. More time passed, and she was nearly in tears, legs straddled wide, hips grinding and seeking, toes dug into the satin pink of the coverlet on the bed.

I tossed the muff aside and worked my hands over her with tender force.

Again we met, joined, this time in the fever of high passion. Nothing stood between us; no rational thought passed through our minds. Our bodies worked in tandem violence with one goal only.

Michelle was first, arching like a wrestler, shaking, vibrating, bringing me along seconds later.

We lay a long time entwined, just breathing together as one, each listening to the inner poetry of the other's body.

"Oh, Jesus! Look at the time," she exclaimed, pushing herself up and off of me. "We've only fifteen minutes to our next class!"

We scrambled for our clothes, doing buttons as we ran out the door. She had to go back to lock the door, wasting precious seconds.

We ran to the school, the lazy midday traffic a blur. We made it up the front steps of the high school just as the bell rang. We clasped hands briefly, meaningfully, and ran in opposite directions.

After school, I waited for her under the oak in front. She ran down the steps to me.

"Oh, God, Steve darling, I'm still buzzing, my head still spinning. What a lunch hour!"

"It was fantastic. Let's go to Vito's."

"I can't my darling. I've got to run home and straighten up the mess before Mom gets there. Sorry." She started off. "Love you," she called back, throwing a kiss. Other students nearby laughed, but I didn't care.

"Me too, Michelle, me too."

I went home and, for the first time in months, took my guitar from its case, tuned it, plugged in the amp and played. I swear it was the sweetest music I had ever played.

But night eventually came, and fear caught up with me. Even forcing myself to think of Michelle, thinking hard about those hours together, couldn't lessen my dread of sleep.

About two a.m., I could no longer fight it, and sleep came to me.

It was the cemetery again. This time the little creek was dry. I looked around and the tombstones were crumbled into somber hunks and pieces all about. The trees were dead, their branches whipping in a bitter wind. The sky, the color of oiled metal, hung oppressively above.

The Abomination stood, horrible in aspect, his body naked and scaled like a python, nearly as tubular. Atop the monstrous otherworldly body was the pale round pie of a face, slitted eyes goat-yellow, hair wild and spiky. He laughed that hideous hellish sound, a clawed reptillian hand groping for me, grasping at me, strangling life from my throat.

A sound pulled me back, brought me to, screaming.

It was the telephone.

I picked it up with sweaty hands.

"H . . . hello?"

"Steven!" The whisper was intense. It was Michelle.

"Michelle? Wh . . . what time is it?"

"Two-thirty. But listen . . . my mother knows! She was driving through town when we skipped out. She saw us!"

I didn't know what to say. I was angry that she would bother me with such a mundane, petty little worry

131

when I had just come back from grappling with a demon straight from Hell. I was also relieved that her call had interrupted that conflict.

"She even knows we made love. She got home before me and saw the bedroom!"

"Calm down, Michelle. At least she didn't come home while we were at it."

"Yes, thank God for that! She had a meeting at the club. But she knows, nonetheless."

"Okay. So she knows. What of it?"

I could tell by her silence that the anger in my voice had hurt her.

"Well, it's okay for you. You don't have parents to give you a hard time."

"Thanks for reminding me," I said flatly.

"Oh, Jesus, Steven, I didn't mean . . . you know I wouldn't hurt you for the world. It's just that you sound so pissed off, like I shouldn't be bothering you . . ."

"No, I'm the one who's sorry. Any problem for you is a problem for me. I'm sorry you had to go through it with your mother. I wish I could have been there with you." I was having a difficult time keeping a sincere tone in my voice.

"I'm glad for you you weren't here. It was horrid!"

"I bet. We'll have to be more careful."

"Yes," was all she said. There was a long silence.

"Michelle, it's late. You'd better get some sleep." It was all I could think of to say. There was still no way I could say the words she wanted to hear. And suddenly, I sensed she could no longer say them, either.

"Well, you're right. I just thought you'd like to know what I went through for you . . . for us."

"Must have been tough."

"Yes. Well . . . see you tomorrow, Steve."

"Bye." When I hung up the phone, I was shaking, still trying to sort out which reality to accept—the dream of Nicholas, or the cryptic call from Michelle. At that moment, I couldn't tell which situation held the most foreboding for me.

Michelle's call must have broken some unknown

pattern, for the dreams did not return that night. I slept peacefully, if somewhat cramped and twisted, on the sofa.

The next day was Friday in that first week of school, 1963. Michelle looked the chided child—a child in make-up and teased hair, a pretty pout on her mouth, eyes downcast.

"Feeling any better?" I asked as we stood out in the warm morning sun awaiting the first bell.

"Now that I'm with you." She smiled a crooked little smile then returned to her pout.

"What exactly did your mother say?" I knew she wanted me to ask.

"She said I disgusted her. She said she could only imagine what went on from the mess in my room." There was a quaver in her voice. "She asked if I was trying to be a little slut." The quaver intensified into quiet crying. "S . . . she called me . . ."

"C'mon now, stop it, Michelle. Everybody's staring. It's okay, really."

She wiped at her eyes with a tissue, mindful not to smudge her carefully applied mascara. Even in her despair, Michelle had an image to maintain.

"Oh, I don't know why I'm making such a fuss. I really don't care what she thinks of me. People can call me whatever they want," she said defiantly, a motion picture heroine before the conflagration of Atlanta. "I'll be a slut, if that's what makes you happy."

That struck me as a truly odd way to pledge her love.

"Wait a minute." I unintentionally backed away from her. "You act like I twisted your arm or something."

"I just mean some of what we did was kind of, well, dirty. Perverted, you know?"

Though I hadn't thought of her specifically and in fact had tried desperately not to think of her at all, at that moment Cat's image leapt into my mind. In particular, I could see her as that precociously mature ten year old in the park, saying that she believed two people in love could do nothing with each other that

133

was dirty if it caused pleasure. At that precise moment, Michelle's attitude, the ease with which her mother's rhetoric had swayed her, made her repugnant to me and made my heart ache for Cat as it hadn't ached since our last parting in early June. I also, at that precise moment, wondered if perhaps Cat might, like me, be Abomination.

The bell rang, and we went inside. Michelle seemed to want me to agree with her new assessment of the physical aspect of our relationship, but I said nothing.

All through Parkhurst's class she tried to get my attention, but I pretended to be absorbed in the lecture.

When the class was over, as we filed out with the others, Michelle nudged against me.

"We doing anything tonight? It's Friday, you know."

"Yeah, I know. Why get ahead of ourselves? What about another extended lunch hour?"

She stopped walking, and the guy behind her almost fell over her.

"Don't be ridiculous, Steven Dalton. After what I went through because of yesterday? Are you insane?"

"Problem, guys?" Mr. Parkhurst walked up to us.

"No, Mr. Parkhurst, no problem. No problem at all," I growled.

"Doesn't sound that way to me. Listen, if you guys wanna talk, I'm free after school, or even at lunch. Sometimes it helps to get a different perspective on a problem, an outside eye."

"Thanks for the offer, Mr. Parkhurst, but we can work it out . . . I think." I wasn't sure there was any reason to even try. I thought of Michelle on the phone, her cooling to the joy of our sex. Looking at her then, the coy act dropped and the sexual hunger gone from her eyes, all I saw was a teenaged girl who wanted not me so much as perhaps the idea of me. I had fulfilled my purpose. She had conquered me, made me admit love I didn't feel, made me feel guilty for wanting only to use her.

"Okay," Parkhurst said, pursuing his offer of aid,

"but my door's open, so to speak. Better split now, or you'll be late."

"Right. C'mon Michelle." I prodded her forward, and she balked.

"I can walk quite well on my own." She strode on down the hall, her patent leather flats clicking out the cadence of her anger on the terrazo floor.

Parkhurst shook his head, a sheepish grin on his face, and shrugged.

"Exactly," I said. "I can't figure her out."

"Sometimes women are an incomprehensible as Brazilian politics, Steve. If you want to hash it over sometime, I probably don't have any answers, but I'd be glad to help you think of some possibilities."

"Thanks. I'd better go."

"Right." He stuck out his hand and I shook it. He had a firm handshake. My dad always told me that meant sincerity, but then again, Dad wasn't right about a lot of things.

The trees were turning. I had managed to get together with Laurel to borrow her car for my driving test and passed with flying colors. Actually, the cop who tested me took a nap until we were through.

"Great, kid. The Secretary of State commends you." He yawned and signed my approval. I drove the nasty black Chevy back to Laurel in White Pigeon, and she slapped me on the back when I showed her the temporary license.

She dragged me into the falling-down old garage saying she had a surprise for me.

The bobbing light bulb on the frayed black cord flicked on, and there sat the ugliest little car I had ever seen. It was a turquoise and white Nash Metropolitan—a two-seater with torn vinyl upholstery and enough rust on the rocker panels to make anyone wonder why the entire bottom of the car didn't just fall off. But it was a convertible, and it was mine. Laurel handed me the pink slip and kissed me on the cheek.

"Happy Birthday, Steve," she said.

"It's too much, Laurel."

"Bullshit. It only cost fifty bucks. My old man and me put the engine back together. Runs like a greased pussy now."

"It's fantastic!"

"It's not gonna take a lot of hard use, but it'll get you around. My advice is, learn somethin' about mechanics and body work quick before this bucket teaches you the hard way, like strandin' you on a freeway up to your ass in mud, rain and piston rings."

"Thanks, Laurel. Thanks a million," I said, and kissed her on the lips. I climbed into the seat.

"Ya sorta have to jiggle the key in the ignition first . . . and don't get too used to it startin' easy, 'cause my guess is, when cold weather sets in, it's gonna be an iron-clad bitch in the mornings."

I jiggled the key as directed, and the little engine popped, sputtered and revved, a good solid rhythmic hum.

She leaned in the open window.

"I can't tell you how important this is to me, how fantastic . . ."

"Hell, Steve, it's nothing, believe me. The first time it dies out in the country and you have to hitch home, you'll be cussin' me out."

"No way, never. Laurel, I love you, you know that?"

"Stop it, you'll embarrass me. Get out of here."

I only made it to the outskirts of White Pigeon before I had to stop and put down the top.

At sixty-five, the front end shimmied like a wet dog, but even at fifty, with the top down, it felt like flying.

The radio didn't work. The ashtray was gone. The fact that those were my first two areas of concern shows the teenage mind at work about automobiles. The hidden complexities of drive-shafts, the internal combustion engine and gear-ratio dynamics are lost to the truly important things. The glove compartment wouldn't open. The rear view mirror was cracked and it flopped. The steering wheel was ever so slightly bent out of shape. I loved it. All of it. The missing, broken parts could detract nothing from my exhaltation and gratitude toward Laurel, probably the most misunderstood person on the face of the earth.

I had to show someone. Michelle was the obvious choice, even though the big chill was still on between us. One of the biggest problems with being a teenager is that old I-want-it-no-I-don't-want-it syndrome, probably more apparent in me than in lots of other people.

Driving past the Bailey house, I saw Mrs. Bailey in the yard, talking to a guy from their lawn service company. I drove on by.

There was a pay phone on George Street near the Methodist Church. That's what we would have been— Methodists—had we ever gone. Mother had been raised a Methodist but had practiced harder at being a Reverend Stoney follower. Seeing the Church, my thoughts switched to my mother somewhere in a looney bin in Kalamazoo, and I felt a twinge of guilt. It was eerie how easily I had pushed all thoughts of her well-being from my mind. I did it again, the guilt with it, just as easily.

I stopped next to the booth, went in and dropped the dime. The phone rang at Michelle's. It rang five times.

"Hello?"

"Michelle?"

"Steven. What do you want?" Iceberg City, here we come, I thought.

"To be friends?"

The silence was so heavy it felt like a liquid weight oozing out of the receiver into my inner ear.

"Oh, how can I be mad when you're so cute?"

"I'm sorry we fought. I have something to show you. Can you meet me somewhere?"

"Why can't you come here?"

"I was there. Your mother was in the front yard."

"Oh. I'll get out. Meet me around the corner on Eisely. Ten minutes?"

"Fine."

137

She was looking as adorable as too-tight Bobbie Brooks separates and Max Factor cosmetics could make her, which was considerably high on the adorable scale.

Her hands flew to her mouth as she squealed, seeing the car.

"You got your license!"

"More. The car's mine, too."

"No! But it's so cute!"

"I thought it was sorta ugly. But it's a convertible, and it runs. Wanna ride?"

"Try to stop me!" She leapt in. "What is it?"

"Nash Metropolitan. About 1954 or something. Where you wanna go?"

"How 'bout Lasky's Woods?" She giggled.

I looked at her.

"Isn't that sort of thing what we had the fight about?"

She got adorably wide-eyed.

"What do you mean, Steve?"

"You know damned well what I mean. We drive out to Lasky's Woods, and things will get out of hand in five minutes. Then you'll be mad at me again because of what your mother said."

"Maybe. Maybe not. I guess we won't know unless we drive out to Lasky's Woods and find out." She smiled slyly and laid her hand suggestively on my thigh.

"I hope we know what I'm getting into."

She laughed out loud and I put the car in gear.

In the country north of town, in the low areas, the trees were already beginning to turn. The sumac was vivid red against purple feathery heather, and oak leaves were matallic bronze on the backdrop of the deep blue cloudless sky.

Lasky's Woods sat on hilly land and the twisting cowpath road was well-rutted from teenager's cars.

We drove deep into the pines and I turned off the engine. Michelle got up on her knees on the seat and took my face in her hands.

"I made a decision. I did a lot of thinking those days we were apart, and I made a mature, adult decision. I decided you were the man I was going to marry, and I would do anything, anything you wanted me to do . . . to keep you, Steven Dalton." She kissed me hard, passionately on the mouth.

I pulled away finally. "What about what you want to do? What about what your mother . . . ?"

"None of that matters. Tell me what you want from me, darling. Tell me what you want me to be for you, and that's what I'll be." She kissed me again, moaning lasciviously.

And again I pulled away, gasping for breath. "It does matter. I don't want to force you into doing things you don't enjoy. It's important to me to know your actions are . . . I don't know, spontaneous, not just doing things for me . . . acting, you know, to keep me happy."

She sat back, studying me, delicately drawn brows slightly furrowed.

"I don't understand you, Steven. You want me to be . . . dirty with you, don't you? That's what I figured out. You need a woman who will do whatever you need, no matter how disgusting . . ."

"No. No, no, no! Michelle, first off you're not a woman yet. You're sixteen. Some girls are women at a much earlier age than that, but you . . . you're every day of sixteen." I massaged my brow. "All I wanted from you was a good time. I thought . . . no, that's not true . . . I fooled myself into thinking that's all you wanted, too. It was a wrong thing, a bad thing for me to do, but God-damn it, you've got such a great body." I looked at her. She was mad. Damned mad. "But there's more to being a woman than great tits."

"You've never minded my tits before. You paw at them just like every other boy I ever . . ." She caught herself before her anger made her say more. "I am a woman, a grown woman. Look at me!"

"It's not age or physical development, Michelle. It's not even mental development, or anything like that. It's . . . it's . . . Hell, I know a girl who was a woman at ten."

"Oh! The mysterious othe girl again. I thought we'd

139

at least progressed past her, whoever she is."

"The sad fact is I may never progress past her. I thought for awhile maybe with you I could forget . . ."

"You were using me? Using my body to get over her! You . . . you sonofabitch! The things you made me do!"

"Hold on, Michelle, I didn't . . . hell, I told you from the beginning . . . it was you, you! I didn't make you do anything."

"Oh, yes you did! All those things, those filthy things you made me do, and in my own home! All products of your filthy perverted mind! Sick, that's what you are, sick and crazy! Crazy just like your parents!"

I didn't mean to do it. My hand lashed out involuntarily, and I struck her face. Shock filled her eyes, then tears as her make-up could do nothing to hide the burning red imprint of my fingers on her cheek.

"Take me home! Oh, damn you, God-damn you, take me home!"

She sobbed all the way back to town. I could say nothing. There were no words that would take back my violence.

She made me drop her around the corner from her parents' home.

"Don't you ever speak to me again! Ever!" She ran from the car. I reached over and shut the passenger door, then watched her disappear around the corner. She was still crying. Oddly, when she was gone, I began to cry, too.

7

Jim Harper loved the little Metropolitan, and I found out he had an innate mechanical knowledge. He showed me how to do minor engine work that would keep the car running smoothly and also tutored me about body work. We went together to buy the Bondo and wire mesh necessary to patch the Metro's rattletrap body and worked on it all one weekend.

Michelle played up to Todd Raintree, and they were soon an item about school. She wore his massive letterman's varsity jacket and his enormous class ring about her neck on a strand of pink angorra yarn. When she saw me coming down the hall, she made a point of stretching up to kiss him. I pitied Todd. I doubted he had the stamina to deal with Michelle's brand of hot/cold affection.

Jim and I discovered jujitsu. We began driving together in the Metro to Elkhart, Indiana every Monday and Wednesday night for classes. We also started weight training. By the time November came, fading late October's brilliant reds and oranges to dull browns and yellows, we had both developed phenomenal upper body physiques. We competed at it, good-naturedly, and both our bodies profited from the effort. Jim claimed it was sexual abstinence that made our muscles bulge so rapidly. I countered with, "What choice do we have? Go queer?" We were teenaged bachelors, monks, unattached males in a society that pushed hard for boys to have girls and girls to have boys.

We never discussed Michelle. We never discussed Debbie Frankwiler. We were both too aware of what we would rather be doing than lifting weights.

Michelle still sat next to me in Parkhurst's class. She spent the hour primping with a compact mirror. She would pat at her hair, repair her make-up, and some-times feign total enthrallment to Mr. Parkhurst. I was not so stupid as to not understand it was all for my benefit, just like her hallway gropings with Todd. She wanted to be sure I knew what I was missing, minute by minute.

"Kennedy's involvement in the Bay of Pigs is crucial to understanding the man . . ."

Michelle dabbed at the corner of her mouth with an extended pinky, removing some imaginery foreign particle from her perfect lipstick.

" . . . beyond a doubt, a powerful man, a decisive man," Parkhurst went on, "history will show this . . ."

Michelle patted her sprayed raven-colored bubble of hair, holding the compact at arms length. She touched a finger to her gracefully penciled brow and removed a fiber of mascara from her lashes.

" . . . the Cubin Missile Crisis shows us what a passionate American . . ."

Michelle adjusted her sweater over her breasts, pur-posely jutting them forward, and caught me staring. She smiled indulgently, then turned full attention to Parkhurst with a deprecating sigh.

Finally the bell rang.

" . . . so that's it for today. Remember what I said last week. It's not too early to begin work on the Kennedy for '64 campaign. If any of you are interested in volunteering for some up-close political activism, be sure to see me. See ya tomorrow."

I stopped by his desk and waited while he spoke to the usual gaggle of breathless girls.

"Yes, Steve, what is it?"

"I'd like to get involved, like you said."

"Excellent. The group is meeting at my place Friday night for Cokes and popcorn. About seven? Know where I live?"

"Yeah. Over on Lilac. The apartment over Lakowsky's Print Shop."

"Right. See you there Friday, okay? Glad to have you aboard. Steve, tell your friends."

* * *

On my way to Parkhurst's that Friday, the Metro
blew a tire. It was only then that I discovered the spare
in the turquoise and white continental kit was bald and
flat. I left the car where it sat and walked to Lilac
Street, dusk and a chill wind settling over Greenriver.

The party was in full swing. Parkhurst's stereo was
blaring Dave Brubeck when I entered. There were
probably thirty people crammed into the tiny
apartment, all talking simultaneously and wolfing
down all the Cokes, popcorn and chips they could
physically consume without stopping the breathing
proccess.

"Glad you could make it, Steve," Parkhurst yelled in
my ear. "Quite a turn out."

"Yeah," I yelled back. "You like Brubeck, huh?"

"You bet. And Miles Davis. Gerry Mulligan. Shelley
Manne. You like progressive jazz?"

"Yeah. Not as much as my father did. He grooved on
it."

"Oh yeah? I'd like to meet him."

"He's dead."

"Sorry, I didn't know."

"It's okay. I still have his record collection. I think he
had some really rare stuff."

"Love to hear it sometime, Steve."

"Sure. Let me know."

"I will. Hey, do you know everybody here?"

"Probably not."

"Are you a good mixer?"

"Oh, yeah. Mr. Mixer, they call me."

He laughed. "I take it that was a bit of wry humor. A
bit sarcastic."

"Me, sarcastic? Never."

"Want me to introduce you around?"

"No, I'll manage on my own."

"You sure?"

"Yeah."

"Okay. Help yourself to the stuff. If you want

143

anything you don't see, holler. Okay?"

"Okay." I made my way through the tangle of people to the bar that separated the tiny kitchen from the tiny living room. I poured Coke over ice in a tall tumbler.

"Isn't it great? All this? The music and stuff, I mean." It was the diminutive blonde cheerleader from my Art class, Mitzie Campbell, standing at my side, trying unsuccessfully to move with the beat of Brubeck's "Take Five." Finding the correct beat in 5/4 time was impossible for Mitzie Campbell.

"Yeah, it's great. You here for the free eats?"

She looked shocked.

"I'm here to, you know, become involved."

"With anyone in particular?" I was beginning to love teasing her. I was starting to understand the beauty of Jim Harper's style of humor. I was probably spending too much time with him.

"I mean involved in Phil's Kennedy thing."

"Phil?"

"Mr. Parkhurst, you know? Everyone calls him Phil." She smiled shyly. "But I think I was the first one he let call him by his first name."

"His favorite, then." Damn you, Jim Harper. I couldn't stop myself.

"Oh, I don't know," she smiled wider, "but it would be great, wouldn't it? I mean, he's really gorgeous, isn't he?"

"Gorgeous." I nodded soberly.

I sipped the Coke. " 'Course, he is a bit old for you."

"D'ya think? I don't. I'm sixteen and he's what . . . maybe twenty-one?"

"Maybe twenty-eight, at least."

"Really? Wow . . . that is old. I can't even imagine being that old."

"Why don't you ask him how it feels?" I couldn't restrain myself. Mitzie was too easy. I should have been ashamed, but I wasn't.

"Should I?"

"Sure, why not? He'll love it. Give you the benefit of his years of experience at being old. He's a teacher, after

144

all. Why shouldn't he teach you?"

"That's right. I'll ask him."

I wanted to be there when she did. I hoped Parkhurst thought it was funny.

Naiveté was a disease in towns like Greenriver in the sixties. No one was immune. Age built up resistance, but the germ lived in the veins of the entire populace. Mitzie had the worst case I'd seen in years, but I too was infected. The sorority sisters of Sigma Alpha Tau in Haines City had proven that.

Parkhurst turned down the music. It was a sh ame, because Miles Davis' "Seven Steps to Heaven" album had dropped and the cool strains of "Basin Street Blues" had just begun to ooze from the speakers.

"Okay, people, you've soaked up enough of my free food and Coke," he said laughing. "Parkhurst's law says if you play you gotta pay. The payment in this case is a strong young adult machine to relect Jack Kennedy to office in '64."

There were cheers and applause from the audience. We had become the audience when Phil Parkhurst opened his mouth. He had done a wonderful job in his classes, converting all of us to Kennedyphiles and subverting us from our parents' unquestioning Republican politics.

Parkhurst stood there. talking on and on about Kennedy, what we as high school students could do in Greenriver to get out the vote, to swing votes to Kennedy. He talked about image—Kennedy's and ours as a movement—and made everything Kennedy had ever done or said into Mom, Apple Pie and Country. He knew how to work a crowd. I wondered why he was teaching instead of politicking himself.

"So who wants to help?"

Hands shot into the air, the room filling with shouts of "I do," "I will" and "Me!"

I was mildly surprised to find my own hand in the air. I had seen Kennedy on TV and had watched much of the Kennedy/Nixon debates. I admired the man. He exuded the personality I wished I had—self-assured, sophisticated but likeable, decisive. I wondered if the man ever had doubts, like other people. I bet he never had nightmares that left him sweating and terrified. He was the stuff of which heroes are made. Becoming involved in Parkhurst's machinery would allow me to own a little piece of Kennedy for myself.

I kept my hand in the air while Parkhurst passed among us taking names. When he got to me, he placed a hand on my shoulder.

"Steven, I want you to be my chief organizer for this thing."

"What? You're joking."

"Not at all. I think you have the same charisma as J.F.K. These kids will follow your lead. Will you let me prove it to you?"

"Sure. Why not?" I drained the Coke and poured more. Parkhurst turned from me and the bar, facing the majority of the people in the living room.

"Listen, everyone. Great news! I needed someone to get this off the ground, someone you could all respect, someone you could all work for without getting ticked off."

The room had hushed to the point where Miles Davis' cool jazz horn was once again audible.

"Well, I thought about it for quite awhile. I went to the people; I asked you and your friends. And you know, the response I got from you was incredibly single-minded, the voice of the people! Now I can tell you, I've approached the one person, your choice, and he's accepted the mantle of office! Ladies and gentlemen of the young people's committee to reelect John Kennedy, I give you Steven Dalton!"

There was an embarrasing pause that seemed to me to last forever. Then a smattering of applause began in the back of the room, over by the dying philodendron. It spread, and grew; there were cheers, and people stood, applauding louder. It was suddenly unanimous. I was elected to I didn't know what by a crowd that didn't know why. Parkhurst was a magician. Or a mesmerizer. Like Mandrake, he must have gestured hypnotically.

"Speech!" someone yelled, then they were all yelling it, clapping and stomping in rhythm. Parkhurst stood there grinning at me, then he winked.

"Go ahead," he said. "It's your crowd." He held up his hands, and there was silence.

I stood up and said some things, God knows what. Parkhurst said something about putting together a projects committee to work with me.

" . . . and then we can get rolling," he said. That's the only part I really caught. I was in a daze.

He strode to the stereo and cranked up the music. A new record had dropped. It was Earl Bostic's "Let's Dance" album. The dirty sax boomed out on "Blue Skies."

The rest of the party was exasperation with a capital E. I spent most of my time trying to corner him, talk to him, but he bobbed and weaved like a prize fighter among the crowd.

Guys and girls, people I had only seen in the halls at school, people I didn't know, would stop me, slap my back and congratulate me. Girls kissed my cheek and beamed at me, wordlessly—political madonnas greeting their virgin-birthed son.

I nodded, smiled, mumbled my thanks, told them I'd do my best.

Finally the crowd began to thin. It was after one before most of the people were gone. Those that remained, five or six, were females, all hanging on every word Phil Parkhurst uttered. Brubeck was playing again, and Mitzie Campbell was still trying to find the beat to move with, but it was hopeless.

By two o'clock I had drank so much Coke I was wired like a blinking Christmas tree. Parkhurst packed the last google-eyed girl out the door. Mitzie Campbell, of course, and switched the music to Miles Davis' "Birth of the Cool."

He turned to me, grinning, and brushed the maverick

147

shock of sandy hair back from his forehead.

"Are we finally alone? Would you mind explaining?"

"Explaining what? I just made you the most popular guy in Greenriver High. Don't I get any thanks?"

"For what? Did it ever occur to you I didn't want to be the most popular guy in school?"

"Don't be ridiculous, Steve. Everybody wants to be popular, to be accepted."

"Sure of yourself, aren't you?"

"Shouldn't I be? I'm a political scientist. Whims of the populace are my meat and gravy."

"Yeah, well, I'm not the potatoes."

He cocked his head and lifted an eyebrow.

"Very good, Steve. Quick use of related metaphor. Shows an agile mind, light on your feet. A prime prerequisite for politicos."

"I'm not a politico. I'm not the least bit politically minded."

"A clean slate. All the better to write upon."

"I'm telling you, I don't want to be written on."

"Sure you do. Leave it to me. You and I are going places. Now if you don't mind . . . it is late . . . finish your beer. Hate to kick you out, but I'm bushed. See you Monday in class. Night, Steve."

I was out in the dimly lit hall making my way down the stairs from his apartment before I knew what was happening.

The beer was trying to counteract all the caffeine I'd ingested in the gallons of Coke, and it left me in a strange confused state of mind.

I looked about for awhile, trying to find my car. Then dim recollection seeped through the fog, and I remembered the flat, no spare tire and abandoning the little Metro on the way to Parkhurst's apartment.

Fog existed not only in my mind, but on the cold prewinter streets of Greenriver as well.

Fog in a two a.m. small town is about as surreal as Midwestern weather can get. There is no movement or sound except that made by the person moving through it, and even those sounds seem to come from elsewhere.

Fog smells of dank underwater things in towns that have rivers—things best unknown to the above-water world.

Yet what is fog, but water thickening the air, the wetting of that which dry-land animals breathe? I knew this fog, all of it, was created from mist moving across the tiny stream at the cemetery.

I walked, trying to clear my head, but the muffled and at the same time echoing sound of my footsteps made me believe I was not alone.

The fog thickened, and in my confusion, I could not recognize the houses or the streets. It was as if I had been transported by some demonic magic to another place, another time.

I hurried along, the sound of my footsteps multiplying. I was followed by one, by two, by a legion of unearthly entities. I fancied for a time that those who followed me traveled on all fours.

The street lamps reflected light back onto themselves, becoming ghostly featureless heads atop poles along some ghoulish taunting gauntlet.

I stopped, heart racing, the sound of my own breathing rasping in my ears.

Calm, I told myself, be calm. It's only a fog. Minutes ago I sat in Phil Parkhurst's apartment, beer in hand. I was only minutes from the well-lighted place. If I wanted, I could go back, simply retrace my steps and return to that safety. All I'd have to do was . . . I turned around and took a few faltering steps. No, I thought, not that way. I'd have to turn left . . . or would it be to the right?

I was lost, lost in the tiny town that had always been my home. The realization made me a bit crazy, and I laughed as the fog thickened still more about me.

Find a street sign, I thought. All I had to do was find a street sign, and I'd know which way to go.

I ran to the nearest corner. The sign had been ripped down. A wind, a storm, maybe a Halloween prankster had torn away my hope of salvation from the confusion caused by the cold pulsating fog.

The next corner. I would simly go to the next corner.

I felt the street slope downward. That should have meant something to me, should have told me what street I was on. Hadn't I ridden my bicycle up and down every street in the God-forsaken hamlet of Greenriver?

The street lamp was out at the next corner, and the damnable fog had thickened so, I could not read the sign in the darkness. I flicked on my lighter, but all it illuminated was my hand, white and shaking, fingers of fog wisping, moving about it.

I used the lighter to ignite a cigarette, tried to calm myself. It didn't work.

I hurried on down the sloping street. Two o'clock. Two a.m. Not a God-damned car, not a person, not a single light in a single damned window of the houses that rose like dead hulks along the street.

I flung the cigarette into the face of the fog, and the tiny red flare was hungrily gobbled up. I began to run. I felt like screaming, but I only ran.

Sidewalk became grass, grass and ground become spongy, wet, wet from the fog, fog from the river, tiny stream of a river in the . . . .

. . . . cemetery. I was in the cemetery! I stumbled over a headstone, scrambled to my feet and slammed into the side of a mausoleum.

Recoiling from the ice-cold fog-slimed marble, I ran in another direction. The soggy loamy ground disappeared from beneath my feet. I was in the air, borne on the thick fog itself.

I came to earth again, falling heavily on my side. I crawled, crawled like an injured beast, mindless of direction, knowing only faceless pain, wanting only escape.

Cold running water wet my face. The river! I was in the old part of the cemetery. My flight through air must have been when I went over the river bank. I tried to stand, but my legs were like rubber.

My dreams, those horrid dreams—wasn't this one of them?

When would I hear the laugh, his laugh? When would his tentacled reptilian fingers seek and close about my throat? I had to get up, get away before it happened.

I scrambled to the near bank, clawed at the cold mud and clumps of dead moss. Panic made my efforts useless. Every movement forward, upward, allowed the mud to pull me back down toward the river. From my dreams, I knew, on that opposite bank. . . .

Don't think of it, don't think at all, I told myself. Calm, I said, be calm. Find a handhold, something to brace a foot against.

It began to work. The cold November air moved the thick fog around me as I defied the mud and gravity and moved up the bank.

I was almost at the top. I sought one more handhold, fingers numb from the river water and the cold mud that clung to them. I could find nothing to grasp.

Then a cold dry hand clasped about my wrist—a strong hand, small but strong—and it pulled. I was on the bank, on the cold stiff frosting grass, flat on my back.

I was torn between two emotions—glad to be up on the bank and paralyzed with fear wondering who or what had hauled me up those last few feet.

A voice came out of the fog, a woman's voice, soft and vaguely familiar with a mocking edge to it.

"Lose your way in the fog? Or just out for a stroll?"

I couldn't speak. I crab-walked backwards, away from the voice, trying to get far enough away to stand up and run.

"Don't be afraid . . . I won't hurt you. You must be freezing. Come warm yourself in my home. I live just over there . . ."

I was near one of the mausoleums. Did the phantom female voice mean . . . ? No, no. Be calm. Calm! I stood, fell to one knee, rose again with the aid of a leaning tombstone.

"Please . . . let me help," the voice cooed. So familiar.

"I . . . don't need help. G . . . got to get home."

151

"Why, your teeth are chattering. Come home with me. I'll light a fire . . ."

"I can't see you! I don't know you! Get away!"

"I only want to help you." The voice was near again. Run! Why couldn't I run?

"I think I know you . . . Steve Dalton, isn't it? You don't have a home to go to, do you? Not a proper one. Your daddy's gone, and your mother . . . well, your mother is away, isn't she? Put away, where she belongs. A wicked, bitter woman, you know. Always was. Come on, Steven Dalton. Home. Home with me."

"No! I don't know you!" Finally my legs responded, numb with cold though they were. I ran, but not for long.

A gnarled oak tree root jutted up in the darkness, grasped my foot, threw me headlong, face-first against a tombstone. I went down, and consciousness escaped like a nightbird in flight.

I was warm and dry. My head hurt and my eyes would not open, but I was warm, dry, and there was light on the other side of my eyelids.

"Awake, are you?" the female voice crooned.

That opened my eyes. She had me, and I'd better be awake, up and awake, ready to run for my life.

I expected to see—I don't know what—the inside of a crypt, a dungeon, a torture chamber—my imagination stoked by fear could supply any possibility. What I saw was a cozy living room, nicely furnished with worn but comfortable furniture. I lay under blankets on a flowered sofa before a fireplace ablaze and crackling with a warm friendly fire.

The woman of the voice moved into the firelight. No ghoul, no hag of the grave, but a slender pretty-faced woman with soft curls of chestnut hair falling to her shoulders. She wore a chenille bath robe, blue in color, well-worn and frayed a bit at the ends of the sleeves.

"Coffee? Hot cocoa? Maybe something stronger? Brandy, maybe?"

"I . . . don't . . . know you . . ."

"Susan St. Charles . . . Jenny's mother . . . Catherine Charlene's mother. Billy is about your age, isn't he?"

"M . . . Mrs. St. Charles? How . . . ?"

"How did you get here? Well, it wasn't easy. You're a real load when you're out cold." She might have laughed to ease the tension in the room, but she didn't. There was a grim, slightly sardonic smile on her pretty lips, full lips that would pout easily like Cat's.

"Brandy, was it? I could use some, too."

"I've got to go." I started to scramble out of the tangle of blankets, then realized I was naked.

"My clothes . . . I . . ."

"Were a mess. I took the liberty of removing them. Tossed them in the washer. Should be out of the dryer in a few minutes. You have time for the brandy."

I heard the clink of glass off in the darkness, away from the fire's orange glow. She returned with two glasses and sat by my feet on the sofa, handing one of the glasses to me.

"You're lucky I couldn't sleep. Insomnia, you know. I've had it for years. Ever since . . . well, never mind. For a long, long time, anyway. Lucky for you. Mind telling me what you were doing floundering about in the river at this time of the night?"

I sipped at the burning liquid.

"I was . . . lost, I guess."

"Lost? In Greenriver? You should be ashamed."

"I . . . got turned around in the fog. Confused, afraid."

"Afraid? Afraid of what?"

Your God-damned mutant son, I thought, but couldn't say it. After all this time, after all the dreams, I still couldn't wholly convice myself that what I thought Nicholas St. Charles was could really exist in this world or any other.

"I don't know. Just afraid of being lost and alone, I guess."

Her face softened, the sardonic twist of a smile left her lips. She looked sad. She reached out, stroked the hair away from my brow.

153

"Lost and alone, yes. Yes, I know that feeling. How often I've felt the same, I couldn't say. Feeling that way has been with me for so many years . . ." She pulled her hand away as her words trailed off into nothing.

The crackling pine in the fire was the only voice that spoke for a long time.

"Why?" I asked, my voice croaking after another burning sip of the brandy. "Why did you send Cat away?" I hadn't meant to ask that, hadn't meant to bring it all up.

The lines of her face hardened, nearly eradicating the prettiness. In the warm glow of the flickering firelight, she was a cold thing, a being of ice or stone.

"I had reasons."

I expected her to rail at me, lay the fault at my own feet. She did not.

"It was best for her to be away. And not so much her, but, well . . . him."

I knew who she meant. I saw the glint of fear in her eyes . . . in *her* eyes!

"You see, Catherine can handle him, sort of. I don't know why . . ." Her eyes moved about the room, as if she expected to find him standing near, listening. I also, from some indefinable nuance of her manner, got the distinct impression that she *did* know why Cat could handle Nicholas.

"Are you saying . . . you're admitting it's true, then."

Her eyes would not focus on me.

"I . . . I don't know what you mean."

"Yes. You do. Of course you do. My dreams, that day in the cemetery . . . you know! Damn it, you know! Your son, Nicholas. I know what he is, and so do you!"

"Oh yes? Then tell me! You tell me what he is. He came out of my body, but my God, I don't know." She was on her feet, over me, a threatening posture with fists in hard little balls and trembling with rage and pain and fear.

"It's true, then," I mumbled to myself. "Oh dear Christ, I was afraid so. I didn't want it to be. No, I kept telling myself, but no . . . true, all true." My hands, palsied like an old man's, grasped the glass and I drained it, the brandy going down like water.

"I think you had best go now. I'll get your clothes."

She left the room, but I barely noticed. I was in shock. Five years I had carried it all inside—five years of night terrors and waking dread. Five years of denial culminated in just a few moments, when his mother confirmed my worst fears.

My clothes were laid carefully at my feet on the sofa by the woman who had given life's breath to the Abomination. She moved off into the shadows, away from the fire's light.

Mechanically, I dressed, shaking with a chill not caused by my nakedness on a cold November night.

I left. I saw her, in the corner, staring at the wall, running her hand up and down the vortex where the walls met, as if seeking some doorway that once was there but had disappeared.

The fog had lifted. It was raining.

I had my answer. I had no answer. I went home.

The dream did not come. It didn't have to. It had served its purpose, keeping his image ever-present in my mind for five years. Now I knew. It was over; it was the beginning. I did not need the dream to bring his image to mind. He would be with me every waking, every sleeping moment of my life from then on.

Morning came. The rain was snow. It was Saturday. I did not go out. I ate very little. I moved from room to room in the big empty house, thinking nothing, doing less.

The day passed, the night came. It seemed no amount of time would ever erase or ease the shock of my ultimate realization that Nicholas St. Charles was some kind of mutant being, some inhuman creature, some demon from Hell.

8

The Sunday morning snow kept coming down. It seemed winter was setting in with some degree of certitude.

I made a conscious decision to go on with my life, to proceed as if the realization had never come. There was nothing I could do. Nicholas St. Charles was some kind of supernatural being, attributant powers unknown. He could have caused my father's death and my mother's insanity—maybe not. There was no way I could be certain. By the same token, he might indeed possess powers to cause my death. If so, I was helpless to alter the carrying out of his threat on my life. The only tangible certainty was that I lived as one marked for a horrible death, a dead man already.

I got out of bed, forced myself to eat a good breakfast of eggs, toast, milk, bacon and coffee. I brought my weight bench and free weights down to the living room. Physical exertion would help, the regimen of body-building would make my mind work in acceptable geometric patterns.

I worked until noon, ate a lunch of bologna sandwiches and milk, then went out to where I'd left the Metro, removed the tire, took it to the Sinclair station, and had it patched. I put the tire back on the car in the deepening snow and drove home. I went back to working the weights.

By five o'clock, my entire body ached. I warmed Franco-American spaghetti, ate, then showered. I settled in the living room on the sofa with a copy of *Profiles in Courage* and one of my father's books on American politics. Phillip Parkhurst had provided me with an activity I could immerse myself in, I would play his game to the hilt. I hoped that between school, weight training, jujitsu classes and Parkhurst's Kennedy thing, I could effectly shut out all thoughts of Nicholas St. Charles—if not shut them out, at least minimize them.

I spent a lot of time at the Greenriver Library, the old Georgian brick building—courtesy of Andrew Carnegie —on the corner of Main and Larch. I read every magazine article I could lay my hands on about John Kennedy, his father, his brothers, mother and sisters. The more I read, the less it mattered that Parkhurst had railroaded me, for reasons unknown, into my currect position as political activist. I felt good about working for Kennedy's reelection. I was beginning to feel as if I knew him, like he was an old friend.

I perused the magazines for the pictures after I had read everything. I chanced on a section that showed Marilyn Monroe at the Washington D.C. birthday party where she sang Happy Birthday to J.F.K. The photo was black and white and showed her poured into a glittering low-cut gown, a wash of spotlight on her, halo-lighting her platinum blonde hair, snow white in the picture. My thoughts—damn them!—drifted to the white-haired beauty, the obsession of my life—Cat! What must she be doing right this instant, I wondered. But I quickly flipped past those photographs of the dead Marilyn Monroe, dead then for over a year, and immersed myself anew in the study of John Kennedy. The vision of Marilyn Monroe conjured thoughts of my Cat, and thoughts of her brought Nicholas to mind. Better to study photos and words of the living man, J.F.K., then the disturbingly sensual and familiar pictures of a dead actress.

Thursday of that week, as I walked into Parkhurst's class, he pulled me aside. I could see he was excited.

"I just heard from the guys at the Kiwanis Club. Their weekly meeting is today at noon in one of the conference rooms of the Auditorium. They want you to speak about Kennedy."

"What?" I was immediately petrified.

"Pretty good, huh? Don't worry, I've got a speech

written up for you, all about Kennedy's trip to Texas. I've got a spare tie and sport coat in the teacher's lounge so you won't even have to go home to change. This is it, Steve. We're on our way."

"Listen, this is all pretty sudden. I don't think . . ."

"Don't bother to think, Steve. That's what gets politicians in trouble. Just read the speech and be charming."

"But I'm not a politician . . . and I'm not running for anything."

"Oh yes you are. You're running for Junior class president."

"We already have one. I hate to point that out . . . spoil your fun."

"No, you don't have one. Mark Hagenborn's father has just been transfered to Chicago. Mark leaves in two weeks. There will be a special election before Christmas break. I arranged it all last night with the principal."

"Okay, so I am running for something. I'll go along with that. I may not like it, but I'll go along with it. I still don't see what speaking at the Kiwanis meeting is going to do to help me or Kennedy's reelection."

"Ah, but there's me to think of. You see, Mark Hagenborn's father was on the city council. So are two other Kiwanis guys. You are my introduction to the fine folks."

"Yeah, well, it all becomes clear. Pretty amazing how your little scheme is falling right into place with events."

"There's nothing little about it, Steve. The sky's the limit. Besides, this speech today will help spearhead the work of our reelection committee. Believe me, it all works out."

That noon we ate rubber chicken from the Greenriver Auditorium's redoubtable kitchen, and everyone applauded when I finished giving the speech Parkhurst had prepared for me. Before we left, there was a lot of glad-handing and shoulder punching between Parkhurst and the other men. I stood, literally in his shadow, nodding, smiling sincerely, and occasionally saying, "Yes sir. That's correct, sir."

Friday morning, the snow was melting, the eaves were drizzling icy water, and the sky was the color of dirty pewter.

I was inordinately depressed. Parkhurst was running my life. I wanted to do something altruistic for the Kennedy reelection movement in Greenriver, but it was slowly dawning on me I was being steered to personal aggrandizement by a power-drunk political science teacher. He told me after class that in the next two weeks I would be speaking before the Lions, the Rotarians, and Knights of Columbus, the Oddfellows and the League of Women Voters.

I went to Lit class, my depression deepening. I didn't hear a word Mr. Evans said. I daydreamed, gazing out at the sky, trying to imagine summer's soothing greens and blues.

At eleven o'clock, I shuffled down the hall to Art class.

I got out my sketches and tried to decide whether I should throw them away or start slopping acrylic on my gessoed canvas. Noon came before I could make up my mind. The sketches looked disturbingly like my nightmares of Nicholas anyway.

I went through the line in the cafeteria, taking whatever food the hair-netted old woman shoved at me. I was eating alone. Jim Harper, my usual lunch companion, had somehow gotten involved with Mitzie Campbell, and the word was out they were a hot item. I saw them in the food line, Mitzie yammering away, Jim tagging after, seemingly enthralled by her conversation.

I couldn't concentrate on eating. It was as if there was something hanging in the atmosphere, about to happen.

I left my food and went out to the parking lot. I sat in the Metropolitan and smoked five cigarettes in a row until the first afternoon bell rang.

I skipped study hall and went to the gym. Deacon Doakes opened the weight room for me, and I worked up a really good sweat. At ten 'til the hour, I took a quick hot shower and shuffled off to Chemistry with dripping wet hair.

After breaking three test tubes, I settled back and did nothing but mope for the remainder of the hour.

World History class was taught by a sweet little old lady named Cavanaugh, and her love of her subject beamed from her eyes. She had spent her summers ever since college traveling to the sites of the events she taught about. Her classes were ninety percent slide shows of her trips.

On that Friday, November 22nd, 1963, the lights were off and the school projector's fan hummed and wheezed behind Miss Cavanaugh's love sonnet accompanying the click-swish of changing slides she had taken of Greece.

I was nearly nodding off when the school principal's voice crackled over the public address system.

"Attention, attention please." There was at least a full minute of dead air.

"NBC news has just announced that President John F. Kennedy . . ." There was a gasping, snuffling noise over the P.A. " . . . that President Kennedy has been shot and killed in Dallas, Texas."

I was stunned. Shock drowned all sensation.

Miss Cavanaugh fainted, going down to the floor, lying there like a limp pile of empty clothing. I stood, stepped over her, and walked out the door.

There were sounds of crying and sobbing coming from the open doors of classrooms I passed. From some came the sounds of prayer; from others, silence.

I passed the door where Michelle sat in her Literature class. She saw me and rushed out to my side. I didn't slow for her. I just kept walking down the deserted hallway.

"Steve . . . Steven! Oh God, Steven, are you all right? Look at me . . . oh God, don't look like that! Are you . . . are you all right?"

I didn't answer. I walked out the rear doors of the school and made for the parking lot.

"Steven! Your coat! You can't go out like that . . ."

The freezing rain spattered on my head, drenching my clothing in seconds. Michelle hesitated only a moment, then followed me out.

I fumbled at the door lock of the Metro. I couldn't get the key in the hole. The keys slipped from my fingers, falling into the slushy snow and mud. I stood there, staring dumbly down at my feet.

I watched as Michelle's delicate fingers fished about in the icy mess, coming up with the keys. I started to take them from her. I noticed her perfect fingernail polish was ruined. Her fingers were blue.

"No. I'll drive." She led me around the car, unlocked the passenger door and guided me inside. I sat staring out the windshield as the rain tattooed the canvas top over my head and attacked the glass before me. Michelle unlocked the driver's door and got in. She started the car, even though she didn't know the secret of jiggling the ignition key. Some people are blessed with a sort of psychic mastery over malfunctioning mechanical things.

The Metro chugged and jerked its way out of the parking lot into the deserted street. It was as if the entire town stood still, the mourning already begun. The death of a President transcended normal political sympathies. It was like the death of America.

I was too numb to be aware of where she was taking me. I was in such a state of shock I could not even remember why I was upset. I looked over at her, shivering as she drove, wet to the skin, black hair streaking down her face. Her eyes wept, adding salt water to the rain that wet her cheeks. I could not recall who she was. It didn't matter.

She took me home, putting the Metro away in the garage and escorting me, invalid that I was, into the house. The words played over in my mind, a child's rhyme of nonsense. Invalid. In valid. Sounds like no longer valid. That's me, I thought, that's me.

We had no fireplace, and Michelle didn't know what to do about getting more heat out of the coal furnace. I was too numb, too much the mute to tell her, too deep in shock to go stoke the old metal beast in the basement myself, so she stripped me out of my wet clothes, wrapped me in a flannel blanket from my parent's bed and set me on a kitchen chair near the opened door of the gas oven. She turned it up to three hundred degrees and left me there.

Some increment of time passed, and I was warm and dry. I seemed to awaken from a sleep, though I knew I had been wide awake the whole time.

Trailing the blanket like a too large shroud, I went up the stairs to my room. I got dry clothes out of my dresser and sat on the bed to put them on. It was then that I noticed Michelle in a fetal ball under the blankets on my bed. She had a bath towel wrapped around her wet hair. She must be freezing, I thought, whoever she is.

She didn't awaken until I was tying the sneakers I had pulled from the back of my closet.

"Steve? What are you doing?"

I finished tying the shoes and stood up. I stood there, staring into the cool air of the room.

"You're not going anywhere, are you? You can't."

I turned and stared at a different patch of air.

"Steve Dalton, come to me, stay with me. You can't go."

"Walk . . . going for a walk."

"No . . . stay. You're hurting, and I can help. Like before, like at your birthday party."

"No!" was what she said, that stranger in my bed, as I left the room and left the house.

The dirty pewter sky was darkening and the rain was almost hail. It stung my skin, tore the tears from my eyes.

I cried as I walked, then laughed when my tears wouldn't come anymore. I laughed because I had on sneakers and ice was making the wet canvas stiff. I cried again, howling when no tears could be shed because a man was shot dead in the hot afternoon sun of a Texas town. At least I could remember why I had such pain.

When I got back to the house, there were no lights

on. I took the spare key for the Metro from the eight-penny nail driven into the two-by-four stud next to the door in the garage.

In an hour, I was in Kalamazoo.

It took some talking, it took persuasion and cajoling, it took a lot of words uttered by a mouth I didn't recognize as mine, but they let me see my mother.

She sat in a straight-backed enameled metal chair by a window cross-hatched with stout wire. The fading light cast the diamond pattern shadows over her frail shrunken body. Her hair was dull and straight, lank strands of greying dead straw framing her face, falling across her eyes.

"Mother . . . " I said, my throat dry, my tongue thick. A shaking hand cuffed at the hair to clear her vision. Those eyes, when revealed, were chillingly vacant. She did not know me. She may not have even known I was there. I had never expected it to be so bad.

"Mother, they shot the president. President Kennedy was murdered today in Texas."

Her head cocked a bit to one side.

"Ed . . . ?"

My throat constricted still further.

"No, Mom, it's Steve. Steven. Dad is dead, remember?"

Her head dropped, sending the lank strands of hair slapping against her bosom.

"Told you, told you, told you, Ed, about those people. See? Now you see, don't you? I was right. Told you."

"Right . . . ? About what, Mom?"

"Those people. I told you, those people, didn't I? Didn't I always tell you? Didn't I say, Susan's not right, she's not right. A bad girl. A really bad girl. Old man. Told her. I told her, too, shouldn't be around that old man. Too old."

"Mom . . . Mother . . . what do you mean? What are you talking about?" I couldn't bring myself to touch her.

A nurse came by the open door. She stepped in and

touched my arm.

"What are you doing here?"

She was young, perhaps twenty-four. She was plain, with a severe set to her mouth.

"My mother, she's my mother."

"Oh." Some of the severity about her mouth vanished. "She really shouldn't have visitors. It's nearly time for her evening medication. Come on now." She started to lead me away.

Without warning, Mother lept from the chair, came at us, bathrobe fluttering bat wings about her body. In the dim light, her face was wild, eyes crazy, lips snarled back showing clenched teeth.

"Wouldn't leave, couldn't leave them alone, could you? Could you?! Well . . . now you see. I know you do!" As suddenly as it had come, the violent outburst passed and she crumpled to the floor.

The nurse released my arm and went to raise my mother from the floor. I helped. We got her into bed. Mother's hand vised onto my wrist.

"Oh, Steven, the dreams, the dreams!" Her voice was pitiful, pleading. "He comes with my dreams. I can't stop him. I can't. It's like he's right here, sometimes in the room, all the time in my head! Stop him, Steven! He makes me say, makes me act . . . " Her eyes darted about the dark room, tiny wild lights in her skull . . . "makes me act crazy sometimes."

The nurse pried mother's hand from my wrist and led me out of the room.

"Don't be concerned. It's all just part of the illness. That's why we don't want her to have visitors unless she's been recently sedated. No point in upsetting the people who care for her."

My mother's behavior hadn't upset me. I knew then why she couldn't help herself. I knew then she would never, never recover.

The rain fell on the Kalamazoo open-air mall. People were leaving the theater, the seven o'clock showing of *Dr. No.* I went into a tobacco shop and bought more cigarettes. I returned to the Metro and pointed it out to the highway that went back to Greenriver.

9

Michelle was on the sofa, wrapped in three blankets and still shivering in her sleep. The house was cracking and thumping in the rafters and joists from the creeping cold. I went to the octopus-armed furnace in the basement and built a new fire, starting with pine kindling, then larger pine boards, and finally shoveling in three big coal-shovels full of bituminous lumps which glittered diamond-like in the light of the basement's single naked bulb.

By the time I returned to the living room, the heat was already spreading through the house.

I stood over Michelle, looking down at her sleeping form. In the light from the standing lamp by the couch, she looked pale as death. Her hair was straight and shiny since it had dried, and her pale face, though pretty without make-up, was unremarkable. I felt a deep need within me to hold her to me, not a need born of love or desire, but rather a need to steal from another human's flesh whatever comfort I could.

I picked her up, blankets and all, and took her to my parents' bed. It was the closest and it was a double bed.

I entered her and used her, finished before she was fully awakened by the rain water dripping onto her face from my still-wet hair.

"Steven," she crooned, gasping air with my rhythm. "So cold . . . love me, darling, love me."

I rolled over, feeling her hands, her kisses, hearing the vague words of one lover to another, and fell into a deep pit of sleep.

No dreams came. I had no dreams anymore. There was nothing but blackness. There was no need for dreams. I knew what the blackness meant—for me, my mother, my father, everyone I had ever really cared about.

Saturday morning, November twenty-third, 1963. 7:45 a.m. Barbara Walters' voice came from the TV as I dressed in the bedroom.

> "The streets of New York were deserted last night. Broadway theaters were closed. Radio City was closed. The only night club not deserted was the Stork Club, but the people there were like the people there on Christmas Eve . . . people with no home, no place to go. The department stores stopped decorating. All the candles were lit in St. Patrick's Cathedral . . ."

I came out in my slacks only, fastening the zipper and belt. Michelle was on the couch staring at the TV. Her hair was teased into her usual perfect bouffant, her make-up all in place. I hadn't realized until seeing her wet and rain-washed how much she looked like a fantasy of a female. That pale clean-faced being I had seen the night before was more real but less beautiful. To hell with reality, I thought. We need all the fantasy and illusion we can muster just to get by.

"Morning, Steve. They're doing all this stuff about President Kennedy. It's really depressing."

"Then why are you watching it?"

"I don't know. It seems like the least I can do now that he's dead."

So that was how it was to be. Millions of Americans all across the land, mourning via TV. They would sit in the comfort of their familiar living rooms and watch network TV dissect every microsecond of Kennedy's trip to the grave.

I made a breakfast of Cocoa Wheats for us both and sat beside Michelle on the sofa. She put seven teaspoons of sugar in hers before she could eat it.

Hugh Downs was speaking on the TV. It was 8:50 a.m.

"Throughout the land, people are mourning. All

parties in Washington have been canceled. Embassy flags are at half-staff. In Chicago, night clubs are closed. Disneyland is closed. Beauty pageants have been canceled, sports events, the Harvard-Yale game . . ."

"Too bad. Where are Americans going to go for a good time today?" I asked the TV.

"Don't be so cynical, Steve. What do you want the man to say? He's just trying to give people some idea of how universally felt the loss is."

"I know what he's doing. I'd just hate to think all Kennedy's death means is an off day for retailers."

"It means more than that, and you know it." She spooned Cocoa Wheats into her mouth without gettting a single bit on her immaculately pink-lipsticked lips.

"Yeah, well, I guess I know it. But really, what about all those Republicans out there, looking for a good time? What about the guy from Minnesota who saved for a year to get his five kids to Disneyland today? What about all those alcoholics out there looking for a drink? What about the bartenders? Do they have the day off with pay?"

"For God's sake Steven! What's wrong with you? Everyone feels the loss. People all around the world!"

"Really? Do you really think so? What will it all mean in twenty years? In five, even."

"You disgust me. You really do."

"That's a hell of a thing to say to a guy in his own house. A guy that just fixed your breakfast."

"You call that brown shit breakfast?"

"That's enough for me." I got up, went up the stairs and pulled clean clothes out of the closet. I found my old corduroy Norfolk jacket and put it on. My winter coat was still in my locker at school.

Back downstairs I got a fresh pack of cigarettes from the carton atop the refrigerator.

"Hey, Steven, I'm sorry. I know you're just upset. So am I."

"That's the breaks." I opened the kitchen door to the garage.

"Where are you going?"

"Out."

"Well . . . how long will you be gone?"

"I don't know . . . long as it takes."

"Well . . . how do I get home?"

"You could try walking. Call Todd. I don't care."

"God damn you, Steve Dalton, God damn you to Hell!"

"He already has, Michelle, he already has."

It took ten minutes to start the Metro. The rain was still falling. It was cold. I drove over to the Parkhurst's apartment.

He was still in his bathrobe. The TV was on. Pauline Frederick was broadcasting from the United Nations.

> "There is silence here. Yesterday, after hearing the news, the delegates stood in hushed groups. The blue U.N. flag was lowered to half-staff. There will be no business conducted here until after the funeral. Then there will be a memorial. The people at the U.N. remember John F. Kennedy's two appearances at the General Assembly and his challenge for peace."

"Come in, Steve."

"Thanks." I moved past him, my attention still on the TV. Charles Murphy broadcast from Dallas, Texas.

> "Governor Connelly's condition is improving. He has been told the President is dead."

Parkhurst glanced over his shoulder at the TV.

"Pretty grim stuff. It's as if the whole world is standing still, heads lowered in remorse."

"Yeah. Even Disneyland is closed."

He cocked his head and squinted at me.

"My, my. Sardonic wit. Not becoming of a rising politician."

"I'm not a rising anything, Phil. That's what I'm here to make sure you understand. It's all over."

"No, no, no. Don't say that. Come on and sit down." He ushered me to the sofa. "This changes nothing. Admitted, we don't have the reelection thing as a thrust, but with the play the funeral is getting, it's just as good . . . maybe better. I can present myself to the city council as a man wounded, but a standard-bearer for Kennedy's decisive policies on a local level, nonetheless. And you . . ."

"That's disgusting, Parkhurst. At the risk of flunking your asshole class, you make me sick."

The quizzical look on his face made him seem even more boyish.

"You surprise me, Steven. I figured you for a winner."

"You'd better shut up before I smash your face in."

"The Neanderthal emerges, eh? Violence is not the way of the winner, Steven."

"Oh, yeah? Tell that to John Kennedy. He lost. I've lost. The whole fucking world has lost. Even you, Parkhurst, you've lost, but you're too thick to understand it. I don't know why I came here. I knew what you were. I guess I just didn't want to believe you were as crass and shallow as I thought."

"What's all the fuss, Phil? Oops!" There stood Mitzie Campbell, wrapped á la Bardot in a bath towel, stepping into the living room from the bedroom. Okay, so she was a poorman's Bardot at best—especially when compared to my Cat, who, in my mind, surpassed even the French actress, the archetype of insouciant sensuality for the sixties.

"Oops is right, Mitzie," Parkhurst said dryly. "Mr. Dalton was just leaving, right, Mr. Dalton?"

"Yeah. Leaving."

"Oh, Steve, please don't say anything to anyone . . ." Her hand reached out to me as I turned to the door.

"Not even Jim Harper?" I shot it at her like a bullet. My words struck her right between the eyes, and she looked like she might just fall over.

"Jim . . . ?"

"Yeah. You remember Jim. The guy who follows you around drooling. You know, I should have known he was just a temporary stopover for you on the way to Parkhurst."

169

"I never meant to hurt . . ."

"Talk about violence, Parkhurst. I hope Jim never does find out. He'll surely kick your ass if he does."

I left. I hoped I'd scared his sanctimonious cocksure ass a bit. I had half a notion to tell Jim. But if I knew one thing, if I'd learned anything from Phil Parkhurst, it was that I couldn't use someone to achieve my ends the way he did.

Then I remembered how I had taken Michelle the night before. It certainly wasn't against her will, but it hadn't been with her intent, either. I felt badly about it. There was no way I could take it back. Maybe it was all for the best. Maybe she would banish any thoughts of pursuing me further.

I drove the Metro home and put it away. The house was deserted again, but the TV was still on.

Sander Vanocur spoke from the White House.

> "The Kennedy family will view the casket at 10:30 a.m. today. Former President Eisenhower and former President Truman will be here tomorrow."

Yes, I thought, the former President Kennedy is wearing a mask of mortician's wax, the rictus of death-pain massaged from his face by skilled formaldehyde-stinking fingers.

I turned off the TV. Let the rest of America mourn before the cathode tube, bathed in its bluish light, bags of Fritos between their thighs.

Sunday saw Lee Harvey Oswald shot and the cameras probed the face of Oswald's young widow unsympathetically, unceasingly.

Monday there was no school. A single black horse, stirrups reversed, followed the caison bearing Kennedy's body, indicating that the fallen leader would never ride him again.

When I saw that sight on the TV while eating my lunch of boiled ham sandwiches, I wept uncontrollably. I had thought it was all over—the emotionalism—but that black riderless horse let me know I would carry it within me forever.

170

Tuesday, I avoided individuals and steered wide of groups of two or more people. There was only one topic of conversation, and I didn't want to hear it.

Parkhurst tried to stop me as I entered his classroom, but I pushed past him roughly and took my seat.

He began at once eulogizing John Kennedy. I tried my best to shut out his words.

" . . . perhaps Mr. Dalton could say it better . . . Steven?"

"Shove it up your ass, Parkhurst. Find another puppet."

There were gasps, exclamations to Christian deities, then uncomfortable silence.

Parkhurst was visibly shaken. He truly believed I would fall easily back into his realm of influence. He fumbled with his textbook.

"Yes . . . well . . . on page 158 of your text, there is a discussion of the formation of the electoral college . . ." His voice shook. President John Fitzgerald Kennedy's name was never spoken in that classroom again.

Christmas that year promised to be depressing. I had no immediate family to be with, and I had shut myself off from my friends once again. I lived in a cocoon that enveloped me whether at home or at school. I worked the weights, I read, I did my homework, I worked the weights some more, and I slept dark sleeps in empty black voids. Such was my life.

The stores in downtown Greenriver were open late every evening, except Sunday, of course. Nothing was open Sunday except the town's one drug store and the newsstand/bus stop.

People shopped, red-faced from the wind and swirling snow, while carols were piped from speakers rigged on every fifth lamppost. Whether it was contrived or not, Greenriver, like most other small mid-American towns, prospered from a wave of general good cheer which washes over all its populace in the Christmas season. People spoke to total strangers, laughed, and went out of their way to be polite and helpful. Motorists relinquished the right-of-way at four-way stops, waving other cars ahead out of sequence to the point where traffic jams were maddening possibilities even in Greenriver.

I would park the Metro on Main Street just to watch it all. It lifted my spirits to watch people enjoying themselves and, for a change, enjoying each other.

I called Aunt Jane and Laurel, hoping to get an invitation to have Christmas dinner with them. As it turned out, Laurel was in California with her latest "old man," and Aunt Jane was flying to Florida until after New Year's.

I drove downtown. I did my Christmas shopping, which consisted of a sweater for my mother, a gold neck chain for Aunt Jane, and a new Harley T-shirt for Laurel. That was the extent of it, the entire circle of my "loved ones." I took the gifts home and wrapped them. I put Mother's wrapped package in a larger box, tied it with string and took it to the post office. Laurel's and Aunt Jane's would sit at home until they returned to the frozen north from their sojourns in sunnier climes.

The Kiwanis Club was selling Christmas trees in the parking lot of the Buy-Low market. I bought one for six dollars and had to put the top down on the Metro and tie the tree across the back of the seats and trunk. It was a cold ride home.

It took me half an hour to find the decorations that we had used every year.

In the garage, I followed the ritual I had learned watching my father. Cut two inches off the trunk because those jerks up north cut the trees in July then ship 'em down to us in December. The cutting done, you nail a cross of one-by-threes on the bottom. Then you get one of the straight-sided ten gallon buckets Dad used to haul furnace ashes to the dump. You take it in where the tree's going to be. Then you go get the tree. You bring in the tree and stand it up in the bucket. Before it all falls over, you put your bricks in the bucket, alternating them, to lodge the tree in the bucket and give the whole shootin' match some balwast.

Then you stand back to see just how God-awful crooked the tree is. If it's too crooked, you have to take the contraption apart and start over. Usually, a couple well-placed shims of shake shingles will do the trick. You fill the bucket with water, drop in about six aspirins and cover the ugly sucker with a strategically draped bed sheet. Imitation snow.

Then it's time for the decorations. The lights are good for at least four hours of bulb-testing and blaspheming. Putting them on the tree is like Chinese needle torture. It made my hands itch. The broken needles filled the house with pine scent, though, and it smelled like Christmas. Except I was painfully aware I was all alone.

Tinsel next, then the colored glass bulbs. I had never been allowed to touch them before. "Hand-blown in Germany," the tiny sticker on each of them said. They were beautiful. I spent hours as a small child staring into their reflective depths, watching the lights glimmer and shift.

We always saved the icicles. Mother insisted they be put on one strand at a time. Christmas over, they were taken off one by one and stored neatly away until the next year. We even kept them in the boxes in which we had bought them.

Dad, Brian and I used to make fun of mom's anal-compulsive ideas about icicles. I thought back on it then, and I realized it must have been difficult for her at those times, when we all ganged up on her for a laugh at her expense. Though she always took it well, I wondered if all those times might have accrued to help push her over the edge after Brian left home, then after Dad died.

I put the icicles on her way.

When it was lit, it was beautiful, gay, and at the same time, a bit sad. No, very sad. I unplugged it and went to my room.

I drove the main street back and forth for hours, watching the snow, the shoppers, catching snatches of refrains from the broadcast Christmas carols.

On impulse, I pulled off Main Street and aimed the

Metro down Iroquois Street toward the park—and the cemetery.

I slowed to a crawl as I approached the St. Charles house on Willow.

A huge black Buick pulled into the drive just before I reached the house. I stopped the Metro by the opposite curb and lit a cigarette.

An expensively dressed black-haired woman in a black fur coat got out on the driver's side of the black Buick. I waited; I watched. She took packages out of the trunk.

The passenger door opened.

It was her! It was Cat! Her snowy hair swirled in the wind about her ruddy face. She wore a white rabbit fur coat and beret. She looked like a White Russian princess stepping from the royal coach at the palace amid a St. Petersburg snow storm.

I leapt from the Metro and slogged through the slush and snow drifts, a mixture of joy, surprise and unnamed dread churning within me.

"Here . . ." I breathed smoke, out of breath from the running and the thudding of my heart. "Let me help."

Cat was bending into the depths of the trunk trying to reach an elusive package. The scent of Shalimar from her warm body, born on the cold wind, made a new exciting fragrance.

She straightened. Her face went white as her coat beneath the wind-whipped pink of her cheeks.

"Steve!" Her pretty mouth worked, but no sound came out. Her body wanted to move in close to me, surrender itself to me, but evidently the presence of the other woman made her restrain the impulse.

"I take it you know this person?" The woman in black had a sultry voice, deep for a woman but not in the least masculine. It was a voice you would expect to hear in a bedroom in some tropical locale at night. I tore my eyes from Cat long enough to view the speaker.

She was gorgeous, with a mature female beauty that was at once entrancing and frightening. The high-fashion make-up she wore emphasized the whiteness of

174

her face and the drama of her deep-set dark eyes. Her ebony hair feathered about her face in the wind like ravens' wings. Looking back to my Cat, I saw the same affectation in make-up style, the resemblance of features. They could have been mother and daughter, exquisite exotics from the pages of a glossy men's magazine. They were more—idealized women, fantasies, symbols, one white, one dark.

"Y . . . yes," Cat stammered, answering the older woman's question. "This is Steve Dalton. I . . . I've told you about him."

"You mean the one you speak of incessantly." She laughed and extended a gloved hand to me. Her laugh was pleasantly disturbing like a hot summer wind, her handshake firm and lingering.

"This is my aunt, Steven. My Aunt Delilah from Detroit."

"Pleased to meet you," I said, my eyes darting back to consume Cat. Only six months since last I had seen her, and yet she seemed to have matured, to have bloomed even more.

"No, you're not pleased. You wish I'd disappear in some puff of smoke so you might be alone with your Cat."

We both looked at her, Cat and I. Her sensuous laugh was her response to our surprised expressions.

"Well, you get your wish. I'm going in. Have your friend bring in the rest of the packages, Cat."

She went up the ramshackle steps in her high-heeled high-fashion boots and into the house. We waited for the door to close behind her before we faced each other and spoke.

"A very beautiful woman, your aunt. Almost as beautiful as you, Cat."

"Thank you, Steve. She is lovely. Strange though . . . no one has ever called me Cat except you and Bill . . . and Nicholas." Her voice trailed off at the mention of his name, her China-blue eyes cloudy. "I don't believe she knew that was your nickname for me."

"Maybe she read my mind. When I'm near you, I feel

175

like I'm sending out bolts of electricity in all directions."
I touched my frozen bare hand to her cold cheek. She held it in her gloved hands and pressed her warm full lips against it's palm.

"I feel it, Steve. I feel the electricity. God, it's good to see you. I never thought . . ."

"Catherine!" The bass voice called from the porch, and she spun around, throwing my hand from her. "Come in now, Catherine."

He was bigger—or my fear made him seem more giant than ever. She dropped the one small package she had been holding, and it sunk into the snow at her feet. She rushed up the steps, careful not to allow even the hem of her coat to touch him as she hurried past into the house.

I bent and retrieved the package, brushing snow from the wrapping of silver metallic paper.

"Bring them, Steven. Bring the parcels to me."

I obeyed. I gathered all the remaining packages from the trunk, took them up the steps and laid them, offerings to the god, at his feet.

"No . . . bring them inside. Everyone will want to see you." The sickening doughy face attempted a smile that was more a grimace. I knew the older he became the more the muscles of his face were forgetting how to mimic the expression of human beings.

I gathered the packages in my arms and followed him into the house.

Both Delilah and Cat looked out of place in the humble surroundings. They seemed misplaced mistresses of the manor, visiting the serf cottage, bringing the holiday greetings from the lord to the commoners.

Cat looked frightened. Her mother, Susan St. Charles, was uneasy, which was magnified when she saw who was following her mutant son into her home. Bill sat staring into the fire, refusing to look up. Delilah had a bemused smile on her face.

"Put the parcels on the table, over there." I did as the Abomination directed.

"Isn't this a happy holiday group?" the bass voice asked no one in particular.

"I think not," Delilah said, making a show of removing her tight leather gloves. "Steven, I must ask you to leave, much as it pains me. I would dearly love to chat, to learn about the young man who possesses the heart of my favorite niece, but we have family business to discuss."

I left without a word, only a stolen glance at Cat. Her eyes begged for deliverance, but I was not brave enough to oblige.

I slammed my fist into the fender of the Metro, and a rain of rust peppered the snow on the ground.

I couldn't sort my feelings. They were mired together, and the more I sorted through the ooze, the more confused they became. There was nothing firm enough to grasp. All that was left was the familiar numbness.

I drove home. Night had fallen. The snow kept coming. I sat in the dark loneliness of my living room and stared at the dead silence of my Christmas tree.

About midnight, there was a knock at the front door, so faint I thought I imagined it. Then it came again.

I stubbed out the butt of my cigarette in the ashtray overburdened with twenty more like it that I had smoked over the passing hours.

The opened door revealed Cat, tears streaming down her cheeks. She threw her arms around my neck, pulled herself to me and covered my mouth with hers. I tasted the luscious salt of her tears as I kissed her face.

"Steve . . . I have to go. Delilah's in the car. We're going back tonight."

I saw the big car black and lurking there in the drive, snow swirling before its headlights, waiting to swallow up my love, my life, and take her away once again.

"Cat . . . stay with me . . ." I knew how impossible it was before I said it.

"No. I can't."

"But I'm so confused. I need your . . . I need to know . . . what your life's like, what do you do, how do you get by, day to day . . . I need to know, I need some answers . . . I need something . . ."

"Oh, Steve, I can't give you answers. I don't know them myself. But I'll write you, I promise. I'll tell you what I can. I wanted to stop by before we left, before we had to pick him up . . . I had to stop. I had to say goodbye in person." She kissed me again.

"No . . . no . . ."

"It's no good, Steve. It never was. We're too young. Too old, too young, I don't know. Sometimes I feel as old as the earth, old as the sky. We can't control what's going on, and all that we share is distance and pain. Goodbye."

She broke from my possessive embrace, from the hunger of my arms and my body, and ran out into the snow, out to the brooding, waiting car.

"Goodbye," I said, but only the snow and the night heard me.

I want to forget the days that came after that night. Christmas came and went. New Year's passed. Aunt Jane called from Florida to say she was staying awhile longer.

School resumed the second week of January, but I only moved through it all, an automaton, oblivious to human emotions and contact.

It was February before the letter came. The paper was pink and silky, perfumed with her scent.

Dearest Steve:

How can I ever explain to anyone what my life is like? You asked me to tell you, so I will try. I will speak of the things I can.

You know about Nicholas. At least, you know as much about him as anyone. Mom sent me away to Detroit with him because in a big city no one notices very much how different he is, and she knew Delilah and I could deal with him in ways she could not. There are still times when he slips away, when he's gone and we don't know what

178

awful things he's done. There are other times when we know all too well.

Delilah is fabulous. She's more like a sister to me. She owns a dance studio, and it was she who got me started at the Arts school. She says I have the natural grace to be a great dancer. Ballet is out, though. I'm too "top-heavy" for that. Ha ha! Right now I'm studying jazz and interpretive dancing. It's fun.

So I want you to know I'm okay, most of the time, and Delilah makes life worth living. She buys me nice things, and when Nicholas is "sleeping," she takes me to nice shows and restaurants and beauty salons.

I have a few girl friends from school and the studio that I see away from the apartment. I don't want any of them to know about him.

Nicholas is the reason I had to say goodbye to you, and he's why you have to forget about me. I know he's caused you pain. I know what he's done to your family. I can't change what has happened in the past, but maybe if we stay apart, I can save you from him hurting you any more.

You see, Nicholas is jealous of you, of us; ever since that day in the cemetery when he saw us. He showed you what he was that day to scare you. He knows how I feel about you, and all he wants is for you and I to be apart. Please don't try to see me ever again. Don't even think about me. He hurts me when he knows I'm thinking about you. He gets in my mind, and makes me—

Oh, never mind all that. I just don't want him coming to you, hurting you and your family anymore. I love you, Steven. I will always love you.

> Goodbye.
> Catherine Charlene St. Charles
> (forever your Cat.)

I folded the single sheet carefully and put it in my wallet. Life was over; life goes on.

10

The next year and a half of my life was unremarkable.
History happened about me, without drawing me in. I
had learned my lesson with John Kennedy.

The Beatles invaded America that same February,
causing the greatest cultural revolution in our country
since R&B went white and showed up on the radio.
Vietnam became a word heard daily. High school senior
males became worried about the draft.

I graduated from high school and, to my surprise,
won a full college scholarship for studies in Literature
with a paper I wrote Mr. Evan's Senior American Lit
class, an advanced course for college prep students. Mr.
Evans had associations with some very good professors
at Haines City College, and he convinced me to use my
scholarship there.

Parkhurst got on the city council, then became mayor
the year I left town. I wanted to tell everybody what an
ass he was, what an opportunist, but I knew no one
would listen. Another of life's little twists, bitter as gall.
I was leaving town in September; I didn't care. Greenriver had elected him; he was Greenriver's problem.

I thought enrollment in college gave me a deferment
from the draft. I didn't know what good a degree in
Literature would do me in four years' time, but the
school counsellor, Miss Rialto, told me a liberal arts
degree at least would allow me to teach in junior
colleges, even without a teaching certificate. Sounded
as good as anything else.

I passed the summer between high school graduation
and evacuation to Haines City in ways I never would
have suspected. It all began with a knock at my door.

Geoff Prang stood there with Kamii, the oriental girl
from Haines City College. He had his arm around her

shoulder, and she had a hand in the back pocket of his jeans. Geoffie Prang, in jeans that his mother hadn't ironed creases into, and wire-rimmed glasses, had a much cooler ambiance than I remembered.

I invited them in.

"I came to you because of what I know you can do, man," Geoffie said. Kamii smiled at me but said nothing. Geoffie sat in my father's chair, and Kamii sat at his feet, pretty as a Siamese cat and just as unpredictable, I thought.

I lit a cigarette, stayed standing.

"I'm getting a band together, and we want you to front it, man."

I sat down.

"You've got to be joking. I haven't touched my guitar in almost a year."

"I can dig it. You were into the weight lifting thing. It'll all come back fast. You were too good to lose it."

"I don't know. Who else will be in the group?" I was excited, in spite of myself. Music's importance to me had never dwindled.

"Me on bass. I've really worked at it, and I have some unbelievable riffs now, Steve. Paulie on keyboards, Todd on drums. The core group. Like old times. And something else, man. Unbelievable. We're gonna have girl singers, like the Supremes, you know? Like white Supremes, yeah."

"I'm afraid to ask who they might be."

"No need to ask, man, I'm about to tell you. Mitzie Campbell, Debbie Frankwiler and Michelle Bailey. Don't say it . . . I know all about your hassles with some of these people, but it's cool . . . trust me, man. They all voted. It was unanimous. They . . . we all want you."

I looked at Kamii. She nodded encouragement and smiled at me.

"Let me think about it."

"You got it, man." He looked to Kamii, who nodded. He got up to leave, giving her a hand which she ignored. She stood in one graceful movement.

"Before you go, you have to tell me," I said.

181

"Tell you what, man?"

"I don't want to offend you, Geoffie, but you used to be kind of twerpie. Now you seem just the opposite." A hip twerp, I thought, but I didn't say it.

"It's Kamii. I've been seeing her every weekend since we first met. Sometimes she drives down, sometimes I take the bus up there. She's taught me many amazing things, man." He smiled at her and she giggled.

"I'm afraid to ask. What?"

"Lots of things. Stuff about her culture and mine. Oriental and African history, ya know? And . . . other things."

"I bet."

Kamii shot me a playful look that said everything; I didn't ask any more questions.

After they left, I went out to the backyard. The June sun was out, climbing high, but it was early enough in the season to still be rather cool. We had a big backyard, not much wider than the house and garage, but quite long, extending almost one hundred yards back to the C&O tracks. There were the overgrown remains of Mother's flower garden, and the twelve foot pine tree I had planted as a seedling. I drew strength from that pine, seeing how it grew and continued to grow, straight and tall. I felt akin to it. As it grew and thrived, I at least felt I could continue, could go on.

What were the designs of human life when compared to the greater strengths, the mysteries of nature? None of the people Geoffie had mentioned had done anything, any permanent damage to me. In fact, I had made the decision to abstract most of them from my life.

I felt I had been guilty of putting my problems before the worth of friendship. Todd had more or less dissolved the band, because of Ginger and Paulie. Michelle had forced my actions because of her one-track view of our relationship. Mitzie only had shown me further Parkhurst's feet of clay. Boiled down, none of it was worth the loneliness of my self-imposed isolation. It was time to mend these relationships, and the action needed to do so was mine. Besides, I was going away in September, and I might never see any of them again.

I called Geoffie within the hour. We agreed to have the practice sessions at my house, starting the next morning at nine.

Todd's van pulled up at ten minutes of nine. Punctual, and a bit eager, I thought. Good. I had spent all of the previous day loosening up the muscles and hardening the calluses of my fingers. They hurt like hell. My strings were a little dead, so I made a trip to the music store for a new set.

Todd came up the steps grinning his old familiar grin, carrying his brass drum under one brawny arm, two tom-toms under the other. Behind him came Michelle with his cymbals, and behind her was Jim Harper with the P.A. amp.

"Jim! Are you part of the group?"

"Me? No, I can't carry a tune in a mason jar. I'm equipment manager, like for a sports team."

"Glorified go-fer," Michelle giggled.

"If I'm to be the group go-fer, please don't glorify me. We go-fers have our dignity."

I saw the sparkle in Jim's eye and knew he took no offense from Michelle's remark.

"Nothing's changed, has it, Jim?"

"A few things have changed." It was Geoffie at the door with Kamii. She carried his bass case, almost as big as she, while Geoffie lugged a new Vox amplifier up the steps. It was the model called the SuperBeatle. "The biggest change is that Todd and Paulie are friends again."

Todd was bringing in more drum equipment.

"Yeah. I decided I was a real asshole about all that Haines City stuff."

"Todd! Language!" Michelle said, only half joking.

"No, I mean it," he continued, watching Paulie's car drive up. They exchanged waves. "Those girls up there —including my own sister—they were just playing with us."

"I know, Todd. And we let it ruin the band."

"No, Steve. *I* let it ruin the band. And I'm damned sorry." He clapped his paw of a hand on my shoulder. "Hey. Remember those punches we traded up there? In Haines City? Well, the way you've built yourself up, I'd have a hell of a time taking you now, Steve."

"I hope it never comes up. I'd hate to have to place a bet on it."

He offered me his hand, and we shook.

"It will never come up, Steve."

Paulie walked up carrying his torn-down Fender Rhodes.

"I see we're all buddies again," he laughed. "Where's the other two-thirds of the girl group?"

"Mitzie and Debbie will be along in a minute or two. Our costumes came in down at Orlando's, and we wanted to show you guys how tough they are." Michelle giggled, handing Todd his cymbals.

"So, guys, what sound are we after?" I asked.

"You didn't give him the whole story, Geoff?" Paulie stopped setting up his piano to give Geoff a dirty look.

"No, man, I didn't want to scare him off, you know?"

"Okay. What did I get myself into?"

"It's cool, Steve," Geoff said hurriedly. "See, we're already booked through the summer for a weekly gig."

"Before you knew I'd say yes."

"Come on, man," Geoffie smiled, "I knew you'd say yes when the idea first germinated in my mind."

"Germinated . . . ?" I laughed.

"Immaculate conception," Jim deadpanned.

"You still haven't answered my question. The sound . . . what's the sound?"

"Well, now, Steve, it won't be like the stuff we did in Haines City. That was a great sound, but it's not what the management wants."

"The management?"

"Yeah, of the place we're playing."

"Let me get this straight, Geoffie. We're putting together a sound just for the gig? A special order?"

"Don't get so worked up, man. It's gonna be okay. The bread's good."

"Come on. How good can it be? What are we talking about here? Four-piece group with three singers?"

"And a go-fer," Jim added.

"Eight," I said.

"How does one hundred and twenty-five dollars each per gig sound?" Geoffie asked.

"Right. I'll play waltzes and polkas for that."

"That's what I thought. The sound will be like the Beatles go Motown," Geoffie said.

"Or the Stones go Memphis," Paulie said.

"Don't we need horns and strings for that stuff?" I asked.

"Once you see the girls' outfits, you'll realize the audience won't notice if we have horns or not," Todd grinned.

"That true, Michelle?" I asked.

She gave me a frank look with a bit of a sardonic twist to the corners of her smile. "Let's just say that it ought to fit right in with your view of what a woman should be."

There was suddenly an electricity in the air that everyone could feel. I shook it off. I wouldn't let her try to manipulate me again.

"The girls' outfits are part of the arrangement, man," Geoffie explained. "The management wants a sexy act. That's a direct quote."

"Which brings up another burning question," I said. "Where are we playing?"

"A nightclub in uptown Detroit."

"Oh, man!" I let my anger show.

"One hundred and twenty-five bucks apiece. Cash. Every week," Geoffie said, smiling sheepishly.

"Right," I said.

At that moment, Mitzie and Debbie came in carrying boxes, banging them against the door jamb, nearly dropping them, nearly tripping over furniture they couldn't see because of their loads.

"There's more in Debbie's car," Mitzie said, out of breath with excitement and exertion. Debbie had inherited her sister Deanna's car when Deanna flew to

185

Berkeley to become an anthropologist a la Maggie Mead.

"Sounds like a job for Super-go-fer," Jim said with mock seriousness and went out for the remaining boxes.

"What is all this stuff?" I asked, surveying the mountain of fancy Orlando's garment boxes.

"Our outfits," Mitzie said, incredulous at my stupidity.

"That's a hell of a lot of stuff for three girls," I said.

"No, man. The management wants us all to . . ."

"Geoffie, no. Not uniforms again."

"Yeah," he admitted, suddenly very interested in tuning his bass.

"They're really cool, Steve," Mitzie urged.

"I bet."

"Come on, girls," Michelle said. "Let's put our outfits on. That will convince ol' sourpuss Steve that it's going to be great." She winked at Debbie and Mitzie. They gathered certain boxes and went into my parents' bedroom to change.

"I have to tell you, Geoff, guys . . . I don't care for this much so far."

"Play along, Steve, ol' son," Paulie said. "Keep remembering the bread. Our first gig is this weekend. By September, we'll each have over a grand after expenses."

"Okay. But you know, our music used to be worth more to us than just the money." After I said it, I wished I hadn't. They all looked as if I'd slapped their faces with a cold cod fish. I decided to play along, as Paulie suggested. After all, it might be fun. If Michelle became less virginal, and I didn't feel like too big an asshole in whatever queer uniform Geoffie had picked out for us. I said so. The guys didn't answer, but Kamii did.

"It seems quite a bit of complaining, Steven. Geoffie told me about the original band. Your music meant more to you than the money because there wasn't that much, not at first. Sure, just before you broke up you were doing okay. But you spent a lot of weekends playing for Cokes. As far as Michelle goes, I'm working on her attitude problem. She will be okay. And if you feel like an asshole in the costume, that's your problem."

Those were as many words as anyone of us, barring Geoffie, I presumed, had ever heard Kamii string together at one time. I had the distinct impression right at that moment that it was she, not Geoffie, who had coordinated all of this.

The girls came out of the bedroom. They wore matching floor-length gowns of gold lame, sides split to the knee, the shoulder straps supporting a backless and nearly frontless bodice. In Michelle's case, the resultant visual effect was eye-catching, to say the least. The other girls suffered only in comparison to her.

Mitzie was still cheerleader cute. Debbie was quite attractive, especially without her glasses. Bat-blind but attractive.

Michelle led them in a series of spins, turns, arm gestures and bows. They had only minimal trouble doing it gracefully in their pointed-toed high stiletto heels, even on the carpet.

"They've been practicing every night," Todd beamed, eyeing Michelle with lecherous approval.

"They're good," I admitted, "but can they sing?"

"Who gives a damn?" Jim asked my libido.

"We've been practicing that, too," Debbie said. "We're not great, but I think we're pretty good."

"I think we're real good," Mitzie said.

"Face it, ladies, we're fantastic," Michelle tossed her head. I noticed she glanced at Kamii for approval. Kamii smiled, nodded, and Michelle twitched her hips at me, in a gesture that was at once defiant and alluring.

"Let's try something," I said.

"How 'bout 'Where Did Our Love Go?' " Mitzie suggested. "That's one we've worked on the most."

"Key of?" I asked.

"E, what else," Paulie said, and played an elaborate arpeggio.

"It ain't rock'n'roll if it ain't in E," Todd said

thumping the bass drum pedal. "Let me try this back-beat, to make it a little different than the Supremes' version." He kicked the bass drum into a syncopation with his ride cymbal and snare side-beat that I had never heard before. It was a wicked, wicked sound. Made you wanna dance dirty. I fell in with stacatto four-beat chords, and Geoffie laid down a fantastic run. The girls started to move. Paulie came in with a complicated extrapolation of the basic melody, and I started to sing.

"Baby, baby, where did our love go . . ."

The girls came in with sweet oohs and shoop-shoops. It was righteous. Somebody had taught Mitzie how to find the beat. Again, I suspected Kamii. Inscrutable.

By the end of the day we had fifteen strong tunes together. I taught the girls how to get a growl in their voices, like Etta James and Tina Turner. I showed Geoffie some even wilder runs and bass-walks than he had managed to work out by himself. Todd showed us all some funky stop-beats and hesitations that raised goose bumps on my arms.

"We'd better meet every day this week." I put my Gibson Firebird away, wiping down the neck and strings with a soft cloth. The new strings I had put on the night before were slick with the oil from my fingers. My fingers felt like there were needles jammed under my nails.

"Leave the equipment set up. Nine tomorrow," I said.

General confusion followed, as the girls went into the bedroom to change and called out questions as to who was riding where with whom.

Michelle came back out, still in her gown, to place a cool hand on my arm. She glanced over at Kamii before she spoke.

"I'm glad we're back together again, Steven," she whispered.

"We are not back together, Michelle, as anything but friends."

She withdrew her hand, but kept smiling. "Oh, I

know. I meant it was good to have all of us together. Your old band . . . Mitzie, Todd and Jim . . . you know . . . all of us."

"Right."'

"Do you think I'm sexy in this dress?" She spun in a slow circle for me.

"Yes."

"Sexier than the other girls?"

"Don't start, Michelle. There's nowhere it can go." I glanced at Todd. She followed my implication.

"Don't worry about Todd. We broke up. All he wanted was my body." She frowned.

"You seem to forget that's all I wanted, too. Sometimes, that's all anybody really has to offer."

"Humph," she grunted. "Still the great cynic. I hoped you had changed."

"I think I have, Michelle. But our whole problem was that we never saw things the same way. You started off leading me to believe all you wanted was an exchanges of the hots. Then suddenly it was hands off unless we're gonna get married. I told you from the start I couldn't get that involved."

"Oh, yes, I remember quite clearly," she said, the bitterness creeping into her voice. "Your famous mystery girl friend. Well, I found out who you meant. I've heard a few things about Miss Catherine St. Charles, about her whole family."

"You'd better stop right there, Michelle." I lit a cigarette.

"I can say what I want. People say her mother was a whore, her sister was a whore, and . . . well . . ." She made a vague gesture with her hand. "Now that I know who your little heart burns for, it's no longer any wonder to me that you wanted me to act like a whore, too. But I can't compete with a professional."

It was the most difficult thing I had ever done, but somehow I managed not to kick the shit out of her then and there.

"Well, you've said what you had to, Michelle. I hope you feel better. Now forget it, and get the hell out of my sight. I won't have this kind of shit break up another band of mine."

The rest of the people had ambled outside, and I joined them.

Paulie offered me a Newport and I took it. I had left my Benson and Hedges in the ashtray inside. The mentholated smoke tasted good in the late afternoon June sunshine.

"Michelle and you have a big conference?" Jim asked.

"Just straightening out a few old loose ends," I said.

"That's a hard thing to do with Michelle," Todd said, taking a cigarette from Paulie's pack.

"Yeah," Paulie acknowledged, lighting Todd's purloined cigarette for him. "Sometimes Michelle's loose ends are fairly tangled, ol' son."

In a few minutes, Michelle came out, changed into her street clothes. She walked by us without a word, straight to Debbie's car, where Debbie and Mitzie waited. Geoffie and Kamii had already left.

"So," I said to Jim, "who are you fucking these days . . . Debbie or Mitzie?"

Everybody laughed the way guys do when somebody says something like that. They all hope they won't be the next one asked.

"Neither. More's the pity. As far as I know, Debbie doesn't do anybody, and Mitzie doesn't seem to either, since Parkhurst kicked her out of bed."

"You knew about that?" I was surprised, to say the least.

"Hell, yes. Everybody did. Mitzie ain't bright enough to be subtle." Jim frowned and took one of Paulie's cigarettes, too.

"Michelle tells me you two broke up, Todd. I'm sorry," I said. It was the thing to say.

"I'm not. Damn! I took more cold showers with that girl," he grinned. "She kept telling me she wouldn't do it with any guy until she had a wedding ring. 'Course you went with her long enough to know how it goes with Michelle."

"Yeah," I said. I hadn't expected her to tell Todd all

190

about us, but I never expected her to go so far the other way. But then, in the sixties, all small-town girls prized the illusion of virginity, hoping that that and just enough tease would land them a rich undemanding husband.

"All of which brings us to the obvious, ol' son," Paulie said stubbing out his cigarette on the porch railing. "Who are you slippin' the ol' sausage to these days? You must be 'bout ready to put a revolving door on this place, for all the chickies who go in and out of here."

"Hate to disappoint you guys, but I'm practically a monk."

They all laughed.

"Come on, Steve," Jim poked at me with an accusing finger. "With this set-up? A house all to yourself? How many beds do you have in there, anyway? Shit, you dumped these guys, then you dumped me. If it wasn't because you thought we'd cut in on your action, why the hell was it?" There was a seriousness behind his kidding that showed me the hurt he felt.

I could have told them why—why I had chosen a life without friends—but I didn't. There was no point. Besides, I didn't have the guts to tell them.

"No, really, guys. I'm pretty much alone most of the time. Anyway, we haven't heard from Paulie. How's the poor little rich boy with the Southern charm doing with the ladies?"

"As Gen'l Lee said to Grant at Appomatox, things don't look too fuckin' good. But never fear, boys, the South shall rise again."

We all laughed.

"Sounds like we're all pretty much in the same situation. Some hot-shot rock stars we are."

"Yeah," Todd grinned, "the only one who's getting it regular is Geoffie. Who'd a thunk it?"

"Two years now," Paulie said, "every damned weekend. Oriental-style, yet." He shook his head. "He probably knows ways we couldn't imagine if we'd been raised in a Memphis whorehouse."

"All this is doing nothing but making me horny," I

191

said, "and given my current prospects, nothing lies in that direction but real pain."

"That's true," Jim said. "I think I'll go home and spend some time with Dad's latest Playboy."

Jim and Todd got into Todd's van, Paulie slid into his mother's Avanti, and I waved as they drove off.

The next day's practice was even better than the day before. Each session we improved dramatically and the tensions between us lessened as the music and sound became most important to us all.

Saturday arrived, and we had Todd's van loaded by nine a.m. We were all high as kites on nerves, anticipation and fear.

Jim rode with Todd and the equipment. Geoffie and Kamii knew the way, so they would lead the caravan in Kamii's shiny little Volkswagen. That left the three girls and myself to follow with Paulie in his mother's Avanti. Michelle insisted on sitting in the front passenger bucket, which put me tightly sandwiched in the back between Mitzie and Debbie.

All three girls had their hair puffed and sprayed in elaborate bouffants. Though they wore their usual summer street clothes, their hair-dos and make-up made them look like big-city girls—or visual aids from a Reverend Stoney Miles sermon about the damnable sluts, the WHOres of BABYlonia, SISters of the A-BOMB-ination.

Driving along, we decided on a name for the band: The Seven Wonders of the World.

The club was located in the most decayed section of an all-black slum on Detroit's east side. In a long block of low two-storey store fronts, windowless, gutted, littered with raw-crawling debris or windows boarded and spray-painted with messages to kill whitey, sat the ugly purple painted door to Levon's Showbar and Lounge. The two by three foot neon sign that proclaimed Levon's location swayed on a rakish angle, hanging from only one tired S-hook.

Inside, everything was purple fur and black vinyl. It

was like a cave. We couldn't see hands before our faces as we made the many stumbling trips to get all the equipment through the front door, through the maze of unseeable tables and to the stage at the end of the long narrow room.

Two tired heavily painted black women watched wordlessly from seats at the bar which ran the entire length of one side wall.

We were all set up and tricked out in our flashy clothes—the girls in their slinky gold lamé and spike heels, us guys in our gold lamé tux jackets, black pants and black ruffled shirts with the gold Thunderbird ties. To say we felt uncomfortable and out of place was the understatement of the year.

Geoffie directed us back to a single dressing room.

Paulie picked something up from one of the twelve littered tables before twelve uniformly cracked lighted mirrors.

"What are these?" he asked.

"I've seen those," Mitzie said, the shock of recognition making her voice loud. "Strippers wear those things!"

"They're called pasties and g-strings," I said.

Paulie dangled the sparkly tassled thing in front of Geoffie's face.

"A strip club, Geoffie? You booked us into a strip club? A nigra strip club?"

"Watch the innuendo, man," Geoffie warned.

"Right, Paulie, don't let Southern prejudice color the issue, if you'll excuse the pun," I said. "It certainly doesn't matter if it's a black or white strip club. It's still a fucking strip club, Geoffie."

I pretended violent anger—which was only partially pretense—grabbing Geoffie's shirt front and bringing him inches from my face, like Al Capone on the "Untouchables."

Geoffie forced a laugh.

"It's cool, man. They do that during early hours, before and after us. You know . . . business man's lunches, the supper crowd, the insomniacs. We're the headliners, man, the main attraction."

"You think it's a different crowd?" I asked, letting go of his shirt.

"Yeah, man, I do."

"Come on, Geoffie, this place is the pits," Michelle said, taking the pasties and g-string from Paulie for closer examination. "How in the world do they keep these little buggers on?"

"They don't. That's the whole point," Debbie said.

"I bet they use glue or something," Mitzie offered, watching intently as Michelle held the glittering blue star-shaped swatches over the ends of her breasts and inspected herself in one of the grimy cracked mirrors.

"It can't be as bad as you're all making it out," Todd said. "If it was, how could they afford to pay us so much? They must get a class crowd in here, and the entertainment hours are probably when that happens."

"All I want to know is how you found this place, Geoffie Prang," Debbie said accusingly.

"Uh . . . Kamii . . . er . . ."

"It is all right to tell them, Geoff," Kamii said. She stepped forward, and everyone focused their attention on her. She so rarely spoke, it was a real event. "My parents are dead and I was not left well off. I have few relatives in America. If I wanted to go to college, I had to pay my own way. I had to find a job I could work short hours, hours of my choosing, and one that would give me high returns for my invested time."

"What are you saying, Kamii?" I asked.

She took the pasties from Michelle and held them over the tips of her own small pointed breasts. "I am saying this is where I work. I am one of the strippers. I take off my clothes before the people who seem to frighten all of you so very much, even though you have never seen them. You girls fly in horror from such a thought, yet it excites you, too, I think. You boys drool over such a thought, and wonder how Michelle, Mitzie or Debbie would look dancing in these." She held up the tiny offending articles of an ecdysiast's wardrobe. "I think you all should be more honest about your sexual desires. Sex is not dirty. For me, showing my body is a means to an end. No different from digging a ditch for money."

"Well, if Kamii says it's okay, I say let's do it," Mitzie said.

"Me too," Michelle agreed. "God, it's starting to excite me!"

"That's the spirit." Geoffie grinned. "Let's get out there. Levon wants to see a run-through."

"*The* Levon? We are to be honored by an audience with *the* Levon?" The mock awe in Jim Harper's face made everyone laugh. "I'll go out and crank up the amps." He ran out.

"Let's go," I said, and we filed out to the stage.

The two tired black women still sat at the bar, sipping amber liquid out of tall glasses.

A fat bald man with a gold tooth flashing even in the dim light waddled out of a door to the right of the stage. He took his smeared glasses off, cleaned them on his broad floral necktie and placed them once again on the bridge of his broad nose.

"So this be it, boy?" his gravelly voice grunted.

Geoffie lept down from the three-foot-high stage.

"Yes sir. We call ourselves the Seven Wonders of the World."

The man grunted. He eyed the three girls very closely. Debbie was the most nervous. Without her glasses, she couldn't tell if fat Levon was a man or one of the tables.

"Kamii honey, c'mon over here to Levon," he rasped.

Kamii obeyed. Fat Levon said something to her that we heard only as a low droning, like a jar of angry bees. Kamii kept nodding. Occasionally she whispered back at Levon. Once he nodded and let out a deep rumbling laugh from deep in his belly.

He approached the stage.

"Kamii says you all good girls." He didn't seem to give a damn about whether or not us guys were all good guys. "I wants you to understan' what Levon's Showbar is all 'bout. My clientele, understan', wants to see a little skin, know what I'm sayin'? 'Specially white skin." He let out another belly laugh that made the girls jump. "Now I don' mean you gals gotta strip off. I got other girls do that." He gestured vaguely at the two black girls at the bar and at Kamii who still stood beside him, nodding silent encouragement and approval to the girls.

"What I wants is for you girls to be real sexy, understan, but ah . . . wh . . . what the word?"

"Aloof," Kamii supplied.

"That's it, that's what I want. Sexy, teasin', you know, but aloof . . . understan'?"

Michelle nodded for all three. Her boobs jiggled and jumped when she did, and fat Levon laughed some more.

"Uh . . . what about the music?" I asked, more than a bit pissed.

Levon eyed me through his thick glasses. He waddled over to where I stood. Even though I was on the stage and he was three feet below me, I instinctively stepped back as he approached.

"This here boy tol' me you boys was good . . . tha's good enough for me. I tol' him what I wanted, he say you could play it. Tha's all I need to know. What I'm concerned with is the visuals, understan'? My customers is used to gettin' a helluva show. These three white-bread gals you got, they gon' be the show, understan'?"

"I understand. I'm just not sure I like it," I said.

"You don't gotta like it, boy. All you gotta do is play that Gawd-damn gui-tar."

"It's okay," Michelle said quickly. "Mr. Levon isn't asking us to do anything immoral, are you, Mr. Levon?"

"Levon's mah firs' name, sugar." He showed her his gold tooth. "An' that's right. Nothin' dirty, jus' bad, understan'? Teasin', tha's all."

"I'm not sure what you mean," Debbie stammered, aiming her remark at a table instead of Levon. I knew she couldn't tell the difference.

"Gladys. Jonelle," he rumbled. The black girls at the bar slid off their stools with the fluid grace of snakes coming off sunbaked rocks. They minced over to his side on spike heels that made our girls' shoes look like flats.

"Take these whitebread girls into my office and show 'em some steps."

The two black women nodded and motioned lethargically to the girls on the stage.

When they hesitated to follow the strippers, I interrupted again.

"Listen, I don't think . . ."

"It's okay," Kamii said. "I'll go, too."

The three girls filed down the side steps of the stage and followed the black women and Kamii through the door from which Levon had entered the bar.

"Now, boys, let's hear this music you so worried I don' care 'bout."

We ran through some numbers, and fat Levon cocked an attentive ear. After awhile, he held up a gold ring-filled hand. We stopped.

"Gawd-damn! You boys are Gawd-damn good!" He rubbed his fat fingers over one of his many chins. The gold rings clicked a tune that sounded like money, like coins jingling together. "Tell you what . . . the crowd likes you tonight, you go over big, I'll bring you in on Friday nights, too. That'll double yo' income. How 'bout it, boys?"

"You bet," Todd grinned from behind his drums.

"Todd . . ." I whispered.

"Listen," he whispered back. "My folks are strapped and I don't have a scholarship to go to college like some people. I need all the money I can get this summer."

I looked to Paulie and Geoffie, and they nodded in agreement with Todd's words.

"Okay. But I do on record . . . I don't like any of this."

"Who would have figured Steve Dalton for the stick in the mud." Todd grinned.

"It's all cool, man. Trust in Geoffie, okay?" Geoffie adjusted his wire-rimmed glasses.

"Let's get changed, get the girls and get out of here until tonight," I said, putting my guitar on the stand

and turning off my amp.

"To where?" Todd asked.

"Hey, we can go to the river. Over to Belle Isle, Bob-Lo . . . 'cross the bridge into Canada." Geoffie seemed eager to be the tour guide.

"Something," I said, "somewhere other than here. I don't care what or where."

Geoffie went to fetch the girls. He was gone about fifteen minutes. The rest of us were in our street clothes, smoking, trying to see further than five feet away in the bar's starless night black interior.

"They don't want to come, man," he said on his return. "They want to go out shopping with Gladys and Jonelle."

"I don't know . . . will they be safe?"

"Sure, man. Kamii will be along. Besides, black people don't do you damage just because you're white. You're starting to offend me." Geoffie smiled.

"Yeah, well, I suppose that 'kill whitey' shit out there on the buildings was a love note." I tossed my cigarette on the floor and ground it out.

"That's just white males, man. White women aren't any good dead." Geoffie laughed. "Loosen up, it's okay."

We waited for Geoffie to change. Todd came over and lit my third cigarette for me.

"Y'know, they're all big girls. They're making their own decisions here. Why are you so upset?"

"I don't know, Todd. But you're right. Debbie and Mitzie are older than I am. I guess it's that old thing about chivalry. Like a guy is supposed to take charge when there's a woman around. Besides, I wonder how their parents would feel if anything did happen . . . shit, they probably all told their parents they're at a slumber party in Greenriver."

"Yeah, I can dig it. But Kamii knows her way around. And I don't think Geoffie would say it's okay if it isn't. These are his people."

"You forget he was raised in Greenriver, and he's just as dumb-ass hick-stupid as you and me."

"Okay. But there's nothing you can do anyway. The one we've got to watch is Paulie. Look at him. He's petrified."

I saw that it was true. Paulie was chain-smoking Newports, lighting one from the butt of another, casting his eyes about like searchlights.

Geoffie came back in his street clothes.

"Let's go," I said. I didn't have to say it twice for Paulie Gibbs.

We crossed the border to Canada and we wandered around Windsor, bought packs of Player Cuts cigarettes because supposedly the Beatles and the Yardbirds smoked them, and headed back to the U.S. of A. The cigarettes tasted like camel shit.

It was about seven-thirty when we left Windsor crossing the Ambassador Bridge, the sun dropping into hazy smog sending out brilliant oranges and purples across the dusky sky.

The deepening twilight put me in a lonely mood, even though I sat shoulder to shoulder with Jim and Todd in the back of the speeding Avanti.

While the others laughed and joked about our day's adventures, my lonely mood led, as lonely moods always have, to thoughts of Cat.

A million things ran through my mind. I ought to find her, now, while I'm here, I thought. But I had no leads. I didn't know her aunt's last name. I didn't know the name of the dance studio. The letter she had sent me a year and a half before, still in my wallet, bore no return address. There was no way. No possible way.

"You gettin' out, or you gonna stay there all night?" It was Todd. Everyone else was outside the car, standing on the sidewalk under Levon's precariously swaying neon sign.

I got out.

Night came fast in the city. It was only around eight p.m., but the sun was down and the golds and oranges of the sunset were changed to blood reds and deep violets.

We opened the door to a juke box blaring Smokey

Robinson. The bass beat thudded against my groin.

"Great sound," Geoffie yelled at my ear. "Hitsville U.S.A. They plug the bass right into the board over there."

"Where?" I yelled back.

"The Motown studios. I went over there with Kamii awhile back, man. I even met Eddie Holland."

"Great," I yelled. I had only a vague knowledge that Eddie Holland was one of the guys that wrote songs for the Supremes.

Fat Levon met us at the door.

"Long towards mornin'," he growled, showing us his gold tooth in a snarling smile. "We were worried 'bout you white cats. Your white honeys is all tricked out and ready to gig. They're in the dressin' room. You boys go on in and get ready. I'm gon' start you early, 'bout thirty minutes. The customer is restless tonight."

"He means the natives are restless," Paulie yelled in my ear.

As we walked through the club, all conversation, all movement ceased. All eyes were on the four white boys following fat Levon and Geoffie through the club.

Paulie's nervous condition was infectious. I saw it in Jim and Todd's eyes, and knew my own eyes held the same fear. Geoffie Prang and his family were the only blacks we had ever seen up close. All the others we had ever seen had been on TV or on the Three Rivers football team.

The dressing room door closed behind us, cutting out most of the noise. The only females in the room I recognized were Kamii and the two black women from the bar. The other three women were utter strangers.

After a moment, I realilzed they were Michelle, Mitzie and Debbie. They looked like women out of a Fellini film about Italian streetwalkers.

"This dress is so tight I can't even breathe," Debbie complained.

"It'll help you hit the high notes," Michelle laughed.

"The dress doesn't bother me," Mitzie said. "It's these shoes. How high are these heels? They feel like stilts. My calves hurt."

200

"Six inches, darlin'," the woman named Jonelle said. "Here, have some of this. Help you cool out." She passed a sweet-smelling cigarette to Mitzie.

"No thank you, I don't smoke."

"Neither do I, baby. This more like medicine. Calm yo' nerves."

"Oh. Okay." Mitzie took the cigarette and inhaled. "Nice." She coughed a bit, then took another puff. "Hey, it does help."

"Then give it to me," Debbie said. "I need all the help I can get in the nerve department. I just got another look at myself in the mirror. No way would my folks approve of the way I look tonight!'"

Soon all three girls were huddled about Jonelle, passing the cigarette.

I still couldn't believe how they looked. Debbie was right. Dressed and made-up as they were, in Greenriver they would have been slapped into jail, no questions asked. They were definitely dangerous women by hometown standards.

The dresses were made of the same material as before, but a lot less of it. The side slits went all the way to their hips and their legs glistened in shining black hose. The shoes were new—black patent leather and with heels high enough to tip the girls forward. The toes were so pointed they could kill cockroaches in tight corners.

They all wore shoulder-length black gloves, their wrists covered in flashy rhinestone bracelets. Bulky rhinestone chokers adorned their throats and long heavy matching earrings hung and swayed almost to their bare shoulders.

I had thought the puffy hair-dos they had done in Greenriver were elaborate. I was wrong. Their spectrum of hair colors—Michelle's black, Mitzie's blonde and Debbie's red—glistened with fine sparkly dust. The rats, teases, finger curls and folds of hair on each of them increased their heights by almost a foot.

Then there was the make-up. As I said, they looked like Fellini's streetwalkers. The black lines around their eyes winged so far to the sides they were lost in the curls

201

of the fantastic hair-dos. Purple metallic shadows went from the black-lined lids up to black arched eyebrows. Their lips looked like wet cherry candy, while their cheeks were bruised raspberry red.

All of the other guys were staring, just as I was, mouths gaping.

These were not the small-town girls we had known. These were the instruments of lust, the downfall of men Reverend Stoney Miles had sweated and seethed about all those mornings on black and white TV in the late 50's.

"You guys better get dressed," Michelle said between puffs on Jonelle's cigarette. "Levon said he'd announce us anytime."

We stripped down to our shorts. The girls paid no attention. Only Jonelle and Gladys watched with amused interest. We hurried.

A knock came at the door.

"Five minutes," Levon's gravel voice shouted.

"What's first?" Michelle asked.

"Is my lipstick smeared?" Debbie checked the mirror nearest her. "Shit! I can't see a thing without my glasses."

Jim stared at her. We all did. None of us had ever heard her swear before.

"You look fine, Red," Gladys drawled. "Have 'nother hit." She passed a fresh cigarette to Debbie.

"Let's do 'Stop in the Name of Love' first," Mitzie said. "It'll knock 'em on their asses."

"Let's go," I said.

I opened the door.

Levon was on stage, one of our mikes before him.

"Ladies and gents, cats and groovy chicks, the Showbar proudly presents the Seven Wonders of the World!"

They all followed me. When the girls filed out of the dressing room onto the stage, a chorus of whistles and catcalls greeted them. I watched closely as I strapped on my guitar. The girls seemed to love the attention.

I nodded to Michelle, and she nodded back. I faced

the other guys in the band, my back to the audience. I counted it down silently, mouthing the numbers so they could see.

"And-one-two-three-four-"

We all hit staccato eighth notes together for a bar and the girls came in.

"Stop!" they sang, palms of both hands extended to the audience.

We were quiet, frozen for two bars.

Michelle moved closer to her mike and breathed, in the sexiest female voice I had ever heard—

"—in the name of love—"

The other girls moved up and breathed with her.

"—be-fore you break my heart—"

The band came in strong.

"—think it oh-oh-ver . . . think it oh-oh-ver."

Michelle and I stepped to our mikes, the other girls stepping back. Michelle and I sang the verse together, staring into each other's eyes.

"Baby, baby, I'm aware of where you go, each time you leave my door—"

Debbie and Mitzie moved up with a full spin for the chorus.

For the next verse, Michelle moved over to my mike. She put her fingertips on my lips and sang, so sexy, almost moaning.

"I've known of your, your secluded nights, baby, I've even seen her maybe once or twice . . . but is her sweet, sweet expression worth more than my love and affection . . . this time before you leave my bed and rush off to her instead—"

"Think it oh-oh-ver," the girls sang.

"Haven't I been good to you—" Michelle moaned.

"Think it oh-oh-ver," they crooned.

"Haven't I been sweet to you—"

"Stop! In the name of love," we all sang the chorus.

Michelle and I moved to the single mike, our lips millimeters apart, and sang together.

"I've tried so hard, hard to be patient, hoping you'll stop this infatuation—"

It was all I could do to keep from kissing her.

We finished the verse, everybody came in for the chorus, and I hit a screaming double-time quitar lead while the girls did in unison one of the most erotic dances I had ever seen.

After the guitar lead, we shifted keys and went right into "Baby Love."

"Oooh, baby love, my baby love, I need ya, oh how I need ya," Michelle breathed into my mike.

When I came close for the back-up vocal, her lips brushed mine. A second later she licked her lips with her tongue, eyes half-closed. If she was acting, she was damned good! She had not only me going but had the audience in the palm of her hand.

When she sang, "I'm so deep in love with you," it sounded positively obscene.

The rest of the set went the same way. The music was perfect, the singing electrifying, and the new choreography, provided surely by Gladys and Jonelle, was lewd enough to jump-start a dead lecher's heart.

When I announced our break, it was met with shouts of "No, no way, man, do it again," and "More, more, more!"

We ran to the dressing room and the juke box blared out the Temptations.

All of us were out of breath with the excitement. We all hugged and kissed. Michelle clung to me, gasping for breath, and I clung to her, holding her close.

Todd put it in words.

"Jesus Christ! You guys," he indicated the two other girls, "were fantastic! You two," he pointed at Michelle and me, "you two almost made me come!"

"No shit," Jim said. "I couldn't believe my eyes! And the audience, oh my God, the audience! They were goin' crazy!"

Michelle laughed and kissed me hard on the mouth. Jim had his arms around the waists of both Debbie and Mitzie, and he kissed them both. Todd kissed Kamii, and Debbie kissed Geoffie and Paulie. Michelle kissed me again. Hell, we were all at fever-pitch.

"What can we start the next set with? How can we do anything that won't disappoint them after the last set?" Todd asked, taking a cold Coke from Levon.

"I know," Michelle said, checking her lipstick in one of the mirrors. "That Mary Wells song that came out in April last year. 'My Guy'."

"We've only practiced that once," Debbie protested.

"That doesn't matter," Michelle said applying a fresh candy-coating of lipstick. "I've got some ideas that will make the roof cave in. No male back-up, for one thing. You girls just follow my lead."

We drank Cokes and smiled at each other a lot. The fifteen minute break couldn't be over soon enough.

Back on stage, the audience cheering like mad, Michelle turned to us in the band.

"Give me a real hard beat, guys."

"You mean uh, uh, uh, uh, accents on the down-beats?" I asked.

"Yeah. Like that. Real hard."

"Okay. One-two-one-two-three-four-"

She shimmied up to the mike. Shimmied!

"Nothin' you could say would tear me away from my guy . . . nothin' you could do 'cause I'm stuck like glue to my guy . . . I'm stickin' to my guy like a stamp to a letter, like birds of a feather we . . . stick together . . ."

With every stroke of the four-beat, she twitched her pelvis against the mike stand.

We did an instrumental break after the first verse, and she moved over to me.

"Nothin' you could do could make me untrue to my guy . . ." She ground her hips into me and my guitar with the beat. She ran her fingers through my hair and kissed my neck. The audience was screaming!

She ended the song sliding up and down my leg.

"—there's not a man today who could take me away from my guy—"

"Whad yoo say?" the girls sang.

"—there's not a man today who could take me away from my guy—"

"tell me mo'!"

"—there's not a man today . . ."

The applause from the audience drowned the rest of the fade.

We did about nine more numbers, ending the set with "Chapel of Love."

The fifteen minute break was a repeat of the one before, only more intense. Michelle spent the entire time sitting on my lap, kissing me.

We opened the last set with "Leader of the Pack." It was such a steamy version that I thought the men in the audience were going to jump the stage and ravish all three girls. Actually, it was even money whether the audience would do it or the guys in the band. We were all nearly drooling.

For our final number, we did "Stay," with Michelle singing lead.

"Stay . . . just a lit-tle bit lon-ger . . . please, please, please, please, say that you're gon-na . . . now my momma won't mind, you know my daddy won't mind, and my sis-ters won't mind just . . . say you will!" She groaned as if it hurt, and ground her hips, bumped her hips, whipped her hips as if in the throes of ecstasy.

Then they did rush the stage. Levon was up there in an instant, moving fast for a fat old dude. He held them at bay while we made for the dressing room.

"God! I hate for it to be over," Michelle sighed. "I don't know whether to laugh, cry or shout for joy."

We were all going through the same orgy of emotions.

"Let's get changed and head for home," Todd said. "It'll be two-thirty before we're in Greenriver."

"Home? I don't want to go home. I'm too high," Debbie laughed.

"Here's an idea," Michelle said. "Why don't we all just spend the night at Steve's? We can have an all-night party to celebrate."

"That's a great idea," Mitzie agreed. "We can make the calls from there. We can all tell our folks we're spending the night at each other's houses. It always works."

"I can get beer in Coldwater when we pass through," Todd said. "I buy there all the time at this little mom and pop all-night party store."

"Great," I said, carried along. "By the way . . . where's Jim?"

"Loading the van. He's the go-fer, remember?"

"Let's not change clothes," Michelle said. "I feel good in this get-up. It's starting to feel natural."

Geoffie and Kamii didn't join the returning caravan. They were going back to Haines City for the rest of the weekend. Jim rode back with Todd in the van. Paulie drove the Avanti, with Debbie in the passenger bucket. I sat in back with Michelle on one side, and Mitzie on the other.

"You know, those were the greatest cigarettes those girls had . . . I forgot to ask what brand they were."

Paulie laughed. "Down home we call 'em reefers. I don't know what they call 'em in Detroit."

"Still, I wonder where you'd go to buy some," Mitzie said.

"Down home, it was any good dark alley in 'Lanta."

"Paulie Gibbs, what do you mean?" Mitzie said, exasperated.

"He means," I said, "that you were smoking dope. Marijuana."

"Oh, my God!" Mitzie cried. "I'm a dope addict!"

We all laughed. There was nothing we could say to console poor Mitzie.

I put my arm around her and she cuddled close.

"Hey! How 'bout me?" Michelle pouted. I put my arm around her, too. She moved in with amorous intent. I didn't object. We were past Clinton when Mitzie had forgotten about her worries over being a dope fiend, and she too was kissing me.

I thought again of Reverend Stoney. How could I wipe that fat-assed evangelist from my mind? The answer, of course, was that I couldn't. Nicholas was Abomination. I was. Michelle. All of us were. Menage á trois? Abomination, definitely.

By the time we stopped behind the van in Coldwater

so that Todd could get beer, things in the back seat were pretty intense. Todd glanced in, said something to Paulie I didn't hear, and Paulie got out of the car. I heard the trunk open, shut, and Paulie got behind the wheel again.

In thirty minutes we were in Greenriver. Paulie wheeled the Avanti into my drive.

"All right, children, time to break the clenches. We has arrived."

"Where's Jim and Todd?" I mumbled. My lips were tired. "Weren't they in front of us?"

"They copped out, Steve. Not enough females to go 'round, the way you're goin' at it, you greedy bastard." He laughed. "He dropped three sixes of beer in my trunk, though. The guy's a real sport."

We went inside. Debbie warmed to Paulie's expert advances immediately after her first beer. Mitzie and Michelle didn't need any beer. Neither did I.

11

I didn't awaken until noon the next day. Everybody was gone. The living room was scattered with empty and half-empty beer bottles. It smelled like a brewery. I cleaned up—first the house, then me.

About halfway through my lengthy shower, Geoffie called. His information left me speechless. Levon wanted us Friday nights as well as Saturdays. Kamii would find us a place to stay between the two nights. Nine more weeks, Levon wanted us, for sure. He said Michelle had it all figured out down to the last penny, but roughly it would mean over sixteen grand, total. Then he hit me with the heavy stuff; there would be record company execs at the club Saturday night. This cold be the break—the big break that the original group had joked about, dreamed about, prayed for two years ago. I was to be part of it, and all because I had finally decided to seek and accept the friendship these people kept offering me, despite my moody introversion. All because I had gone along, hoping to have fun and hoping to forget my own problems for awhile. I had just played along as Paulie had requested. Good old Paulie.

Kamii's lodging arrangements in Detroit turned out to be a loft over a tool and die company about six blocks from Levon's, which meant it was in the same depressingly ghetto-esque neighborhood. One big ugly room, it had a floor of rotted asphalt tile and walls of peeling white paint. The windows were painted black and the ceiling sagged in several places where it leaked rain. There were five naked spider-web-festooned light bulbs. No chair, no beds. A cracked porcelain toilet squatted out in the open in one corner, with a tiny lavatory next to it. The bowl of the sink was streaked red from the iron-laden water that constantly dripped out of the green corroded faucets.

"Eeyuk!" Mitzie said, expressing the feelings of the entire group. We all decided that even if the loft were free, we would gladly foot the expense of a hotel rather than stay there.

There was some kind of paperhangers convention or something, so we ended up at the Fort Pick-Shelby, miles from Levon's. The girls shared a double, Paulie and Todd agreed to room in another double, and Jim and I took a single.

"I think our go-fer is trying for a raise, sleeping with the lead guitarist," Michelle said, laughing.

"Small minds," Jim said.

We had a little time before making the crosstown drive to Levon's. The girls seemed content to do each other's hair and talk about the ideas Kamii had laid on them a week before—sexual freedom, women living their own lives motivated by their bodies' own biological needs, and other mysterious conceptualizations.

Todd and Paulie decided to cruise the neighborhood, and Jim and I, by mutual agreement, abstained.

After ten minutes the faded lime green walls of the ten by ten room depressed the hell out of us, so we took the rickety elevator down to the lobby.

The carpeting was badly worn and of an indiscernible color. I wondered where seedy hotels got pre-worn carpets and pre-torn leather chairs to furnish their shabby lobbies. I was sure the Fort Pick had never seen better days. It had most probably just sprung up from the city pavements in its current state of delapidation.

Whores began to populate the lobby as dusk fell. The desk clerk must have known why they were there, but he chose to ignore their presence. Or perhaps he got a cut of the take.

Jim and I were hit on like fingers in a piranha tank— at least ten times—on our short trip from the elevator to the coffee shop. Some were attractive enough to be tempting, but they were all old enough to have given birth to us, some possibly old enough to have whelped our parents.

We sat in the dingy coffee shop drinking coffee out of stained mugs heavy as boat anchors. They were probably lead lined, to withstand the corrosive effects of the black liquid they held.

We finished our coffee in silence.

The hookers were no less intent on soliciting our funds on the trip back to the elevator. They couldn't remember we had turned them down only a few minutes before. We were just faceless, walking opportunities.

It was showtime at Levon's Showbar before we knew it.

We went on stage to thunderous applause. The club was packed beyond a fire marshall's nightmare. People stood shoulder to shoulder at the bar, and lined up right to the entrance.

We began to play. Michelle's body movements were

210

even more sexually graphic than the previous week, and like the word changes she had done in "Stop in the Name of Love" then, she altered the lyrics in every song we sang from thinly veiled innuendo to outright obscenity.

Levon sat at a table near the stage and showed his gold teeth, all of them, to everyone.

Todd, Paulie and Jim got more and more uneasy. I could see it on their faces, and I could feel it in my gut. Jim moved like a ghost about the stage, checking amp wires and mike cords, always with a disapproving eye on Michelle.

Michelle was taking over, and the other two girls went along with the flow. Geoffie seemed oblivious to the drift of things.

At the break, we all went back to the dressing room for Cokes—all except Michelle. She went out on the floor to mingle with the paying customers—her fans.

The exuberance of the previous week's gig was missing. Debbie and Mitzie chatted in one corner about the clothes and hairstyles of women in the audience, but even they were subdued. Geoffie sat in another corner with Kamii, exchanging whispers. Todd, Paulie, Jim and I sat with our ten-ounce bottles of iced Coke, smoking, wondering what it was all about, but exchanging no thoughts.

The second set was almost disastrous. Michelle was so involved with herself and the audience's reaction to her gyrations, she stepped all over our solos.

At the end of the set, she started out into the audience again. I grabbed her arm, perhaps with a bit too much force.

"Watch the merchandise, buster," she spat.

"Merchandise is right," I grunted. "We need to talk. C'mon back to the dressing room."

"Absolutely not. My public awaits." She laughed too loudly.

"I'm not taking no for an answer, Michelle. C'mon." I pulled on her arm. She tottered after on her high heels.

"Hey!" she yelled.

A big black man nearby stood up and moved in close.

"Need any help here?" he said to Michelle, iron in his voice.

"No," I said, turning to Michelle, hoping he wouldn't be there if I looked back.

"Yes," she said, the anger strong in her voice, her eyes burning into me, still trying to free her arm from my grasp. I let the flame of my anger escape my eyes, too, and she wavered. "I mean, I could use a drink. Could you have the bartender send a Manhattan to the dressing room?" She batted her false eyelashes and he melted.

"Sure, darlin'. My pleasure."

"Thank you," I said tersely, and still holding her arm, towed her into the dressing room where the others waited.

Only once inside, did I release her arm, and she rubbed at the red spot with her gloved hand.

"You'd better have a really good reason for man-handling me like that, Steve Dalton!"

"I do. You're screwing up the whole scene."

She searched the room for friendly eyes. Even Mitzie and Debbie looked away. Kamii was studying the toes of her shoes.

"Look, I'm just trying to sell the songs." Still no one met her searching eyes except me.

"You ungrateful bastards! If it wasn't for me, you'd die out there!"

"I think we'd all admit you're the star attraction. You're just forgetting you're not up there alone."

"Well, maybe I should be! I'm working my fanny off out there, and you're all dogging it!"

"You know that's a lie. Everybody's doing their best."

"Well, maybe that's just not good enough."

"I don't hear any complaints out there." I jerked my thumb toward the dressing room door, at the crowded club on its other side.

"I mean not good enough for me."

I sighed. "If that's how you feel, fine. Just tone it down. You might find it a bit tough to get up there a cappella."

"After this, I'm about ready to try." She wasn't pretty when she was angry. She looked like a pouting little girl in her mother's make-up.

"We're committed to tonight and tomorrow, anyway. All we have is a verbal contract, right, Geoffie?"

"Uh . . . right."

"If you want to split after this weekend, so be it. We'll just limp by without you."

"Maybe. Maybe if I talk to Levon, he'll find me a new band and you'll be limping, all right, off into the sunset."

Kamii stood up. She put a tiny hand on my arm. "Let me talk to her alone."

Great, I thought. I figured she was the primary cause of Michelle's burgeoning ego in the first place.

The door opened just then, and the big black man who had tried to run interference in my little confrontation with Michelle smiled warmly and handed her the Manhattan.

"Why, thank you. I can't tell you how much I need this."

"My pleasure, darlin'. Call on me anytime."

"I'll just do that, thank you."

He made a pistol of his hand and mimed a shot at Michelle. She returned the gesture, making a pretty O of her mouth to blow away the imaginary smoke from the tip of her finger. Then she drained the glass in one lusty swig. Luckily for her image, he shut the door behind him before she started choking violently on the whiskey.

Kamii took Michelle out of the dressing room, behind the stage and into Levon's office.

I shut the door to the dressing room. No one would look at me, talk to me.

I grabbed another iced Coke and slumped into one of the folding chairs. The only sound was the booming jukebox filtered through the flimsy veneer door. The Four Tops were singing their brand new release, "I Can't Help Myself."

The minutes ticked by like on the $64,000 Question, only it was me in the glitter suit, not emcee Hal March. It's amazing how long fifteen minutes can seem in an uncomfortable situation. Five minutes before it was time to go on stage, the door opened letting the full blast of the juke box and Michelle Bailey in. Kamii came in behind her and shut the door.

"I see now where you all might think I was in the wrong," she said, hurt and defiance dripping like venom from her words. "I will not apologize, but to keep the peace, I will do as Steve Dalton so boorishly demanded." There, I thought, just like Kamii told you, you bitch!

"I'm quite sure we all thank you," Jim said with an outrageous bow.

"You shut up, Jim Harper! You have no say in this whatsoever!" She turned to one of the mirrors and played with her hair, so stiff with lacquer it couldn't have been messed up by a tornado.

"That's where you're wrong, Boobs. I'm a human being, just like you, and as such, I'm entitled to my opinions."

"Well, it's a free country," she singsonged, still fussing at the mirror, "so you can say whatever you want, I guess. What I mean is, your opinions aren't worth a hill of shit to this group."

"All right, God-damn it!" I shouted and jumped up from my chair, hurling my Coke bottle on the concrete floor, sending slivers of thick green glass scuttling like frightened mice around everyone's feet. "That's enough! This whole thing is way out of hand. The only reason I did this was for fun. And it was fun—the practice sessions and that first fantastic performance last Saturday night. Now it's all bullshit. A pain in the ass. I want it to be over. In fairness to Geoff and the arrangements he made with Levon . . . hell, in fairness to Levon, we owe him tonight and tomorrow." I wheeled on Michelle, strode to her, my face inches from her layered make-up. "I don't give a shit if we go on from here without you. You either shut the fuck up right now, act like a normal human being on and off the fuckin' stage, or I'm gonna take you out behind this stinkin' rat-hole building and beat the livin' shit out of you!"

"Are you finished?" She was putting on a marvelous act, but her voice shook with anger, fear and hate.

"That's up to you."

"I think it's time to go on again." She walked toward the door.

I grabbed her arm and spun her to face me.

"Not until you do two things. One, promise not to show off anymore, and two, apologize to Jim and everyone else here for being an asshole."

"I will not . . ."

"Yes, you will, God-damn it!"

Her eyes flew furtively to Kamii. Kamii nodded so quickly, the motion was almost imperceptible.

"I . . . I promise."

"Promise what?"

"I p . . . promise to be good," she said in a little girl voice, on the verge of real tears.

"And what else?"

"I apologize . . . to Jim . . . and everyone else?"

"For what?"

". . . what do you mean?"

"For being such an asshole. Say it!"

"F . . . for being such an asshole."

Everybody jumped up, nearly running out the door. Kamii put her arm around Michelle when I released her and gently led her out the door. I grabbed Geoffie's arm and pulled him back into the dressing room.

"You see Levon after. You give him notice. And by the way, get everybody's damn money. Give mine to Jim. Don't tell him it's mine. Tell him Levon coughed it up for expenses." I let go of his arm.

"Right, man, whatever you say." There was fear in his eyes, too.

The first song was very rough. Michelle just stood at the microphone, a garden statue, a thing of stone. She missed all the cues and forgot half the words. The other girls tried vainly to cover for her—we all did—but it was embarrassing.

By the second song, she was more into the swing, but still she sang without emotion, without movement.

By the third song, she was fully recovered, but she stood stock still, glaring at me as she sung. It became a game. She was trying to screw up.

In the middle of the fourth song, I noticed the change in the audience. They still tapped their feet to the beat, still patted out time with their hands on the table and on their drink glasses, but their attention was no longer riveted to the stage. So be it, I thought. If rapt attention can only be achieved by being a freak show, so be it.

The set was over. I spoke to no one. I put away my guitar, wrapped up the cord to my amp. Jim and Todd already had half the drums out the back door and into the van. We had to move them out. The strippers were due to move in.

I hauled my amp out myself. The night air was cool, but smelled of gas fumes and garbage. Jim, Todd and I loaded the van. The girls and Paulie were gone. I saw Geoffie talking with Levon when I cleared the mike stands off the stage. Levon was clearly angry, though I couldn't hear their words from where I stood. The juke box was thudding out "The Stripper," and Gladys and Jonelle pranced out of Levon's office and onto the stage in scanty costumes and spike-heeled shoes. I hauled the last of our equipment out the back door as they began to grind to the beat.

"Let's get the hell out of here," I told Todd and Jim.

"You got it, chief," Todd said, jumping into the van's driver's seat.

As Jim and I got in, Geoffie came out the back door of the club.

"Need a ride?" I offered.

"No, I'm staying with Kamii in Haines City."

"Levon's pretty steamed, huh?"

"To say the least, man. He threatened to sue us until I pointed out we were all under twenty-one."

"So? Did he pay up?"

"Yeah. I'll get it to you tomorrow night, okay?"

"Cool," I said.

He started to walk away from the van, then turned back. "By the way . . . he said the record company producers are still coming tomorrow night. For what it's worth, man."

We were in the hotel rooms by one-thirty.

The impending demise of the band was all I thought about as I lay in my jockey shorts on the hotel bed staring out the open window at the hot Detroit night. Jim lay silently beside me, arms folded behind his head, flat on his back staring at the cracked and peeled ceiling paint.

"Jim?"

"Yeah?" his voice cracked and he cleared his throat.

"You think I was out of line with Michelle?"

"No way."

"I mean, do you think I came on too strong?"

"Only way she'd understand. Even so, I don't think she wants to go along with what you said. Weird little Kamii convinced her."

"Yeah, right. It's just that everybody else seemed really upset. With me, I thought."

"Naw. Not even Debbie and Mitzie. You heard Todd. Everybody wished they had the guts to lay it on her that way. I think you woke up the other two girls a bit, did something to lessen Kamii's influence on them."

"Okay . . . I guess. It's just that I don't think I'll ever forget the look in Geoffie's eyes. He was afraid of me."

"Well . . . you've got to understand, Steve, you're an imposing cat when you let your temper go. I don't think you realize how much all that weight training built you up. Shit, there's guards on college football teams who aren't muscled-up the way you are."

"Were you afraid of me?"

"No . . . well, hell. Yeah, a little. I've seen you sad and I've seen you upset, but I've never seen you that mad. It was like watching God throw thunderbolts at sinners. When you broke that damned Coke bottle, shit! I thought you were gonna kill her."

"Really?"

"Just for a second or two. Then I remembered who you were."

"Yeah? And who's that?"

Jim was quiet a moment. He shifted his weight on the bed, jostling me with the movement of the tired springs.

"What do you mean?"

"You said you remembered who I was. I thought since you said that, maybe you had some kinda clear-cut idea of who that might be. I sure as hell don't."

"Listen, Steve. Don't get hung up on that routine. I don't think anybody knows who they are inside, not really. Other people are bound to see you in a certain way. Maybe even in a way you can't imagine."

"How do you see me?"

"Too personal, man. I don't want to get into it. I think you're basically an okay guy."

"Whaddya mean, too personal?" I sat up on the bed, startling a pigeon sleeping on the ledge outside the window. He fluttered away clumsily with coos of complaint into the Detroit night.

"I mean, you don't want to hear it. I think some good things about you, some bad."

"Skip the good. I want to hear the bad."

"No way."

"Yeah. C'mon. I wanna know."

He sat up and faced me, fumbling behind himself to the bedside stand for a pack of cigarettes and matches. He lit up.

"Okay. Here it is. You're so damned hot to have somebody run you down, you gotta pick on me. Okay. Number one, you're so involved with feeling sorry for yourself, you tend to drift through everything. You're afraid to be happy, damn it!"

"That's funny coming from the great stone-faced comedian."

"With me, it's a way to get laughs. Mostly laughs inside for myself. I'm having a ball most of the time, inside."

"Okay. I'll let that go. What's number two?"

"Number two is you're afraid to get close to people, and if you do, it's short-term. You go along, tight as a Catholic girl's knees, with someone for awhile, then suddenly it's over and you're gone."

I knew he meant my treatment of him, and I said so. I apologized.

"Not just me, man. This isn't some vindictive thing I need to get off my chest. You asked to hear it, remember? You did it to Goeff, Paulie and Todd. You did it to Parkhurst . . . even if he did deserve it. You did it to the whole junior class after Kennedy croaked and you abandoned the race for class president. You even did it to Michelle. And you know what? Much as I dislike the bitch, I think you should be aware you're partially to blame for her bein' so weird now.

"Michelle was a tease, a well-known tease. She would lead guys on, do a little heavy petting with them, then turn cold as hell, pulling that Greenriver good-girl crap. You came along and she let out all the stops. Don't deny it. I know she did. Then you pulled your Mandrake act with your emotions, cutting her down at the knees. She gets angry, gets bitter, runs to Todd. She had Todd on the old act-hot-play-it-cool routine she was famous for. When she tired of that, she tried a different route. Voila! The new improved sex-freak, Michelle."

I took the lighted cigarette from between his fingers, and he lit another for himself.

"Maybe you're right. I don't know. She helped me forget some things . . . I know I used her . . . but I also told her from the start I couldn't get totally involved."

"And it didn't strike you at any time that she was involved, despite what you said?"

"Well . . . yeah."

"I rest my case, Steve."

"Yeah, well. No real revelation, I guess. I knew all that stuff about myself. There isn't any more, is there?"

"Not right now. I'll let you know."

There was a soft rapping at the door.

"Yeah, who is it?" I yelled.

"Todd. Let me in, okay?"

Jim was closest, so he got up and opened the door. Todd stood there in jeans and T-shirt, sandals looking ridiculous on his big feet.

"Get dressed. We gotta go look for the girls and Paulie."

"They're not here yet?" I asked, trying to see my wrist watch in the dark. I moved off the bed.

"It's almost three," Jim said, noticing my wrist inches from my eyes as I tried to see my watch in the sick yellow glow of the hall lights outside the door.

"And they're not back yet?" I said again, trying to find my street clothes, piled somewhere on the floor.

"That's what I said, wasn't it?" Todd was not a night person.

Jim and I got into our clothes. Mine fought me all the way. Todd stood, jittery and scowling in the doorway, while I searched under the bed for my shoes.

Down at the van, Jim spoke again.

"Where the hell are you gonna look?"

"I know where to look," Todd growled. He herded us to the van and we drove through the depths of the Detroit night.

Eventually we passed Levon's. The pathetic neon sign flickered feebly in the night illuminating four black women dressed in flashy short-skirted evening clothes leaning against the buildings and the parking meters.

Todd stopped the van in front of the defunct tool and die shop where Kamii had meant for us to stay.

"See?" He pointed up. There were cracks of light showing around the edges of the blacked-out windows upstairs. He parked the van, we got out and he carefully locked up. I saw Paulie's mother's Avanti then, parked just around the corner.

"Okay, we know they're here, so let's go back to the hotel and get some sleep," Jim said, trying to be reasonable.

"No. I want to make sure everything's cool," Todd said.

"I really don't want to go up to that roach-hole again," Jim said.

"Then stay with the friggin' van!" Todd's teeth ground together.

"What's the big deal, Todd?" I asked. "You know, Jim's right. There's the car. There's the lights on up there. They don't want to see me, so why can't we just split?"

"Because . . ." He seemed to be struggling with something. Then he blurted it out. "Because I want to make sure Michelle's okay. All right?"

"Yeah," I said, "yeah, it's cool. I'll come, too. Jim?"

"Sure. I always enjoy uncomfortable scenes. Why not?"

Before we were halfway up the rickety stairs, we could hear the booming of the music. The door was slightly ajar. I pushed it open. What was revealed looked like a scene from a film epic on the decadent ways of ancient Rome.

The loft was still filthy, still in its advanced state of ugly dilapidation. A portable stereo blared out the Stones' "It's All Over Now." The floor was covered with naked blue and white striped mattresses. Stroh's cans and Gordon's gin bottles lay everywhere. Easily thirty bodies in various stages of dress and undress writhed to the beat of the music, some vertical, most horizontal. The air was thick with a yellow haze of smoke from marijuana cigarettes.

Paulie was in his jockey shorts, shoes and socks, on one of the tacky mattresses, rolling about with two black girls who were trying valiantly to make love to him, while he, just as valiantly, tried to simultaneously drink a beer and smoke a joint.

I was relieved to see that all three girls, Mitzie, Debbie and Michelle, were still dressed in their stage costumes. They were dancing and partaking of the liquid as well as gaseous entertainment.

"Well," I shouted to Todd over the music, "what's the plan of action?"

"I say we leave them to their own devices," Jim yelled. "Or vices, as the case may be."

"No. We have to get them out of here. Even if by force."

221

I looked at Jim and shrugged.

"Okay," I said. "We'll each grab one. Save Michelle for last. She's gonna be the most difficult."

Todd zeroed in on Mitzie, while Jim grabbed Debbie around the waist and lifted her from the floor. That left me with Paulie.

"S'cuze me, ladies," I said as I pried the two black girls off of his body. "C'mon, Paulie, where'd you leave your pants?"

"Aw, Steve . . . JoJo and Connie were jus' gonna show me a few little tricks they know . . ."

"I'll bet. What would your daddy say if he saw you with those girls? He'd leave brown spots on those nice white sheets he used to wear in dear ol' Georgia. C'mon, whitey, you've had enough cultural exchange for one night."

By the time I found his clothes and jiggled him into most of them, Jim and Todd already had their loads stashed in the Avanti. I tossed Paulie into the passenger bucket.

"Are we ready to tackle Michelle?" I asked. "I mean that literally."

Todd was about to answer, when the night was shattered by twirling red and blue lights and the raucous scream of sirens.

Five police cars pulled up before the building.

"Oh, sweet Jesus!" Todd exclaimed.

"You two jump in the van. I'll drive the car," I said.

"But Michelle . . . Geoff and Kamii were there too . . ." Todd sputtered.

"To hell with them," Jim rasped. "Listen to Steve. Let's move!"

Todd didn't resist as Jim dragged him by the arm over to the van. I got in the driver's seat of the Avanti, fished through Paulie's coat pockets until I remembered where he always kept the keys. They were above the driver's visor. The cops were all upstairs when I pulled away from the curb.

All the way back to the hotel, my passengers giggled,

laughed and protested their unseemly exit from the party.

We hustled them up the freight elevator, each of us holding our hands over their giggling mouths in an attempt to pass through the hotel to our rooms unnoticed.

It was a wonder, but we delivered the three safely to their beds. Todd stayed with Paulie, I volunteered to make sure the girls didn't cause any more disturbance, and Jim went back to our room to sleep. He was the only one of the group that got any that night.

Being nursemaid to two girls in evening gowns through the dry-heaves and mid-morning roaring hangovers was an olympic event I vowed never to repeat, if at all possible. Todd had about as much fun with Paulie. After a brief ten a.m. consultation with Jim in the girls' bathroom, while I held Mitzie's head up out of the porcelain receptacle and swabbed Debbie's forehead with a damp washcloth where she lay on the ceramic tile bathroom floor, Jim agreed to track down the whereabouts of the rest of our ne'er-do-well friends.

By seven p.m., I had the girls fed with a meal they kept down and fortified their general well-being with about a dozen Excedrin each. I also had their gowns sent out, cleaned and delivered. I urged them every step of the way in putting on their street clothes, loading them and their plastic-bagged costumes into the Avanti, and drove them to Levon's.

Todd drove a grey, pinched-faced Paulie to the same destination. I was determined that Levon would have a band of some description for that one last performance.

The five of us arrived at the door of the club's dressing room at the same time, entered, and found Kamii, Geoffie, Michelle and Jim waiting. Michelle had dark circles under her eyes that make-up wouldn't hide, no matter how thick she troweled it on, but she was dressed and, for all intents, ready to perform.

Ice hung in the room like a Day at the Glaciers.

"I hope you're happy, Steve Dalton," Michelle said

flatly, her voice almost a full octave lower than normal.

"I'm not happy," I said, "and I can't imagine why you think I should be."

"Simple. I spent the night in this city's jail and it's all your fault."

"Mine? Did I tell you to go to that pit to have a party?"

"No, but I wouldn't have felt the need to release all that tension if you hadn't been such a prick."

"Ah . . . I see you've added a new word to your vocabulary. Obviously the high-class company you've been keeping lately."

"Okay, let's cool the World War III stuff," Geoffie said, trying to make his voice as pleasant as possible. He seemed wary of incurring my wrath. "Levon asked us to go on at eight, and I said we would."

"Great," Mitzie groaned. "It shouldn't take more than an hour for me to squeeze into that damned dress again."

"Well, you'd better hurry. I'm not going to blow this performance for anything," Michelle said, coughing to clear her throat. "Those record company guys are already out there. I personally couldn't care less if you all went straight to hell, but me, I'm going to go all the way. None of you," she leveled a venomous gaze at me, "none of you is going to fuck this up for me."

"Another pearl not to be found in Webster's," Jim said. "You're right, Steve, Michelle has blossomed here in Motown. Must be the clean pure air. Brings out her best qualities."

"Shut up, you slimy shit-head," Michelle growled. "Somebody give me a God-damned cigarette."

I gave her one and lit it for her.

"Thank you ever so much," she said in a phony sugar-coated voice and blew smoke in my face.

Through some miracle and with Kamii's silent aid, Debbie and Mitzie got dressed, coiffed and made-up. They looked nearly human when she finished with them.

Geoffie got me aside as we slipped into our gold and black tuxedos.

"Don't get crazy, man, but there's a problem."

"What might that be, Geoff? I mean, other than the fact that most people in this room hate each other and I spent the night being puked on by two girls whose biggest worries used to be how soon they'd marry Mr. Right and settle down in the vine-covered cottages in Hicksville, U.S.A.?"

"You've got a right to be uptight, man. Angry at me and Kamii. But you're not the only one who's been put out. How deep do you think the shit's gonna be at the Prang house when Daddy Prang finds out his son spent the night in a Detroit jail for consorting with known prostitutes and drug dealers?"

"I admit I wouldn't want to trade Thom McCans with you, Prang. So what's the new problem?"

"Levon went our bail, and we aren't going to be paid."

"Nothing?"

"Not a cent, man."

"Well, these little life-lessons don't come cheap, do they, Geoff! What say we go out there on stage and knock 'em dead for Stevie Wonder?" I slammed a fist into the wall and left a hole the size of Geoffie's head. He backed away and ushered the girls out of the dressing room door.

Our first set lacked real conviction—primarily because all three girls and Paulie winced as every note boomed out of the amplifiers. I took real pleasure from playing high octave screaming guitar leads.

As we laid down our instruments to leave the stage for the first break, a middle-aged white guy with shoulder length hair that was obviously a wig, wearing Brooks Brothers threads and wing-tips, approached the stage.

"Far out, cats and chicks. Say, who's the leader of this dynamite group?" He talked like a DJ.

Everybody looked at the guy in the wig, then at me.

"I used to be," I said unplugging my guitar, "but I've abdicated to the dynamite chick in the black bee-hive with the humungous knockers."

"Well, groovy. I'm Jerry Fair, agent extraordinaire, as I like to say. What's the lovely chick's name?"

"Michelle 'Boobs' Bailey," I said, jumping off the stage, "a.k.a. Queen of Cell Block 49. Call her Boobs . . . she'll love it." I went to the dressing room. I looked back over my shoulder to watch Michelle turn on the gushy charm, even though the effort probably made her head pound like Ringo Starr's bass drum.

I got a Coke from the dressing room and sneaked out the back door to the alley to be alone for a smoke.

When I went back in fifteen minutes later, everyone was back on the stage except Michelle. She was at a table chatting gaily with Jerry Extraordinaire and two fat white guys with cigars as big as baby's forearms rammed in their faces.

I hung my guitar around my neck like an albatross and gave the downbeat for "Do Wah Diddy Diddy." I sang the lead out loud and strong.

"There she was, just a-walkin, down the street . . ."

Michelle stayed in the audience for the whole song, still yakking.

I lead the group into "Ticket to Ride."

"She's got a ticket to ride, and she don't care . . ." I sang directly at Michelle. When the suits she sat with weren't looking, she flipped me the finger.

I reached a point in the set where I couldn't do another number that didn't require Michelle for lead vocal.

We played the intro to "He's So Fine" four times before she decided to slink unto the stage.

She was back to the bumps and grinds, singing for the three fat cats alone. The next number was Nino Tempo and April Steven's 1963 update of "Deep Purple," with me doing Nino's part and Michelle doing a credible imitation of April Stevens doing her breathy Marilyn Monroe impersonation. The fat cats loved every second of it.

We ended the set with "The House of the Rising Sun" and Michelle had the fat cats by their shriveled balls.

I went out the back door again.

In the third set, she was so worked up, I thought she'd start stripping off. I couldn't even bear to watch.

Neither could the rest of the band, including the girls. The set ended, after an interminable length of time. I felt sure I would look in those dirty broken dressing room mirrors to discover I had gone totally grey-haired.

Michelle minced off the stage like a showgirl, and Jerry Extraordinaire helped her down.

Everybody except Jim followed me into the dressing room. We all began to change into our street clothes wordlessly.

When I was out of the black and gold monkey suit, I turned to face them.

"Anybody want to join Miss Bailey and her record world friends to discuss our brilliant futures?"

"God, no," Mitzie groaned, wiping the gobs of make-up off with tissues and cold cream. "I just want to go home and never leave again."

"Me too," Debbie said, almost in tears. "I don't know if I'll even be able to listen to music again."

"Somebody ought to find out what Michelle's plans are about getting home," Todd said.

"Not this ol' boy," Paulie said. "Anybody takin' the Avanti express had better be in it in ten minutes. I'm gonna go help Jim load the van."

Geoffie still stood there, in his monkey suit costume, looking forlorn. "Kamii and I will get her where she wants to go."

"I think Michelle can manage that for herself," I said, and dropped my gold and black outfit into the waste-basket.

The girls went with Paulie, while Jim and I got into the van with Todd.

My last glimpse of Michelle was one of a girl become a woman alien to me, sitting with three men of likewise alien origins, all of them speaking the language of another world, another dimension in time and space. I wouldn't realize just how alien their world was until years later.

Jim's parents were gone when we returned to Green-river about three a.m. Sunday. There was a note tacked to the refrigerator with a magnet that looked like a banana. The note said they had taken a weekend trip to Sandusky, Ohio. Jim and I spent the remainder of the night drinking coffee in the kitchen's eerie white light that reflected off the red formica table top and chrome chairs. We said absolutely nothing. There was little enough anyone could say.

12

I walked home at about ten a.m. and found the front door of the house unlocked. In the living room Brian sat in the uniform of a Green Beret watching an ancient rerun of a 1958-vintage Reverend Stoney Miles on TV. My mother sat on the couch staring into space, looking at nothing at all.

Before I could recover enough to even say hello, Brian stood and handed me an official-looking letter. There was a sadistic grin on his face.

The letter was Uncle Sam's invitation to come to Detroit for my draft physical.

"Welcome to the U.S. Army, squirt." He shook my hand, trying to crunch the bones. I squeezed back, saw his upper lip twitch back from white teeth, and he retracted his hand.

"What a welcome. Hi, Mom."

A fleeting smile passed over her ravaged face like a wraith. Her eyes glanced at me and darted away.

"She barely knows anybody, but the doctors said there was no sense paying for the room up there anymore. She's not dangerous to herself or anybody else. They gave me an open prescription for her. Strong stuff, I guess. Lets her sleep without bad dreams."

I could imagine what horrors those dreams contained. I wondered if I could sneak some of her drugs for myself.

I drew Brian into the kitchen.

"I don't mean to sound selfish, but I'm going to college in the fall. How can I take care of her here?"

"Well, don't look at me, squirt. I'm off to Nam in two weeks. And you," he tapped the letter in my hand, "may just be going along."

"So why the hell is she here?"

"I told you . . . the doctors . . ."

"Has the army dulled your brain, Brian? If neither one of us is here, who takes care of her?"

"That's your problem, squirt. Hey, it's a great out from the draft for candy-asses. Just plead hardship. You have to stay home and take care of your loony old lady." That nasty mocking grin I remembered so well cracked his face again. I recalled that when he was a teenager, he had been good-looking. In the Green Beret uniform with his close-cropped hair and eyes that had grown cruel, he repulsed me.

"I'm going to college in September, Brian. That's it. I can't take care of her. I saw her in that place in Kalamazoo. I can't help her. No one can."

"Well, I've got a contract with Uncle to kill slants in Nam, squirt, so you'd better figure something out." He went back into the living room, sat in Dad's chair and engrossed himself once more in the ravings of the evangelist.

I slammed my fist into the refrigerator leaving a circular dent and causing the motor to kick on.

Damn! I had successfully disposed of all feelings for my mother—good, bad or indifferent. Well, not exactly. I was a long way from indifferent, and bad was the direction my feelings were headed.

Two years on my own—two years burying emotions

like love and compassion to better bear hurt and pain—
had left me with nothing to combat adversity except
anger.

Why the hell couldn't she have just stayed in that
place? Why couldn't she have died? Why couldn't the
Abomination just murder her, like he did my dad?

My spine froze, as I realized what I was thinking,
wishing, praying for dark fate to bring about. She's my
mother. She gave me life! So what! I thought. I didn't
ask for this, any of it, especially not for the things that
had happened to me and around me since the dawning
awareness of my puberty. But then, neither had she.
Wasn't it me that had incurred the wrath of Nicholas by
loving Cat? Hadn't I brought on my father's death and
my mother's insanity by goading the Abomination, no
matter how unintentionally?

I had to think, I had to have a plan. I tossed the letter
from the government onto the kitchen table and
stomped through the living room to the front door.

"I'll be back in awhile," I growled.

"That will be nice," Mother said in a thin abstracted
voice. "Come see us again. Maybe Ed will be in next
time."

I let the screen door bam-bam-bam behind me and I
ran.

I ran to Willow Street, the street that backed the
cemetery, the street where the St. Charles house sat
among the pines and willows.

I hammered at the door. I beat with my fist until the
thin wood screen door cracked.

Finally, the inner door opened. The inside of the
house was a dark cave. Cold air wafted out at me from
within, chilling the perspiration on my face.

"Yes?" the tired voice said weakly. "Oh, it's you.
What do you want?"

My eyes adjusted to the black beyond the threshold,
and the black became grey, forming into shapes. Susan
St. Charles stood in a robe made for a fuller, healthier
figure, her once shining chestnut hair hanging in limp
grey-streaked dullness around a sallow haunted face,

gaunt from sleepless nights untold.

"I want to know where Cat is," I demanded.

"You know. Detroit." She started to shut the door. I yanked open the screen, pulling loose the upper hinge. It hung there crazily as I slammed the flat of my hand against the inner door.

Mrs. St. Charles didn't struggle against my brute force.

"Detroit's a big God-damned town. I know. I just left there. I want an address. A phone number. Delilah's last name."

"Why? Why can't you just leave it alone? He's left you alone, hasn't he? Well, hasn't he?"

"Yes," I whispered, remembering the dreams, recalling the sleepless nights and torment. "But I need help. I need to know what to do."

"There's no help for you in Detroit." She started to shut the door again, and I let her.

I couldn't imagine what had sent me running to her, why I so desperately needed Cat again, right at that moment. Maybe I thought if I could see Cat again, it would rekindle Nicholas' jealousy, his hatred of me and my family, and perhaps he would seek revenge—on what remained of my family.

I sat on the greyed wood of the St. Charles front steps and sobbed. What was wrong with me? Why did I wish death on my poor insane mother? How could I go on living, if such thoughts came so easily to me?

I stood unsteadily. It was decided. I would atone for my evil selfishness. I would go to my draft physical and would plead hardship, as Brian suggested. The army would not take the last son, not with the elder one already scheduled for tour of duty in Vietnam. I would forego college in the autumn and would care for my mother, for as long as she lived.

The bus for the Detroit draft physical trip left from Centerville, the county seat, at eight a.m. The draft headquarters shared a tiny one-storey building with a live bait and tackle shop.

Maple trees whispered secrets overhead and the sun shone in a beautiful blue sky as we boarded. There were potential inductees from all over the county; some I half-recognized, others were total strangers. Jim Harper was among those I knew well. We sat together on a ripped seat near the rear of the bus.

"What a bitch," he said.

"That's an understatement."

"Haven't seen you since the big hullabaloo in Detroit. Todd still has your guitar and amp."

"He's welcome to them. I won't be needing them. Especially if things don't go well at Fort Wayne."

"Don't remind me. Hey, I heard from Geoff. Michelle signed with those record guys."

"As a solo, huh?"

"Yup. They pay the freight for her back-up group, costumes, material, studio time, the works. They're taking her to Las Vegas or Los Angeles or something."

"Yeah, well, I'll tell you what . . . I wish her all the luck in the world."

"Don't give it all away, Steve. We're gonna need some in Detroit."

"Probably." I ignored the hand-painted no smoking sign suspended up front, slapping the space above the windshield as the bus jolted along the road. I lit up. "You know, I believe I'm gonna do one of those hookers at the good ol' Fort Pick Hotel."

"That may be rough. I understand they double guys up and the rooms are assigned."

"If she doesn't mind being watched, I sure don't," I said. I flicked the cigarette out the window and settled back, legs sprawled under the seat before me. I closed my eyes.

When I awoke, we were pulling into Fort Wayne. Not the historic part, but before a nondescript one-story brick building where the inductee exams and physicals were given.

A sergeant about fifty years old welcomed us with the usual bullshit speech about not screwing off, doing what we were told, being where we were supposed to be when we were supposed to be there or else they'd slap us on the first available transport to Nam, even if we were green, three-legged and queer.

They fed us mystery meat and runny mashed potatoes, gave us fifteen minutes free time, then ushered us into a big examination room with what looked like surplus grade school desks wall to wall.

Some guy we didn't know came up to Jim and me and said, "All you gotta do to stay out is fuck up the written exam real good." He walked away, chuckling.

"He's got it figured out," Jim said sarcastically.

"Yeah. He'll come out with the intellect of a monkey, pass the physical, and be the first one on the plane."

"Cannon fodder," Jim agreed.

"That's okay. There's guys here who look like they'll spend the night figuring out how to study for their urine tests."

"Right, and they'll probably flunk it. Miss the cup or something."

"I'm okay so long as I don't have to pee in a test tube."

The tests were handed out. I finished mine in half the time allotted. I got a ninety-nine. Jim was done shortly after me. He got a ninety-eight.

"O.C.S. all the way." The young lieutenant who graded them grinned.

"Right," I said. "That's what we're after. Officers have about a two minute lifespan in Vietnam, don't they?" I eyed his shiny new silver bars. That made him nervous.

"Go have a smoke. The bus takes you to the hotel in an hour."

"Thanks, chief," Jim said and saluted. We went out on the lawn for a smoke, as directed.

"What you figure those whores at the hotel charge?" he asked.

"Damned if I know. You probably need a lawyer to figure out what to ask for, then to determine if you got what you paid for."

"Do you tip a hooker?"

"Fast friendly service? I don't know that either. I do know how to find out, though. Ask 'em."

"Sure. See any hayseed around here we can sprinkle in our hair so we look the part, too?"

"How much money did you bring?" I asked.

"Twenty."

"I've got a hundred. You need any, I'll make you a gift, okay?"

"That's sporting."

"I'd feel bad if I got laid and you didn't have the price of a ticket."

"Hell, I guess that's what bein' friends is all about, Clem," he drawled, suddenly walking like he had two inches of cowshit on his boots.

We goofed around the area, making fun of the steel-plugged cannon aimed at downtown Detroit, and the seagull crap all over the statue of General Wayne. Jim wanted to know if his first name was John.

The others filed out of the building about half an hour later. The same sergeant who greeted us gave us a speech about no drinking, no carousing with loose women, and damned well being aboard the buses at oh-six-thirty hours, sharp, bright-eyed and bushy-tailed.

We got on the bus and rode to the hotel. When the bus doors opened, the occupants scattered, some with war whoops, others with lewd raucous laughter. Jim and I had been to the big city before. We would eat the free meal on the government, then troll for hookers.

Mutual agreement led us into the coffee shop. It must have been break time 'cause all the hookers were in there.

We seated ourselves at the counter. A man of twenty-odd years and indeterminate ethnic origin came over for our order.

"Coke," I said.

"Coffee," Jim said, "black and strong. Worked here long?"

The counter man seemed shocked to be asked a question. He looked askance at Jim, probably wondering if he was really expected to answer.

" 'Bout two years," he mumbled, slopping my Coke as he sat it down.

"Guess you know the hookers pretty well, huh?"

"Hookers?" He looked at Jim quizzically.

"Yeah," Jim said, extending an arm expansively to indicate the dozen or so girls in the coffee shop, "the hookers."

"Oh, you mean the hoors." I'd never heard anybody pronounce "whores" that way before. I nearly laughed Coke up my nose.

"Yeah." He looked self-satisfied. "Yeah, I know quite a few of 'em. You might say I know 'em intimately." He chuckled.

"Okay, so which ones do you recommend?" Jim asked.

"Oh. Shoppin' around, eh? I see how it is." He leaned toward us conspiratorially, elbows resting on dirty plates and flatware behind the counter. "Well, some likes 'em young an' cherry, an' some likes 'em experienced. You fellas look like you'd like experienced, am I right? Huh? Huh?" He poked at us with a food-caked spatula.

"Yeah. Experienced," Jim said, feigning eagerness like a nephew coaxing a punch line from a boorish rich uncle.

I had this strange feeling we were with a seedy salesman shopping for a new car. Or rather a used one. Low mileage? Dependability? A cream puff? A hot little number with lotsa power under the hood?

"Well, take Sally over there in the corner. By the window." He aimed the spatula at a slender woman in her forties. Short platinum blonde hair. Thin-lipped. Large expressive eyes. "She quick and slick, but knows all the tricks. For the right price, she can do ya six ways from Sunday.

"Or take Carmella." The spatula singled out a woman of about thirty with thick curtains of coal black hair hanging about her face and trailing down her back to her butt. She wore a tight red mini-dress that ballooned her smallish breasts into appreciable mounds.

She was dark-skinned and full-lipped with beautiful Hispanic eyes. "She don't speak much English, but she understands around-the-world, I'll tell ya!

"Or her! Jesus, yes, I didn't see her at first! Sheila!" His emphatic gesture with the spatula caused a glob of food to detach and fly across the room.

"Good, huh?" Jim asked.

"Christ! Best there ever was!"

"Little old, isn't she?" I said, finishing my Coke.

"Age is experience, and experience is the best teacher, I always say. There's rumor, I don't know if it's true, but they say she screwed a guy so hard once, he was crippled afterwards. 'Nother guy told me she could suck the piston rings out of a V-8 Impala."

"Sounds like my kind of woman," I said, eating my ice.

"I don't know. I think I'd like the Mexican chick."

"You could do worse than those two, a lot worse," the counter man said.

Jim and I sat half-swiveled around, staring at our chosen targets.

Serendipity took over. The woman named Sheila stood up and walked by the table where the girl named Carmella sat. They exchanged words we couldn't hear, and a laugh. Sheila glanced up and saw us ogling them. She smiled and waved.

"C'mon," I said. "There will never be a better time."

Jim followed me off the stools.

"Hi," I said, trying to sound nonchalant.

"Hi yourself, honey," the Amazon said.

"Ah . . . how much would it be . . . I mean . . . we have rooms upstairs and . . . well . . ." I couldn't get the words out. I had no idea what the words should be.

Sheila laughed. "Whatsamatter baby, you want some?"

"Yeah. We both do." I indicated Jim, who nodded vigorously, a look on his face like a basset hound eyeing a choice steak.

She sidled up to me and looped her arm through mine. Her perfume was strong, almost suffocating, but not unpleasant. She was a bit taller than me in her heels and nuzzled easily into my throat for a kiss. "How much you wanna spend, lover?"

The Mexican girl was following all of this. It almost seemed she knew Jim wanted her and was letting the Amazon, Sheila, negotiate for her.

"What would fifty each get us?" I asked.

"Honey, whatever you want," Sheila answered nibbling my ear.

"About how long would whatever we want take?" I asked.

"That depends on your staying-power, honey." She licked my cheek. Licked it!

"Well, we're here with the army group and we're sharing rooms with other guys . . ."

"No problem, sugar. I got a room upstairs of my own. Let's go."

She motioned to Carmella, who came immediately to Jim's side.

The room had two double beds with a night stand between them. We removed the night stand and shoved the two beds together. The women stripped quickly, expertly, then helped us out of our clothes. I paid them, and they each tucked a fifty away in their purses. They were even more friendly after that. We left the lights on.

Almost two hours later, we all lay back naked, smoking cigarettes.

"So. Do you make a good living doing this?" I asked.

Sheila laughed.

"You get asked stuff like that a lot, eh?" I felt stupid.

"Not as often as 'how did you get started,' 'what's a nice girl like you, et cetera,' and 'where did you learn how to do that?' I do okay. It's easier than bein' a line-rat for Ford or GM. I can pick my hours."

"Did you ever want to do anything else?" Jim asked.

"I used to think I could be an actress or a model maybe. I had a pretty good voice, maybe a singer. I don't know. That was years ago. Hookers are made, not born. Why don't we ask our little taco? Hey, Carmella, you want to be something other than a hooker?"

"Oh, si! I would like very much to be a dancer."

"Yeah?" Jim seemed genuinely interested.

"Si. I take lessons from a very lovely Senora . . . Senora St. Charles."

I nearly knocked Sheila out of bed and sat my chest hairs on fire with my cigarette.

"Who? St. Charles who?"

Carmella pulled back, frightened. She probably thought I was about to get violent, another crazy trick.

"No comprende . . . I . . ."

"Please, please, Carmella, this is important. Is your instructor's name Delilah?"

"Si. Senora Delilah St. Charles."

Of course! How could I be so stupid! Cat had said Delilah was her aunt. Her father's sister, not her mother's! I could've looked her up in the fucking phone book! Now I had an even better line. Carmella would actually know where Delilah's studio was located.

"Can you tell me how to get to her place? Her studio?"

"Si. I go there twice a week. I know very good where is it."

"Right. Okay. Where is it, Carmella? This is very important to me."

"It is on Jefferson Street, past the bridge that is to Belle Isle . . . I have the address of this place in my purse." She scrambled out of bed, no longer afraid. She took a crumpled piece of cardboard from her purse and thrust it out at me, her small naked breasts bouncing with the movement.

"You can keep," she said smiling, pleased to be of help.

It was a business card.

St. Charles Studio of Dance, it said. Modern, Jazz, Ballet. In the bottom right-hand corner was Delilah St. Charles' name, a phone number and, God, an address.

I pulled Carmella to me and kissed her.

"Jesus! This is amazing. Fantastic! Carmella, I love you!"

238

"Oh," Sheila feigned a pout, "you know how to hurt a girl."

"No," I said, "I just mean . . ." Look at me, I thought. I'm apologizing to a hooker about love.

"You like the dance?" Carmella asked in her broken English.

"No . . . I mean, yes . . . I guess. What I mean is, there's a girl, Delilah's niece . . ."

"Oh, si! The beautiful one with the hair like mountain snow. Si, I know her, I talk to her. She is nice."

"A nice niece," Jim deadpanned lighting another cigarette.

"Are you trying to say you've got a girl friend in Detroit?" Sheila asked, applying a fresh coat of crimson to her lips, without the aid of a mirror and doing a perfect job. "Baby doll, I'm jealous!"

"I . . . I'm sorry," I said stupidly. "I've got to go. I've got to . . . I can't stay." They all stared at me as if I were crazy as I danced into my clothes, muttering about having to go.

I left them both to Jim. My mind had room for only thoughts of Cat, my Cat. Even as a child, she was better, had stirred more ecstatic feelings than that seasoned pro, Sheila, who had worked my body like clay on a potter's wheel.

I spent the night smoking, wondering if the following day I would actually get to see Cat. My stupid Greenriver morality, my blind sense of duty to authority, would not allow me to blow off the physical, to run to her and find her. Dawn finally came, and I got on the bus to Fort Wayne with Jim and all the others.

The physical was so ridiculous, I would have laughed out loud, if I hadn't been half frightened by the army regulars' shouted and growled threats. It's easy to be threatening when you're the only fully clothed person in a room full of guys in their skivvies and shoes.

I felt especially dorky in my white jockeys and black suede pointy-toed Beatle zip boots from Flagg Brothers in Kalamazoo, clutching my paper bag of valuables. The most fun was thirty guys doing a military about-face, bending over and spreading cheeks for a gruff old army medico who walked down the rows peering cautiously where the light don't shine.

The urine test was interesting—forty guys grasping tiny collapsing paper cups trying to pee on command while the cups cooperated by recollapsing just as the flow began.

"I can't pee," one guy whispered urgently to me, thrusting his cup under my pathetic trickle. I was terribly swollen from my night with Sheila. "Drain a littla that goose in mine, eh?" I obliged. What's a little urine between total strangers?

A guy in the corner bit a hunk of flesh from his thumb and squeezed a drop of blood into his cup. Another sprinkled in sugar from a paper restaurant packet artfully concealed until then in the fly flap of his jockey shorts.

We all filed up to a Dutch door affair, where a grey old Negro was testing the little paper cups of yellow stuff with litmus paper.

"The blood'll do it," the guy in front of me confided. "It'll do it, no shit!"

"Name." The old doctor's bored voice droned it out.

"Caulfield, James," the guy with the blood almost

snickered, handing over the cup, purposely splashing a bit on the man's fingers.

"You son of a bitch!" the man stood up, throwing the cup at Caulfield. "You drafted, boy!"

A burly sergeant appeared out of thin air and grabbed Caulfield with a meaty paw. There was a sadistic grin on his face. He led the wild-eyed sputtering Caulfield from the room.

The Negro doctor washed and washed his hands, swearing interminably. Finally he turned back to the opening and sat in the creaky wooden chair.

"Jeez," I said, jerking a thumb in the direction of Caulfield's unceremonious exit. "What an asshole!"

"Shut the fuck up, boy," he snarled. He gingerly took my cup in one hand, slapped a strip of litmus in it with the other, and in one motion, without looking at it, tossed it in the polyethylene-lined trash barrel.

"Name," he said in monotone.

"Dalton, Steven."

"You okay, boy. G'wan."

I went.

Somehow, the day managed to drag by. Late afternoon sun filtered in the high dirt and dead-fly-encrusted windows. I was on the slivery bench waiting my turn to talk to the army shrink. All the guys with papers describing 'special problems' had to see the shrink.

I sat at last on the cold metal folding chair, army green of course, opposite a tired-looking immaculate man with a colonel's bird on each lapel.

I handed him my papers and he read them gravely.

"This all true, son?" he asked in his tired voice.

"Yes. Uh . . . yes sir, it is."

"Your mother's . . . at home now?"

"Yes sir."

"And your brother . . . Captain Brian P. Dalton. Off for a tour of Nam?"

"Yes. Yes sir. Within the week."

"Well, I guess it's pretty clear-cut, in your case. Your family's sacrificed enough. Go get dressed, son." He stamped my papers at least a dozen times and kept them. He handed me a card. "After you've dressed, find the room number on that card."

"Yes sir." Oh shit, I thought I was done. Wrong.

The room was full of social workers.

There was an atmosphere in that room that made my flesh crawl.

I was beckoned by a mousy brown-haired woman with thick glasses and no chin. I went to her army green desk and sat on the army green chair as she indicated with a chubby social worker's hand.

"Mr. Dalton, is it?" she said in a voice that dripped honeyed pity.

"Yes, ma'am. Steven Dalton."

"Mr. Dalton, this interview is meant to help you cope with your problems by providing you with a list of agencies in your state, county and community which you may enlist for aid, free of charge, as needed." She handed me three sheets of paper. State. County. Community. The community one was almost blank. It listed a high school counselor's name who evidently worked on retainer for the county. I recognized the name—the guy was a geek, a well-known geek. I couldn't imagine anything he might say that would solve anyone's family problems.

But then, mine weren't exactly family problems. Oh, I had to figure out how I was going to adjust to taking care of my mother, how I was going to deal with not going to college, what the hell I was going to do to make a living, but my big problems were way beyond the resources of the services listed on those sheets of paper. Where was the name of a good exorcist?

"Thank you, ma'am," I said, as self-deprecatingly as I possibly could manage.

"It's my job, Mr. Dalton. Now . . ." She folded her hands primly on her desk, atop my file. I wondered where that file and its triplicate copies would end up. "Is there anything you need to talk to me about immediately? It's not usual procedure at these interviews to get involved, but I feel . . . well, having read your folder

242

. . . I feel you must need to open up to someone, someone understanding, about your . . . home situation."

I tried to hesitate long enough to make her believe I was really thinking it over, soul-searching.

"No, ma'am. I should really just get on home to my poor mother."

Her eyes watered behind those thick-lensed glasses.

"Yes . . . yes, Mr. Dalton. Please utilize those lists to the betterment of your home situation." She pawed in a desk drawer. "And . . . and here's my card." She folded my hand over the bit of paper. "If you need to talk, Mr. Dalton, please don't hesitate to call me. Collect. Anytime."

"Thank you, ma'am." I got up slowly, as if the burden of my home life bent me low. I was playing a game because of my lack of respect for the woman, but I realized it might also be because it was easier to adopt the Jim Harper method of viewing problems with a wry attitude than to face them head-on.

I stopped an officer, a lieutenant, in the hall.

"Excuse me, sir, who do I talk to if I don't want to take the bus back home?"

He looked at me as if I were speaking some exotic incomprehensible tongue.

"Do I look like a bus driver, mister? Did the uniform throw you?" He strode off down the hall, muttering about recruits and assholes.

Outside the day was waning rapidly. I approached a black corporal near the tired waiting buses.

"Excuse me, are you in charge of the buses?"

He frowned at me, adjusted his trousers on his lean hips.

"Why you ask me about buses, sonny? You figure 'cause I'm a Negro in this man's army, I'm gon' know 'bout buses?"

"No, I just . . ."

"You just nothin', sonny. Your momma's callin' you."

And he marched away.

Finally a group of men ambled toward the buses and I recognized our driver.

"I'm Steve Dalton from Greenriver. Who do I tell I'm not going back on the bus?"

"You just told him." He grinned. "They must want you pretty damned bad to keep you. Hell, most guys get a couple days before they ship out to the swamps."

"No, I just . . . yeah. They want me pretty bad." It was easier to go along than to explain. Besides, what would I say? I need to see this girl I laid when I was eleven?

Next I had to find Jim.

He was slumped on the ground at the base of the statue of General Wayne.

"Been looking all over for you," I said.

His face was ashen.

"What's wrong?" I sat down beside him and offered a cigarette from my nearly empty pack.

"Would you believe I've got an uncle in the soldier business who wants me?"

"Oh, Jesus, no, Jim!"

"Yeah. I have two weeks to get my affairs in order."

"Can't you appeal?"

"Doesn't appear it would do any good. Seems I'm just what they're after in the soldierin' material department. How'd you make out?"

"Hardship deferment. 'Cause of Mom and Brian's already in and earmarked for Nam."

"Yeah. Well, I'm not jealous. I'm happy for you."

"You really have to go?"

"Yeah. Guy I talked to said there's always a slim chance I'd stay in the U.S. Or get shipped to Korea or Germany or Greenland or something, but he didn't sound too convincing."

"This is awful."

"It is. No doubt about it." He stubbed out his cigarette on General Wayne's metal boot.

"You goin' to see that St. Charles girl?"

"If I can track her down."

"Got any money left?"

244

"No."

"Here." He dug the twenty out of his jeans.

"You sure you don't need it?"

"Naw. I'm just getting on the bus. When I get to Greenriver and tell Dad, he'll buy the beer. Hell, he loved the army. Get the fuck outta here. That girl must be somethin' special."

"She is, Jim." I stood up. I stuck out my hand and he clasped it firmly.

"What can I say, Jim?" I asked.

"Nothing. Not one damn thing. I'll be okay."

"Sure you will. Write me?"

"Whenever I can." He stood up. A chilling breeze came up off the river, and a tug horn sounded, making gulls wheel and cry out.

"See you. Take care." And I walked quickly away.

The city bus ride was a jerky stop-start toss-the-passenger-around kind of ride, but it was cheap and fast. The sun was a molten ball of red lost in car exhaust fumes of the western sky when I got off the bus.

A fast walk three blocks up pedestrian deserted streets brought me to a three-storey building of dirty white brick with windows made of thick blocks of glass that would let light in but provide no view of the interior.

The place looked deserted. My watch read 7:15. There was a sign on the door that said "St. Charles Dance Studio," but there were no hours posted.

I knew I had to get in. A sixth sense fired by an aching longing told me I had to get inside that building.

The door in the back alley was formidable, but the hasp and Yale padlock weren't strong enough to lock out my growing anxiety and pain. I grasped the thin lip of door edge and pulled until my arms shook from the strain, pulled until the wood jamb yielded the screws and the door broke open, the sudden release sending me sprawling on the rough gravel of the alley.

It was dark inside, but I didn't want to use the lights. I groped down a hallway with three or four doors that opened on small offices. A double door to my left gaped open on a huge empty room with mirrors and a railing running the entire length of one side. Identical double doors on the other side of the hall were shut tight.

My palms were dripping sweat as I grasped the cold brass handles and slowly opened the doors. Music blared at me even with the doors cracked the tiniest fraction of an inch. It was jazz—Pharaoh Sanders wailing away in mystical frenzy.

The lights in the room were subdued—blues, purples and reds from a stage-like overhead lighting system. I was immediately aware of motion, but it was a motion so perfectly synchronized with the music, in the vague light it was as if the Pharaoh's jazz had materialized in human form.

The swirling halo of white-turned-blue hair told me the dancer was Cat. My Cat.

I was at once overcome with simultaneous urges to run to her and feel the heat of her body against me, and to stay, frozen as I was, drinking in the raw poetry of her body in motion.

The music and her movements described pain, anguish, hot anger and passion, lust unfulfilled, the torment of souls lost beyond the finding.

Then the record ended. I heard the automatic changer click to a halt. Cat ended the wild dance face down on the floor, and I held my breath an eternity waiting for her to move. When she stood, I could see her exhaustion, her heavy breathing raising the moons of blue flesh out of the scooped neck of her black tights.

She saw me at the door, and her breathing stopped. Even across the vast expanse of that blue-lit polished wood floor, her recognition was instantaneous. She did not move to me, but she spoke, voice breathless.

"Steve . . . you shouldn't be here . . . you can't be here . . ."

"But I am. I had to see you. I love you."

The only sounds in the room were the thudding of my heart and the rushing in and out of her breath through her open mouth.

"I love you, too . . . but . . . we can't be together . . . you know why."

"I don't care. I need you. I've got to have you." I moved from the doors.

"Don't . . . come any closer . . . it just gets . . . more difficult . . . confusing . . ."

"There's nothing to be confused about. We were made for one another. Some plan, some cosmic plan . . ."

"No!" She held her hands out in front of her, warding off the danger of my desire for her.

It didn't work. I strode to her, took her glistening perspiration-damp body in my arms, pulled her hard against me and kissed her, abusing her mouth with mine.

She opened her mouth with a moan of submission and our tongues touched, arcing electricity through our bodies. My hand closed roughly on one breast and the passion of our kiss deepened. Animal sounds came from her, almost grunts, as ecstasy enveloped us.

Suddenly I was flying through space, crashing against the wall of mirrors, sending splinters and slivers of quicksilvered glass waterfalling and glinting through the purple-blue light.

I felt the sticky warmth trickling down my neck from the back of my head and my jarred brain fought to recognize shapes from the blurry images my eyes transmitted.

Huge iron-muscled hands dug into my ribs, lifted me, slammed me back, and more glass arrows skittered across the floor. I could hear her voice screaming in terror. I could smell a strong odor, ophidian, like the dark hot smell of the reptile house at the zoo. My brain cleared enough for me to see, but I didn't need to see to know what had me, crushed me again and again against the ruined mirrored wall—Abomination!

Cat's screams continued, rising in pitch, hysterical, and the rhythm of my abuse slowed, lessened, until at last the iron hands let go of me and I slumped to the floor amid the glass shards and a growing pool of blood.

She was on me, straddling my splayed legs, sobbing, crooning, placing feather-light kisses on my face that made her lips blood crimson and dripping, trying to stop the blood from flowing with the touch of her gentle lips and fingertips. But she was not a mystic healer—I continued to bleed.

I saw the horrible hands close around her shoulders, dwarfing them. They pulled her up to her feet, a limp doll. They clasped her against a massive chest and that unearthly voice I knew too well from dreams boomed out in the emptiness of the room.

"Tell him, say it to him!"

"No . . ." Cat whined.

The terrible claws cut into the flesh of her shoulder, crushed her against the huge chest and flat-muscled stomach. "Tell him, or I kill him now!"

"S-S-S-Steve . . . go . . . get out . . . p-p-please . . ."

"Tell him!" the voice thundered.

"I d-don't want you," she whimpered. The enormous hand flexed and a gasp of pain escaped her trembling lips. "I don't want to ever see you again. I h-hate you! I hate you, I hate you!" she screamed at me.

I stood slowly, bits of glass dropping from my scalp, from the ruins of the flesh on my back.

I watched helplessly as the curved scythe-like talon of one hand snagged the fabric of her tights, leaving a long ragged rent on the material from neckline to groin.

The Abomination let a deep rumbling chuckle hiss from between those ugly thin inhuman lips as a massive hand closed over her breast and squeezed until she sobbed and twisted against the pain.

"Tell him," the voice rasped, as if heavy with lust.

"I don't have to . . ." she whispered under the pain. "He knows."

I felt my gorge rise. I slipped and nearly fell on the bloodied bits of glass as I scrambled to be out of there, out of there and away. I heard Cat's scream of pain and revulsion as I crashed out the rear door in the alley. I heard the hideous, victorious, mad laugh of the Abomination.

Even bloody and torn, no one looked at me in the bus station. The old black attendant in the lavatory helped me pull the chunks of glass out of my back and wash the wounds.

"Wait just a second," he said, winking, trying to put on an air of mirth as he scrambled through the lockers along one wall of the dirty marble washroom.

" 'Bout yo size," he said, holding out a worn chambray workshirt. "Los' an' found," he explained. "Don' worry, iz clean. Washed it mah own sef." He helped me into the shirt. The material stuck to the lacerations. "Bes' I kin do, boy."

"It's fine. Thank you. I wish I could pay you . . . I only have enough for my bus ticket home."

"Don' worry. You jes' owe me. Nex' time you in the Motor City, boy, you stay the fuck outta them bars . . . you listen to ol' Jerry now."

"I will. I promise."

"There you go. 'Bye." He waved at me as if sending me off on a world cruise. Bon Voyage from Jerry, the men's room attendant.

The bus ticket to Centerville was $18.75. I bought two packs of cigarettes with what was left and got on the bus. Fifteen minutes later we were speeding through the night.

My mind went, quite literally, blank. What else could it do? Once again I had run, filled with terror and revulsion, instead of doing whatever was necessary, once and for all, to end this madness. Now, my revulsion spilled over onto Cat.

I did not sleep, but neither was I awake or aware. In Centerville, the bus driver had to physically carry me off the bus. I sat on the wooden bench letting dew wet my body and watched with unseeing eyes as the sun rose.

I thumbed and walked the dozen miles to Greenriver.

Laurel's mean black Chevy sat impatiently in my drive. Laurel was on the front porch in faded jeans and a tight Harley T-shirt.

"Where the fuck have you been?" she growled. She must have realized from the blank look on my face that something was wrong. "They didn't draft you, did they?"

"No," I muttered. "Hardship. Got to take care of Mom."

She grimaced, making her face ugly under her mask of too much make-up.

"Kid, there's no easy way to say this, but you don't gotta sweat takin' care of your mom anymore. Nobody does. She's dead."

"Oh, Jesus," I moaned, dropping to my knees on the porch. "Oh, sweet baby Jesus! He did it again! The bastard, the sonofabitch bastard!"

Laurel dragged me to my feet. "I don't know what in hell you're ravin' about, but come on inside. Christ, your neighbors have been eyein' me all morning as it is."

The house was still morning cool. All the shades were drawn and it smelled like disinfectant, like a hospital. Or a morgue.

"County coroner has your mom. Happened about midnight last night, they guessed. Strangled to death on her own phlegm or some such shit. Christ! You wouldn't of believed the look on her face, like she'd seen the Creature from the Black Lagoon. Aw, Jesus, here I am goin' on like this, and you're upset."

". . . Brian . . . ?" I asked.

"He split. Went back to the base or some such shit. Called my mom yesterday and said he couldn't put up with your mom anymore and was headin' out. That's why I'm here. Mom sent me over to watch her. Jesus, I'm one lucky bitch, ain't I? Why'd she have to pick me to die on?"

"She didn't . . . " I muttered. "He did it. Did it again. Just like Dad. Because of Cat. I saw Cat. My fault, just like Dad."

"I don't know what the fuck you are on about, Steve.

250

Don't you go crazy on me. Here." She dug three small blue pills out of her tight jeans pocket and shoved them in my mouth.

"Chew 'em up . . . taste like old sheep shit, but they work faster that way."

I obliged. I didn't notice the taste. Ten minutes later I was limp, weak and high as a kite.

Laurel stayed with me and kept me pumped full of the little blue pills for the next several days. I was a zombie at the funeral; I was a zombie at home. I spent the time at the funeral with my unblinking glazed eyes locked—not on the coffin that contained my mother's wasted body—on the back of the St. Charles house, sad and brooding with its peeling paint, the branches of giant willows whipping the house lethargically in the early summer wind.

At home I lay in my bed at night, glassy eyes fixed on the crack in the ceiling over my bed. Not one single thought crossed my mind. I was so stoned, I hardly remembered to breathe.

Laurel slacked off on the pills. I awoke one morning almost a week after my mother's funeral—which I could remember nothing about, still can't to this day—and the world actually seemed semi-lucid to me.

"I can't stay with you forever, Steve. You gotta find some way to get your shit together," Laurel told me, sitting in my father's chair, fixing me with a pitying yet half-pissed-off look.

"Give me more pills."

"No way. You've had twenty-five bucks worth already. Get your act together and move it on down the road, man. What you gonna do?"

"All sorta pointless. Doesn't matter."

"The hell it don't. You got that scholarship for college, don't you? You ought to plan on doin' that."

"That's September. How do I get there from here?"

"Good question. If I was you, I'd get a job. Hard work, somethin' to do twelve, sixteen hours a day that wears you out, keeps your mind from workin' 'cause your body's too busy."

251

"Like what?"

She thought a minute. "I know exactly what. My ol' man knows a guy who works road construction. He can get you in."

It was settled, so far as Laurel was concerned, and a week later, I reported for work.

I liked working construction. I strained, I perspired, I ached, and worked some more. The best part was, just as Laurel predicted, my body's pains allowed my mind to think of nothing else.

Before I knew it, July became August, and the August sun rose each day a few degrees further south. The mornings were cooler and the afternoons not quite so scalding hot.

My shoulders were broad and straight, and my back rippled with muscles even weight lifting couldn't give them. My skin was almost chestnut brown, and my light brown hair and eyebrows were sun-bleached blonde. Other than being a few inches shorter in height, when I looked in a full-length mirror, I saw muscle man Todd Raintree.

Sometime in mid-July, I confirmed my registration by mail at Haines City College. I had all the papers telling about course confirmation, classrooms, campus maps, time schedules and dorm reservation together on the center of my dresser at home.

A late August heatwave of 90-plus heat and matching humidity brought my career as a construction worker to a close.

I had two weeks before college classes began, and it was the first time all summer when I wasn't working my butt off or resting from having worked my butt off. I went out and bought some 45 rpm's I'd been hearing on the radio: the Byrds' version of Dylan's "Mr. Tambourine Man," the Stones' "I Can't Get No Satisfaction," and the Beatles' "Help" album. I also went to Coldwater to see the Fab Four cavort in the movie.

I forced myself not to think too long about my mother's death, particularly the why and how of it. The guilt I felt about having quite literally forgotten her after Dad's death and the onset of her mental problems weighed heavily enough.

The court upped my allowance to seventy-five dollars a week, and Aunt Jane's lawyer had an investment broker working with the insurance settlement money from my father's and mother's estates. I was told I would inherit a substantial amount of money when I turned twenty-one. Like everything else in my life, the news left me untouched and numb, not knowing what to feel.

By an eighteen-year-old's standards, I was already wealthy. All the money I had made working construction over the summer was in the bank, and it totaled nearly three thousand dollars.

I took my summer's earnings and some of the weekly allowance money from Dad's insurance settlement I had been stashing away and paid cash for a beautiful black shiny new Mustang convertible with white top, white leather interior, and rear deck chrome luggage rack. I bought Samsonite luggage, a complete set. So far as I knew, it was the first time anyone in my family ever had a matching set of luggage. I bought a complete wardrobe of college clothes, using the ads in Playboy as a guideline as to what was cool. Media formed my generation more than parents. I called the luggage, the wardrobe and the Mustang my birthday presents to myself. No one else remembered.

I said goodbye to Laurel and Aunt Jane over the phone. I had grown very cold, unfeeling. It was best not to get involved with people, period. The Sunday before classes, I made the trip to Haines City, solo flight, in my new wheels.

I was assigned room 509 in Charles Jameson Hall. My roommate's name was Joe Harmon, but classes began Monday without my seeing hide nor hair of him. In fact, I wouldn't see him at all, except for one black midnight in October.

My classes seemed too easy. The atmosphere was so much more relaxed and unregimented compared to high school. Just having the option whether to attend classes or not was a relief. It was also a nagging temptation for many students, who flunked out their first semester, not from the curriculum being too rigorous, but simply from burgeoning apathy.

I took the free time I had from breezing through my studies to explore Haines City and Ann Arbor, afoot and in my trusty Mustang.

In my travels, I found a karate school off Williams Street in Ann Arbor that was run by a small grey-haired oriental named Che. I enrolled in his group class and quickly moved on to private sessions with the Master.

It was already mid-October, the campus trees aflame, and I still hadn't seen any indication that anyone resided in 509 Charles Jameson Hall except me. The elusive Joe Harmon, my supposed roommate, seemed nonexistent, though when I asked after him at the desk, the log showed him signing in and out each weekend. For all that circumstantial proof of his living with me, no one on the fifth floor knew him or could give a physical description of him.

I certainly didn't mind Joe Harmon's absence. I made the room my own. It was pleasant having the sanctuary of a private room in which I could ponder, brood or despair without fear of interruption.

Paul McCartney crooned the poignancy of "Yesterday" on every radio or juke box I passed, and it was easy for me to fall into the wistfulness of Michigan autumn. I bought a portable stereo, and the records I bought to play on it reflected my shift in taste—Donovan; Peter, Paul and Mary; Dylan; Simon and Garfunkel.

I had heard nothing from home.

I wanted to hear nothing from Detroit.

Master Che taught me advanced Karate, refined the moves I had learned in jujitsu, and gave me an inkling of Eastern philosophy. The classes and daily practice of the moves filled the time between my academic classes and sleep. The mental regimentation necessary for karate helped organize my thoughts and shut out those images, scenes and memories in my life I could not bear to relive. I was not happy with my daily existence, but neither was I unhappy. But routines are made to be interrupted.

One evening as I sat at my window, watching the October night wind in the ruined oak and maple leaves below, a soft triple knock came at my door. A girl in big round glasses, dirty jeans and workshirt, tattered buffalo-hide sandals and waist-length dull brown hair stood on the other side of my threshold.

"Good God," she said in a vaguely familiar voice. "What . . . you been eating your Wheaties? You look like King Kong."

"Excuse me?"

"Aren't you gonna invite me in?" She shouldered past me into the room. "*That's* your stereo? Where does the little crank go? What do you do for entertainment? Jerk off? I figured to come up here and get my ears blown off listening to some good blues tunes on a real power box. My stereo's on the fritz."

It dawned on me slowly. This person was Donna—the sorority sister of Ginger Raintree who had taken me to her room on a bet over two years before.

My peevishness at her manner turned to honest anger. "I'm surprised you had the guts to come up here. I know all about the little game you girls were playing last time we met."

She shrugged. "What did you expect? True love? It was just a little fun. Nothing to get bent out of shape about. Where's your roomie?"

"I don't appear to have one. Now I'd appreciate it if . . ."

"Look, when I heard you were on campus, I didn't rest until I found out where you were. After two years, it ought to mean something to you that I went to so much trouble . . . it ought to be worth something that I even remembered your name. Now come on."

"You don't get it, do you, Donna? I don't want anything to do with you. I don't like being made a fool, and I don't count people who go out of their way to make me a fool as my friends."

"You're right. *I'm* being a silly ass, not you. Let's try

255

it this way: Steve, I apologize for using you the last time we met. It was a stupid sorority dare, that's all. I didn't think about how you'd feel if you found out. I'm sorry. Okay?"

She looked like a waif, eyes big behind the round glasses, unruly hair falling in her face. I gave in.

"Oh . . . shit. Okay. Apology accepted. Let's get out of here. Beer and pizza?"

The Haines City Hideaway was a college crowd hangout. It was dim lights, music by the Stones and Yardbirds, rustic initial-gouged tabletops and benches instead of chairs. The pizza—I insisted on a basic pepperoni and double cheese—was excellent.

"I don't even know your name . . . just Donna."

"Donna Siegal. J.A.P."

"What?"

"Jewish American Princess. Doting father, typical chicken-soup-toting Jewish mother. They think anthropology has something to do with the study of ants." She laughed and snatched another piece of pizza from the pedestal tray.

"I always thought anthropology would be an interesting area of study."

"Everybody says that. What that means in translation is you can't believe how boring it sounds."

"No, really . . ."

"Don't worry, you can't offend me. I'm used to the stereotype. The female anthropologist, a frustrated frigid woman who can only get it off crouched in the bushes writing down the rituals while watching Maoris fuck."

The waitress brought another pitcher of beer. I filled our mugs.

"Actually, I find most of it boring myself. All those dragged-out ethnographies citing the intricacies of Maraboutic lineages in southeast Persia, et cetera. That's why I've sort of swung into the occult. There's a fine line between accepted anthropological treatises on primitive societies' magical belief systems and, say, Aleister Crowley's ravings in the Equinox books."

"You lost me."

"Small wonder. You're a Lit major, aren't you?"

"Yes. Does it show?"

"No. I checked."

"You did go to a lot of trouble to get to me, didn't you?"

"Yeah. I have a strong sense of like for you."

"Like?"

"Yeah. That's about as strong as it gets with me. So. Pizza's done. You know my full name, ethnic origins and kinky propensities . . . now can we go back to your room and screw?"

The beer had mellowed my anger, and I conceded defeat. Besides, Master Che had not been able to give me an oriental philosophy that did much to sublimate my occidental hound dog urges.

Sex with Donna was energetic, if somewhat academic. She kept citing positions used by primitive groups of people in various underdeveloped areas of the world. It was more like a travelogue than satisfying sex.

Afterwards, she lay on the bed nursing a cigarette while I sat in one of the straight-backed scarred oak chairs, staring out my window at the night cloaking my trees.

"Tell me about your occult studies," I said.

"You mean you have an interest in the Black Arts? Necromancy, voodoo, human sacrifice, the works?"

"Maybe not all that. What do you know about people who can alter their shape . . . or at least their appearance?"

"Shape-shifters . . . you want vampires and were-wolves, like on the late show?"

"No . . ." I didn't know how to ask about the Abomination. I wondered if Donna would be his next target if I did.

I saw her acknowledge my pause with a quick nod of her head. She examined the glowing end of her cigarette minutely.

"There's all kinds of literature on shape-shifters. African lion-men, Indian tiger-men, French loup-garou,

Jivaro jaguar-men, Nordic berserkers . . . nothing in modern times, though, which is why all the current analyses of these ancient accounts are critiqued by Jungian and Freudian psychiatrists. They figure they are just hallucinations couched in the individual cultural belief-systems."

"What that means is, modern science thinks these people were all just crazies?"

"More or less. You ever see a werewolf?"

I paused again, and her eyes darted to mine. She hauled her naked body off the bed, straddled my knees while holding my face between her hands, so I could not look away.

"Look at me," she demanded, and her eyes lasered through her glasses into mine. "God-damn it, if you know something, if you've seen something . . . you have seen something, haven't you? I can tell, don't lie."

"Why would you believe it, if I did tell you?"

"Because I want to believe it, damn it! Now spill it!"

"I won't . . . I can't. Maybe for your own safety."

She peered at me awhile longer, then her naked shoulders shook with a deep shudder and she released her grip on my face.

"This is scarier than I'd imagined. Oh, I've toyed with the thoughts before—what would it be like, how would I react! You've really seen, really experienced something, haven't you?"

"I can't say. I just want to find out things right now. How do I start?"

"God! Ask me. Ask me questions!" She lit another cigarette with trembling hands.

"I don't know what questions to ask. That's my problem."

She was pacing now.

"Okay. Let me think. There's some books I can get for you . . . transmogrification, transformation of matter, shape-shifting . . . all theoretical stuff, obviously. Some case histories—unsubstantiated, of course. You read 'em, then ask me the questions." She stopped pacing and looked at me thoughtfully, head cocked, long hair drifting over her shoulders and small breasts.

"There's a man you can see. I can introduce you. But you've got to spill it to me first. I don't want to look like an idiot."

"I tell you, for your own good, I can't do that."

"Okay, okay. This guy is a Crowleyan Mage. Pretty weird, but really knowledgeable about all this stuff. I met him in Ann Arbor at a seance."

"Sounds like a nut."

"Don't be so provincial. You want knowledge about unorthodox occurrences, you gotta look in some pretty unorthodox crannies."

"You're right. I shouldn't throw stones."

"You aren't going to tell me, are you?"

"Not a word."

"Bastard! Okay. I'll get you the books. I'll drop 'em by tomorrow night."

She dressed quickly and left.

Donna phoned my room two days later. B.F. Trevor, the Warlock, as he called himself, was holding a Halloween Black Mass, and Donna had wrangled a special invitation for the two of us.

"I don't know if I really want to attend a Black Mass . . ." I'd read the books she had procured for me, and I didn't like what they had to say on the subject.

" . . . it's the only way Trevor would agree to talk with us. He's sort of on a recruiting drive . . . Satan's evangelical quest or something. Do you want to see him, or not?"

" . . . I guess . . . I want to. Should I bring a broomstick or just the human sacrifice of my choice?"

"Funny. Listen, I've got to warn you . . . this guy is deadly serious. Just do what you're told, or you'll blow the whole thing."

"Have you been to one of these get-togethers before?"

"No. But I've heard rumors."

"What sort of rumors?"

"Delicious ones," she laughed. "I'll pick you up about ten p.m. on the thirty-first."

"Ten?"

"Yeah. He doesn't start the ritual until midnight. The Gateway to All-Souls." She imitated a fiendish laugh of glee worthy of any Renfield anticipating arrival of the Master of the Undead, and hung up.

She came at ten on Halloween night, in her usual jeans and workshirt. The unusual thing was that she wore make-up and her hair was neatly brushed and shiny-clean.

"Ready?" she asked, standing in my doorway, her eyes glinting with excitement behind her glasses.

"I guess. I'm not ashamed to tell you I'm scared. I just don't know what to expect."

"Necromancy." She giggled like a twelve year old with a lewd secret.

"That's . . . magic done by raising the dead?"

"That's it, babes. I hear Trevor can really do it."

"You don't honestly believe that."

"I'd sure like to. We'll find out one way or another tonight."

14

The night was perfect for scary stuff like attending a Black Mass. The trees were bare skeletons under fog-draped lampposts, and evil jack-o-lantern faces glowed and flickered in house windows as we drove past. Trick-or-treaters were off the streets by then, adults were at costume parties, and the town seemed devoid of human life.

Trevor's house—mansion, actually—was on the river in Ann Arbor's exclusive east side hills off Geddes Road.

It was a multi-level modernistic spider of a thing, crouching with legs grasping up and down the sloping bank to the river below. When imagining a frightening house on a Halloween night, something tall and Victorian comes to mind, but the cold gaping eyes of glass, the flat forbidding planes, the intimidating angles of Trevor's house held more inexplicable terror, causing the goose-flesh to more readily crawl down my arms.

The long circular drive off Riverview was dotted with Cadillac Eldorados, Mercedes, and even a late model Rolls.

A lighted walkway, like a yellow tongue lolling between the juniper bushes, led us to the blood red mouth of the double doors.

A tall, broad-shouldered bulky man with severe horn-rimmed glasses and a shock of snowy hair above an expensive grey business suit opened the door. His eyes were puffy slits behind the thick distorting bifocals and beneath thick thunderclouds of brows. Jowls sagged in porcine folds over his stiff white collar and school-striped tie, and a white-grey beard hid most of his face beneath the glasses. He seemed to tower over my six feet, though in truth, he was probably only six-one or two. His height, unlike his width, was attitude more than inches.

"You must be Donna and Steve," he said, a smile spreading his fleshy jowls, revealing small pointed teeth, all seemingly of equal size. There was something unsettlingly familiar about his voice. I shuddered.

"Yes," Donna said, hands fluttering like nervous birds with no purpose or destination.

"Do come in. The coven is complete, the novices are present, and the intitiates await below."

"Sounds like the fun's about to begin," I joked.

Trevor—for that was who the man before us was—lost his smile. The slit-eyes closed up even more, the thundercloud eyebrows bunched, and the fleshy jowls quivered below the beard.

"I do hope you are not a skeptic. I will not allow a

skeptic to enter the sacred chamber."

"Oh, he's not a skeptic. Steven is the one who has had paranormal experience. Remember I told you?" Donna was nearly sputtering.

Trevor's face softened again. "Yes. Yes, I recall. A joke, then. You were making a harmless joke."

"Yes, that's all," I affirmed.

"I apologize, then. You see, Steven, we all take the rituals very seriously. Come into my home, partake of my hospitality, the warmth of the hearth, the camaraderie of my friends . . . but do not belittle the rituals."

"Understood," I said gravely, though I felt a real urge to giggle.

There were fourteen others in the spacious den— Trevor's coven of twelve and two novices, I discovered after some minutes of conversation. The night was special, it seemed, because two of the more experienced coven-folk were leaving that night to form two splinter covens, the novices to become full participants, taking the places of those leaving. The initiates—those who "waited below," as Trevor so ominously put it—were to become the novices-in-training. A sleepy-eyed redhead of about forty-five lusciously well-preserved years kept telling Donna and me how lucky we were to be allowed to watch all this terribly important status-changing happen. We nodded politely and agreed, not having the slightest clue what she was on about.

The drink was strong—a mulled wine heated over the open fire in the fireplace, supposedly concocted from a medieval Cornish book of shadows discovered by MacGregor Mathers. The thick burgundy-hued drink had aphrodesiac properties, according to the sleepy-eyed redhead. She must have told us that easily a dozen times as she eyed Donna and myself with democratically equal amounts of lust for each. After my third mug of the stuff, I was beginning to believe her. Each time her flour-white hand stroked my neck, I felt an urgent need to thrust something of myself into her nearest hungry oriface.

I guessed the aphrodesiac qualities of the wine were not to be underestimated.

The redhead was nuzzling my neck with her full red lips and I had an erection that threatened to split my zipper. She was moving to that vicinity of impending disaster when Trevor shook off an adoring blonde and a sultry brunette to announce the time had come to prepare for the ritual.

Donna released her death-grip on the neck and body of a middle-aged dentist-looking type, both of them gasping for breath from the passionate kiss they had been exploring in all its vivid nuances.

Sleepy-eyes smiled as she rose, following the others out of the den. Donna clung to me as I helped her up and answered Trevor's beckoning hand.

Stairs led a winding path downward. I could only assume we were going back into the bank on which the house was built, but because of the numbing disorienting effect of the wine, I could not be positive.

At length, we were in a smallish room. There was a rack of robes. Donna and I were given coarsely textured brown ones, while the other men donned black and the women blood-crimson robes of material that seemed to be silk.

Trevor lit a huge candelabra before we moved on, the fat guttering candles providing an eerie flickering yellow light.

I realized we all were naked under the robes only as an after-thought when I felt the rude cloth on my skin, since I could not remember a room full of naked people, nor the act of stripping myself nude. The wine had taken total control of me, and I was only aware that the sackcloth material of my robe felt alive on the nerves of my body.

The hall seemed narrow and cave-like, but by then I was having trouble seeing, so I couldn't be sure. The hall was rising and falling under my bare feet, the walls and ceiling breathing.

We entered a large high-ceilinged room. I knew it was large only because the candelabra illuminated no walls nor roof, only the immediate area around Trevor.

On the black floor in white luminous paint was a huge double circle, inexplicable runes dancing between the inner and outer circumferences. In the center of it all was a draped table—an altar, I guessed.

Donna and I were gently pushed into kneeling positions on either side of the altar. It was made clear we were to wait there.

The twelve entered the outer circle. Trevor lit some pungent incense and some fat black candles at the four cardinal points of the altar. He extinguished the candelabra by squashing the flames beneath the palm of his hand. Somewhere behind us, a roaring conflagration sprang to life in some sort of open fire pit.

Trevor stood majestically behind the altar and lead the coven in a chant made up of Latinate words, none of which were recognizable to me from my two years of high school Latin.

The chanting continued. A black hilted sword was passed about, and each coven member kissed the gleaming point. After the sword, a huge golden goblet was passed, and those who drank from it were left with disturbing red stains on their lips. Both the sword and goblet were kept from Donna and myself.

The next thing I knew, the coven was disrobed, all save Trevor, and they danced counterclockwise about the great circle, Trevor watching from his elevated position behind the altar, chanting and clapping in time to a music I found totally unfamiliar.

He ordered Donna and me to disrobe. Before I could make a decision, yes or no, two coven members raised me to my feet and removed the coarse material for me.

Trevor said something about flying, traveling to the magical plane, and I vaguely recognized the voluptuous sleepy-eyed redhead approaching me with an urn of ornate Florentine design. She dipped her hands into the narrow mouth and began spreading a thick green ooze over my body. My skin tingled with the first touch. She paid special attention to my wrists, my palms, the soles of my feet, armpits and groin.

The sensation of weightlessness came over me, then I seemed to float up, above the scene. I could see the altar, the circle, and the dancing coven below. I soared. The room was without height, as I penetrated the night sky. Trevor's sprawling spider-house lay below, as well as the river and the city lights. Then I was among the stars, breathless, freezing, hot, rising, soaring. The multitude of stars, at first dense as sequins on the black velvet gown of some temptress, became sparse. Then the black hole of oblivion engulfed me and sucked men to its vortex.

I was back, somehow, in the subterranean room. My eyes opened as from a deep sleep of death. I was dancing, rubbing bodies with the others, the touch of their flesh, male and female alike, electric. The dancing became frenzied, and the frenzy became sexual debauch. Trevor moved among us, robed, regal, gathering spent seed into the goblet. He muttered arcane magical words that were palpable in the darkness.

The initiates were brought forth, a male and female, nude, blindfolded with scarlet cloth, hands bound tightly behind them. They were made to kneel before the altar. A many-tongued whip appeared, and each coven member in turn scourged the bodies of the initiates, who writhed in agony as ugly red stripes multiplied on their bodies. Donna and I had our turns at flailing, and ecstasy filled me as I watched the bodies twist under my administration of the scourge.

They were made to kneel again, trembling, weak and moaning, at the altar, and Trevor forced them to drink from the goblet. They were placed side by side on the altar, and each of us—the coven, Donna, myself—took them in all imaginable forms of fornication, by turns violent, passionate, cool and kind.

Hours, days, eons passed in this manner. Through it all a sexual stamina and a carnal need possessed me so utterly, all I could do was probe, prod, grasp, trying with desperation to sate an insatiable lust.

At length, oblivion came again. When I awoke, my

brain throbbed, and my body was trembling and weak, used up beyond capacity. I was dressed in my street clothes, as was Donna, who lay beside me in a heap on the floor of the room where the robes were kept.

I tried to stand but could not. Donna began to stir, moaning "my head, my God-damned head," and then a door opened, flooding the purple room with light. There was Trevor, white shock of hair disheveled, thick glasses on his pudgy face, clothed in silk lounging pajamas with oriental lettering on the pocket.

"And so you awaken . . . finally. Come into the den. Tell me how you enjoyed our little gathering." He held open the door for us with the deference of a servant. My legs were rubber, but somehow I got Donna and myself up the many stairs to the den.

Trevor gave Donna a concoction for her throbbing head and ordered breakfast for us. I was surprised to see dawn breaking over the river outside the den's panoramic window.

"And so you shall speak . . . did you appreciate the ceremony?"

"I don't recall much of it. What was in the wine to make me experience that flying sensation?" I asked.

Donna rubbed her glass against her forehead. "Not the wine. The ointment. Aconite . . . or henbane . . . a psychotropic, anyway. Produces the hallucination of flight . . ."

"There you go. You college-educated types." Trevor shook his head, mildly angry. "Can't you simply accept the fact that you did fly? Is it so difficult to forget the narrow scope of your mundane existence? Sensation of? Hallucination of? No! Flight! The magic, part of the ritual."

"Okay, okay." His tone irritated me. "But what about the necromancy? I don't recall . . ."

" . . . of course you don't. You were unconscious." He got up and began to pace the thickly-piled carpet. "I assure you, spirits were summoned, and demons were called. They appeared to us, did our bidding, and were sent. Is it my fault you could not master the power given

266

you by the ritual . . . could not control the perception . . . that instead, your weak minds and wills chose oblivion? We blessed the new coven leaders and initiated the novices . . ."

" . . . that part I remember." The memory of the floggings came back so strongly I wished I could in turn be beaten as penance for my participation in that sadism. "The girl seemed so familiar . . ."

"She should," Donna moaned, still nursing her headache. "It was Candi Jones. Remember? Ginger Raintree's party?"

"Oh, my God." I turned to Trevor. "Where do you get off beating people up in the name of this stupid coven of yours?"

"Careful, young man. You are in my house, and offended, I can be quite destructive. The power cone of the coven centers on me, you know." He brought himself back to a modicum of civility. "Don't be a prude. Read Crowley, my boy. Sex is magic. Magic is sex. The flagellation excites the senses of full enjoyment of the sexual act. The sexual act in turn generates the power necessary to perform magical acts. The Powers of Darkness feed on the energies of lust. They feed on it, boy. Man's obsession with sex is the tool of Evil. Read your Bible. The painted harlot, the temptress, the Earth Mother with enormous breasts to suckle her damned offspring, her hungry sensuous lips, her engorged vulva —view the ancient artifacts of civilizations where sexual magic was revered above all else. Look at the medieval woodcuts of women lustfully kissing the Devil's hind-parts, fondling, kissing his rod of power—nothing has changed through the eons, boy, only the name. Christian religious leaders call it perversity; we call it homage to the Master." Calming once again from his fervent dissertation, he smiled at me. "And in answer to your question, both Miss Jones and her companion were willing conscripts. They knew full well the nature of the initiation rituals in advance. They gladly accepted the honor of being admitted as novices to our ranks." He lit a slim brown cigarette, taking it from a gold box on the ebony table before the couch. "Power, young man. Miss Jones understands the power of the coven. All our members are respected figures of power in this community. Yet before their admission to my coven, they were struggling, sniveling nobodys."

"You're full of shit," I said, and abruptly stood up. I wobbled, nearly making a mockery of my planned scornful, defiant exit. "Coming, Donna? I've had enough of this air bag. He can't help me. I was foolish to think anybody could."

"No. I'm not coming. I'm staying."

"Fine. Since we came in your car, I'll walk."

"Don't be hasty, boy," Trevor thundered, his fat jowls trembling beneath the beard. "You dare not incur my wrath . . ."

" . . . go to Hell, Trevor. I've incurred the wrath of forces you're just pretending you understand so you can ball young girls and exploit your sado-masochistic tendencies. God! You make me want to vomit!" I made my way to the door.

"Wait!" Trevor shouted. "Tell me what you know, what you've experienced. Let me . . . help you conjure the demon that bedevils you."

I was out the door and down the walk. The wind off the river was cold and it made my head split into aching halves.

After that Halloween night, I became even more the recluse. I shunned Donna like a leper, avoiding her calls, pretending not to be in when she, or anyone, knocked at the door of my door room.

I avoided all women. Something in what Trevor had said soured me on them. I beame a monk as well as a recluse. I went to my academic classes; I went to my karate classes. I studied; I built muscles on my muscles at the college gym. My celibacy was promoted by my mastery of sublimation. I had learned. The sex drive was replaced by academic and martial arts excellence. It was difficult. The women I had contact with in my classes were interesting, some pretty and even tantalizing, but none could compare for beauty with Catherine Charlene St. Charles—and she was lost to me. The agony for me was increased knowing that she resided a scant thirty-five miles from the campus, and I could never ever travel that short distance to see her.

As far as I knew, Cat's sister Jenny still operated the little convenience store near Haines City College campus. I went out of my way rather than pass even near that place.

Despite my regimen, despite my sublimation, occasionally the dreams came. Not the same as when I lived in Greenriver. Different. Disturbing as much for their difference as from their total incomprehensibility.

Once the dreams returned, they came back every few nights. The dreams took me not to the Greenriver cemetery, but to an unfamiliar cityscape. Unlike the reality of the other dreams, the clarity was blurred, like a camera filming through gauze.

I saw a platinum blonde, wearing too much make-up and too few clothes. I didn't recognize her. She stopped a man passing by, and they exchanged words I could not hear, but the implication was clear.

The dream made me watch, made me follow them as they went down litter-and-garbage stewn night streets, dirty stray dogs growling and side-stepping as they passed. Street bums, collapsed in boarded-up doorways, saluted them with brown bag-wrapped bottles.

The two went up ruined wooden stairs, side walls close and inscribed with the urban hieroglyphic of graffiti.

Room of night, room that had seen many such meetings, was furnished with pain and despair as well as a sagging dirty bed and a broken-leg dresser with a cracked mirror. A curtainless window let the black night in.

She undressed and got on the bed. The man stripped to his underwear, nervous, looking about. Money went from his wallet to her purse.

Legs spread in a reluctant invitation, and the man was on her.

I saw a closet door across the room slightly ajar, as if some unseen thing watched the contortions and exertions on the bed.

The unseen manipulator of my strange dream pulled my focus to the man's back. I saw sweat stain his undershirt and drip to the woman below, whose face was averted from my view, as if she knew I watched.

I heard the closet door squeak open. I knew somehow it was the closet, though in the dream I saw only the man's sweating back.

Then the sweat gushed red, the man's scream of pain short and guttural. Blood splattered over the platinum hair, over the blue and dirty white ticking of the pillow, over everything. Her face turned up to my view, features unrecognizably painted, drowned in the man's blood. She was sobbing out of control, her mouth wide in a rictus of horror and pain. The blood oozed in. I awoke. And waking, I sought not to analyze the dream. If I had, I certainly would have known what it meant.

I saw Candi Jones after that Halloween night. It was nearing Christmas and snow blew continuously on the northern winds. I saw her walking without a coat across the winter campus. Her vivacity, the beauty I remembered from that time at the Sigma Alpha Tau sorority when she frolicked with Todd Raintree in the van, was gone, wrung from her like water from an old dish rag. Her eyes were sunken, hair lackluster, hanging in strings about a wasted sallow face. Despite the overall look of ruin on her once lovely face, a quirky sad smile seemed permanently fixed to her countenance.

"Candi," I called out as she approached. "Candi," I said, touching her frigid arm. She didn't stop, she did not turn, she didn't even blink, but walked on, through the blowing snow.

I stayed at the school over the holidays, talking long distance to Laurel on Christmas Day. Aunt Jane was in Florida again, and Laurel threatened to hop in her Chevy and brave the snowbound highways to Haines City so I would not be alone on Christmas. I talked her out of it, by promising to go down on Easter Sunday. I knew I would not. I think she did, too.

Over the break, I walked the campus endlessly, seeking solace, diversion, any respite or hiatus however brief from my memories of Cat and my fears and terrors that I carried always within me.

On one such walk, I chanced upon Donna. She sat huddled on a bench the maintenance crews had forgotten to put in storage back in October.

She was crying.

"Donna, what's wrong?"

She looked up, startled. I saw the wasted ruin I remembered so vividly from the face of Candi Jones.

"You haven't heard, then."

"Heard what?"

"The police found Candi Jones' body in the river early this morning."

"I'm not really surprised. I saw her a few weeks ago, and she looked like walking death then. Was it Trevor's coven that did her in? Or was it suicide?"

Her eyes had the look of a cornered rabbit.

"Don't say that! Don't say that to anyone about Trevor, do you hear? We . . . they had nothing to do with it!"

"You said 'we' . . . did you join up with that crazy bastard?"

She pulled her eyes away and studied the snow piled on the toes of her soaked-through brogans.

"Answer me, damn it!"

"Yes. I did! What if I did? He can do it, you know. He can raise the dead. I saw . . ."

"You saw nothing. He's a sick old man. There's nothing to that hocus-pocus, nothing."

"You just don't know. He showed me."

"He showed you nothing. It's the drugs he uses. He destroyed Candi Jones with them. I saw that on her face. I see it on your face, Donna. Get the hell out while you can."

"No, no, no! The power, it's there. I saw!" Her manner changed abruptly. She rose and began fawning over me, patting my chest and face with cold shivering hands.

"The power can be yours, Steven. Candi wasn't alone in the river. The other initiate was with her. Joe Harmon. He's dead, too, and now there's room for you. Trevor asks about you. He wants to know about your experiences with the demons . . ."

"Joe Harmon? My roommate? He was the other initiate? Donna, did you . . . did the coven murder . . . ?"

"Please, Steven, please? If I bring you back to Trevor, why, he'll probably advance me to the next rung of the Ladder of Omniscience. He saw, you know, that you had experienced the touch of the demons. He saw it in your eyes . . ."

"Donna, you have to get out. He's a sick perverted man. He's destroying you."

"No." She started backing away. "He is the Way. He is the Truth. He is divine!" And she was gone, running and stumbling away in the snow.

I didn't call the police. What could I tell them? That I had participated in the sadism inflicted on two young people who were now dead? That I knew a poor Jewish girl who was probably the next to end up in the river? My familiar reaction set in. I closed in on myself, avoiding everyone and everything.

I still attended classes, but that was it. I was certain Trevor had murdered Candi Jones and Joe Harmon, my phantom roommate, whom I had never met—other than to beat him mercilessly as an anonymous victim while I was under the influence of Trevor's exotic drugs. In the long run I was just as guilty of those peoples' deaths as Trevor.

I took an overload of classes in the winter term. I enrolled for the summer term. That tiny dorm room became my world.

Time passed. I continued to go to school year round, almost doubling my load each term. I was an honor student. I had my Mustang stored on blocks. I went nowhere I could not walk. I knew no one and spoke to

272

no one. Even Laurel's attempts at keeping the fires of our relationship stoked dwindled because of my increasingly cold response. By my twenty-first birthday, I had enough credits to graduate. The lawyers of my parents' estate contacted me two days before I was to leave the familiar sanctuary of my dorm room for good. I insisted we meet in Haines City. I did not want to return to Greenriver. Ever!

We sat in my neat little dorm room, windows overlooking my trees and my campus, and signed the papers. I was twenty-one and wealthy, just as I had been promised. I retained the lawyers to continue managing my money. I could afford to do anything I wanted. Except one thing. The one thing in the world I wanted was unattainable, held from me by threat of a being not of this world, held from me by powers no amount of money could serve to conquer.

I got the Mustang, almost in assembly line condition, out of storage. I would travel the country. Get as far from Greenriver, Haines City and Detroit as I possibly could.

15

The times, as Dylan's song promised, were a-changin'. Campus unrest hit Ann Arbor with a vengence just as I left on my odyssey. Abbie Hoffman, Jerry Rubin and the rest stirred the fires of anarchy in Chicago among Daly's bulldogs, yippies, hippies and aghast Democrats.

Then Martin Luther King Jr. was dead. Bobby Kennedy was dead. Four dead in Ohio, Crosby/Stills/Nash

& Young sang plaintively. The Doors sang about when the music's over—and it was. For the country, and for me. I wandered the country in my aging Mustang, looking for peace in a land that was rent with violence between generations and ideologies. I wandered, none of it touching me, all of it wounding me.

Before I knew it, it was the 1970's. Linda Ronstadt and the Eagles sang of love and pain with a country lilt, and the wounds of the country took on a semblance of healing. Nixon pulled us out of Vietnam to win an election, to save our great country from further divisiveness, then sold us all, along with presidential respectability, down the river. The first comic president took office as Disco damned the airwaves, then the peanut farmer with the gentle attitude took over. Hostage days countdowns began and dragged on forever. Then without warning, it was 1980. Then '81. '82. '83. Reagan healed unemployment and the economy by expanding the National Debt to monstrous proportions. Tons of cheese for the needy rotted in Detroit. George Orwell's estate burgeoned with profits from book sales —all those people who hadn't read the damned thing in the preceeding forty years—and now it was 1984. I was thirty-seven—on the brink of middle age, a monied drifter, an observer of life. I was a writer.

It happened by accident rather than design. I scribbled down the pain of the nation and of myself, and once in a drunken stupor at a party showed the scribbles to a man who claimed to be a publisher. Damned if he wasn't. The next thing I knew, I owned an IBM Selectric. Typing paper and white-out became my chief life expenses.

Women in my life? There were always women in my life. But it's probably good to confess my sins.

In the late sixties and early seventies, I learned such new terms as male chauvinism, sex-object, consciousness raising, women's rights and sexual equality. Damned if it didn't seem I was hearing Kamii talk to the girls in Levon's bar all over again.

Like most males of the species, I had never considered

my view of women as derogatory in any way. These new terms and their application to American society made me ashamed, uncomfortable, and took all the fun out of my sexual fantasies.

I realized, of course, being of the liberal bent, that women had a good case and deserved to be liberated from the goddess-whore-slave stereotypes. Even though I tried to fight all discrimination of thought and deed in myself, my libido had been formed by the media exposure I experienced growing up. Need I mention the name of Stoney Miles again? The fantasy women of the Frederick's catalog from Billy St. Charles, or the Playboy Philosophy? Growing up in the sixties, when women's fashions played most heavily on the male reaction to the blatant sexual display?

I am a victim of my enculturation, as Donna Seigel would have said. And strangely, throughout my adult life, traveling about the country on research trips and book promo tours, I never had a problem finding women who loved the old goddess-whore-slave stereotypes more than liberation—for one night stands, anyway. I maintain staunchly the fundamentals of E.R.A., but sadly plead guilty to perpetuating the outdated male attitudes toward women's beauty and sexuality that keep the female gender up in arms.

Somewhere in there, in a bar in Amarillo, I found a topless dancer that looked enough like Cat to be her sister. I married her. She could do some incredibly professional things with her body and mine, but it wasn't enough. I divorced her, and she became rich. Even that did nothing to dwindle my cache. Those Greenriver lawyers just kept investing in America's successes and failures for me, and I kept on being a fatter and fatter cat.

1985. I am a writer. My novels are well received by critics, mostly unread by the public. Thank God I don't have to live off the royalties. I am a very wealthy man, as I have said. I couldn't have done better if I'd won the

Publisher's Clearing House sweepstakes every year for ten years.

The letter reached me, God knows how, in Fort Lauderdale, Florida, where I languished on the beach daily, a greying man, ogling the beach bunnies, regretting my misspent life, wishing for and fearing poetic finality to it all.

The letter was from Todd Raintree, a poetic name in itself, out of my dim past, when music meant more to me than making a profession of transferring favorite songs from records to tape for use in my car's cassette player.

It seemed old Todd was in charge of organizing our high school class's twentieth reunion.

It was as if Fate itself had hand-delivered that letter to me. The moment I read it, Thomas Wolfe's literary abjuration aside, I knew I must go home again. I wired Laurel to prepare the family manse for the prodigal son's return.

Laurel called my hotel the next day as I sat, sucking a Benson and Hedges—the Ultra Lights, and I had degenerated to menthol some time before—trying to decide whether to pack or simply buy clothes when I got there. Greenriver. The place I swore would never see me again. But hadn't the dreams stopped somewhere in the distant past? Hadn't the systematic elimination of my family members ended? Oh, sure, Brian was M.I.A. in Nam. So were a lot of other poor schmucks. Maybe even Jim Harper. God knows, I never heard from him after that day at Fort Wayne. That day—that last time I had seen Cat. She was like a fairy princess from some horrible Brothers Grimm tale, a Rhine maiden caught in the clutches of the ogre king. A trite but surreal movie in my mind, a busty Brigitte Bardot playing the part of Cat. Another blow to my mind's vivid fantasy life, when poor Ms. Bardot lost her breasts to radical mastectomy. Cancer, cancer, burning bright. If only those affected portions of my mind, my memory, could be excised so easily by the surgeon's unemotional knife.

Laurel's call interrupted these pointless musings.

"What the fuck, are you crazy?" In the background I heard a male voice say, "Jesus Christ, Laurie, watch the language. The God-damned kid'll hear ya." To which Laurel hollered, only partially away from the receiver, "Shut the fuck up. I'm talkin' ta my cousin. It's long fucking distance."

"Problem, Laurel?" I asked, amused.

"You damn well know there's a problem. That rundown house of yours has been boarded up for seventeen-eighteen years. It'll take an army and a damned fortune to clean it up in time."

"Hire as many armies as it takes, and spend as much as you need. I'll call the bank and have them release the money to you. I really appreciate your doing this, Laurel."

"Well . . . sure. Okay, then. Hey, you could write me once in awhile, ya know? Whoever heard of a writer who can't write a letter now and then."

"Sorry, Laurel. I'm looking forward to seeing you again. Have you been getting the checks okay?" I hated asking, but sometimes it took months to get the cancelled checks back. She must have struggled with an inner pride that forebade her accepting the money each time one of the monthly checks arrived in the mail.

"Yeah, I'm gettin' 'em. I've told you before, I don't need no charity."

"And I've told you before, it's not charity. It's the least I can do for someone who gave me so much support in those years when I needed it most. Spend it. Enjoy it. Pamper yourself with it. I can afford it."

"Yeah, yeah, yeah. Listen, I'll get the house fixed up okay. And yeah, the old man says hi."

"How's the little pride and joy?"

"Stephanie? You won't recognize her. She's twelve, y'know."

"Twelve! My God. It's been that long? She won't recognize me. That time you brought her to Chicago when I was at the A.B.A. convention . . . what was she? Six?"

"Five. She still talks about her cousin Steve. She

drools over them pictures of you on the backs of your books. Damn! I sure wish you'd tell me what the fuck you're talkin' about in those books sometime."

"Nothing important, Laurel." I laughed. "How's Aunt Jane? She must be getting right up there in years."

"Off boogeyin' in Florida again. Surprised she hasn't looked you up."

"I'm probably too slow for her, not enough action."

"Probably right. The old biddy makes me dizzy sometimes. Well, this is costin' a fortune. You need to be picked up in Detroit?"

"No . . . I'll rent a car at the airport. Thanks again, Laurel. And Laurel . . . I love you."

"Shit," she said and hung up.

I decided to buy the clothes when I needed them rather than lug a suitcase. I called the airline and made reservations.

A week later, I boarded the jet in Fort Lauderdale, sat for an hour in Atlanta waiting for the plane change, and got off at Detroit Metropolitan Airport two and a half hours later. It was raining, September rain.

I got a rent-a-car, an Olds Cutlass Brougham, and headed out of the airport. Something made me veer right too early, and I found myself heading east on I-94 instead of toward Ann Arbor, Jackson, and points west.

I cursed the mistake, then analyzing it, realized it was no mistake. My subconscious had willed the Olds to take me to Detroit, to take me to Cat.

Fighting the rush hour traffic headed out of the city, it took me almost an hour to reach that little dance studio on Jefferson.

I was surprised to find it still there—surprised and upset. I think I actually wished it were gone.

I parked the Olds, writing off the wire wheelcovers as I did so. I only hoped they left the car in operating condition. There were guys in that part of Detroit who could strip an Olds, Buick, a Caddy in five minutes flat. Then they'd burn 'em to cover the thefts. These weren't penny-ante guys—with gas at a buck thirty a gallon, they had to lay out at least five bucks to torch a car right.

The front door was open, which I thought was trusting and optimistic, considering the deterioration of the neighborhood; it had been bad enough back in the mid-sixties. Since the riots of 1967, it had gotten much worse.

I went down the hall to the practice studio where last I had seen Cat. The room was empty, and I ran my hand over the mirrors where he had slammed me against the wall, the only audience this time the multiple refections of me, wall to wall, back and front views, again and again. I shut my eyes against the mental picture of him standing there, grasping at her body with those horrible hands, her hands clenched in anger, repulsion, then limp, hanging at her sides, resigned.

Hands. A hand touched my shoulder lightly. My eyes opened to show me a raven-haired woman of medium height reflected next to me in the mirror. Her deep, penetrating, mystical eyes were at my shoulder level.

"What are you doing here?" her smokey voice asked, a hint of a smile on her blood-red lips.

"I . . . I'm Steve Dalton, I just . . ."

"I know who you are. I asked what you were doing here."

"You're just as beautiful as you were twenty years ago when I met you at the St. Charles house in Greenriver."

"Twenty-two years, and flattery will not soften me, Steve Dalton. Call me Delilah," she said, smiling. "Come. I'll give you some coffee in my office."

Her sexy well-muscled dancer's body flowed before me down the hall, and I watched every self-assured step intently. Even in my confused, troubled state of mind, I thanked the Powers That Be silently for the invention of Danskins.

The office was all in black and silver, futuristic, yet comfortable—dramatic, like the woman who used it.

She got me coffee in a black mig with a metallic

interior that shone like chrome. Taking another mugful for herself, she sat behind the gleaming black desk. I sat opposite her. The desk top was empty, like starless space between us.

"I repeat my question."

"Isn't it obvious?" I sipped the coffee. It was rich and delicious.

"Obsession, Steve Dalton, is a dangerous thing."

"I know that. I have sufferred for it many years."

"And your family."

"Yes." So she knew it all.

"I can prove to you how dangerous, how fatal my little nephew can be. Perhaps even now you need to know the extent of his . . . shall I say . . . appetites?"

She pulled a large leather-bound book from a desk drawer and slid it across the expanse of desk to me.

"Clippings, Steve, from Detroit newspapers. It is by no means complete. Many of his victims will never be found."

I took the book. Clippings were Scotch-taped to every page. A scrap book of horror. Page after page of newspaper descriptions of murder . . . a teenaged girl here . . . two infant children there . . . a corporate executive . . . a union labor boss . . . a dime store heiress. But the bulk of the articles named middle-aged men. Hundreds upon hundreds of them.

Page after page, some front page stories with photos and banner headlines, some a few tiny column inches. The link seemed to be that all bodies were horribly mutilated and there were no suspects, no leads, no witnesses, no clues.

I looked up from the book, the question in my eyes, though I knew it's answer.

"Nicholas. All of them. And your parents. Yes, he is quite remarkable. He prefers to do this thing one-on-one, but he can, of course, perform long distance."

"And the dreams . . ."

"Oh, yes. He can make you dream what he wishes. Sometimes he warns . . . sometimes he does it as play, to show you something he wishes to hurt you with." She drank quickly from the mug to mask the twitch in the muscles around her mouth. "He is quite capable of every depraved, abominable action you could ever imagine."

"The Abomination," I murmured.

"Pardon?"

"The Abomination," I said aloud. "My name for him." I lit a cigarette and she produced an ash tray from somewhere in the desk. "I can't believe we are sitting here, calmly discussing all this. I won't even ask why you kept a scrap book on his exploits like he was some kind of football star in high school."

She made a vague gesture with her hand, dismissing the book. "I don't know what else can be done, other than calmly discuss Nicholas. Who would believe such nonsense had they not experienced dear Nicholas for themselves, as you have?"

"Doctors . . . run tests on him . . . surely he's not human."

"True. Though he was born of woman, there is nothing human about him. Or perhaps there once was —I'm no expert on this—but as he has matured the human cells in his body have mutated, been eaten as if by cancer. You know of course he can change himself. The semi-human form that he shows the world, gangling and misshapen as it is, is nothing more or less than an elaborate mask. His true form . . . God!" She covered her face with her hand for a moment, then recovered her composure with what seemed a practiced effort. "But you see, doctors, hospitals, police . . . all out of the question. He is too powerful, has been too powerful for years now. That's why Susan St. Charles gave him to me. Not that I could control him, but rather because his appearance and . . . nocturnal pursuits could go unnoticed in a large city."

I tapped the book with my hand, cigarette ashes cascading down it to the thick black rug. "Not unnoticed by these people."

"Nor by you, me, or our dear Cat."

"Which brings us to the answer to your original

question. My obsession. My twenty-five-year obsession over a person I cannot see, let alone possess. Cat. My Cat."

She shook her head and sat the mug with a clunk on the desk top.

"And that's the greatest shame. She too has been torn all these years by a like obsession for you. I can't explain it any more than I can explain Nicholas's existence. The two things may even be intertwined in some odd cosmic way. The two of you were destined for each other, soul-mates, for lack of a less cliched phrase. And perhaps the two of you, somehow, are the answer to Nicholas's destruction. God knows, the two of you have most directly borne the pain of his being. You, with the death of your family members, and Catherine Charlene with . . . well, let's just say with the death of her soul."

"What does that mean?"

"I can't tell you. In the final analysis, all you need know is that Cat is lost to you forever."

"She's . . . dead?" I couldn't keep the trembling fear out of my voice.

"No. God, I only wish she were. No, she is with him. She must always be with him. She keeps him from breaking out, loosing mass destruction. I shudder to think what he is capable of . . . if angered, if set free."

I slammed the book of untold horrors onto her black starless night desk.

"I can't accept that! All these years I've wanted her, lusted, burned for her! She was meant for me, you said it. I told her the same thing long ago, and long before that, she said it to me. She's mine, God-damn it! And I am hers. We were meant to be. All the rest of this . . . this supernatural bullshit . . . Nicholas the shape-shifter, Nicholas the Abomination, Nicholas the boogey-man . . . it's all illusion, like magic on a stage, like tricks, like, like . . ."

"No!" Her hand cast the coffee mug against a wall where it shattered, taking a Napalachenko print down with it. "It's reality, Steven! Let me tell you about it. You think you've suffered? It began with my brother.

He read the books, he collected them . . . rare books, books from auctions, estates. His interest in the occult began early in his teens. He read Waite, Crowley, Blavatsky. He read Poe, Lovecraft, Machen. Oddly enough, his knowledge seemed to grow greater after reading the stuff that was supposedly fiction. He even claimed that Lovecraft's fictional creation, the Necronomicon, existed, and he had a copy!

"I laughed at him, called him a fool. He told me he would show me. Someday, he would show me. Well, I guess he did. You know he did. I know it more than you."

She came around the desk, leaned against it, displaying her voluptuous body to me.

"Do you think I'm attractive . . . pretty, sexy?"

"Yes, but what does that . . ."

"How old do you think I am?"

"I'm not good at that . . . you look about thirty-five, but I figure you must be around forty-eight."

"But I haven't changed, have I, since you saw me twenty-two years ago in Greenriver?"

"No . . . but . . ."

"Well, Steven, I'm seventy-two. Shocked? Come back in thirty years. I'll still look the same. You see, my looks, my physical condition, my cheating of time's normal ravaging are all due to my brother's first success with the Black Arts, what you call trickery and illusion. He said he would show me. He asked what I wanted more than anything in the world, and being a vain woman in my early thirties, growing old and ugly were the worst things I could think of ever happening to me, to anyone. I asked him—to humor him, you see—for eternal beauty and youth. He said, it's yours. That simple. I laughed at him and forgot about it.

"It took time to realize it, of course. Other women my age grew crows-feet around their eyes; when they smiled, lines formed at the corners of their mouths that didn't go away as soon as they should. I attributed the supple quality of my skin to a good diet, good genes. It wasn't until a day in 1947, when I was crossing a street in Detroit, that I realized my brother had fulfilled his promise. I was hit by a truck, you see . . . it ran over me, all its many wheels passing over my body. When it braked to a stop, I stood up and dusted myself off."

I could only shake my head in disbelief.

"He got in deeper. I don't know all about it. I don't know if it was something out of Faust complete with Mephistophelian devils or not, but he made a pact. He was rich and powerful; he had money. In return, he provided a gateway for evil on earth.

"He had been busy, going from town to town, looking for the proper atmosphere, the proper girl. He found the ambiance in Greenriver, by the cemetery, the right girl in the person of Susan Sorrel. Even though she was a high school girl and he decades older than her, she fell victim to his charm.

"Their first child was normal. My brother made an error in his incantations, chose the wrong moon phase . . . something. Who knows how complicated the ritual must have been? He tried again and failed, but he felt closer. He tried once again, and came very, very close. The fourth time, he succeeded. The results of his matings with Susan Sorrel were Jennifer, Billy, Catherine Charlene, and of course, Nicholas. When he was positive he had succeeded, he left them, left poor Susan to raise them all alone. I helped as much as I could, when I finally found them, but I was having troubles of my own. Immortality is not such a sweet prize as one would imagine."

"I hope you aren't offended, Delilah, but I don't give a shit about all this. It doesn't help me find Cat . . ."

"I had hoped you would understand. Understand that my brother does have power, that Nicholas is real . . ."

"Because you stand here and tell me you should be an old hag? That because of your brother's hocus-pocus you are instead damned to live forever in this beautiful body? Poor baby!"

"Don't be sarcastic with me. You had better listen and pay heed. I could prove my age to you, but men who choose to be blind shall forever see nothing. My age or the problems and the horrors I have experienced because of my brother's damnable gift to me are inconsequential. What I want you to realize is that Jennifer was normal. Billy had a taint . . . of a dark side. Nicholas was the completely non-human baby."

My anger let it seep through very slowly. I couldn't believe what she was implying.

"Say it straight out, damn it!"

"Catherine, your dear Cat, is half and half."

"Incredible. Not the story . . . the fact that you believe it. It's been a lot of years, and over those years, I've experienced a lot of life. I've been all over this country, and I've never encountered anything even close to this. It's all *got* to be illusion."

"Do you think this is the type of thing that people would tell a drifter? How many people have you ever been able to confide in about Cat and Nicholas? Be that as it may, this is a one-time, one-of-a-kind occurrance. Believe it, Steve. It's your death if you don't. You used to know that. That's why you spent all those years wandering, trying to forget. I'm telling you go back, back to your life of quiet desperation. It's better than the stark horrid reality of Nicholas and Cat."

I left her there, sitting behind her night black desk, shaking her head, a weariness weighing on her. "God," she moaned, "I tried. I hoped to God you'd understand, you'd believe. I've lived it so many years . . . so many years . . ."

I had no idea why she felt she had to concoct that elaborate story, that explanation. She was just part of the conspiracy to keep Cat from me.

She was unbalanced, that was clear. She truly believed she was seventy-two years old. I felt sorry for her. But as I left her there, shaking her head in despair in her silver and black world of the dance studio, I realized she didn't look forty-eight, either. She looked a young thirty-two, younger than me.

The car, miraculously, was still where I had parked

it, wheelcovers and all. I pointed it west and headed for Greenriver.

16

It was the same, still the same, always the same. Some of the old stores had changed hands; there were new names lettered on the plate glass windows. City planning had murdered certain ancient oaks and pines in the small parks, and the gazebo in the town square no longer had roses growing up its trellised sides. But basically, fundamentally, intrinsically it was the same Greenriver I had left at the age of eighteen.

The front door was unlocked—you could do that in Greenriver, I supposed, even in 1985. There was a note from Laurel on the table by my father's chair.

"Did the cleaning myself. You can't get people to do shit the way you'd do it yourself. Come see me as soon as you can. Stevie wants to see her famous cousin really bad. Don't be too surprised when you see her. She's into Cyndi Lauper, Madonna and Prince. I swear to Christ she looks like a street slut half the time. Anyway, come see us.

Luv, Cousin Laurel."

I smiled to myself, folded the note and put it in my pocket.

I didn't tour the house—I couldn't. I could not even dwell too long looking at my father's chair. I undressed in darkness and slipped naked between the sheets of my parents' double bed. Sleep came—thankfully, dreamless.

I found some clothes and albums for little Stevie in a boutique on Main Street that I figured for about a six month life expectancy before it went bust. The prices were exorbitant, the selection skimpy. I guessed at the sizes of the clothes. That was one thing about record albums for gifts—as long as you knew the person's musical tastes, they always fit.

Freddie, Laurel and Stevie Kolzicky now lived in a small but pleasant Cape Cod on Greenriver's north side. Like most small Midwestern towns, civilization ended abruptly at the city limits. A farmer's barbed wire fence formed the boundary for the Kolzicky backyard. Beyond it lay acres of grazing land for sheep.

When I pulled the Olds Cutlass to a halt in their gravel and rut driveway, the screen door burst open. A girl, nearly tall as me, came running at me, arms outstretched.

"Cousin Steve, cousin Steve," she screamed and flung her arms around my neck.

Stephanie had indeed grown up since last I saw her. She had her father's long lean frame and the incipient mounds that would balloon into breasts of proportions equal to her mother's. She also had her mother's fundamentally pretty face, hidden behind Egyptian-style eye make-up, shadowed by a razor-cut shock of blonde hair tinged with shades of blue and scarlet. She was, as the vernacular has it, punked out. I fought hard to remember Beatle cuts, zip boots, sport jackets without lapels and pegged pants. I shelved my xenophobia, and it was cool. Irrationally, as we walked to the house carrying her booty, I entertained notions that I liked the way she looked.

Lanky Freddy Kolzicky rose from his recliner in front of the tube blaring motorcross finals and shook my hand. Five seconds later, he was emersed again in the hopping, crashing, sputtering cycles, riders masked like dirty Darth Vaders.

Little Steven raved on and on with each new bag she opened, extracting my gifts to her and kissing me on the cheek for each one. I fought the urge to recall passages verbatim from Nabokov's most famous book and maintained an older cousin-like demeanor.

It was difficult talking to Laurel. Oddly, she seemed as embarrassed and uncomfortable as me. The relationship we had once known was gone. She could no longer be that wild, free spirit, not with a husband and an almost grown child.

I made a quick end to the discomfort by quoting a lame excuse about business I had to attend, phone calls to make. Stevie dragged at my sleeve, pleading that I stay, but relented at my promise to return the next day. I got another kiss on the cheek from her, a mumbled goodbye from Laurel and a passive hand wave from Freddie, muttering to himself and the TV about Chink bikes as a guy on a Suzuki won the race. I didn't stay to tell him Japanese people weren't Chinks.

I spent time strolling the business district, lolling at the gazebo in the town square that was really a circle, and kicking pebbles off the concrete bridge over the river. Dusk was threatening, and I decided to check out Todd Raintree's bar. Alcohol was another of my vices—smoking, liquor and loose women.

It had to be Todd's bar I had seen in my wanderings. Who else would name a bar Raintree's?

The name was painted on the facade in letters two feet high. It was big as a billboard, on the north side of the square where the gazebo stood.

Inside, it was dark and intimate. Tables stood on little raised and railed platforms all about the room.

Todd Raintree's unmistakable high school football star frame stood by the cash register, his meaty hands busily working a tiny pocket calculator as he eyed the journal tape of the register.

"The erstwhile businessman, plying his trade," I said. "Barkeep, draw me a draft. Or is that redundant phrasing?"

He looked up. His eyes seemed not to focus for a

moment, as his facial muscles danced through a dozen expressions. With a swiftness and grace that startled me, he leapt the high bar in a single motion, and bear-hugged me 'til I thought my ribs would pop, all the while hollering, "God-damn! God-damn!" at the top of his lungs. Simon and Garfunkel had been harmonizing "Homeward Bound" softly over the p.a., and the early tenants of the bar looked shocked and appalled at Todd's raucous greeting.

Eventually, he let me go.

"Jesus K. Crimeny, you look good! Hell, you're almost big as me! Did you get a body transplant, or what!"

"You look good, too, Todd. How's business?"

"Great, just great. Ronni," he bellowed at a sulky looking brunette at one end of the bar, "take over for me. This is God-damned Steve Dalton! Bring us a couple Molsons. No. A God-damn pitcher."

He slapped my back about every five feet on the forty-foot journey to a table by the bandstand.

"I can't begin to tell you how glad I am to see you. Jesus! Of all the people I never expected to answer that letter . . ."

The sulky brunette named Ronni brought the pitcher and two iced mugs. She began to say something to me, smiling, but Todd waved her away impatiently.

"So tell me," he said, "how's it been?"

"Okay. I travel a lot. Book promo tours . . . signings, talk shows, that sort of thing. Boring and time-consuming." I looked around the bar and lit a cigarette. "This is a great place, Todd. I never figured you for owning a bar."

"It'll be April of 2050 before I own it. But I run it for the bank," he laughed.

"You tell me how it's been, Todd. You're the home-town boy. I haven't been here since I was eighteen. Catch me up."

"Well, I went to Michigan State on a football scholar-ship and screwed up my knee the first game out of the box. Athletic Department couldn't see their way clear to keep somebody who couldn't run a running game, so I dropped out after my freshman year. My grades sure as hell wouldn't have kept me in school.

"The knee kept me out of the service, and I kind of drifted from job to job . . . here, Kalamazoo, around. Then my old man retired from his job, and offered to cosign for me on a bar business. Said he always wanted a place he could go drink for free. So that's how I became a bartender."

I eyed him for a moment, then decided what the hell. Maybe he would know. "Heard anything about Michelle?" I could not fathom why I asked after her first, of all the old gang. Maybe it was because we both had been her victims, Todd and I, an eternity ago. I couldn't begin to read his expression. The pause before he spoke was more uncomfortable than I had imagined possible.

"Yeah. Yes. She came back . . . and I married her." He chugged almost a full mug of beer in one gulp. "She . . . she had some bad times . . . I mean, she sang in some big-time places. Atlantic City, Las Vegas, San Francisco, L.A., New York, Chicago, New Orleans . . . she even did a gig at Albert Hall in London."

I decided to cover my shock over the idea that the two of them had wed by skipping over it, just as he had done.

"I had no idea she was that hot. I mean, I've never really lost track of pop music . . ."

"Oh, well, her records didn't make it big over here," he said it quickly. "Big in Europe and England especially."

"I'd love to hear her."

"She sings here. She'll be on at ten. You probably can't stay . . ."

"I wouldn't miss it."

"Oh. Well. Okay."

"Can I talk to her? Is she here yet?"

"Why do you wanna talk to her?"

"Don't be so defensive, Todd. She's your wife. I'd just

like to apologize to her for all that shit that went down all those years ago. Life's too short to let a twenty-year wound like that fester forever."

"I don't know how to ask this without sounding stupid . . . but would you please just leave her alone? I mean, it's not like I'm afraid anything would happen, it's just . . . well, she's had a tough time. I don't think she'd want to see you."

"Todd, this is a tiny little town. I'm going to be here for a couple of weeks, maybe longer. I had my cousin get the old house cleaned up. If I hang around, Michelle and I are bound to bump into one another eventually."

"Not necessarily. Gina doesn't go out much, doesn't socialize around in Greenriver."

"Gina?" I was confused, to say the least.

"That's what she wants to be called. Regina is her middle name."

His attitude, his sudden nervousness, the change from gaiety to depression when the subject of the conversation switched to his wife, all disturbed me. Todd was having some kind of major problem.

"Damn it, Todd," I said softly, "what is it? What's eating you alive about Michelle?"

"Oh, God, Steve," he was almost in tears. "I can't begin to tell you what they did to her."

"They?"

"Those record guys. Record guys, shit! Oh, they were in the entertainment business," he said bitterly, "but not records. They ruined her, Steve. They nearly wasted her."

"Easy, Todd, easy. Your patrons are watching."

"Right." He cast an eye about the bar, faked a smile, nodded at the few of the closest people who were indeed looking with some concern in his direction. Maybe they thought I was mafioso in town to shake down the local bar owner. Todd turned back to me, whispering this time."

"It's just, you know, I'm the one who holds her head when she cries until she pukes her guts out remembering what it was like. Thank God she can't remember all of it. The drugs made her insensible half the time, I guess."

"Drugs, Todd? Michelle was into drugs?"

"Hey. Nothing small, either. She was a smack-freak for almost ten years."

"Jesus," I whispered.

"Well, like I say, it made her forget all the other stuff."

"Other stuff, Todd?"

"You don't want to know. If you ever cared for her, even a little bit, believe me, you don't want to know. They forced her into prostitution, porno movies, worse. Much, much worse, believe me."

"I don't know what to say, Todd."

"There's nothing to say. I try to make her life as pleasant as possible. She enjoys singing here, but she refuses to see any of the old crowd . . . Debbie, Paulie, you know. I mean, if they come in here, she pretends she doesn't know them. That's why she likes to be called Gina. She . . . wants Michelle Bailey to be dead."

"Okay. I'll play. Introduce us like we're strangers. Listen, it might help. I'm sure a psychologist would say it's wrong to feed her delusions, to go on letting her hide, but I know what nightmares can be like. I'd do anything to help her believe those nightmares aren't and never were reality."

"Do you really think it will help?"

"To have me reinforce her fantasy life? Can't hurt to try, Todd."

There were tears on his cheeks now. He fisted them away.

"Thanks, Steve. It's not many friends that would . . . after twenty years . . ."

I put a hand on his arm. "It's best to look back to only the good. Life's too short, like I said."

He toasted me silently with his beer mug and drained it.

Ten o'clock came. A small band had set up on the stage—guitar, bass, drums, piano, and a sax man. They played a few soft instrumentals, generic ballad jazz. They were pretty average, though better than what expectations would have allowed for a town of Greenriver's size. The sax man had an extraordinary lyrical sense to his playing. I listened, drank the beer that Todd kept coming, and smoked my cigarettes.

"Thank you, ladies and gentlemen," the sax man breathed into the mike. "Now we'd like to bring out a fabulous songstress, by name, Miss Gina Raintree."

There was moderate applause. A woman stepped up to the mike, out of the shadows of the small bandstand. If I hadn't spoken with Todd, I would never have recognized her as Michelle Bailey.

"Thank you," she whispered, as the applause died. She brushed back her long straight black hair, silvered with streaks that told of her years of turmoil, letting the spotlight illuminate a narrow hollow-cheeked face with large dull eyes. Her imitation smile faltered as she adjusted the mike stand. "I'd like to sing a song for you called 'Fumblin' with the Blues.' "

Her voice was rough, throaty, as she did the Tom Waits tune in a slow, almost dirge-like tempo. When she finished, I applauded loud and hard. Her set consisted five blues songs and ballads, each more full of pain than the one before. As she thanked the audience and left the stage, I had to wipe the tears from my eyes.

Todd brought her to the table. I stood up and watched as her hands began to tremble, her mouth gaped and her eyes widened in disbelief.

Quickly, I took up her hand and shook it.

"Great set," I said. "Todd probably didn't tell you, but he and I used to play in a band together a couple lifetimes ago. I'm pleased to meet someone who can handle the blues as well as you do."

"I . . . that is . . ." she stammered, eyes looking at everything in the room but me.

"Please. Sit down. Let me buy you a drink. I'd like to get to know the woman who finally snagged Todd Raintree. He was sort of God's-gift-to-women when he was in his prime." I laughed and pulled out a chair for her.

She didn't know what to say, what to do. Clearly, she knew who I was. I believe I had convinced her I did not recognize her, though.

"Uh . . . Todd tells me you're a famous writer. What do you write?"

"Words. The test of a successful writer these days isn't so much what words he writes, but how many. My agent gets grey hairs when I turn in anything less than five hundred pages."

She laughed, and for a fleeting moment, I saw something of the old Michelle in her. Todd sat with us, watching her like a mother watches a sick child who might overexert and collapse.

We chatted about insignificant things—nothing that would call up old memories, nothing that would shatter Michelle's fragile faith that her charade was a success.

After a time, she rose to do another set with the band.

"Thank you," Todd said when she had gone. "It worries me that she wants so desperately to be some other person, but she seems to get a little more confidence, get a little better each day."

"Is she seeing a doctor?"

"She won't. I know she should, but she won't."

"She must be thirty pounds thinner than I remember her. If she won't see a psychiatrist, would she at least see someone to make sure she's not anemic?"

"It's the pills. She still alternates uppers and downers depending on what she needs to make it through, but she's off the hard stuff. I'm gradually replacing the speed with sugar pills. Eventually she'll be off all of it. It's just a matter of time."

"You're playing a dangerous game, Todd, with her life. Or what's left of it. She may not have the time. I'm no doctor, but she looks bad. She looks very sick."

"It'll be okay. It'll take time. You can't know what it's like to want something so bad you'll do anything in the world to get there. Those bastards kept telling her fame and fortune was just around the corner, telling her the sex and drugs were just little unpleasantries on the way. She hit the drugs hard when some part of her realized

294

she'd never get any of it, that she'd sold out every ounce of her decency for hollow promises. You can't know what that's like."

"Obsession," I mumbled, "can lead us to just about anything."

"What?"

"Nothing. You're right, I'm sure you're right. Just watch her closely, Todd. The day may come when you have to force her to see a doctor . . . I've got to go."

"Thanks again for what you did, Steve. Come back tomorrow . . . anytime. The drinks and eats are always on the house for you."

I was up early the next morning.

Fortified with eggs and bacon Laurel had thoughtfully stocked in my refrigerator, I was putting on the tan cord sport coat, new jeans and Addidas I had bought the day I shopped for Stephanie, when the doorbell rang.

I recognized Mitzie Campbell immediately. Her hair was shorter, an expensive beauty shop shade of champagne blonde, her clothes richly tailored, her carriage elegant. Her face was the same—less baby fat with the beginnings of hard lines around her mouth, but fundamentally unchanged from when last I'd seen her. Only her eyes were different. Gone was the innocent wide-eyed look of the ingenue, replaced by sharp calculating eyes of a woman who has seen much, suspected more.

"Am I too early to get a coffee? Or too late."

"Mitzie. Come in."

We embraced. She touched her cheek to mine and made a kissing noise with her lips. It was a prefunctory greeting, totally without warmth or emotion. She sailed past me into the room, taking it all in.

"Nice to see some things never change, Steven. The house is just as I remembered it."

"No one's been in it for twenty years, Mitzie. Have a seat. I'll get your coffee."

I brought the coffee to her, and she set it on the table

before her, as if she had no intention of drinking it, the request for it just having been something to say to get in the door, get a conversation started.

I sat opposite her in my father's chair.

"Well, well, well. Steven, time has been a friend to you. So distinguished looking. And quite a success, I hear. Still single, too."

"The last part is true, at least," I said sipping my coffee. "What have you been up to, Mitzie?"

"You haven't heard? My God, if you've been in town more than five minutes, I would have thought someone would have brought you up to date on my life's history."

"Can't say anyone has." I smiled. I wondered why the hell she had come.

"I'm quite the talk of the town, you see. I just finalized my seventh divorce. You know how Greenriver feels about divorced women. Why, I simply must be a Jezebel." Her laugh was hollow and unpleasant. "If not that, at least a fortune hunter."

"To be blunt, you look as though you found a bit of fortune here and there."

"True, too true. All my dear ex-husbands were well to do. 'Were' is the telling verb in that sentence, Steven, I had a very good divorce lawyer."

An awkward silence followed, during which I nervously sipped coffee and Mitzie looked me over unabashedly.

"Uh . . . may I ask why you wanted to see me, Mitzie?"

"Well, I dropped by Todd's little establishment about midnight last night for a nightcap, and he told me you were in town. To be honest, I wanted to see if you were as good-looking as I remembered. I'm happy to report you are, dear."

"So now that your curiosity is satisfied . . . ?"

"Why, I thought perhaps we could exchange financial statements to see if there was any point in our getting seriously involved with each other."

I nearly spat coffee at her.

"Mitzie . . . I . . . I'm not looking for a relationship . . ."

"Oh, dear . . . have I made a fool of myself?"

"Not really. At least we have it out of the way without any messiness."

"True, too true." She must have upgraded her diction from watching old British movies on the late show. "So. Shall I simply go, or can we chat?" Or old Bette Davis movies.

"Do you see any of the old gang? Besides Todd, I mean."

"And Michelle?"

"I didn't think . . ."

"Oh, dear. Has Todd snowed you with that long dreary story about Michelle being some stranger named Gina? God! How long will he play that silly game?"

"He believes it will help Michelle . . ."

"Help her what? My God, the woman's just a burnt-out whore. Everybody in town knows it. Why, my ex-husband number two even had a collection of her quaint little films . . . ever seen one?"

"You're not being very charitable . . ."

"Are you forgetting how she treated all of us before going out on her own to seek fame and fortune? You of all people should remember. God! I still have nightmares about your little temper trantrums in that sleazy Detroit bar. Michelle always played her little games. They simply got out of hand, that's all. They backfired on her, and I say she only got what she went after. Play with fire . . . burny, burny."

"Still, if the tables were reversed . . ."

"Not a chance. I never wanted fame. Just fortune. So far as that goes, the big difference between Michelle and little Mitzie is she let the system use her and *I* use the system. I succeeded; she failed. Her sexcapades are on film, while mine led to lucrative marriages."

"Is that what makes her a whore, then? Her failure to achieve what you did?"

"Remember Phillip Parkhurst, now Greenriver's illustrious mayor? If he taught me one thing, it was that the end does justify the means."

"So if Michelle would have become rich and famous from the . . . films . . . it would have been okay?"

"Of course. Then she could have bought them all up and destroyed them. It happens all the time in Hollywood."

"I think I liked you better when you were a dippy cheerleader." I lit a cigarette. Mitzie seemed unruffled by my denunciation of her attitude toward Michelle.

"Well, you should look up Debbie and Paulie Gibbs, if it's middle-class charming that you're looking for. I swear, they are the toast of Greenriver society, perfect in every way."

"That would be refreshing. I'm tired of hearing about screwed-up, wasted lives."

"Surely you don't include me in that evaluation. Why, I swear, I'm perfectly happy. Ecstatic."

"Do you ever see Geoffie Prang and Kamii?"

"I'm sure you mean Rashim Mohammad Abdul and his oriental courtesan?"

"I beg your pardon?"

"Little Geoffie Prang, Greenriver's unhip Negro, went to U. of M. for two years, straight A's, then under Miss Kamii's guidance went from oriental philosophy and African lore right into acid, speed, cocaine, et cetera, et cetera. He dropped out, hard, and they both went back to the land north of town. They did take a side trip first to Berkeley, got involved in somebody's liberation army or something, ran into Deanna Frankwiler, who had gone native long before, getting degrees in anarchy and psychedelics, and invited her home to Michigan with them. Deanna was ready, I guess, because she had spent a year in a Turkish prison when she tried to bring a whole Gucci shoulder bag back to America filled with hashish.

"The few times I've seen them, their inner peace was too damned loud for me. Real freaks. God knows what they do for money or food. They probably have inner connections with whoever's really in charge and are provided manna daily."

"I can't believe it . . . Deanna?"

"Oh, believe it. Drug City. Her father, I swear, her father had a heart attack when he saw Deanna in her sackcloth and beads. What a sight! Mousy little Deanna Frankwiler! Sounds like the old crowd went to hell in a handbasket, huh?"

"Hmmm. By your analysis, you're a survivor."

"Damned right. And you, too, apparently."

"Not really, but that's too long a story."

She adjusted her cape-like coat about her shoulders.

"Well, I guess the real fun is next Saturday night when we all get together at the reunion, right? At least I've forewarned you on some counts. Too bad you can't see your way clear to a little hanky-panky with little Mitzie. See you Saturday." She stood abruptly and made her way across the room.

"Let me see you out."

Mitzie had barely left the drive in her chocolate Mercedes when the phone rang.

It was Laurel, her whispering voice sounding choked.

"Listen, Steve, I don't know if I should tell you or not . . . Jesus, this is too weird!"

"Laurel, what . . ."

"A friend of Freddie's is kind of a burn-out, see, so he does deliveries for people in town 'cause all he owns in the world is this old beat-to-shit Chevy pick-up."

"Laurel, I don't understand . . ."

"So he got this steady gig haulin' groceries for Von Weimer's groceries. Now, Von Weimer cut out deliveries back in the '50's but these people pay double to have their food trucked to them."

"Laurel, you aren't making any sense . . ."

"So Freddie's friend has been takin' groceries out to the old castle of a house on Mill Road, y'know the one, that gangster built in the '20's. When this guy gets liquored with my Freddie, he'd rave about this beautiful rich woman out at the house that would pay him when he delivered. Freddie figured this guy was bull-shittin', because, like I say, he's a burn-out. And that could even explain last night, if it wasn't for . . ."

"Laurel, stop it! I . . ."

"Last night he came runnin' in, see, eyes buggin', breathin' like a bagpipe, screamin' about monsters, monsters. Steve, he just came back from that house on Mill Road, but instead of the beautiful woman, he said he saw a monster."

"Laurel!"

"Like I say, I'd a thought he was trippin' but he told me the name of the woman. Steve, her last name is St. Charles, and he said she had hair like the clouds . . . the clouds, Steve."

"Jesus," I breathed.

"Steve . . . ?" Laurel said at the other end of the line, but I had hung up.

This was it. Fate. This was why I was back in Greenriver. I had to do it this time, I had to. But as I saw myself in the hall mirror, I saw an aging man whose weight lifting and construction work-built body was sagging—sagging too much to be the avenging Conan.

But I had to go and see for myself.

Cat.

I drove the car slowly up and down that stretch of Mill Road past the ludicrous stone castle of a house a half dozen times without stopping. Finally, I gave in to the stabs of nervous pain in my stomach, and headed back to town.

Not defeated, just scared close to death.

There was nothing special about Wednesday. Just another lovely early autumn day in Michigan. It was the day after my thirty-eighth birthday. There was no eclipse of the sun or moon, no special conjunction of stars, nothing in trine—absolutely nothing about the day to specifically recommend it for the battle and defeat of Evil on earth. There was nothing special about me, either.

I had no talisman, no chant, no magical sword when I pulled the Oldsmobile into the drive at the stone castle-like house. I had no idea what powers he possessed or from whence they came. I didn't know if he was a demon from some Judaeo-Christian Hell, an efreet or djinn, a genetic freak of an unknown law of cellular development, or an illusion of my mind. He could have been any or all of these things. I was in no mood to ponder such philosophical questions as being, existence, cause and effect. Gut level—he had colored my life with black fear, terror, pain and suffering for something over twenty-seven years. He had to die.

The door was not locked. I stepped inside. Too easy.

It was dim inside, windows all shuttered, no lights on. The room was large with high ceilings, decorated with furniture from an earlier, more genteel age that dictated brocades and carved wood.

There was an open stairway at the back of the room, flanked by a rounded archway to other parts of the house.

On the stairway, halfway down, stood the object of my quest. Catherine Charlene St. Charles stood there, not the child, not the teenaged girl my mind held in cherished memory, but a mature woman of breathtaking beauty.

The hair, pure white as virgin snow, swirled about her head, over her shoulders, down her back. There were great clouds of it framing that lovely face. The eyes in that face were still child-like, large, China-blue. The lips were baby-pink and full, but there was no sense of the child, no fresh innocence in the countenance. There was pain behind those lovely full lips; there was terror behind those beautiful blue eyes.

"You should not have come." Her voice was soft, barely audible, without inflection.

"I had to. You know that." I wanted to run to her, but I was rooted where I stood.

"Yes. I know. It's all out of my hands now. I cannot stop you. I cannot stop him. What happens from here on was determined long ago."

The gap, the expanse of oak floor between us, was no more than fifteen yards, but it could have been miles. I took one faltering step toward her, then he appeared in the archway, filling it. A flowing oriental black silk robe concealed his body.

"Steven . . ." the voice from Hell rasped, "what a surprise. Isn't it, dear Catherine? Have you made our guest welcome?"

"I . . ." Her expression did not change, but her hands fluttered almost imperceptibly at her sides. Her breasts swelled with her rapid breathing beneath the black whisper of her tailored silk blouse.

"You must excuse dear Catherine, Steven. She has little contact with society these days . . . for the past several years, actually, but that's the way she wants it . . . isn't it, Catherine?'"

"Yes," she whispered. Her eyes sought to look anywhere but at my face.

"But we must welcome old friends, mustn't we? What can I have Catherine get for you? What may I have her do for you . . . within the boundaries of polite society, of course." The hideous laughter rumbled from deep within him.

"Who are you?" I blurted. "What are you? Why . . ."

"One question at a time, Steven. Who am I? I am my father's son . . . my sister's brother. You know me. What am I?" The enormous hands spread in a questioning gesture. "There is no answer for that one. What are you? You might as well ask the chair, the fireplace. What is matter that, given a chance arrangement of atoms and molecules might not just as easily be some other thing? A slight glitch in DNA, and dear Catherine might have been you, been me. It's all perception. Rather metaphysical. And your final question?" He took a step toward me. Cat's hands fluttered again; a nerve twitched the corners of her mouth into an imitation smile, then made it disappear.

"Why . . . why do you haunt me? Why is Cat in your thrall . . . what power . . ."

"There you go again, Steven, with those multiple questions. I don't haunt you. My dear sister does. And it's because you refuse to relinquish the childish memory of your crude preadolescent coupling with her, because you refused to leave her alone, leave her to her own kind, that I was forced to take action against you." He stepped a yard or two closer to me. Cat moved down one stair.

"You murdered my father, my mother."

"Your father, yes. Your mother, poor deranged creature . . . I saw that more as a mercy killing. Surely you can see that in both cases, I did you a favor. I gave you your freedom from parental domination at the tender age of sixteen."

"You . . . freedom? You call the life I've lived free? God! I've been tortured by dreams, visions, thoughts of you. I've felt the pain of your existence since I was eleven years old!"

"Twenty . . . twenty-seven years? A wink of an eye—less in cosmic time. The popular view of Hell speaks of suffering for an eternity."

"You should know about that. If you're not a creature sent straight from Hell, then one has never existed."

"Careful how offensive you become, Steven. You will upset my dear Catherine."

"She's not yours," I screamed, blood boiling at my temples.

"Oh, but she is, she is. Tell him, Catherine. She is of my flesh, of my blood."

She didn't move, nod, gesture. He came toward me a bit more.

I was enraged, frightened—curious. Could it be that the thing which drew me back, kept me from forgetting, going on with my life was curiousity alone?

"Possibly," he said. I stared at him a long moment before I realized he was answering my unspoken question.

"Quite possibly it was your innate curiosity, Steven," he continued. "You are, after all, a man of the world, a questing soul, a man of knowledge, letters.

"I, too, have spent the years in pursuit of knowledge. Oh, I haven't a college degree like yours. I could not attend public schools. Dear Catherine has been my teacher."

I looked up at her in time to see the shudder twitch her shoulders and breasts.

"Once I had the rudiments of learning from her, I was voracious." He laughed, making the blood-chilling sound of metal chunking across concrete. "Poor choice of words; I hate puns. But you see, Steven, I too am haunted, troubled. We are kindred spirits, you and I, oh yes! You cannot rest until you know the who, what and why of me, and, oddly enough, neither can I. My existence is as much a mystery to me as it is to you." His moony eyes in that pasty unreal pie of a face followed my longing stare at Cat—beautiful, trembling Cat.

"Oh, yes. You and I, Steven, share many things, including that carnal lust for dear Catherine."

"Enough." Her voice was flat and quiet, but the timbre of outrage vibrated in it, just below audible level, more sensed than heard. "That's more than enough. Steven, you must go. I must ask it, though I know you will not. There is nothing for you here."

"There is. You, Cat. Let me take you . . ."

" . . . away from all this?" She moved down the stairs, a dancer performing restrained drama in a supernatural ballet. "It's far too late, Steven. Keep the memory of me as you fantasize me, but go before the truth shatters your fantasies . . . and you. Better that I am more idealized goddess in your mind than what I really am." She looked so small, there at the foot of the stairs, a yard or two behind and to one side of his gangling, broad-shouldered mass.

"It's not that simple, Cat. It never was."

"No, dear Catherine, he's right. Not that simple." He moved a few feet closer to me. "You've said it before. Destiny. We three have some unknown destiny preordained by some mad deity. We can but play out our parts, as the script demands. Steven, the crusading knight of justice and right; you, as he sees you, the radiant love princess, captive possession of me—the evil demon, personification of all things vile and despicable in the cosmos."

"At least the last part is accurate," I said. "What's it to be, then? Silver bullets? A stake through your heart? Wolfbane? Garlic flowers? A piercing ray of morning sun? The destruction of your resting place? Some ancient Babylonian incantation? Caldean, Sumerian, Egyptian . . . what? What must I do to end your putrid existence?"

"Try them all," he said, still advancing on me, a step at a time. "Dear Catherine has over the years. Haven't you, Catherine? Tell him."

"It's true," she said, the years of misery and dashed hopes dripping from her voice. "Nothing works. He simply grows stronger . . . older. Don't you see how pointless all this is, Steven? You may try to kill him, but in the end, only you will die, and he will still possess me, control me, use me. I was lost to you, the world, years ago. Years and years ago."

"Maybe you're right," I said. In my mind I was reciting Shakespearean sonnets, my social security number, old half-remembered license plate numbers from cars I had owned. If he could read my mind, I had to throw him totally off guard. I made a slow shuffling turn, as if to go out the door, and he came closer. I put my hand on the door jamb as though feeling faint, pausing to still the spinning world, continuing to run nonsense combinations of trivia through my mind. He moved closer still. Out of the corner of my eye, I saw his spatulate fingers caress the edge of the massive wooden door.

I braced my hands against the jamb, and with one lightning move, galvanized all my body's strength and energy into one flying, double-footed kick. I caught him square in the barrel of his chest, and he went down.

I landed, as Master Che had taught me, spun, kicked out at the surprised goggled-eyed pie face and connected. The face gave, seemed to ooze, liquid under my foot. I gathered myself, leaped into the air, and came down, a crushing blow as I landed flat footed on his chest. Bones snapped, splintered and gave.

I stepped back, breathing as Master Che had taught, trying to come down from the fevered pitch of the attack.

He was still. Arms crucified against the oaken floor,

legs twisted unnaturally, as though the pelvis had been shattered. His chest was a ruin—flattened and spread too wide at the sides. The face, once a disgusting pantomime of human features, was unrecognizable, more like a rotted squash, caved in upon its own putrescence. The robe fell open. Naked obscenity lay beneath.

I relaxed my stance. I turned to Cat. She stood, hands covering her lovely face, shaking her head.

"It's over Cat. So easy. All these years, and it was so easy." I took her in my arms. God! How wonderful that felt! There is no description for the joy and passion that electrified my body, my mind. I pulled her hands down and kissed her open, willing mouth. Her tears wet my cheeks.

"No," she broke away. "No, it's never over."

"But it is, it is. I killed him. I. Killed him." I took her again into my embrace. Her flesh was warm, yielding. Her mouth drank the love from my mouth, gave it back transformed into hot lustful passion, all the time murmuring, "No. . . no . . . no . . ." plaintively, the word a sob, a moan, meaningless to me.

Her scream rang in my ear as taloned spatulate fingers tore at me and flung her away. I was spun around, a toy, a weightless doll to face a resurrected, whole, unmasked Abomination, and as he held me still, he laughed, laughed and . . . changed.

The pie face elongated into something between a tusk-snouted boar and a slit-eyed, forked-tongue-flicking cobra. The chest swelled to massive proportions making the laughter rumble within. The arms bulged with powerful musculature. Two new arms were born under the originals and grew and matured, duplicating the others, reaching out to crush other parts of my body. Two more followed, then two more, until the spidery compliment all held me, crushed me, sought to hurt me in new and exotic ways.

One of the massive hands loosed its grip on me and forced its way, a burrowing thing, into my mouth, down my throat. I felt its alien intrusion into my body, forcing, stretching the passage, raping, violating, ruining.

A pain like no other in the universe stabbed my chest. I whimpered and blood gushed from my nose. My eyes felt as if they would shoot out of my skull. The arm came up, came back up, thank God! It was withdrawing. It came all the way out, and a voice not mine but from my throat chanted a mantra of pain and joy. Then I saw. In the hand, in that awful, bloody alien hand, beat a heart—my heart, ripped from my chest, yet beating!

Another of the hands relinquished me, grabbed out, stretching, a rubber telescoping thing, reached out until it pulled Cat up from the floor where she lay sobbing. The arm brought her up beside us.

I raved on, bugged eyes on him, the vital organ that was mine in his hand.

"Eat, Sister, feed," the rumbling voice taunted.

Beaten, suppliant, willing to do anything to speed the end, she took my heart from him, took the beating thing like a wounded bird into her trembling hands, and with a moan of repulsion, ate.

With each tearing, rending bite she took, my mind reeled in crescendoing pain. I howled, banshee howl, eyes bugged, prisoner in his tentacle arms, her sobs mournful, horrified counterpoint to my howling.

She finished eating, blood dripping from her fingers, smeared over her white cheeks, tinting the tips of her snowy hair. Her eyes pleaded for forgiveness, but in my terror, my pain, she was as he was—Abomination, his twin.

"Now see, knight errant, your error," he chided, laughing. "Sister Catherine is as much the demon of your dreams as me. More so—you lusted after her. Now I have had her eat the heart she had stolen. All gone," he said, as if playing pat-a-cake with a child. With a swirl of his fluid body, a simultaneous shove and release of those many arms, I flew—a bird, flying through the open portal out into the day. The hot sun, burned into the emptiness of my body—a husk, empty, without a soul.

I lay by the car, my rent-a-car Oldsmobile. I crawled to it, feeling the hollow rattle of my breath in my chest. My lungs expanded into the cavity left by my recent cardio-ectomy. I felt the blood, idle in my vessels, settling like lividity in a corpse, to my lowest point.

I stretched up, opened the car door, crawled in, and looked back over my shoulder to see them framed in the doorway—Horror's American Gothic.

His white cobra-hooded, boar-snouted face was turned to the weeping, wailing Cat, serpentine tongue laving her bloody face—my blood—as his many hands roamed, fondled, groped and punished her tormented squirming body.

The car started. It was only when I heard the engine roar to life I realized I was still howling. I bent the rear view mirror to my face and saw not my face but a mask of pure horror, blood dripping from lips. Part of me was calm—the calm of deep shock. It wanted me to act normally, but the part of me in ascendancy was a mad raving lunatic whose heart had been ripped out.

I slammed the car in gear, and threw stones and gravel with the front-wheel drive. My body was tossed about, side to side, as the car swerved down the dirt road. My two selves, the calm sane one and the raving howling mad one, fought each other for the steering wheel. The mad one triumphed and the car catapulted a ditch, wove down a hill between sparse birches and splashed into a syrupy bog. The door sprang open and I flew out into the water. The moccasin showed me its white mouth, its slit-pupiled unblinking eye, and slid away through the water.

Willow trees mourned overhead, making the thick swampy water uncommonly cool—cold, almost—cold enough to shock me back into one being. It was the sane, calm being that took dominance as I dragged myself up out of the slimy water, the green algae and tiny snails clinging to my clothes, the rancid raw sewage smell putrid in my nostrils.

I felt for a pulse at my wrist. Did I feel one? There? A dim thump? Didn't my chest bump a bit with the beat of an intact human heart?

I remembered what Delilah had said: he could make you feel, make you see what he wanted. That was it, then. All hallucination. Just a defense. Maybe his only defense. If I went back, armed with a gun, perhaps he would die, as any human would.

Yes. I was sure of it. All hallucination. A gun would kill him. But why, then, did I keep trying to find my pulse, my heartbeat, as I trudged up the hill, down the dirt road, away from the house and toward town?

Five miles is a long walk in the Michigan sun, even in early September. Especially when the odor of swamp permeates the clothing of the walker.

It was late in the evening when I reached the outskirts of Greenriver. I was near Laurel and Freddie's house, but tired as I was, I could not picture myself knocking at their door, reeking of bog water, looking like death, muttering for them to find my pulse because a monster from my childhood may have ripped my heart out through my esophagus.

No. I dragged myself on, by-passing the town square, keeping to the side streets, on, ever on to my family's house.

I burned the clothes in the old coal furnace, surprised to find stains of dried swamp mud on my shirt that looked disturbingly like blood. I walked naked from the coal blackness of the furnace in the basement, up to the second floor bathroom, and took a shower so hot my skin was lobster red when I got out.

I lay on my old bed, thinking old thoughts, reliving old nightmares until long after the moon rose, casting cold silver about the room. I still could not be sure I felt a pulse or a heartbeat, but I knew further speculation in that direction only would bring utter madness. Reality? Gone, gone again.

I allowed myself to sleep, my last thoughts before oblivion centered on how I might obtain a gun before the weekend. A gun—perhaps a reality even Nicholas could understand.

17

It was noon on Thursday before I awoke. I got into some new clothes, snipping off tags and extricating pins for what seemed endless minutes, then walked downtown. I walked straight into Todd Raintree's bar about fifteen minutes past noon.

Thankfully, neither Todd nor Gina, nee Michelle, were there. I didn't think I could stand any more of Todd's hangdog reminiscing, or Michelle's twisted "What's My Line Mystery Guest" identification games.

Who was there was the sulky brunette. She tended bar for a handful of us early-drinking misfits. After she brought my frosty Heineken, she hung close, wiping down the same spotless part of the bar ceaselessly.

"That's you, isn't it?"

"Beg pardon?" Working where Michelle Gina Bailey Raintree hung out, she probably had reason to ask such questions of just about anybody.

"In the pictures. Here, look. That's you playing guitar, isn't it?"

I looked where she pointed, and behind the bar saw framed pictures of my first band, the one with just Geoffie, Paulie, Todd and me when we were sweet sixteen and innocent as puppies.

"God, yes. In another lifetime. That was back before there was hair. Literally. Pre-Beatles."

I almost expected her to ask what's a Beatle, but thanks once again to media hype, the Beatles were well-known even to the under twenty crowd who were twinkles in somebody's eye when John growled out "Twist and Shout."

"Todd says you were better'n anybody. Even guys today like Eddie Van Halen and Stevie Ray Vaughan."

"Todd has a flair for the stretched superlative. How 'bout another beer?"

"Sure. You still play?"

"No. I haven't even looked fondly at a guitar since the sixties. I had a very bad experience with one. Swore off them."

"That's too bad. Todd seemed to think since you guys were all in town together, you could like, you know, play."

"Not a chance. No fools like old fools, and all that. I prefer dignity to depression."

While I waited for my second beer, I absent-mindedly felt for my pulse.

"What's your name?" I asked her, as she set the beer bottle on a new napkin.

"Rhonda. My friends call me Ronni." Her sulky little pout became a sly smile. "You can, you know, call me Ronni."

"Thanks. You can call me Mr. Dalton."

Her face fell.

"Just kidding. Call me Steve."

She brightened.

"So, Ronni, do you believe in monsters?"

"Like, what?"

"You know . . . ghosties, beasties, things that go bump in the night. Things that can rip your heart out and feed it to the one you love?"

"Are you okay, Steve?"

"I guess so. I just wondered, briefly, if all Greenriver was haunted or if it was only me . . . always only me." I drank down the beer, shunning the mug, and ordered a third.

By suppertime, I was well potted, like a geranium at an old lady's convention, and Ronni was giving me a wide berth. Good. I didn't need a youngster coming on to me.

My problem now was that Todd had come in to supervise the service of the Thursday night dinner crowd. In Greenriver, it was suppertime. Only in restaurants and high society in the Midwest is it dinner-time. Midwesterners putting on airs may invite you to dinner, but afterwards in the parlor, when things are cozy, will ask how you enjoyed your supper.

Todd came up, asked me what I'd like for dinner. I knew he meant supper. He was putting on airs. He had to. He was a restauranteur.

"It's on the house," he said, clapping my slouched shoulders with a beefy paw.

"You don't have to . . ."

"I know I don't have to, but as crocked as you are, I can't let you go, so I may as well feed you, eh?"

"I really didn't want to do anything to ruin this buzz. I've been working at it since noon."

"So Ronni tells me. Hey, I think you scared her. Said you were babbling about ghosts and monsters and stuff."

"Didn't mean to spook the help, Todd, pardon the pun."

"She's more than just help, Steve, but that's a long story. So . . . what'll it be for su . . . dinner?"

"Steak. Medium bloody. Baked potato with at least two pounds of sour cream. Salad, French dressing. Oh, and more beer."

"How about moving to a table?"

"Do you have any that will hide me from your other, more respectable patrons?"

"It's not like that, Steve. I don't care if you strip buck naked and dance on the tables. You're my friend."

"And you're my friend," I said as he helped me off the barstool. "Do you have a gun, friend?"

"What?"

"A gun. Do you have a gun? Dirty Harry . . . Clint Eastwood . . . Miami Vice . . . bang-bang, you're dead?"

"No . . . why do you ask?"

I slumped into the captain's chair he pulled out for me at a table near the rear of the bar.

"Usual reason. I need to kill something."

"Listen, Steve, you're pretty high. Let me get your food working. We'll talk more later."

It was funny to see Todd so upset. He was like the mother hen, worried about an erring chick.

I couldn't get another beer to save my soul until Todd brought the food. He kept glancing toward the door as I ate. Then suddenly he got up and rushed to the front to greet someone.

The next thing I knew, a well-to-do-looking couple were standing over me as I fought to keep the sour cream from running out of my baked potato.

"Welcome back to Greenriver, Steve." The voice was familiar, too deeply pitched for my memory to recognize immediately, but none the less familiar.

My bleary eyes struggled in the bar's darkness, but eventually I focused in on an older, plumper, slightly bald Paulie Gibbs. The lovely petite redhaired woman in designer glasses beside him had to be Debbie Frankwiler . . . Mrs. Gibbs.

"Sit down, sit down. Fill thy flowing bowl. Landlord!" I shouted at Todd. "Mead for these weary wayfarers from my darkling past!"

"You're causing quite a stir," Paulie said as he pulled out a chair for Debbie, then sat opposite me. "You have Todd very upset . . . asking about guns and the like."

"Just the ramblings of my fevered brain, old son. You used to call everybody that, you cracker. Old son. Well, how 'bout it, old son, you have a gun? That's a paraphrase from a Longfellow poem, I believe." I laughed, too loudly.

Debbie smiled pity at me. Paulie looked as if he'd rather be in a sideshow biting heads off live chickens. Anything would be preferable to sitting with a ranting drunk in his hometown bar.

"I've read some of your books, Steven." Debbie smiled, her hands smoothing Todd's tablecloth. "Very deep, very intellectual. Some of your thoughts, attitudes . . . unconventional, but stirring."

"That's me, Debbie, old daughter. Unconventionally stirring." I turned to Paulie, reaching across Debbie's smoothed linen to grab his arm. "Did you ever call females 'old daughter'? Or is it part of the Southern Gothic mystique that women are less important than

313

horses, thereby being undeserving of quaint colloquial appellations?"

"Don't be rude to Paulie, Steven," Debbie chided gently. "He's spent twice as many years in Michigan as he did in Georgia. He's the same as you or I. Same mores, same . . ."

I transferred my grip on Paulie's sport-coated arm to Debbie's smooth naked one. My senses told me immediately I prefered Debbie's flesh to wool blend.

"Ah, but there you are incorrect, my Titian-haired beauty. For I am unlike any other human being. I live, I breathe, I walk, I talk, yet I have within this chest no heart. No ugly bloody little muscle thudding sway, ticking seconds like a sweep hand on a Timex. Here, feel for yourself."

I thrust her hand against my chest and held it there. Large nervous eyes darted behind her pretty glasses. They looked pleadingly at Paulie. He looked away. I thought perhaps he would strike me.

"You see? Nothing. No beating beast within this breast. Nothing, nada, zip, zero."

"Whatever you say, Steven. May I have my hand back?"

"Ah, of course you are humoring me. And no, you may not have your hand back. I cherish the warmth of its flesh, would welcome it on my chilling brow. I die, you see, am dying. It's only a matter of time."

"We're all dying, Steven," she said softly, "from the day we are born. It's all downhill."

I laughed and let her hand go. She hid it gratefully in her lap.

Todd came over with Rhonda and helped her clear away my dishes.

"So. How are we getting on?"

"Peachy," I told him. The look both Debbie and Paulie shot Todd did not go unnoticed, even in my alcohol-dulled state. I felt sorry for them. But then, they felt sorry for me. It was a Mexican stand-off in the pity department.

"It must be great, you know," Rhonda enthused,

"you guys from the old band days back together again."

"We still lack the bass player extraordinaire," I said.

Paulie laughed. "That's still the funniest anecdote about those band years . . . our black bass player who didn't have any rhythm."

"A cheap racist shot," I said severely, then melting into giggles myself, the exertion of laughing clearing my head a bit. "I had to show him every fingering, count out the syncopation. Shit, I had to teach him soul!"

We all laughed, even Rhonda, who didn't seen to get the joke.

Paulie was the first to sober. "Too bad he went so weird."

"How bad can it be? A little grass? Hell, lots of people do a little grass . . ."

"No, Steven." Debbie shook her pretty red hair a bit. "It's like 1969 never ended for Deanna, Geoffie and Kamii. They live in a hovel on cushions and pillows instead of furniture, and eat peyote and acid sugar cubes instead of food."

"Well," I said sourly, "we all deal with reality in the best way we can."

"John Lennon said whatever gets you through the night is all right." Todd lowered his hulking frame into a captain's chair dragged over from another table.

"Is that why you own a bar?" Rhonda taunted playfully. "To help people through the night?"

Todd took a smack at her nicely-rounded ass with one of his broad paws, but she danced away, laughing.

"You had better watch your mouth, girl," he called after her, "or somebody else will be payin' your bills and buyin' those designer jeans for your smart ass, you . . ." He stopped suddenly, and the grin vanished from his face quicker than a rabbit at a magician's convention. He looked at me with something like fear in his eyes, glanced at Debbie and Paulie, then frowning, lowered his gaze to his shoes.

"Wait a minute," I said. I could feel the tension like negative ions in the air. "There's something going on here that I'm not supposed to know about. Well, listen

. . . with the day I've had, I'm in no mood for mind games."

"Rhonda lives with Todd and Mich . . . er, Gina," Debbie said. "That's all."

Todd shook his head, still staring at his shoes. "No, that's not all. Rhonda is her daughter."

My mind sobered a bit as the neurons shot electricity around so my brain could comprehend the import of Todd's words.

"You mean, Michelle has an eighteen-year-old daughter?"

"Gina . . ." Debbie interjected, almost frantic to sustain Michelle's alias.

"It's okay, Deb. I already told him about Michelle. And Rhonda's nineteen, Steven. She was born in March of 1966."

"No, wait," I said, rubbing my forehead. "If I remember correctly, that would mean Michelle was pregnant in June of '65 . . . when we did the gig at Levon's."

"That's right, Steven." Todd nodded, his shoes still his main visual interest.

"Shut up, now, Todd," Paulie said. His voice was soft, not threatening, just issuing a warning that Todd should have remembered himself.

"Why shouldn't he know?" When Todd looked up, I could see tears pooling in his eyes.

"What good will be served?" Debbie asked, touching his sleeve.

"Jesus! Quit talking about me like I'm not here," I yelled. Several other patrons looked to our table, frowned, looked away. "Todd, if you are my friend, let me in on this little secret. I can take it. Hell, I can't have a heart attack."

Todd looked at me hard. One of the tears escaped to roll down his cheek. He leaned on me, clapped a hand on my shoulder, and another tear streamed.

"I love you, Steven. I've always loved you like a brother." He looked over at Paulie and Debbie, then back at me. "I've always felt like all you guys were a second family. And I don't know why, but I've always felt sort of responsible, you know, if any one of you needed help."

His hand was a dead weight on my shoulder. I couldn't imagine what he was getting at.

"I always looked up to you, Steven. I would've done anything for you. That time you dad died . . . when your mom passed away . . . I wanted to help, I wanted to do something, but your cousin was there, then Jim Harper, and . . . well, I didn't know how to express myself."

"You still don't." I smiled, and patted his hand.

His face tried to smile, couldn't.

"When Michelle came back, don't you see, it was more out of a sense of loyalty to you than her that I married her."

"Now wait a minute . . ." I started to pull away from him, but he locked me in place with the other heavy arm.

"No . . . not that . . . I always cared a great deal for Michelle. When she came back, I would have done anything to help her, but I probably wouldn't have married her if it hadn't been for Rhonda."

"I still don't . . . oh," I said, smiling. "Forgive me. I'm still a bit groggy from the grog. But a brick doesn't have to fall on my head. Rhonda's your daughter."

He stared me squarely in the eyes. "No, Rhonda's your daughter."

"What?" The other patrons eyed us again. I could barely stay in my seat. Only Todd's restraining arms kept me sitting down.

"That's not possible!" I protested.

"It's not only possible, Steve ol' son," Paulie said quietly, "it's honest-to-God positive."

"But Todd said . . ." I protested. Todd knew what I meant and shook his head.

"All that stuff . . . what Michelle did . . . didn't start until well after Rhonda was born. She refused an abortion because she knew whose baby she was carrying."

317

"But when . . ."

"It was that night after our first performance at Levon's," Debbie said. "That night Paulie and I first got together. Remember? It was you and Michelle and Mitzie in the bedroom . . ."

"Okay, okay. You don't have to paint me a picture. So I was supposedly the last one . . ."

" . . . the only one, man," Todd said. "She was never with anyone else before you or after you until after Rhonda was born."

"Oh, sweet Jesus, Joseph and Mary." I buried my head in my arms, slumped over the table. Todd patted my back. Debbie got up, came around the table and rubbed my back, crooning motherly, comforting words in my ear, kissing the top of my head.

I rose up, gently pushing them away. "I'm okay, I'm okay. So. I assume Rhonda doesn't know."

"All Michelle ever told Rhonda was that her father was a great man who wasn't free to get married. Rhonda has no idea in the world who her father is. I've tried to do what I could, in your place, since Michelle came back to Greenriver."

"Todd, I appreciate that, but I guess I can't feel guilty for something I didn't know about. I don't believe Michelle and I could ever have made a go of it, even if I had known. The only thing I might have been able to do is save Michelle from . . . well . . . from all she went through."

"I doubt anybody could have kept her from all that. She was pretty intent on being a singing star," Paulie said.

My eyes found Rhonda across the bar. Yes, I saw it now. Michelle's coloring, fine-boned face and tendency to be heavy-breasted. My height, my brooding manner, my troubled, searching, deep-set eyes. It's a strange feeling to be thirty-eight and suddenly become father to a nineteen-year-old child. But of course, I reflected, nothing had really changed except my awareness of the biological fact a cell from my body had united with a cell from Michelle's body nineteen years previous.

Certainly, nothing had changed for Michelle. Or Rhonda. Rhonda was still fatherless. I could do nothing about that. No one could make up for nineteen lost years. It would be foolish to try.

" . . . didn't tell you to upset you."

I realized Todd was speaking to me.

"I told you because Michelle needs you to know, I think. Something has to be done to help Michelle, like you said. You can be the help she needs."

"What can I do?"

"I've thought about it a lot . . . what you said about a psychiatrist thinking she should confront her problems. Tell her you know."

"But you said . . ."

"I know. But maybe if one of her secrets she guards so closely is revealed as being inconsequential, she will realize all her pretenses are unnecessary."

"I'm not a psychiatrist. I only said . . . listen, if you had any idea what my life has been like . . . God! I'm not the messiah!"

"Nobody thinks you are, ol' son, but we all think Michelle needs help to start livin' again," Paulie said.

"How about professional help? We're screwing with her mind, here. How about people who are trained?"

"No good. She won't see 'em," Todd said.

"Force her! My God, if you're serious . . ."

"Won't work. You have to be the one. We all always looked up to you. You were the leader of both bands. Maybe Michelle will still key into that, and you can snap her out of it."

"Todd . . . Debbie . . . Paulie . . . how can I possibly tell you? Didn't any of you ever suspect I had problems? All those years . . . didn't you?"

They looked at one another, then back at me.

"What do you mean?" Debbie asked. "Your parents' deaths? We all felt for you, but you shut us out. Besides, it's difficult for a teenager to grasp the pain of such a loss unless they themselves have experienced . . ."

"No, no, no! What I lived with all these years makes that type of emotion almost trivial. There was a girl, a beautiful girl of ten who was my friend . . . no . . . my lover. Wait. Perhaps I should tell of her brother. Not the older one, the younger. He was a monster. Todd, you said it yourself, but you couldn't even suspect . . . a real monster. Abomination. There was this minister on TV when I was a child . . . no. This is too confusing. Just today I saw them. They're here, in Greenriver. I killed him. I know karate, you see, I'm trained. Master Che . . . but that was in college. So I killed him, but he came alive. He came alive and ripped out my heart. Tell 'em, Deb, no pulse or heartbeat, right? Then she ate it. She didn't want to, no, but he made her do it. She's mine, she's still mine. He says she . . ." I was frantic to make them understand. I was sweating, trying to sort it out, ignoring their exchanged looks of confused concern. Then the door opened and she came in. Radiant. No other word. Her beauty, the essence of her being, drew me out of my seat and led me stumbling across the room. She reached out and took my hand.

"Take me somewhere private," Cat whispered.

I ignored the calls of my friends, took her arm and led her outside to the crisp September evening air. It was like a dream. My senses were dead to the night. I knew only her presence beside me, and that was world enough.

It was only a few blocks from downtown to my house. The night was a black backdrop, a stage set complete with mock stars and moon.

We didn't speak; we just walked. Leaves did not move on the trees; time was suspended.

It seemed only seconds from our leaving Todd's bar to when I was fumbling with keys at the door of my house.

We entered without exchanging a word. I flicked on a dim light by the doorway.

She wore a lavender sheath of some flimsy silky material that stretched lovingly over the ample curves of her breasts and hips. The cloth was nearly transparent and I could tell she wore nothing beneath it, wore nothing else save high heels and dangling earrings of amethyst.

She sat on the sofa and patted the cushion next to her. She was not smiling; her full lips were parted and her eyes held the fire of need.

I sat next to her, drinking in the Shalimar scent I remembered and the strong musky odor of her femininity.

A hand, trembling with urgency, caressed my neck, slid to the back of my neck, pulled me to her. Breath sweet and hot scorched my face. Our lips met, and her other hand slipped, like an animal seeking shelter, to my groin.

I freed her voluminous breasts from the confines of the dress, rolling strawberry nipples with the palms of my hands. Her dress rode up as her thighs rolled wide, and my fingers found the syrupy heat and entered with ease. Her head lowered, predatory. She sought her prey hungrily.

The urgency mounted, the tension a taut wire, hot with electricity, and I moved between snowy thighs and plunged to her center.

We fell to the carpet, rolling over and over, the heat like the flames of Hell, licking our bodies, urging us on, quickening our movements, speeding our release.

But it was not release, when it came. It was but preamble to more intricate, exotic ecstasies, pleasures unbounded by natural law, space or time.

The moon hung low, peeking voyeuristically at us through the living room drapes some unknown eon of time later. She would not release me but held me deep inside the sticky heat of her. Her moist mouth would not be still, and it worked over my chest and shoulders, sucked the blood to the skin at my throat as if hoping for eruption, covered my mouth, thick tongue always exploring and darting. Little animalistic sounds of pleasure, pain, need and desire came from deep in her throat, and the moon sank lower still toward dawn.

At last, she released me, but her mouth roamed my entire body, searching, still hot with the hunger, the need, the wanting.

"Cat," I whispered, "oh Cat, make it last forever.

Don't ever leave me again."

"I love you, love you." She gulped air to speak, her intensity mounting again. "I will always, always love you, darling!"

I pulled her to me, kissed her fevered cheeks and lips, hot as branding irons, tried to calm her, cool her.

"Cat . . . we must go, must leave now. Go away as far as we need to, to escape. . ."

"No . . . no, no, no!" She was sobbing now, despair mixing with her unflagging lust. "Never far enough. Can't get away."

"But you are free now. That's why . . ."

"No! He can call me back. He can make me do anything, anything he wants. He owns me—body, mind and soul. I am his."

"No! No, God-damn it! Mine! You are mine! You said it, you said it all those years ago. There's some divine plan that created us for each other."

"There is a plan, yes," she said, pulling away, sitting up in the fading slant of moonlight. "But it is not divine. Unless you include dark powers, Evil, in your definition of divinity."

She was standing now, shrugging back into her clinging dress, sliding narrow feet into her heels. I sat on the floor and retrieved my scattered clothing, a piece at a time, and put it on. I sensed she was about to bolt for the door. I wanted to be ready to give chase.

"But if we can't stop him, we must run and keep running until he gives us up." I stood next to her, lit cigarettes for us both.

"He won't. He can't. It's all part of the plan, the game, the little drama we are all scripted into—to play out our minor tragedy in the scheme of things."

"But it's not fair," I despaired.

"I read a quote once," she said blowing smoke into the air where it rolled like thunder clouds in the last of the moonlight. "It said: 'In nature there are no rewards or punishments, only consequences.' I believe that. After all these years with my brother, catering to his every whim, hiding him, providing for him, doing every despicable thing he forced upon me, I can believe little else. You and I, Steven darling, can hope for no rewards just because we strive to do good. The rights and wrongs of society, of human civilization, are not applicable to us or to my brother. He is as a tornado, a hurricane, an unpredictable, uncontrollable act of nature. He *is* . . . and that is all that can be said. You can't stop him. He is as inevitable as an earthquake."

"There must be some way."

She turned away. I saw the deep breath she drew raise her white shoulders in the moon's silver light.

"I can stop him, I think, but to do so, I must become as he is."

"Cat . . . what do you mean?"

She faced me, tears staining her cheeks. "I am my brother's sister. I, too, can change, can mutate."

I looked at her. "No, Cat, it can't be true . . ." The awful image of her brother in his gelatinous, flesh-mutating state flashed before my eyes. I could not bear the thought of Cat's beauty shifting, changing, becoming hideous and monstrous.

"See!" she demanded. She rushed to the dim light of the small lamp still burning near the door. I watched the beads of perspiration spring out above her lip, on her forehead. She grimaced with concentration and pain.

Slowly, the tendons in her forearm became more pronounced, bulged, turned to steel cables beneath the white skin. She gave a little gasp, grunted like a wounded animal as the fingers of her hand lengthened, knobbed at the joints, as red-painted fingernails lengthened to daggers.

In about sixty seconds, she ended the transformation, panting with the effort. The once delicately-boned fragile white hand was now a yellowed, horny-skinned talon with deadly claws.

"I . . . I can't believe . . ." I gasped.

"It's true, Steven. Feel it." She raked the claws gently down my chest. I shuddered at the sensation. It was real —solid flesh and bone—no hallucination. "I've known

323

for some time I could do this."

"Then why . . . why haven't you freed yourself?"

"Because I don't understand the consequences. No punishment, no reward, remember? But who can foretell the consequences if I allow myself to mutate completely?"

I saw in an instant what she meant. Little enough did any of us understand why Nicholas existed or why we were, the three of us, intertwined in this fate. How could any of us know what awaited Cat if she transformed and destroyed the Abomination? Would she then replace him? Be as he was before her? Would she then become Evil's gateway to this world?

"I see. It's hopeless. What can we do? What must we do?"

She drew another deep breath, her eyes fluttering as she relaxed some inner concentration. I watched as slowly her hand and arm became once again the thing of beauty I cherished.

"I . . . I alone have to do it. I have but two options. One is to never see you again, never to allow us contact ever again." She held up a restraining hand as I began to protest. "The second option is to transform, to battle him, to destroy him, accepting the consequences on the chance that we, you and I, could then be together forever."

"Cat, you know what I . . ."

"Yes. Yes, Steven, I know. After tonight, I know all too well there is only one choice to be made." She stepped closer. Her arms reached up behind my head, her breasts crushing softly against my chest. "I know now, after this night, I have no reason to live if we cannot be together." She kissed me, passion still lying just below the surface of the kiss.

"When?" I said. "I will be with you . . ."

"No. Whatever is to be, shall be, with you there or not. I will wait. Bide my time. Pick the right moment. As difficult as it may be for you, you must forget it and push it from your mind. If somehow Nicholas should read your mind—in a dream—my chances of success are nonexistent. He must not know. You must wait. Patience, my darling. I will choose the time carefully."

"Soon," I pleaded, "make it soon."

"We have both endured this agony over a quarter of a century. Minutes, hours, days—all meaningless now. I will wait. You must wait. I will choose the moment I am strongest, he the weakest. It will be soon, my darling, as soon as possible. I promise."

She kissed me again, the passion hot on her mouth, again, cooled not at all by the rivers of tears from her eyes.

"Promise me, Steven, promise me . . . if I defeat him, you will be with me, stay with me forever, no matter what. Promise me?"

"Cat, of course, it's what I've always wanted, it's . . ."

She smiled then, satisfied—was there mirth in that smile, too?—and she was gone, out the door before I could stop her.

I have no idea how she returned to the stone house on Mill Road.

I had no idea what those last words she spoke, what that odd little smile meant. I think I do now.

18

Dawn found me still awake, smoking cigarettes 'til my lungs and head ached.

I was out of it. Wait. Await the consequences.

I decided to go see Michelle Raintree. If I could not

help Cat, perhaps I could do something for Michelle.

I showered and changed into another set of my newly purchased Greenriver clothes—new jeans, an oxford-cloth button-down, and a psuedo-suede sport coat. Before I went out, I called the wrecker and the car rental company to retrieve their swamp-mired Oldsmobile. The police, I was assured, would be by later for a statement. Cat was right—societal laws were inconsequential. I had nothing to fear from accepted reality.

Michelle was wearing tight faded jeans and heels with a too small sleeveless T-shirt that said M-TV on the front. Avant-garde gold earrings dangled to her shoulders, her long raven hair falling free and loose about her face and down her back.

She was surprised to see me at the door of the comfortable Cape Cod she shared with Todd Raintree and the unplanned product of our loins, Rhonda. She was surprised, but the emotions behind the surprise ran the gamut from hate to pleasure, and showed on her face in confused sequence like a French movie without sound or subtitles.

"May I come in?"

"Yes." She stepped back, widening the door opening.

"Michelle . . . Todd asked me to see you." She did not bridle at my use of her real name; she seemed resigned to the inevitability of her ruse coming to an end.

"I can guess why." She sat on a red velvet lounger. I chose a Boston rocker opposite her.

"Oh?"

"Yes. I . . . I guess I've known all along nobody bought this routine about me not being Michelle Bailey. I was just . . . so ashamed . . . embarrassed, really. I suppose Todd told you everything about what I did in Vegas and Hollywood?"

"Yes."

"Good old Todd," she sighed. "But that's okay. I make no apologies for that stuff. That's why I was more embarrassed than ashamed. I just wanted . . . needed so desperately to make it, to be somebody."

"Everyone has that need. Some more than others."

"Well, I had it the worst. Especially after all those changes I put everybody through at Levon's."

"I think that was a fairly typical reaction to the situation, looking back on it. You smelled success. Nothing could keep you from going for it. Maybe you had more guts than the rest of us. Maybe we were all too scared, too small-town."

"Or maybe just more sane." She looked down at her hands in her lap as they twined and untwined nervous fingers. "I couldn't sort it all out, Steve . . . my feelings about breaking out of Greenriver, my feelings for you. I've thought about it a lot as the years went by. Sometimes I think I threw myself at fame and fortune because I couldn't have you."

"Michelle . . ."

"No. That's just sometimes. Other times I realize you were just a game I was playing, a role. I thought because you technically took my virginity, you owed me the rest of the package—marriage, the whole bit. Kamii didn't help me sort it out. Her ideas just made me run off headlong away from you and Greenriver, away from finding out who I really was . . . straight into Hell. I know now there was nothing wrong with Kamii's ideas, though I'd love to blame somebody else for the way I ended up. For the longest time, I enjoyed blaming you for my Hell."

"People make their own Hells, Michelle. Oh, sometimes we all have help. But even that's a choice—free will."

"I know that now." Her eyes met mine. They were clear and untroubled, only resigned to the truth of her past.

"Why does Todd think you're on the verge of a breakdown?"

"Because I was . . . until you came back to town. You should have seen me, just two weeks ago." She laughed, straining at it a bit. "I was playing it to the hilt."

"I admit you looked bad, even just the other evening when I first saw you. I guess it's that you looked so different. Right now, talking to you this way, you seem as mentally well-adjusted as anyone I know."

"Your being here, coming back to Greenriver, made me realize I couldn't keep hiding." She looked down again, watching her hands as they petted the red velvet of the lounge. "Did . . . Todd tell you about . . . Rhonda?"

"Yes."

An enormous sigh of relief left her body.

"You know, I called her Rhonda because of the song we used to sing together, 'Help Me, Rhonda?' Somehow it was a link to you without letting you know she was our daughter."

"Why didn't you ever let me know?"

"At first, it was pride . . . and selfishness. I was so mad at you all the while I was pregnant, because the pregnancy was delaying my fabulous career. Later, when my fabulous career turned into drugs, porno and prostitution . . . well, I couldn't admit my defeat, you see, couldn't admit you were right all along."

"I've never been right all along, Michelle. I reacted one way to a situation, you another. If you only knew how much the first incarnation of the band ached for a chance at the big time—that's all we talked about, day in and day out—and I backed out of it. My life has been no better than yours in some ways, all because of decisions I made or failed to make. I don't mean to say I know what pain and torture you experienced. I can only know my own. We all suffer from our decisions in different ways, in different degrees. Funny, it always seems the worst possible consequences to the person experiencing the pain."

"I know what you're saying is true. When they finally turned me loose, because I was getting too used up on drugs to even be a passable whore, all I had was Rhonda. That was five years ago. I think it was her strength alone that helped me find my way back to Greenriver. She was the only one with me those long weeks when I went through withdrawal from heroin. She got me here and found Todd. I needed constant care, and Todd and Rhonda gave it to me."

"Did Rhonda understand all of what you were doing?"

"She must have. We never talked about it. Even now we don't. God knows how screwed up her head really is."

"What kind of a person is she? What kind of relationship do you have with her?"

"She has a good strong relationship with Todd . . . not father-daughter. He's more like an uncle to her. She and I . . . she tries to be nice to me, but I robbed her of her childhood, jaded her, I think. When we came here and I insisted on going by a fake name, she didn't speak to me for almost a month. The name on her birth certificate is Rhonda Lee Bailey. When I forbade her to use her name here, she was in effect disenfranchised completely. Todd insisted we get married, as much to give Rhonda a name as anything, I think. Things have gotten steadily better between us over the past three years. Things will get even better now. I know I have to make the effort."

"How does she feel about the father she never knew?"

"She only knows he's an important man . . . that he was unable to marry me. I told her not to ask questions, but she always did. When she did, I'd describe you."

"I don't live up to my publicity, I'm afraid. If she ever finds out I'm her father, she's going to be greatly disappointed."

She rose from the lounge, came to me and kneeled at my feet.

"No, Steven, never. You're all the man I described to her."

"Michelle, if you knew, if you only knew . . ."

"No." She hushed my lips with a cool finger. "If my memory of you is exaggerated, idealized . . . don't tell me. You're my saviour. Don't tarnish my memories."

"Michelle, I can't be anyone's saviour. I can't even save myself."

"Allow me to be selfish once again, Steven. I need to draw strength from you."

I stood up and pulled her up with me, off her knees.

"What about Todd? Can't he be your strength?"

"Oh, he is. But in a different way. He helps, but he lets me get away with being wholly self-indulgent. You never did. I needed your presence. I needed to fear your anger again. I needed the myth of you, the dreams, the way you were, the might-have-been."

"Fantasies are dangerous ground to travel. I know."

"It can't be any more dangerous ahead than where I've been. At least now I'm not afraid to be Michelle Bailey, with Michelle Bailey's past and a hope for her future." She kissed me, and I responded on some very basic level. "Thank you," she whispered.

"Okay," I said, and pushed her gently away. She smoothed her hair, licked her lips, attempted a smile and brought it off successfully.

"Will you be at the bar tonight? I can promise a good performance. The debut in Greenriver of Michelle Bailey."

"I wouldn't miss it."

I went home and got some sleep. It was a sound, deep, good sleep.

I awoke just in time to dress for dinner and Michelle's appearance at Raintree's.

It was a brisk evening, the September sun having dropped a few more fractions of degrees south, seeking out its winter route across Michigan, letting the ground lose warmth more rapidly into the cloudless night. Stars bristled out of the sky like shining nail points driven through black velvet, and the wind came up chill, brushing at the face of the moon.

Todd's was full. I had to take a place at the bar. There was expectancy in the atmosphere of the room, or at least, I imagined there was.

Rhonda served me my Heineken with an uncharacteristic smile and a pat on my hand. Her moody eyes sparkled.

"Can I like, talk to you later?"

"Why not now, Ronni?"

"I'm pretty busy. How 'bout in ten-fifteen minutes?

330

We can step out in the rear alley where we can, like, hear each other."

I nodded. As she went back to serving the others at the bar and getting up orders for the waitresses serving the tables, I wondered if Michelle could have possibly told her. I decided her attitude would not have been so blithe were that the reason she wished to speak with me.

I watched her. She seemed to continually juggle at least two beer mugs, a bottle of whiskey, two shot glasses and a lit cigarette. She was quite professional. I had a brief surge inside me I thought must be the emotional stirrings of the proud father. It was a queer feeling.

I gazed at the crowd with a writer's eye, looking for little idiosyncracies of the people I might later use for characters in a book.

Ronni tapped my arm and gestured with her head toward a door at the back near the restrooms. I followed her out.

The night was even colder, and a strong wind made the ragged newspapers, leaves and bits of trash in the alley dance an odd hornpipe.

Ronni turned to me, waded between my arms and kissed me on the mouth.

"There," she said, obviously pleased. "That's for what you did for my mom."

"Ronni, I did nothing . . ."

"Oh yes, you did! God, for the first time in like nineteen years she's acting like a real person. You did it. She told me you did."

"I really didn't do . . ."

She moved in again, zeroing in on my mouth with hers. "The first kiss was for what you did for Mom," she breathed. "This one's for what you do to me." Her arms locked like shackles behind my head, and her lips covered mine. Her tongue parted my teeth, and I struggled violently to push her away. The shock at being kissed in such a manner by her made my struggles ineffectual.

"No!" I commanded, between her assaults.

"Why not? You're a man, I'm a woman . . ." And she kissed me again, moaning a bit.

I pushed away again. "Absolutely not! Ronni!"

"Oh God, you make me so hot! Your eyes, your body . . ." And again she invaded my defenses and kissed me.

With a supreme effort, I finally broke free of her grasping arms and hungry mouth.

"God-damn it, Ronni, stop it! I'm your father!" I was shaking uncontrollably. In the dim light of the reeling moon and stars, I could see her face. She couldn't decide whether to laugh or cry. She chose laughter.

"You're kidding, right? I mean . . ."

I shook my head gravely.

" . . . you're like, not kidding, are you?"

"No."

"Shit!" She stomped her foot like a small child in a tantrum. "Fuck! I don't believe it!"

"Listen, Ronni, this isn't the way I wanted you to find out . . . fact is, I didn't want you to find out at all."

She cocked her head like a puppy and looked as if she would cry. Then the anger took over again. "Shit! Fuck!"

"I can understand your anger. I . . . I just found out about you yesterday."

"Don't hand me that bullshit!"

"No. . . it's true. Ask Todd. Ask your mother."

"That's just something to say, to get you off the hook. Shit, they'd back you up on it."

"No. It's true. Right after your mother and I . . . right after you were conceived, I never saw or heard from Michelle again until this week."

She cocked her head, again on the verge of tears.

"Really? Oh God! Why me? Why was I ever born?"

"I can answer that one. So that Michelle would have someone to care for, someone of her flesh to care for her."

She gave me a weak smile. "You are a bullshitter, aren't you? Okay, I believe you. But I'm still pissed. It's gonna take some time to stop thinking of you as somebody whose bones I'd like to jump, and start callin'

332

you Daddy." She poked a finger in my ribs. "You sure I can't have it both ways, Daddy?"

" 'Fraid not."

"Y'know, I'd just decided I could settle in to a real serious affair with a guy like you, and suddenly we're related. Damn! Well, I'd better get back . . . Todd counts on me a lot, you know. C'mon. You're next Heineken is on me, Dad." Her acceptance, her bravado was almost believable. Almost.

I followed her in. My stool at the bar was still vacant. The lights dimmed as I sat down, and the drummer with the combo on the bandstand bent to his mike.

"Raintree's is proud to present, for your listening enjoyment, Michelle Raintree."

Scattered applause ushered her on stage. She could still manipulate hair, make-up and clothes to work the magic. And she radiated beauty from within. Her gown was black sequins and gauzy chiffon, she wore black opera gloves, and her hair swirled like a cloud, black and stormy.

She grabbed up a gold-plated Shure microphone with real style, a broad smile on her face that made her gorgeous.

"I want to take a moment tonight before we start . . ." She turned to the drummer. "Boys, give me a little back-beat."

The drummer and the bass player started a low funky rhythm. The guitarist hit some chords, while the keyboard man did some fills.

"Mmmm. That's nice. As I said, I want to take a moment to pay tribute to someone in the audience." She shaded her eyes from the stage lights. "You are in the audience, aren't you? Yes, there you are. Ladies and gentlemen, I give you a man, once the greatest guitarist Greenriver—perhaps the whole Midwest—ever knew, the wisest man I ever met, and the man who saved my life. Steven Dalton. Stand up, Steve. C'mon. Let's hear it!"

Everybody applauded, but I was sure none of them knew why. I stood reluctantly, gave her a little wave of my hand, then sat, spun to the bar, and hid behind hunched shoulders.

"Everybody in this room should know a man like Mr. Dalton. Steve, this one's for you. In fact, all the songs tonight are for you."

She signaled the band. They stopped playing and picked up the beat with quarter note hand claps. The drummer booted in bass drum eighth notes and Michelle sang:

"Baby, baby . . . where did our love go? . . ."

She did it the way I taught her, like the Supremes but with delayed phrasing and syncopation. It was beautiful. I stood and applauded. The room followed my lead. Michelle Bailey was back with the world.

Todd showed up about halfway through the second song, "Baby Love," with Paulie and Debbie Gibbs. They all came over to me. Todd embraced me, tears in his eyes, shouting, "Thank you, thank you, thank you for giving her back to me," in my ear.

Debbie was crying, and Paulie smiled from ear to ear. "Welcome home, ol' son," he shouted over the music. Todd embraced me again.

"Michelle told me," he shouted, "I've got only you to thank . . ."

I shushed them all. "Listen!" I commanded. "She's perfect."

Todd hustled us up a small table near the bandstand, and Ronni brought us drinks. She patted my cheek and said, "Drink up, Dad." Todd heard and stared at her in amazement as she went back to the bar.

"She knows?" he hollered at me.

I nodded.

"Jesus," he said, and Michelle and the band segued with a chord change into "World Without Love." We applauded until our hands were red. She ended the set with another announcement.

"Now a song for a young woman I couldn't live without. My lovely daughter, there at the bar, Rhonda Raintree."

"Dalton," Rhonda called over the crowd noise.

Michelle hesitated only a moment, flashing a glance at me. I nodded. She smiled with real joy and gave the band the downbeat for "Help Me, Rhonda."

She came down off the bandstand amid a standing ovation and shouts for more. She kissed me, she kissed Todd, and she kissed Paulie and Debbie. Ronni came over, and they exchanged kisses. For a few shining moments there that night, we knew bliss. The happiness that's so hard to find—the kind only old friends, separated for decades, may experience with such a reunion, when old wounds are healed. To paraphrase Dickens, reunions can be the best of times or the worst of times. That Friday night at Raintree's in Greenriver, we had the best. The worst was yet to come.

19

Saturday I was a bit hung over. The phone rang. Even Michigan Bell didn't want me to sleep it off.

"Steve? Todd. All set for the big night?"

"The reunion? Yeah, I guess. What kind of turnout are you expecting?"

"Out of a class of two hundred fifty-four, one hundred and two people R.S.V.P.ed. That's classmates minus spouses. I figure the total attendance at about one seventy-five. We're catering for two hundred. I've had extra cooks working since seven."

"You're catering it?"

"Yeah. And the group that backs Michelle is providing the tunes."

"Big night at the high school gym." I laughed, but it made my head throb to laugh.

"Yeah, I guess."

"So how's Michelle today?"

"Great. Just great. We . . . we even made love last night."

"Todd, I don't think I need to hear . . ."

"No, it's important. It was the first time since she came back to Greenriver that I actually felt like we were both present for the act. She even told me how much she loved me, apologized for all she'd put me through. I can never thank you enough, Steve. You literally gave her back her life."

"Todd, all this hoopla has gone far enough. I did nothing. She did it all. Sure, she claimed it was my presence, the fact that I came back to Greenriver that made it happen, but honest to God, that's all I did. Your wife is a strong woman. I'm happy for you and her. I'm happy for Rhonda."

"That's . . . really why I called, Steve. It's Rhonda."

"What about her?" My stomach tightened. I fumbled with a cigarette and lit one. It seemed my emotions had just been waiting for something like fatherhood to pump acid into my stomach and bile into my throat at the mention of Rhonda's name.

"Well, she had a long talk with me at breakfast. She . . . wanted to know if I'd talk to you."

There was a silence at the other end of the line.

"So you're talking to me. Spill it, Todd! The suspense is killing me."

"She wants to know if she can live with you."

"What?"

"She wants . . ."

"I heard. I just can't believe."

"She says she deserves to live with her rich famous father. She says you owe her at least nineteen years of easy livin', as she put it."

"Christ, this is . . ."

" . . . unbelievable, I know. I guess Michelle built you up so many years to Rhonda, she thinks you're Moses on

336

the way to the land of milk and honey."

"Aptly put. But my lifestyle won't accommodate a full-grown daughter. I'm on the road, either for research or promotional tours, two-thirds of the year. Hell, even now I'm ignoring three deadlines just to be here in Greenriver."

"I know, Steve . . . or at least, I can understand what you're saying. She may not appreciate what Michelle and I have given her here, but at least here she now has a solid home environment. I tried to explain all that to her but she wouldn't listen. Maybe if you tell her . . ."

Great, I thought. Another conflict. Just what I've been seeking to spice up my otherwise dull existence. "I'll do what I can," I said. "Where will she be today?"

"She's supposed to be working, helping with the food for the reunion, but she told me with a rich old man like you, she expected not to have to work another day in her life."

"Christ . . . sounds like a spanking is what she needs, not a talk."

"Well . . . she is your daughter. Better late a father than never, Steve. She's at the community pool. You can find her there."

"A million thanks," I said, and hung up the phone. I don't know why I bothered wasting sarcasm on Todd. He never did well with sarcasm or irony. Lit terms were taught one of the semesters in high school when his mind was on music, sports, or tits.

An hour later, the rent-a-car people delivered a Pontiac Sunbird to my door.

The community pool was new to me, having been constructed about 1970 within a stone's throw of the new high school. It was an indoor pool, so it could have year-round use.

Rhonda was lounging in a reclining chair, aloof, eyes closed, a subtle self-satisfied smile on her full Michelle-like lips. Her long slender body dripped beads of water onto the ceramic floor. Her full, also Michelle-esque breasts swelled provocatively from the scoop of her suit's neckline as she breathed. It was difficult to look at her and maintain a fatherly stance . . . especially since I was so unused to the role.

"Hello, Ronni."

She opened one heavy-lidded eye. Her smile twitched wider.

"Daddy dearest . . . like, help yourself. Did you come to sweep me off to Paris for the weekend?"

I pushed her calves to one side and sat next to her feet on the end of the lounge chair.

"No, but it's that whole misinformed view of my life which I do want to speak with you about."

A look of mock concern made her face seem childish.

"Did the stock market crash? Did the yacht sink? Oh, Dad-ums, are we down to our last two million?"

"We're a bit below our first million, Ronni . . . about five hundred grand below. That's what I mean. I'm no Jim Michener, no Stephen King. I don't write the kind of books they do as TV mini-series or make movies of, with the author picking up a couple mil for screen rights, points and residuals. I'm . . . moderately successful. I'm comfortable."

"Good. I want to be comfortable, too. Let's be comfortable together." She flirted, twitching her little ass in the chair.

"That's the other thing. Though I'm sure you're a wonderful person, I don't know you, and you don't know me. I think you'd have a really difficult time adapting to my lifestyle."

"What's to know? You're my father. You have to take me in. You're like, my real father."

"Let's clear up something, Ronni. You're nineteen. I don't legally have to do anything concerning you."

She sat up, her jiggling breasts thrust out defiantly at me.

"I bet if I hired a lawyer, I could get a judge to see it different. Like, a poor, disadvantaged child, living with a two-bit bartender, raised by an ex-whore . . ."

I slapped her face. Hard. Too hard. Blood trickled down her chin, dropping little red spots on her breasts.

She rubbed at the red imprint on her jaw.

"You'll never do that again, mister."

"I hope I don't need to. I never want to hear you refer to Todd and Michelle in those terms again. They love you."

"Does love change the truth? Did I say anything that wasn't true?"

"Maybe not, to both questions. But judging people, categorizing them, degrading them can only lead to misery for all parties concerned. Who are you that you can act so superior to them?"

She stood up and turned away, but not in time to hide the incipient tears.

"You know who I am." She laughed. "I'm a bastard. The fucking bastard child of a big-time writer who doesn't want me and a recovered smack-addict-porn-star-hooker—and don't you dare hit me again! Truth is truth." She spun around to face me. "All I want is what's coming to me. Damn it, I deserve my slice of the pie, and you're the one with the knife and fork!"

I could say nothing in the face of her anger. In a way, she was right. Just because I had been unaware of her existence for nineteen years didn't mean I was absolved of all responsibility. Like they say when you break a law you didn't know was a law—ignorance is no excuse. Maybe this was one of those cases of cosmic right and wrong. Maybe I did owe Rhonda nineteen years of fatherhood. She had paid her dues, if what Michelle had told me was accurate. Imagine growing up knowing your mother was a prostitute; imagine being sixteen and being the only person around to help your mother through cold-turkey withdrawal from heroin.

"Okay. But when you get tired of following me from coast to coast and back again, don't say I didn't warn you." How it would all work into my life—the existence or demise of the Abomination . . . Cat—I had no idea. I played it as it came.

She wiped at her eyes, eye make-up smearing and turning her into a raccoon.

"You mean it?"

"Yes. I'll try to be the father you need, that you needed nineteen years ago. If I fail at that, I hope at least we can be close friends."

"You really mean it?"

"Yes."

She threw herself at me with so much force, she toppled me off the end of the lounge chair to the ceramic tiles surrounding the pool. There we lay, me flat on my back, she straddling me, kissing me repeatedly.

"Hey, you two, none of that," the lifeguard's voice boomed across the pool. "This is a family place."

"We know," Ronni shouted back, stumbling to her feet and helping me up. "We're family. Close family." She squeezed my hand and half-ran, half-dragged me to the shower area so she could dress.

She was brushing out her still damp ebony hair as the Sunbird took us down the main drag of Greenriver for the sixth time. I was cruisin', wasting time in Greenriver, just as I had so many times as a teenager—living, passing through time, always waiting for something to happen.

"So what's the first father-daughter thing we're gonna do?" She tilted the rear view mirror to her and applied a thick coat of mascara to her top and bottom lashes.

"Figure out what to tell Michelle and Todd and figure out the possibilities of how they're going to react."

She put on eye liner. Too much, I thought, being a father.

"It'll be okay," she shrugged blithely.

"I meant what I said last night about you being here to help Michelle along. She needed you when she was coming out of the drugs. I think she needs you now just as much. She needs your love . . . she needs to love you."

"But she's got Todd," Ronni whined, then pooched her lips to apply lipstick. Too bright red, her father thought to himself. " 'Til you whipped into my life, I didn't have anybody . . . not really. I mean, Mom was

340

always on the edge of bozo-city, and Todd was there trying to keep her from falling in. You know?"

"If you say so. I just don't know if Michelle will be willing to let you go. She told me it was always thoughts of you that got her through the rough stuff."

"I care for Mom and Todd—don't get me wrong— but I don't owe either of them a thing. I've paid and paid."

"Okay, okay. But let me think of the right words and pick the right time to let them know."

She dabbed perfume behind her ears, down the deep cleavage between her breasts, and on her wrists, all the time staring intently at me.

"You're not . . . like chicken, are you?"

"Damn it, of course not," I barked, looking directly at her, ignoring the road. "And for God's sake, pull your skirt down. And button up your blouse!"

"Yes, Dad-ums." She giggled.

We ate at an Arby's in Three Rivers, fed the pigeons in the park by one of the rivers, and drove back on secondary roads, meandering so we could go over the old one-lane covered bridge in Centerville. She told me what she remembered of her childhood with Michelle in Vegas and L.A.—not a lot of laughs. I told her what I could—about the good times with Michelle and me, about the band, about how good her mother was at picking up the lyrics and style of the music I had taught her. I could not, of course, tell her of the fear, the horror, the terror—the obsession her mysterious father had lived with since childhood.

Before we knew it, evening was upon us. What we had discovered was that we shared a basic viewpoint— cynicism tempered by unreasoning romanticism. It wasn't unusual that we should share a life-philosophy, considering the things in our pasts, but the likenesses cemented our relationship.

When I dropped her at the Raintrees' Cape Cod, Michelle came to the door, smiling, and waved to me enthusiastically as I pulled out of the drive.

I had just time enough to go home, clean up, change

341

and buy some cigarettes before the festivities got underway at the gymnasium.

20

The school lot was filled to overflowing. I ended up parking the little Sunbird illegally almost a half mile from the doors.

On the sidewalk before the entrance sat a gleaming black dinosaur from my past, from the past of the class of '65: a shiny 1965 GTO convertible with black vinyl interior—black on black, we called it then. It was a beast. It reminded me of a cross between Laurel's old monster '57 Chevy and my sportier '65 Mustang. I wondered what it was doing there—perhaps for ambiance alone—and I wished like hell I could drive it.

The gym was dark, darker than the deepening twilight outside. Balloons and crepe paper hung from the high open rafters, and the stage was backed with flats that had been used since time immemorial as scenery for Junior and Senior class plays. Tonight the flats were covered with eight-by-ten blow-ups of the entire class of 1965. People wandered behind the band, looking for their own pasts or the memories of forgotten sweethearts.

The band played softly, instrumental renditions of songs from 1960 through 1966. I recognized them all.

What I didn't recognize were the people. Oh, I saw Paulie and Debbie across the room, and Mitzie in her baby seal white furs with a geezer on his last legs drooling on her neck and cheeks constantly—but the rest of them? I had no idea who these bald, fat, matronly middle-aged men and women were. They surely weren't the all-state athletes, the star cheerleaders, the high-stepping marching band members, the prom kings and queens, the debating team, the aspiring thespians. These people were lawyers, accountants, grocery store checkers, factory workers; they were homemakers and parents; they were prescription-drug junkies and alcoholics. They were boring, they were mundane, they were strangers.

The name tags acquired at the door from bubbly, freshly coiffed housewives were no help. I read them, searched my memory banks, and came up blank.

Someone slapped me on the back, causing me to sputter bourbon all over the sleeve of my camel-colored fake-suede sport coat.

"Hey, man!"

I turned and gawked. There was a light-skinned black man in a dirty Jamaican shirt and dread locks. I thought it was Geoffie Prang. It had to be. He was the only black person in our graduating class. The final tip-off was the short oriental female at his side, with straight black hair falling down past her tiny butt.

"Geoffie?"

"No, man." He pushed smudged moon eyeglasses up the bridge of his nose. "Rashim. Rashim Mohammad Abdul. I didn't feel right with the anglo slave name my biological parents laid on me. Kamii helped me discover my true name in a transcendental trance way back . . . uh . . . back . . ."

"In 1971." Kamii smiled, her eyes unabashedly crawling up and down my body. "I'd like to share my body with Steven, Rashim."

"That's cool," Geoffie/Rashim said, nodding reflectively.

"Uh . . . so how are things, Geo . . . Rashim?"

"Great, man."

I expected him to say psychedelic or far out. He and

she were throwbacks, people caught in a time warp that began in 1967 and ran to 1972, over and over again like a tape loop.

"When would you like to share the secrets of the temple of my body, Steven?"

"Kamii, I, uh, appreciate the offer, but I'm . . . well . . . otherwise involved."

"Relationships should be free and open, man," Geoffie/Rashim said. "If they aren't, they probably aren't worth the psychic energy necessary to fuel them."

"I can dig it," I said, unwillingly falling into the vernacular. "But some relationships are best left closed."

"No." He shook his head vehemently. "No man, that's a trap." Then with the fluidity of thought only a person long conversant with drugs could manage, he said, "Hey, Deanna's here someplace . . . I can find her for you, but she's taken a vow of silence this week."

"Uh . . . I see Todd just got here. He . . . uh, wanted to see me about a private matter. Catch you two later, okay?"

"Far out!" Geoffie/Rashim nodded.

Lying to him made me feel as though I had lied to a child, hiding the candy and saying it was all gone.

Todd set a chafing dish down on the long table to the left of the stage, the table already groaning with the weight of assorted victuals. He waved as he saw me approaching.

"So . . ." He grinned at me. "You ran into nature boy and Sheena of the jungle."

"Yeah. Stimulating pair. He can't place the decade and she wants to share the secrets of the temple with me."

"Wants to jump your bones, eh?"

"Right."

"Don't feel too flattered. Eighty percent of the guys in this county know the secrets of the temple." He laughed, but behind the joking, there was something he wanted to say to me. I could see it when I studied his still handsome face.

344

"Is anything wrong, Todd?"

"You told Ronni she could go away with you."

"Yes, I did." I half expected him to punch my nose, but he didn't. His serious face broke into his broadest grin.

"You know, I thought it would be a problem, for Michelle I mean, but you know what she said when Ronni told her? She said, 'Good. Ronni can get to know Steve, and I can get to know Todd.' That's what she said. She also said there were paybacks to be made, all 'round."

Just then Michelle breezed in the door, in a smart lavender jersey dress, almost the same hue as the dress Cat had worn the night before. That gave me a twinge, churning up the old worry and fear, but Michelle floated over to us and kissed me on the mouth, then Todd. She looped her arms through ours and led us into the crowd.

"Let's mingle, you stodgy old alumni," she said, laughing melodically.

We mingled first with Debbie and Paulie Gibbs. Conversation was exchanged about Michelle's previous night's performance, how good she looked and sounded, and she countered with how good she felt. No one mentioned my blitherings on Thursday night at Todd's, about being heartless, et cetera. I guess old friends are allowed one night of drunken ravings without explanation or comment. Michelle told of my plans with Ronni, and I was commended, all around. Then Michelle made some lewd wifely comments about further explorations of Todd's bod.

Mitzie Campbell strolled over with her old lecher in thrall and started right in on Michelle.

"So good to have you back with us, Michelle dear," she meowed. "The whole town is abuzz. Gina was such a bad choice for an alias . . . like an Italian streetwalker or something."

"It's good to be back," Michelle said, ignoring Mitzie's insinuation.

"And how's that wonderful daughter of yours? Does

she plan to always work in the bar?"

Todd was on the verge of attacking Mitzie with harsh words—at the very least words that, I was sure, would have been lost on her—when Geoffie/Rashim and Kamii oozed over to us.

"Man, this is great!" he drawled, his eyes exceedingly bloodshot. "Hail, hail, the gang's all here." The smell of weed off their clothing was overpowering at close range. They must have just seconds before done refresher tokes.

"Almost," I said. "Only Jim Harper is missing."

"Yeah, literally," Paulie said. "Nobody's heard from him since he went off to Nam."

"I had heard he was in San Francisco," Paulie said.

There was a commotion at the doors, but a crowd was gathered there, so we couldn't see. A voice rose up from that direction over the crowd noise and over the band.

"I can get the fucking thing myself, thank you," a male voice bellowed.

The crowd parted, and a wheelchair moved down the pathway toward us. In the wheelchair sat a man wearing an army jacket over a loud Hawaiian shirt. His hair was mostly white, shoulder length and wild, falling around his face, which sported an equally wild reddish-brown-and-white beard.

His arms worked the wheels rhythmically, and soon he was before our little group.

"Together again for the first time," he said to us, his face, what we could see of it behind the hair, expressionless. The only thing I could read was a defiance that burned from his eyes like Hell-fire.

"Jim . . . ?" I said tentatively.

"Who else, fearless leader?"

"Far out, man," Geoffie/Rashim said. "We were just this second rappin' about you. What happened to your legs, man? You crippled or somethin'?"

Debbie and Michelle shot Geoffie/Rashim a look that would have killed him if possible. Mitzie laughed behind her hand. Kamii just stared and smiled. All I could think was that Kamii wondered how to show Jim the secrets of the temple without being injured by the wheelchair.

"Nam happened to my legs, Geoffie, and crippled is the something I am. Look up crip in the ol' Webster's, and there's my picture." Still no trace of emotion crossed his face.

"Jim . . . you never wrote . . ." I stammered. "You said you would write."

"At first things were too crazy, I was too crazy. Later . . . well, later there was a damn good reason for not writing."

"Anyway. You've got to catch me up on your life since 1965. God, I've missed you ."

"Don't get sloppy sentimental on me, Dalton. I'm the guy you toughened up with, remember?"

"Yeah, I remember. Weight lifting, jujitsu. You know I got up to first degree black belt in karate when I was going to college?"

"That's ludicrous. You're too damned musclebound to be graceful. Christ, you look like Todd the Bod." Everybody laughed, a bit nervously. No one had ever been too sure how to take Jim's stone-faced humor. Hearing it from a wheelchair made it even more difficult to ferret out—to understand if he was making fun of himself, or us, or not joking at all.

"So. The group may be back together, for tonight, anyway, but your roadie is definitely ready for the old roadie home. You guys are just gonna have to schlep your own shit from now on." He turned the wheelchair away from us. "Now if you'll excuse me, I think I'll visit with some of my other great good ol' friends from the G.H.S. class of '65."

"He didn't have any friends besides us," Mitzie sniffed as Jim wheeled away.

"Let's grab a table big enough for all of us," Paulie said, "'fore they're all gone."

"I think we women will invoke our feminine prerogative and all go to the powder room together," Michelle said, batting her eyelashes in broad imitation of Scarlett

347

O'Hara. Ronni and Debbie followed her without question, but Mitzie moved off with her septuagenarian lover without a word of parting. It was clear she thought herself a notch above us all.

Kamii and Geoffie/Rashim just stood where they were, smiling, smiling, smiling.

Paulie, Todd and I went over to a large table to stake our claim.

Jim Harper wheeled over to us. It was apparent to me he just didn't want to be anywhere near Mitzie, and I couldn't blame him.

"Mind if I join you? Or haven't you come to terms with my little ol' veteran's disability? It's not catching, you know. Mortar shell wounds rarely are, a decade after the fact."

"Mortar shell, huh?" Todd said, nodding as if he knew what that meant.

"Yeah. Fragments in the old spinal cord. Thank God they didn't get me in the front. At least this way, my dick still works. I just can't feel it. It's a bitch to look down and see you've got a hard-on and didn't know it."

"Where did it happen?" Paulie asked.

"That's the bitch of it. Saigon. Loading the friggin' kids and social workers on the choppers and planes. I was a hair's breadth away from bein' out in one piece. 'Course, so were the kids and social workers."

"You went in '65, didn't you?" I asked, trying to piece together the chronology.

"Yeah, but I liked it so much, I kept re-enlisting. The Cong gave me hotel space for a lot of the time. They liked me. I was one of those guys Barry Sadler sang about."

"Green Beret," Todd said, still nodding gravely.

"Brian was a Green Beret," I said, simply for something to say.

"You might say that. You might also say Brian was a fucking murderer."

My back stiffened. My last few encounters with my brother all those years back had been far from pleasant, but hearing Jim bad-mouth him nonetheless stirred familial loyalties.

"How do you mean?" I asked, my voice tight.

"He was solely responsible for wiping out a whole battalion of our guys in '68. I was there. I watched it all happen."

"Misfortunes of war, ol' son." Paulie shook his head. "I'm sure Steve's brother didn't . . ."

"Like hell he didn't," Jim interrupted. "It was like he was possessed, like some demon from Hell made him give the orders to cut through where he knew the Cong lay in wait. The sonofabitch was laughing, laughing as his men got cut down!" He wiped spittle from his beard, slumped back in his chair and lit a Camel.

"Maybe you know what happened to him . . . I mean, he's still M.I.A.," I said, some of the anger at Jim gone. I believed his story about Brian. I remembered what Delilah told me—"He can make you do whatever he wants . . . even long distance"—even all the way over in Nam?

"Yeah, I know what happened to him . . . but I ain't sayin'. Suffice it to say the bastard is where he belongs."

"Why don't we change the subject?" Paulie said, shifting uneasily in his folding chair. "What you been doin' since you got back?"

"Well, employers didn't come lookin' for me. Not only was I a reminder of Vietnam, I was a trained killer. A crippled trained killer. That's like bein' an attack dog without any fangs. I mean, I woulda made a shitty bodyguard. The C.I.A. said I was definitely out." He grinned humorlessly behind his beard. "I got a G.I. loan and bought into a bookstore in San Francisco. Sold a hell of a lot of your books, Steve ol' pal. Must be nice to be so successful."

"I'm not all that successful," I protested, for the second time in one day.

"Don't put yourself down, man. There's nothing wrong with success. Hell, you're all successes at what you do. Look at Paulie, he changes the world with a stroke of a solid gold pen," Paulie put his hand self-consciously over the gold pen protruding from his jacket pocket, "signing contracts, stock deals and checks, big business personified, proof that capitalism and

349

nepotism still flourish in this glorious land of ours. Hell, he even donated that GTO out front as a door prize." He stubbed out his Camel and lit another. "Yeah, Steve's a big shot writer. His pen doesn't change anything, just forces his thoughts into other people's brains. Even Geoffie is a success. He's the most successfully weirded-out individual I've ever seen." He puffed at the unfiltered cigarette. "He was always pretty good at being white, too. Kamii's the perfect meditation freak . . . she can meditate alone or in groups . . . I understand she can meditate the hell out of a group of five or more guys. Debbie's the perfect mother . . . the proud mother . . . I wasn't in the room here for five minutes before I saw the same two pictures of her kids three times.

"And Todd . . . I've been checkin' up . . . you're the most successful of anybody. Most guys, all they want is to own a bar and marry a whore. Shit, you've done both, boy."

Todd jumped up, nearly overturning the table, fists rolled big and threatening. I stood too, barring access to Jim in his wheelchair. It took all my strength to hold Todd back.

"Don't get jacked out of shape, Raintree," Jim went on. "No offense meant. I've seen some of her movies. Looked to me like she was a success at what she did, too. Hell, man, we're all whores. Bein' good at it is somethin' to be proud of."

Todd took no comfort from Jim's philosophy, and I was still using all my strength to restrain him from punching out Jim.

"I think we should change the subject again," Paulie said.

"Whatever you say, man. Who am I to argue with big business? Just a crippled-up bookseller from 'Frisco."

"Todd," I said, "let's go get everybody drinks from the bar . . . my treat."

"Okay," he said, the set of his shoulders relaxing a fraction, but fire still smouldering in his eyes as he stared at Jim.

We made our way across the shiny tongue-and-groove boards of the basketball court floor to the bar at the opposite end of the room from the stage.

"He had no right to say that about Michelle," Todd said as we moved through groups of middle-aged white people doing the Monkey, the Frug, the Boogaloo and the James Brown.

"No . . . it was tactless. But I wonder if you or I would be less jaded, less cynical in his condition."

"He got a bad break, no doubt about it, but so what? He better not say anything like that to Michelle. I'll kill him."

There was nothing I could say to calm him. I bought the drinks, though Todd ordered them. He knew what everybody would want.

The bartenders were two of the cute little table girls from Todd's restaurant, and they flirted shamelessly with him as they put the drinks on two trays. He didn't notice their flirtations, or if he did, he was immune to them. We managed to get the two trays of drinks back through the gyrating crowd to the table without spilling anything.

Michelle, Ronni and Debbie had returned from the ladies' room, and Jim was monopolizing a conversation about the sixties.

"Yeah, the greatest protesters of the sixties were the soldiers in Nam. We were sent over there ostensibly to allow the South Vietnamese the right to a democratic government. The fat cats in D.C. read that as all the high moral precepts of free market capitalism, moral cleanliness and all the apple pie you can eat. We soldiers created the black market, owned whores by the scores, and traded apple pie and mom for smack and coke."

None of us had anything to say about any of that.

"Remember the clothes we wore? The hair styles?" Debbie ended the uneasy silence.

"The make-up?" Michelle said. "I swear I went through the sixties looking like an anemic Cleopatra."

"We all started to. Remember the get-ups we wore at Levon's in Detroit?" Debbie said with a wink at Michelle.

"I remember them," I said. "That exaggerated, almost trashy sort of femininity still gets a rise out of me."

"Hey, yeah, that's true." Todd grinned, tired of glaring at Jim. "I guess we're kinda locked into that time, huh?"

"I know I still daydream about you guys in skintight pegged pants with Beatle haircuts," Debbie said, laughing.

"Well, now that's a new side to you, darlin'," Paulie said. "I never realized you were droolin' through all those teenaged years. Still waters and all that."

"This all just shows a definite lack of libido development. You guys are still sexually aroused by what turned you on in your late teen years." Jim polished off his straight Jack Daniels.

"You should talk," Michelle said. "You're still stuck in Vietnam."

"Yeah, I guess we all retain the cultural values of the time in our lives that affected us most. Arrested development," he grunted. "Steve still has the hots for puff-haired girls with big tits and too much make-up, and I'm still reliving the experiences of having my ass blown off, and you, you Boobs Bailey-Raintree, are still . . ."

"Shut the fuck up, Harper," Todd threatened.

"No. That's okay," Michelle said, touching Todd's arm. "I'll finish it for him. I'm still a whore as far as you're concerned, right, Jim?"

"That's hardly something I'd broadcast to the world, dear." It was Mitzie. No one had noticed her as she sidled up to the table to eavesdrop on our conversation.

"And I wouldn't be so quick to throw stones if I were you, Mitzie," Jim said.

"Whatever do you mean?" she asked him, eyeing his wheelchair with contempt for it and him, as if it were Jim's own bad taste that led him to use such a tacky means of conveyance.

"I mean whoredom is not a narrow profession. How many husbands for you, Mitzie? And how much were you paid to do what you did to get them? High price and an eventual marriage certificate don't change the basic precepts."

She sniffed at him. "I shouldn't expect any different attitude from someone like you."

"Whatever I may be, I'm not an acid-tongued, money-grubbing, self-deceiving bitch wrapped in animal skins, jewelry and situation morality. For all my practical cynicism, I don't judge these people." He motioned to us all with his empty glass. It was almost a salute. "I'm no better than any of them, so how can I be their judge?"

"It sounds like you're judging me," Mitzie protested.

"That's because I'm better than you. All these people are. I knew it way back in '63 when you decided sleeping with that asshole Phil Parkhurst was the fast track to success, and I was just exercise to keep you in practice."

The old codger drooling at Mitzie's side had stopped drooling, had adopted a quizzical, almost offended look as he gazed at Mitzie.

"I . . . I never . . ." she stammered.

"Save us the meaningless rhetoric. The whole school knew it. In fact, the whole town did. That's probably what got Parkhurst elected mayor the first time. Any guy who can ball sixteen-year-old high school cheerleaders and get away with it is good enough to screw a town the size of Greenriver."

"I don't have to put up with this!" Mitzie stomped away in her fashionable heels. Her companion followed, a trifle reluctantly, wheezing questions about her sleeping habits.

"Good riddance," Jim muttered, fishing in his fatigues jacket for another Camel.

"Jim, old friend," I said, "your humor used to be funny, but now it has grown a bit too caustic. Mitzie's right. You're being just as hurtful tonight as she is."

"You're right. I apologize to all of you. Just trying to hide my jealousy. It's not easy seeing old friends again who have made something of their lives, or turned themselves around from what they used to be . . ." he looked directly at Michelle and favored her with a real smile " . . . while I'm still hawking books in a 'Frisco store front."

"Apology accepted," Paulie said. "Let me get you another drink, ol' son." He pointed to the rest of our glasses questioningly. We all shook our heads. Paulie went to the bar for Jim's next Jack Daniels.

"I suppose with Mitzie gone that blows Todd's surprise," Ronni said, pouting. Everyone stared at her —she had been so quiet, just drinking it all in.

"What surprise was that?" I asked.

"Well . . ." She looked to Todd for approval. He nodded. "See, Todd was going to have all of you perform . . . together again, you know?"

"Jesus!" I said, downing my Beam's Choice. "I'm glad as hell Mitzie left."

"We can still do it, can't we?" Michelle asked, her question aimed more at me than anyone else.

"I don't know." Debbie laughed. "Can you sing, Jim?"

He looked surprised. "Sure as hell can. Nobody ever asked before."

"Not true, Harper," I said. "You told me once you couldn't carry a tune in a handbasket."

"As I recall, I said I couldn't carry a tune in a mason jar. Handbaskets are for flower ladies and fairies."

"Well, why don't you take Mitzie's place?" Debbie said. "You can be our third Supreme."

"I'd rather be a Delron," Jim laughed. "Choreography in a wheelchair." It was good to hear a real laugh from him.

"Why not? It may open all new career paths for you," Michelle said. "Look what singing did for me."

"I don't care what any of you say, I'm not getting on that stage. I haven't even touched a guitar since I was eighteen." I motioned to Paulie before he left the bar. He saw me and went back for a drink to replace the one I had gulped.

"Aw, c'mon, Steve. None of the rest of us have kept at

354

music either. Everybody here is half crocked already. By the time we play, you won't know the difference, either." Todd drained his drink when he finished speaking, like sentence punctuation.

"I'd really love to hear you play again, Steve," Michelle urged, reaching across the table to lay a hand on my arm.

"Yeah, like, c'mon, Dad-ums," Ronni chimed in, pouty and persuasive.

I watched Jim raise an eyebrow, shift his glance from Ronni to Michelle, to me and back to Ronni again. Then realization spread across his face, and he smiled behind his beard. Apparently his wealth of knowledge concerning his old school chums was incomplete after all.

"Hey," Todd exclaimed, "Ronni knows all those old tunes from listening to my records. She could sing."

"Does this mean I'm drummed out of the girl group without even a tryout?" Jim asked.

Paulie came back and set a drink in front of Jim, me and himself. "Did I miss something?"

"Todd has it set up for your old group to play. Even Jim and I get to sing," Ronni bubbled. "Trouble is, Steve doesn't want to." Her moody eyes went sad and she pooched her lower lip at me.

"I'm for it," Paulie said. "Lord, I'd love to hear that sound again."

"That's the trouble," I said. "The sound won't be there."

"Steve always was the perfectionist. I'm for it," Todd said. "To hell with perfection, let's boogie!"

"I agree," Michelle said with a sparkle in her eye. "I even brought my own microphone." She opened her purse and produced the gold-plated Shure she used at Raintree's.

"Pretty sure of yourself, aren't you?" I asked and gulped whiskey.

"There's nothing to be afraid of, Steve," Debbie assured me. "I'm ready."

"God knows I'm looking forward to my debut," Jim

saluted us all with his straight Jack Daniels.

"Then it's settled." Ronni slapped her hand on the table with finality. "Whether Daddy-kins wants to or not. We'll force him. When do we do the do?"

"Strike while the iron is hot," Todd grinned. "I'll go round up Geoffie."

"You mean Rashim," I said sourly. "You'd better take a butterfly net."

The girls disappeared giggling. Still not believing it was happening, a scant twenty minutes later, Todd had dragged me up on the stage. The hired band guys were watching their instruments with unmasked concern as we hooked ourselves up and made adjustments.

"So why can't I play this guy's guitar?" I asked, when Todd took it out of my hands.

"Because," he said, pointing off stage.

Ronni came out with my guitar, my trusty old Gibson Firebird, clutched like a fragile infant to her breast. She offered it up to me as a priest would the transubstantiated wine in the sacred chalice.

"We've been keeping it for you," she breathed, as I took it in my hands.

I was like a gunfighter, feeling the weight, the balance of his old weapon. It felt good, warm in places from Ronni's body heat, cool in others. There were new strings on it, and it was in perfect tune. I strapped it on and plugged into the amp. The guitarist had a fuzz distorter built in to his foot switches. It wouldn't be the same as my old Fender Bassman with the patched speaker, but it would be close enough.

"I'm set, I guess," I said. But looking up, I saw that only Jim's wheelchair sat at the bank of mikes Todd had put up. Ronnie, Debbie and Michelle were nowhere to be seen.

"Where's the girls?"

" 'Nother surprise," Todd mumbled, grinning.

Geoffie/Rashim sidled over to me, the long neck of the Ampeg fretless brass strapped on him looking like a third arm.

"Man, you're gonna be knocked out by my playin'."

That's about all I do anymore, besides meditate. I play my bass. My bass, man, is my friend. The tones are the resonance of the universe. Can we play in D-flat? Y'know, that's the key signature of the cosmos, man."

"I think we'll try for something a little less exotic, okay, Rashim?"

"You're the boss."

Todd hit a side beat that got the crowd's attention immediately. He was still the best damned drummer I'd ever heard. He pulled the gooseneck mike down to his mouth.

"A little surprise," he said into the mike. "Some of you may remember our old band . . ." Scattered applause from the crowd.

"We went by a whole lotta names—the Avantis, Blue Djinn, Sorta Blue . . ." He laid in some hi-hat licks that raised goose bumps. "May I present Rashim Mohammad on bass, formerly known as Geoffie Prang."

Geoffie/Rashim came in with a wicked bass line. More applause from the crowd. "Paulie Gibbs on keyboards." Paulie laid down some treble-clef magic. His fingers still had it. The crowd were on their feet now.

"And the leader of the group, singer and super lead guitarist, Steve Dalton." I hit the high notes, sustained them 'til my teeth hurt, then slid down the E-string to a funky backing rhythm.

"This is the band you knew locally in the early sixties. The band you never heard had a girl group fronting it, and we called ourselves the Seven Wonders of the World. Joining us tonight on vocals is Jim Harper." You couldn't tell the applause from those clapping to the beat. They were all moving around out there now to our infectious rhythm.

"Now let's bring on the girls!" Todd punctuated the words by taking the beat up double-time. The rest of us fell into it like German clockworks.

"Ronni Dalton," Todd screamed, "Debbie Gibbs, and Michelle Raintree!"

The girls strutted out. I nearly dropped my guitar when I saw them. They wore the old skintight gold lamé sheath dresses, the six-inch spike heels, the opera-length black gloves. They had done their hair and make-up as though they had just stepped out of 1965. They did choreographed spins and turns up to the mikes. It was poetry. It was wet-dream nostaligia for a middle-aged sex maniac like me—sexy women and rock 'n' roll.

"Stop in the Name of Love," I shouted, off-mike to the band. The crowd was going wild.

We worked the double-time back-beat up to a four count. I ticked it off with my guitar neck. We all stopped at once. The girls struck a pose. Michelle slowly raised an arm, palm outward to the screaming crowd.

"Stop! . . . in the name of love," she cooed, "be-fore you break my heart," . . . and we all hit the upbeat. Ronni, Debbie, Jim and I came in, "Think it oh-oh-ver. Think it oh-oh-ver," we harmonized.

We ran through a dozen old fabulous tunes. Each one was better, tighter than the one before it. My guitar played itself. I was so high by the time we did "Stay," I could barely breathe. I was hyperventilating from the excitement.

Todd spoke into the mike. "I don't know 'bout the rest of you guys, but this old man is bushed."

Protests from the crowd were loud and long.

"One more," I said into my mike. "From the newest male girl singer of our group." I moved away from the mike. "Jim!" I stared straight into those eyes that had seen so much in the swamp halfway 'round the world— seen those things, maybe, instead of me. "For What It's Worth."

He smiled at me and moved closer to the mike. "Thanks, old friend."

We hit the opening chords to the old Buffalo Springfield tune that in 1968-69 echoed off the Washington Monument and the steps of the Berkeley Administration Building. I'm sure it played on the Japanese radios in the whorehouses of Saigon, too. Jim sang lead. I could see the glint of a tear in his eyes as he sang: "Think it's time we stop, children, what's that sound, everybody look what's goin' down . . ."

They wouldn't let us go. I called Michelle and Ronni to my mike. We went into "Help Me, Rhonda."

At my signal, we broke rhythm, slid into the Beatles' "Michelle." It was like group E.S.P. The three of us shared a mike—Ronni, on my left, Michelle on my right, our lips inches apart. Father. Mother and Daughter. I was shocked and ashamed by my burgeoning erection—at the same time, excited to near ecstasy.

When we finished the Beatles ballad, I hit the chords to "Walkin' Blues," Paul Butterfield's version. To my surprise, Jim Harper pulled a harmonica out of his jacket and played it just like the Butterfield record. I responded with some Mike-Bloomfield-style guitar. Ronni and Michelle sang a close harmony lead, like Don and Phil Everly. Debbie grabbed up a cowbell and a drumstick and beat out the hard four-four time. Geoffie/Rashim was all over the bass neck; Paulie was pounding low chords on the piano with his left hand in triplets while his right hand did syncopated eighth note fills. The crowd was transported. They were no longer mundane people in their thirties. Now they were rejuvenated, revitalized. They were people in love with the moment and feeling every pulse-beat of their hearts, their bodies, and the universe in every beat we laid down.

I was suspended in space and time. It was a relived memory, only better; it was the type of perfection that comes in dreams and fantasies, never in reality. The others on that stage felt it too. It seemed the gymnasium of Greenriver High and all the people in it had been picked up and dropped into a dimension where nothing had ever happened.

Then the doors at the far end of the room opened, and Cat stepped through them. She walked up to the stage, hips swaying with her long slow high-heeled strides. She was smiling provocatively. I could smell her heady fragrance, even from the stage—at least, I thought I did.

Somehow I finished the song, took off my guitar and

propped it against the piggyback Marshall amps. I vaulted off the stage.

"Well, folks," Todd said into the mike, "guess that's it." I never heard the protests from the crowd. I was holding Cat's hands, gazing into those lovely China-blue eyes.

"Introduce me to your friends," she said. "All these years, and I've never met them. They must mean a lot to you."

"They do, Cat, but your brother . . ."

"Too many years have been wasted worrying about my brother. Forget him for now."

Her words were like hypnotic suggestion. I immediately pushed thoughts of Nicholas and the decades of fear out of my mind. For the first time in days, I was aware of the thudding of my heart.

"Take me to your friends. Unless you are ashamed of me."

"Never! God, I want you to meet them. Come on." I was ecstatic. The others had grouped at our table. I walked over to them, my lovely, radiant Cat on my arm.

They were laughing and reliving those stage moments when we approached, but they all quieted when they saw us—saw her.

"Everybody . . . I want you to meet Cat—Catherine Charlene St. Charles. She's my . . ."

"Call me Cat," she said to them. "You must be Michelle." She took up Michelle's hand. "I always wanted to meet you." Before Michelle could respond, Cat moved on.

"And you're Paulie Gibbs. And your wife Debbie. Lovely. So happy to meet you at last." They too were speechless.

"Todd Raintree . . . Geoffie and Kamii." She moved around the table, touching them all with the intimacy of a lover, not a new acquaintance—or was that my jealous interpretation?

"And Jim Harper. At the last, you were closest to him, weren't you?" Jim nodded dumbly, struck by her unearthly beauty, or so I thought. "All, all of you are like a second family to my Steven. And of course, you are Rhonda, the daughter he didn't know he had. A shame. You should have been with him all those years. You would have been good for each other. One never knows when it might be too late to make up for lost time."

Somehow Paulie regained his composure, while the rest of them literally sat with gaping mouths.

"Won't you sit with us?" he said.

"I would be honored," Cat responded. The exchange brought the others to life.

"I think Debbie, Ronni and I would like to get out of these get-ups." Michelle laughed nervously. "Too early for Halloween."

"I like the look," Cat said, appraising the three of them with a direct stare a man might employ. "It suits you . . . it suits Steven, too, I think." She laughed her throaty, melodious laugh. I felt chills but I didn't know why.

"I don't think you ought to change," Todd protested. "You all look like celebrities . . . sexy, too."

"You've convinced me." Michelle laughed, sat down and stole nervous glances at Cat.

"Me too," Ronni said, and sat beside her mother.

"Well, this little piggy is all pinched up in the waist by this excuse for a dress. I'm going to the little girls' room," Debbie said decisively. "It's no mystery to me why women finally refused to wear these things with all the underwires, push-ups and push-outs."

"I'd like to . . . powder my nose. Mind if I come along?" Cat asked.

"Not at all," Debbie said, and the two of them left the table.

We all sat down, no one knowing what to say. Least of all me. I had no clue as to how she knew about all of them, even Ronni. I knew I had never mentioned any of them to her. Our conversations had always been selfishly concerned only with talk of us two.

"So . . ." Michelle broke the silence at our table,

silence surrounded by the noise of the party, "that was my rival for you all those years ago? No wonder I lost out. I've never seen a woman that strikingly . . . sexual before in my life."

"She's right," Paulie agreed. "Your friend exudes sensuality like some kind of jungle cat."

"There's definitely something there," Todd mused.

"Something not quite human," Jim added. "I don't mean to offend, Steve. I mean . . ." He struggled for what he meant.

"There's something almost supernatural, supernormal about her," I supplied.

"Yes . . . sort of," Jim said.

"Cosmic," Geoffie/Rashim breathed. Kamii said nothing, but in place of her peaceful smiling face, there was a mask of suspicion, worry—almost fear.

"Are you two contemplating getting together permanently? Marriage?" Paulie asked. One of Todd's bar girls brought a tray of drinks to our table. She said something about them being compliments of the band. Everyone ignored her, but hungrily grasped a drink and downed at least half of it. Cat's presence was unsettling to all of us, but I sensed only Kamii knew why. I certainly was at a loss to explain it.

"Marriage?" I said, half in a stupor of wonder and confusion. I couldn't for the life of me remember why marriage was out of the question. "I'd like to . . ."

"Look at me," Jim Harper said, holding his hands out over the table, palms down. "I'm shakin', just like I used to when the Cong had us pinned down in the night. I have to tell you, Steve . . . yes, she's beautiful, but there's something wrong . . . very wrong."

"She is very evil, I think," Kamii said softly.

"What do you mean?" I was incensed.

"A feeling only. She is not what she appears."

"You better lay off the pharmaceuticals for awhile," I said to her, trying to laugh but failing.

"No, Kamii's right," Jim said. "I haven't felt this odd since . . . since I totaled your brother in Nam."

"What?" I leapt to my feet. "You're sitting there, Jim Harper, and admitting to my face you are responsible for my brother not coming home from Vietnam? Sure, sure, I get it now. How else could you be so positive he was dead, when no one else in the world knew? You sonofabitch, crippled or not, I'm gonna kill . . ."

"Don't you think they've been gone to the ladies room an awfully long time?" Kamii said softly. Only the eerie tone of her words kept me from Jim.

"I was thinkin' the same thing," Paulie said. "Would someone mind checking?"

"I will," Michelle volunteered. When she rose from the table, Kamii did too, and walked along beside her out of the gym.

"About your brother, Steve, you've got to understand," Jim said, sweating visibly as nerves twisted him in his chair. "He was like a demon possessed, and when I saw, when I watched, this strange feeling came over me, too, and I . . . well, I . . . I wanted to watch him die, just like he watched our guys die . . . I got pleasure out of it . . . I came in my pants when I shot him." His voice was queer, quavering and choked in his throat. "I felt the same odd sensations when that woman of yours touched my hand."

I stood there, trembling. Anger at Jim and wanting to avenge my brother's death, yes, but the odd thing was I knew I was trembling with fear. Fear of the woman I loved, the woman who had obsessed my thoughts for most of my life. She was as goreous as ever, as desirable as ever, but at the same time, I had to admit there was something in Jim and Kamii's words that rang true.

"M . . . maybe somebody else ought to go see . . ." I stammered, tilting my head in the direction of the restrooms.

"Maybe us guys ought to go," Todd said, his macho a bit too watered down to bring off the old men-can-do-anything bravado.

"Count me in," Paulie said, swigging down his bloody mary.

"And me, man. I get nervous when Kamii is away." Geoffie/Rashim stood up with Paulie and they walked off together.

Todd thought a minute, then ran to catch them. I sat

down. Jim, Ronni, and I were left sitting at the large round table. The balloons that were part of the center-piece were losing air, nippling at the ends, becoming opaque.

The hired band had started back up, doing Doors music. "When the Music's Over" took on an eerie implication in my mind.

"What do you suppose is going on in there?" Ronni asked, long fingers nervously plucking at the nipples of the balloons.

"God, Steve, I feel awful . . . I mean, there's some-thin' weird happening . . . I grew a sense for danger in Nam. I've got fucking goose bumps all over me."

I felt it too. It didn't take a war in the tropics to train me. It was the Abomination. Something was going on, yes, and I could sense his presence, his hand in whatever it was.

"I'm going," I said. "I have to know."

"No, wait . . ." Ronni reached out to me, but I was gone.

The women's restroom was below the gym, in the front section of the girls' locker room. The lights along the walls of the stairwell were out.

My stomach was grinding against my spine, and my mouth was tasting of brass as I ran my palm down the damp ceramic tile of the stairwell. The door to the restroom was half open. The lights were off in there, too.

They had to have come here, I told myself. The rest of the building was sealed off with floor to ceiling expanding metal gates.

The light switch didn't work. I used my lighter, but it did little to illuminate the large room.

I checked the stalls—all empty. I made my way through the doorway at the far end into the locker room.

A small-wattage light in the towel cage burned feebly near the entrance, leaving large clots of shadow in the far reaches of the room.

I could not call out. I was too afraid of the sound my

voice would make echoing off the tiled walls. I could not speak their names; I could not speak *her* name.

Suddenly a locker door clattered open, and something thudded onto one of the fixed benches and slouched to the floor.

Still holding the lighter aloft, I inched over to the blob of darkness.

The lighter would not stay still in my hand, but I saw enough.

It was Todd—or had been Todd. He was split open as if by a chain saw, from throat to groin, bloody masses of viscera lolling out of his ruined body. Drumsticks were entwined in his intestines. An empty whiskey bottle protruded from his mouth, the bottom end stretching wide his jaw.

My breath came in ragged bursts, my heart thudding blood into my temples. I backed away, inadvertently nudging another locker. It sprang open. I turned in time for Debbie to fall into my arms. The left side of her head, skull and all, was missing. Missing! Torn up photos of her children were stuck into the grey matter of her ruined brain. I dropped her to the floor. Her wide green eyes stared at me accusingly.

The scream wanted out of me, but it would not come.

I went into the showers. God knows what drove me to do so. My lighter flickered, burned my hand, showed me shapes standing along the walls. I knew it had to be them. I was relieved, and at the same time shaking with anger, thinking they could just stand there, knowing Todd and Debbie were dead.

I moved to the first shape, my feet dragging, some part of me knowing it was all wrong. It was Geoffie, standing there. A look of horror distorted his face. His moon glasses were broken, dangling from one ear. There was some kind of white powder smeared all over his face, hands and arms—a little black child wondering what it was like to be white. I shook him, and he fell to the floor. When I knelt to him, I could see the hole in the back of his head where sick grey stuff blobbed to the shower floor. Looking up, I saw the grue dripping from the shower spigot above.

I gagged, stood, and moved to the next shape. Paulie. Head impaled on the next spigot. His gold pen was thrust into his left eye socket.

On the opposite side of the shower room stood Michelle. She, too, was jammed onto a spigot. Her face had been destroyed, the beauty erased as if torn off by sharp fangs. Her breasts had been torn from her body. The plug-end of a microphone cord dangled from her mouth. Looking down, I saw the blood-drenched gold-plated Shure mike hanging from between her thighs.

I could not even vomit, though I could taste the bile as my stomach heaved. My mind reeled. In the far corner lay Kamii. Her legs and arms had been ripped off. Her waist-length hair had been stuffed down her gaping throat. She was in perfect lotus position, only her dismembered arms and legs were interposed.

Yes, the Abomination had been here, had sought to destroy all I had ever loved. My second family, Cat had said, only minutes before. And she was nowhere to be seen.

I rushed back through the carnage, ripping open every locker in search of her.

She wasn't there.

Of course not. The Abomination would want me to watch her destruction.

Then I thought of Jim and Ronni. I had to save them, the last of those I cared for. The last? No, there was still Laurel and my niece . . . .

I had to get Jim and Ronni, then I could get to Laurel.

The band was playing "Sympathy for the Devil" when I got to the gym. Ronni sat alone at the table watching the people dance.

"Jim," I screamed over the music, startled by the terror in my voice. "Where's Jim?"

"Your friend came and got him," she said.

"Cat? You mean Cat?"

"Yeah. Hey, if she was my squeeze, I'd be jealous. She was getting pretty chummy with him, you know?" She giggled.

"Where? Where'd they go?"

"I don't know . . ." She pointed " . . . that way. Toward the back of the stage."

"Stay here!" I commanded and started off. Then I pivoted, grabbed her wrist and yanked her after me.

"Hey! That hurt!"

"Come on! I don't want you out of my sight."

It was dark behind the stage, but some light spilled over the top of the flats and high curtains from the colored spots over the band. Behind the wall of amps, there was only a heavy thud of the bass beats, like the beating heart of some enormous monster.

In the corner by some old wooden risers the high school chorus used for concerts, I saw the glint of the chrome wheels of Jim's chair.

As we neared, I could make out two shapes.

Closer still, and there was Jim in the chair, head rolling as if he were in pain . . . or ecstasy. On her knees before him was Cat, the snowy cloud of her hair moving in a rhythmic dance.

Right next to them, I could make it all out. I could see it all.

Jim's eyes rolled open.

"Steve!" he gasped.

Cat's head stopped moving, then Jim screamed. Cat moved back, and blood gushed from Jim's groin. Ronni and I watched helplessly as Cat's hands, transmuted to claws, reached up and tore open Jim's throat. He was dead in an instant.

Cat stood, her mouth dripping blood, her arms from shoulder to claws scaly, powerful, inhuman transformations. She laughed. Her melodious laugh darkened and became the scraping metal boom of brother's laugh.

The snowy hair fell out in skeins. The trunk of her shapely body ballooned. The face lost the ethereal beauty, mutated until his face smiled out at us. Nicholas!

"You!" I screamed. Ronni was whimpering.

I turned away, dragging her with me, crashing through the curtain, toppling the photo-covered canvas

367

flats on the band. He came after us.

I glanced back as we flew from the stage, tumbling to our hands and knees on the gym floor.

He was fully mutated now, and the six arms made short bloody work of the band. The crowd was in wild, screaming panic.

Ronni was looking back, too. I saw the expression on her face that said she had simply blanked out. Her brain could not accept what it was seeing, so it hid in catatonia.

I had to pick her up and run with her in my arms.

At the doors, I glanced back again. The Abomination was swelling, mutating still more. Arms sprouted from a scaly bulk the size of an elephant. Gaping saw-toothed maws opened on dumb eyeless heads that bulged up from ever-broadening shoulders.

No one was escaping the horrible death. He moved through them all, meeting screaming, struggling people, leaving bloody, unrecognizable chunks of flesh in the wake of his pursuit of Ronni and me.

We were outside. Carrying her, I knew I could not make it to the rear of the parking lot and my rented car. Displayed on the sidewalk was the shiny GTO Paulie was going to give away in the drawing.

I knew Paulie. Had known Paulie. Sure enough, the keys were clipped to the back side of the visor on the driver's side.

The monster engine roared to life, and the GTO thundered away from Greenriver High.

I ran every stop sign and light between the high school and Laurel's house. Ronni sat beside me in Mitzie's gold lamé costume, her teased and sprayed hair only slightly awry, her exaggerated sixties make-up still perfect, but her mouth hung slack, and her eyes reflected the horrors of Bosch's Hell.

There were no lights at Laurel's.

Good, I thought, they've gone away, or maybe sleeping peacefully in their beds.

I crashed in the front door, not bothering with the bell. If all was okay, I'd pay for the fucking door.

All was not okay when I flicked on the living room lights. Freddie sat in his recliner staring at a blank TV screen. Laurel lay on the couch staring at the ceiling. The problem was, their heads had been ripped from their bodies and exchanged, one for the other. Laurel's body lay on the couch, but Freddie's eyes in Freddie's head stared at the ceiling. Laurel's head watched the TV for Freddie's body.

Blood drenched their clothing, the furniture, the K-Mart throw rugs.

"Stevie!" I screamed. A whimper answered from the kitchen. I ran to the sound and flicked on the lights. She was huddled in a corner, a butcher knife held out before her in both hands.

She thrust it at me repeatedly, moaning, her eyes blank as I approached.

I easily avoided the knife, scooped her up in my arms and ran to the idling GTO. I flipped forward the driver's seat and eased her inside. She still had the knife; she would not relinquish it. Ronni stared out the windshield, her expression unchanged.

There was only one place left to go. I would go to the old castle of a house, out in the wild hills north of town. I would find Cat, dead or alive. If she lived, our escape party would be four. If the Abomination had already destroyed her, the three of us—my daughter, second cousin and I—would run as far and as fast as the antique powerhouse of a car would take us.

The night had grown cold, but I drove ninety miles an hour with the windows open. Something about the rushing frigid air kept me going. It did nothing, though, to revive Ronni, nothing to quiet Stephanie's tortured moans.

We were there. I knew time was short. The Abomination would come here first.

I left the two in the car. The front door to the house was ajar, darkness, blacker than the night, spilling out the opening.

My lighter showed me the way to a hurricane lamp on the mantle over the front room fireplace, and with some coaxing, the wick drew kerosene and took flame from my lighter.

Up the oak stairway, through every room I searched —nothing.

I paused perhaps a moment I could not spare to gaze on the room that must have been hers—delicate antique furnishings, immaculately clean. On the vanity, a framed publicity photo of me from my last book tour.

Another room that held my attention was the master bedroom. The bed was enormous, the headboard ornate with hideous forms and unclean symbols. It was his room, his bed. Brown stains of blood covered the bedclothes. On the pillows, strewn about the center of the bed's expanse, was bright crimson blood, so fresh it still dripped down to the sheets and mattress.

I found no access to an attic, though I knew there must be one.

Time was running out. I could feel the Abomination breathing closer, saw his terrible eyes gazing into the open windows of the convertible out on the road that gave no protection to Ronni and Stevie.

The ground floor was empty of life. There was no access to the cellar from within the house.

Outside, to the rear, I found the storm cellar doors I expected.

Wild gusts of nightwind tugged at my clothing trying to warm me of his approach and I discovered the slanting doors weren't latched. They fell back with a clatter that stirred sleeping birds in the nearby enormous pines and oaks.

The hurricane lamp's yellow glow showed me patches of pooled blood on the timeworn wooden treads of the steps leading down.

Tiny rooms catacombed the cellar. They seemed endless, and time ticked away.

An archway opened on the left to the largest cell I had encountered. The lamp blazed brighter as I turned up the wick.

A huge X of timbers dominated the room. Chained with links cutting naked flesh and nailed—nailed!—

at the hands to the rude wood was Cat. Blood dripped from her mouth, from claw slashes on her breasts and stomach and ran in streams from between her legs.

Her head moved a bit. Hooded China-blue eyes tried to focus on me.

"Steven . . ." she breathed, the words a supreme effort. "I . . . tried . . ."

I set the lamp down and began working at the chains, at the nails that pierced her tender milk-white flesh.

I used the same claw hammer that had pounded the nails to remove them. Her arms fell limp to her sides, her feet dangled and the thick chromed chains took her weight, cutting more deeply into her skin.

"God . . ." she moaned, "how he punished me . . ." She twisted feebly away from the pain caused by my trying to free her from the chains.

"They . . . they won't come off," she breathed. "They hold his spell . . ."

At length, all I could do was use the hammer to extract the cleats that held the chains to the timbers. She was right—the chromed chain, all of a piece, solid, no joining link anywhere, encircled her neck, formed an X between her swaying breasts, doubled back around her tiny waist, seemed permanently affixed.

I had no more time, in any event. I swept her up, tried to hold the hurricane lamp away from her thigh and hurried through the cellar maze.

"C . . . can you hold the lamp?" I asked, panting, juggling her and the glass-chimneyed thing clumsily.

"I . . . don't know . . . so weak . . . punished me . . . hour after hour . . . for seeing you . . ."

"Yeah, well, he punished me tonight. Indirectly, as always. He murdered them all . . . every last one . . . all my friends . . . my cousin . . . maybe everyone I've ever known, everyone in Greenriver by now."

"Got to . . . get revenge . . . got to . . . kill . . ." she breathed struggling in my arms.

"No. I want to run more than I want revenge," I said. I kept taking wrong turnings, ending up in cul-de-sac fruit cellars or coal bins. Finally I stumbled on the bottom step to the outside world. I cast the hurricane lamp to the ground, shattering it, letting out purifying fire to destroy the dwelling place of the Abomination, to destroy the chamber of Cat's horror in the cellar, to destroy what was the bed of her horror, her brother's evil obscenity, on the second floor.

"M . . must go to Mother . . ." she moaned as the night air struck us both.

"Why?" I said, using all my concentration to get her to the car.

"Make her tell, make her tell about Father."

"Why?" I asked again, trying to get her into the back seat with Stephanie. Stephanie moaned louder and slashed out with the butcher knife. I backed out with Cat still in my arms, sat her next to Ronni in the front seat and got in myself. Ronni didn't even notice that Cat was slumped against her.

"Only my father can stop this . . . all his fault . . ."

She was right, and I knew it. I could not just run, not anymore. I had let it all go a quarter of a century, sacrificing all those people near and dear to me rather than actively seek some remedy, some nemesis for the Abomination. I had thought giving up Cat would save those relatives and friends he threatened, but of course, his unspoken bargains had been lies. How many others —strangers, people of untold scores, hundreds—had died at his hands over the years? If bowing to my obsession for Cat was the things most important to me in the universe, why then did I turn her over to him? Not only once, but five times throughout my life. What hell had I subjected her to, thinking to protect my friends, my family, myself, only to have friends and family annihilated in the end anyway?

I nosed the long hood of the GTO back toward Greenriver. No, I could not just run. I owed Cat—I owed all of them—more than that.

21

The town was alive with sirens, banshees in the night, all racing to or already congregated at the high school. There were gunshots from that direction, too. At least while the shots were localized there, I knew where the Abomination was.

I careened down the night streets to the little house on Willow by the cemetery.

"I'm better now," Cat said, though her voice was still scant more than a breathy sigh. "I'll come with you. Just . . . just help me a little, please?"

I pulled her slowly, gently out of the car. She had to lean against me, but she could walk a bit now. I put my sport coat over her shoulders. She was still naked. Only her shoulders and back were covered against the chilling night and modesty. Things like temperature and modesty seemed inconsequential concepts in a reality we had long since exited.

I flung open the door. Four people were silhouetted by a crackling fire in the crumbling brick fireplace. I flipped on the overhead living room light. I recognized Susan St. Charles; Delilah, Cat's temptress-beautiful ageless aunt; an older, dissipated Billy St. Charles; and the eldest sister, Jennifer, who was almost nun-like with her severe black dress of little style and drab face without trace of make-up.

They seemed to be waiting. Waiting for us.

"So . . ." It was Delilah who spoke, not budging, not even looking away from the fire to Cat's naked pain. "It has all begun. Now he is free, untethered, out in the open. It is irrevocable now."

"No," Cat breathed, touching a hand to her naked breast, as if to still her racing heart, leaving a stain of blood from her stigmatic hand. "I think . . . he can be stopped . . . and I think all of you know how." She inhaled sharply, wincing with pain as the fire-reflecting chromium chains dug into her. "If you won't use your knowledge to stop him, at least tell us. Tell us finally the whole truth, so that we may try."

"There is no way," Cat's mother sobbed, her once pretty face ruined by the years, wet with tears that would never dry as long as the Abomination she had birthed lived. "Don't you think I would have done it long ago?"

"There's nothing to be done," Jennifer said coldly. "Mother's right. Nicholas wanted Catherine. Only his having her could keep him in check. We all made the decision to send the two of them away to Delilah's, and it worked. It would still be working if you two could only have left it alone."

"Yeah," Billy said, the old pugnacious tone still strong in his voice. "Why did you two have to screw it up?"

"It was never that simple . . . it . . . never . . . worked. None of you can even imagine what I've . . . tell them, dear Aunt Delilah." Cat seemed to be gaining strength, from her developing anger alone.

Delilah turned and looked at Cat's nakedness criss-crossed with the gleaming chains. The hardness left her face and pity replaced it. She made a movement as if to come to Cat, to comfort her. Then, the pity hardened once again to . . . resignation?

"Nicholas has murdered—what?—thousands of people over the years since he left Greenriver. The book you saw, Steve Dalton, was only a compilation of the deaths that made the news."

Cat's mother wept loudly, her face hidden in work-worn hands. Billy lit a cigarette, his expression one of uncaring defiance. Jennifer's prim attitude changed radically. The truth had been hidden from her, apparently, and she resented it.

"Tell them how, Aunt Delilah, how he got his victims." Though her voice was little more than a breathy whisper, venom dripped from Cat's tongue.

Delilah gestured vaguely with her hand, as if trying to belittle what she was about to reveal.

"He made Catherine . . . pick them up."

"No . . . no! Not that simple, not that clean and easy! He made me a whore for his insatiable hungers and desires. He made me get strange men in bars, on street corners, take them to filthy rooms in ruined tenements, take them to him. He made me have sex with them while he watched, hidden. Then he would come out of hiding and force me to look on as he ripped them apart, watch as he ate them." Cat's voice trembled, her whole body shuddering against me as I held her up, the force of the words she spoke draining what little strength she had regained. "Then he would rape me, rape me in the blood on the bed, amid the torn bits and pieces of the bodies . . ." She collapsed against me, her eyelids fluttering as she faded into oblivion.

"For Christsake!" I yelled at them. "For God's sake, you let this be? You all let it happen to her! You are all, all worse monstrosities than Nicholas!" The dream— now I knew the truth of the cryptic dream!

"Oh, God, dear God, oh, dear God!" Cat's mother fell to her knees from the tattered sofa. "Take me! Kill me! Send me straight to Hell!"

Billy covered his eyes, did not move.

Only Jennifer came to us.

"I didn't know. God, I swear I didn't. Let me take her to the bedroom. I'll get her some food . . . soup or something . . ."

I allowed her to take Cat's weight from me and lead her stumbling husk of a body out of the room.

"If any of you have answers, by God I better hear 'em. Now!"

Billy was frozen, his cigarette burning into his fingers. It was as if he had simply ceased to be on this plane of existence. Cat's mother went on praying to a deaf God with words that ran together into nonsense.

Delilah got up from her seat. She moved in close to me. She had not aged a day since before Nicholas's birth. I believe that now. I could believe anything now. She

had to know. She was linked to it so closely. Her brother
. . .

"There is a way. If you can find and destroy Cat's father, my brother, Nicholas's power to mutate at will should cease to be. If not, at least you should be able to destroy him then."

"I don't understand."

"Of course you don't! You are a realist—logical. Your damnable logic has never allowed you to accept any of this as fact, and that's why you've never done anything about it."

Her black eyes glinted with a perverse sort of pleasure. "Well, now you must do something, now that there is wholesale destruction in your little hometown.

"My brother made a pact with . . . whatever power of Evil exists in this universe, call it what you will. He wanted power, unlimited wealth, longevity. He used to share his knowledge of the occult with me, before he bestowed this curse of eternal youth on me. Before I found out he really could do magic and cast spells, I laughed at him, so when he made the pact, I was not involved." She moved closer, touched my hands and I felt an unnatural coldness, the cold of the crypt, that chilled me to the bone.

"He got what he wanted. You and I have covered this ground before. His payment to Evil was the child of Evil—Nicholas. Catherine saw; she was there at his birth. No one was supposed to see, to know, but she saw. A child of two, and she has known since then. And since that terrible night, she has been inextricably intertwined in the fate of the child of Evil. Perhaps, it is only by her hand that Nicholas may be killed."

"No. She tried. That's how she got the way she is . . . the claw marks, the chains, nailed to a cross . . ." I was letting the utter despair wash over me.

"Get hold of yourself. I have told you what I know of how to stop it. Destroy my brother, and all things he has wrought through magic will cease to be with his death."

"There is no alternative. How do I find your brother?"

"You know that. You have known that for some time."

"That's not possible."

"Of course it is. You sought him out once, let him destroy the few people you let yourself get involved with in Haines City."

"Trevor?!"

"Yes. That is the name he chose to live with in Ann Arbor. He used a different name in the years between the birth of Nicholas and when you sought his knowledge in your college years . . ."

"Oh, my God," I moaned.

Jennifer came out of the bedroom to the rear of the house.

"She's coming to herself. I gathered some clothes that will at least cover her. But I can't get those awful chains . . ."

"They bind with a spell as well as with metal links," Delilah said. "As I suspected, much has become clear to Nicholas over the years. His knowledge of the black arts is innate. His mind need only 'remember' them. Those chains were meant to restrict Catherine, to make her unable to battle Nicholas. I'm sure of it."

I told Jennifer to take me to Cat.

The bedroom was tiny, cluttered with cardboard boxes brimming with toys and dolls, detritus of a house once occupied by four children—three children and a monstrosity.

The bedside lamp's shade was draped with a black chiffon scarf, Jennifer's attempt at filtering light from Cat's tortured face.

The pain had softened from that face, which had regained its full radiance of beauty. Cat seemed to be sleeping, her lids closed down gently, her breasts rising and falling with regular breaths. The gouge marks were fading through some miraculous self-healing process I could not begin to divine.

"We don't have anymore time to fuck around," I said. "Where are those clothes you were talking about?"

Jennifer brought them to the bed.

"Sweater and jeans are Cat's from when she was last home. She was what? Fifteen? I know they'll be too small . . . still, nobody else's clothes are going to come as close."

"What about shoes? She will need shoes."

"Catherine wears a five and a half. None of her's are left here at Mom's house. Delilah wears five and a half but all she has with her are those un-Godly spike heels."

"Get 'em. Heels are better than barefoot."

Jennifer complied with my command, returning to the room carrying pointed-toed spiked pumps of black patent leather. At least they had ankle straps. Maybe they wouldn't fall off as we ran from—to?—Nicholas.

Jennifer shook Cat's shoulders gently, and she sat up with a moan, one hand massaging the frown from her forehead.

She swung her legs over the side of the bed with Jennifer's aid and looked down at herself. I thought she might laugh. Her breasts were shoved so tightly together by the material of her old sweater, they bulged like balloons out of the V-neck. When she stood, she noticed how low the jeans hugged her hips. They were so tight, they would not snap. The chrome chain around her waist peeked out between where the short sweater stopped and the too-small jeans began. Cat looked down at the shoes on her feet, and she did laugh.

It wasn't much of a laugh, strained, but I fell in love with her all over again for it.

"I feel as though I ought to be jumping on a Harley behind Peter Fonda," she said. "This outfit is straight from a 1967 cycle flick, isn't it?"

I took her in my arms and kissed her. The life she had led—the life of pain, misery, and degradation—and still she could joke, make fun of herself and our situation. I had to do whatever I could to save her, save us, make it possible for us to share a life free from fear.

"I love you, Steven," she whispered, unwilling as I was to end the embrace, unwilling to again face the horrid reality of Nicholas.

"We must go," I said. Jenny followed us out of the bedroom.

We didn't pause in the living room, though her mother stretched shaking supplicant hands toward us, and her tear-streaked face pleaded mutely for comfort. She wanted some word, some sign of forgiveness, but Cat was single-purposed. She strode to the door and dropped her hand to the knob. Only then did she glance back.

Cat let her eyes fall on each of them in turn: her mother, brother Billy, sister Jennifer, her Aunt Delilah.

"May God, if there is one, damn you all to Hell," she said evenly. "After an eternity there, you might, just might get an idea of what I've lived through, what you all allowed me to live through, because it was easiest for you. I only hope . . ."

Her words were cut short because the front door exploded open, ripping the knob from her hand.

He was there—Abomination, mutated again—long, lean body streamlined and scaled head to foot, built for the speed needed to get us before we could escape.

His hands and feet were webbed claws, good either for pushing wind and space behind as he ran, or for efficient killing. His head was bullet-shaped, cobra-hooded, reptilian. He had a long, thick tail for balance while running, moving in the night with horrible grace.

Coming through the ruined doorway, he reached for Cat, but she nimbly dodged, even his lightning quick grasp, with a dancer's move.

With a like grace and speed I would never have suspected, Delilah crossed the room and struck the Abomination across the face.

"Enough!" was all she said, all she could say, for in the next instant, the Abomination had crushed her larnyx with one of those enormous webbed claws.

I shoved Cat out the door. As we made it to the car, I knew Delilah would not have to worry about the curse of eternal youth any more. Nicholas, the Abomination, had surely killed her.

Stevie was in the back seat, howling, beating the butcher knife's blade against the GTO's side window. The blade would hit the glass, bend sideways and she would strike again, her frightened mind

379

comprehending neither that the monster was no longer outside the car nor that the window stood between her and the night.

Ronni had been shocked back to life by seeing the Abomination in his new mutation. She was screaming, crying and laughing simultaneously in the car's front seat.

I circled the car, holding Cat's elbow, trying to steady her steps as we moved, but she was rock-solid, even in the spindly heels over the uneven ground.

Driver's door open, she dove in, I right behind her.

The power plant roared and I scattered stones twenty feet behind us peeling out.

"They're all dead by now," Cat said cuddling into me and at the same time trying to calm Ronni, like a Commanche with a wild mustang, running her hands over the skittish animal's body, sending calming electricity from one body to the other. It worked. In minutes, Ronni had collapsed against Cat's bosom, her crying becoming manageable sobbing.

Then Cat looked over her shoulder at Stevie, still wild-eyed, still brandishing the knife that had been her only protection when her parents were savaged by Nicholas.

"Give me the knife," Cat said softly, reaching over the seat behind her.

Stevie made an inhuman sound of protest and stabbed Cat's hand. Cat sucked breath sharply, but left her hand hanging over the back of the seat.

"Give it," she repeated, more sharply.

I watched in the rear view mirror as Stevie's eyes followed the dripping of the blood from Cat's hand to the car floor. Slowly she turned the knife end for end and handed it to Cat.

Cat brought the knife into the front seat, and I could see how badly she had been stabbed. The wound was deep, into the miraculously healing flesh where Nicholas had crucified her, but she seemed to be ignoring it.

I handed her my handkerchief. She paid me with a

smile and without a word, wrapping the cloth around her bleeding hand.

By the time we were thirty miles east of Greenriver on our way to Haines City, all three of them were asleep, leaving me and the roaring GTO to battle our way down the night highway alone.

Michigan's Irish Hills at two a.m. can be as lonely and eerie a stretch of road as ever existed. Tiny little towns, scarcely more than wide spots in the road, dot the black night scenery every twenty miles or so all along U.S. 12, but at two a.m., it is as though the people who inhabit them by day have been absorbed into the surrounding woods and fields, reclaimed by the natural elements from which all life is spawned.

I didn't like being alone then. It allowed my mind to settle on certain mental pictures of the past few hours like crows settle on gnarled branches overlooking the carnage of a pitted battleground.

I did not want to think, but I didn't want to awaken any of my traveling companions for a chat, either. I was beyond chatting, just as they were, as we all might be for the rest of our lives. How could anything ever be mundane or normal in the accepted sense again?

The GTO slithered around the switchback curves of the Irish Hills, almost without my aid, the tires occasionally making the sweet poetry of squealing automotive pain. I was playing counting games with the roadside mileage signs versus the odometer figures. I was ready to try anything to keep my mind occupied.

The flapping sound seemed distant at first, like the loose corner of a canvas tarp on a highballing flat bed truck, coming up the highway behind me. It seemed to draw closer and get louder, but there was no engine roar other than the dual four-barrels under the GTO's own hood, sucking air and fuel to fire those eight over-sized pistons.

I checked the rear and side view mirrors. Nothing but black road, white lines and black night.

The sound was louder still, like something big, right behind me—a mammoth truck with a huge piece of loose tarp flap-flapping right behind me. I checked the mirrors again—still no lights, no motor sound.

Then the damned sound, the truck tarp or whatever, was above me! Right above me, and I couldn't see a thing.

I stomped the accelerator to get the hell away from the sound, just as the vinyl and canvas convertible top of the GTO was slashed open by a huge four-clawed talon.

The wind and night screamed in through the gaping hole, and something else, too—the Abomination, in a winged transmutation that gave him the ability of flight.

In the back seat, a foot talon closed on Stevie's thigh and she screamed her pain into the night wind. The other foot clutched the back of the front seat for balance, one hand on the top chrome of the windshield for the same reason.

His right hand claws slashed into the front seat blindly, as his scaly upper torso was still outside the car. He struggled with unfamiliar muscles, trying to fold the enormous wings that the rushing wind sought to bear into flight once again. Maniac screams issued from me as I swerved the car all over the road, trying to dislodge him from his perch, dodging his one free slashing claw at the same time. Cat jabbed up with Stevie's butcher knife until she connected.

He squealed like a slaughtered pig, and she struck again. Blood spattered her face as she drove the long-bladed knife deeply into his obscenely enormous genitals. The right front wheel dropped off the shoulder just then, and when I swung the steering wheel hard to keep us out of the chasm-like ditch, he shifted, slipped, and was gone, his squealing noises fading quickly as we rocketed away.

"Faster," Cat pleaded desperately, wiping at the blood on her face with her handkerchief-wrapped hand. "He won't be incapacitated long. He just mutates until the cells all heal themselves. We may gain only about twenty minutes." She stroked Ronni's face, quieting her terrified sobs, then turned to see how Stevie was. Her thigh was gouged by the Abomination's claws, and blood dribbled slowly down the flesh, pooling in shiny dark spots on the black vinyl seat. She was unconscious, breathing shallowly and irregularly.

"She's not bleeding too badly," Cat reported. "Could have been much worse. I've seen him rip legs right off of bodies with less effort."

The rushing wind fluttered the torn convertible top and teared my eyes. The curves were too radical for the one hundred-plus miles per hour I was pushing the car, but the GTO's tight sport steering helped. Some bestial part of man meant to meld with the machines he makes had taken over, and my muscles steered the car through the black bends of road with a sightless dumb intelligence all their own.

I strained to glance in the tilted rear view mirror and was shocked to see bulging eyes, a mouth twisted with fear, a face familiar and at the same time wildly, insanely alien. I was shocked because the face was mine. Surely, I thought, I must have long since slipped over that invisible boundary into utter madness.

Suddenly we were rounding that last sweeping curve up and around the hill overlooking Haines City, nestled deep in the valley by the river.

Trevor's house was on the river, between Haines City and Ann Arbor. We would be there in ten minutes.

Time enough? Was the Abomination healed, changed? Was he even now catching up, seconds away from again crashing into the open roof of our car?

I hadn't been in Haines City for over sixteen years. I could not remember the one-way streets, the parkways, the boulevards. The area had exploded into the eighties with urban growth like creeper vine on a barren hillside.

Time ticked by. I was lost. The whereabouts of Trevor's house a mystery, the Abomination surely seconds away from breathing down our necks.

"We've been by here before," Cat said, the tension in her voice making it strained, like she was speaking through clenched teeth.

"I know. I'm fucking lost, okay?" I ripped at her with
383

the words, wanting to hurt her, but was immediately ashamed. Her silence, as she petted the teased hair on Ronni's head pressed needfully to Cat's bosom, made my shame all the greater.

"It's been sixteen years . . . I don't remember. I swear they've changed the direction on all these God-damned one-ways."

"So break the law," she said softly. "I can't believe you're worried about going the wrong way on a one-way street at a time like this."

The quiet even quality of her voice was maddening. Of course she was right. I spun the wheel hard and floored the GTO. It did a screaming one-eighty and we were headed for the river, doing seventy the wrong way on a narrow two-lane one-way street.

I stopped the car. The September night wind was walking through the leaves on the street. Only the oaks had bronzed, and their leaves rattled a death call to the still green leaves of the other trees.

Trevor's house, the sprawling spider-like modernistic monstrosity on the hill, waited and watched.

Ronni roused herself from Cat's motherly embrace. She looked around, eyes blinking.

"Ronni, are you okay?" I asked.

She didn't answer at first. She looked at Cat's blood-spattered face with something between wonder and fear in her eyes.

"I . . . guess so," she said.

"She's not all right. She's in shock," Cat said.

"I know, I know. Listen, Ronni, can you drive a four speed?"

"Huh?"

"A four speed, a stick shift . . . can you handle it?"

"Yeah." Finally she stopped staring into Cat's face and looked across her to me.

"The girl in back . . . her name is Stevie. She's my cousin's daughter. I don't know what relation that makes her to you, but it's blood, whatever it is, so take care of her. We're going into that house up there, Cat and I, and you're gonna drive this car the hell out of here."

"N-no," she stammered. "That thing . . . that thing is out there." Her eyes darted all around, trying to pierce the night.

"It's after us now, dear," Cat whispered.

"Right," I said. "So do as I say and drive to the nearest police station."

"No," Cat interrupted. "A church. Any church. It doesn't matter what kind. Just get there, go inside and wait. When this is all over, we will find you." With those words, she motioned me out of the car and slid out after me. Ronni struggled to get behind the wheel in her tight dress. She paused there, a long moment, looking at us through the windshield. Then she started the engine with a roar and gave us a faltering humorless smile that showed me she was, as Cat had said, in deep shock. She let out the clutch and the tires yipped.

She was gone. Stevie was gone. Cat and I stood alone in the wind whispering darkness.

I pulled her into my arms, squeezing her tightly against me. I could feel the hard bulge of the Abomination's chains of bondage beneath her clothing. I kissed her. I knew full well it might be our last kiss.

"Front door?" I said, as cavalier as I could manage.

"May as well." She smiled, hard grim lines at the corners of her mouth. "Kiss me again," she breathed, her tongue touching briefly her full upper lip. Her long-lashed lids slid slowly over her eyes as our mouths joined in a fevered passion born of many kinds of desperation.

I thought for an instant I heard a flapping sound hidden somewhere beneath the sound of the wind in the leaves.

"Come on," I said, and took her by the hand, starting up the long lighted steps to the spider's mouth. Breaking off that embrace was the hardest thing I ever had to do. I wanted nothing more than to spend an eternity exploring the intimacies of her body.

The double red doors were unlocked. I recalled my initial impression of them, sixteen years previously when I stood in the same spot with Donna Siegal. A mouth—a huge spider's mouth—ready to swallow its insignificant prey.

The big doors were unlocked. There was no impediment, yet we stood there, hesitating. In the dead hours of the morning in a big city, the doors were unlocked. I wondered if we were perhaps expected. I checked Cat's face for any expression—there was none. She wiped at the spatters of her brother's drying blood on her face, using the electric blue sleeve of her too-small sweater.

I pushed the door and it swung in effortlessly.

We searched the opulent rooms, one level to the next, finding indications of recent occupancy but no living thing.

I remembered the hidden chamber, down all those steps, the ceremonial room buried deep in the hillside somewhere. I had been drugged all those years ago before the descent, and too mentally unsettled on the return to the upper levels to remember details.

"Off the master bedroom . . . a passage to rooms below," I muttered uncertainly.

Cat nodded. She found the hidden lever that sprung the mirrored section of the wall out, revealing the narrow winding wooden steps. She led the way in without hesitation, as if resigned to our fate—or perhaps, after her life with Nicholas, welcome its finality.

The only thing I could be sure of was that down was the right direction. After an interminable descent on those narrow steps, we finally reached their termination.

Dark halls spidered off in every direction. Tiny bulbs the size of candle flames but casting nowhere near the light were spaced high on the walls about every thirty feet. There was no indication of which way to go.

"You remember nothing from the last time you were here?" Cat whispered, reading my thoughts and confusion.

'No," I said helplessly. I felt stupid, angry at myself for not remembering, and angry at her for reminding me I didn't remember.

"Then I guess it's trial and error. I only hope my brother gives us enough time."

She started off in one direction, when a sound came from the hall directly opposite. It wasn't much of a sound—small, nothing to particularly recommend it for notice, other than there were absolutely no other sounds to be heard in these subterranean hallways.

We glanced at each other, nodded our agreement, and reversed our direction, toward the source of the noise rather than away from it.

Whenever we would pause, wondering silently if we could be going right, the wee small noise, indescribable, unidentifiable, would come again, a little farther down the hall, past the last light, around the next turn.

The immensity of the catacombing itself became awe-inspiring after awhile. Who had done all this under-bround work? Had Trevor commissioned it? Who else knew this giant and farm existed? Or, like the Pharaohs who built the great pyramids, had Trevor silenced all the workers permanently?

To our dismay, the hall rounded a corner, and more steps lay before us. They were old, ancient looking stone, covered with slippery moss and lichen.

I had noticed sometime before that the lights were fewer, and the ones we did pass showed a heavy sweat of condensation on the walls. I assumed we were traveling under the river. Now these steps would lead us still further into the earth.

The stairs were not lit at all and the stairwell itself was no longer finished wallboard, but rather buttressed and timber-supported native earth and rock. There were still signs that the tunneling was man-made, not naturally occurring, but it had been done many years ago . . . perhaps centuries.

What builders? Indians? Some lunatic band of lost Vikings who had managed to portage Niagara Falls, navigate Lake Erie and find their way up the sketchy waterways to Haines City's primordial hills? And if so, why would they dig so deeply into the earth? How would they accomplish it? It was ludicrous. But so were any alternative explanations that might include magic.

With loathing, we felt our way down through the

darkness, our hands brushing bloated unseen vegetable and fungal matter, sliding through oozing mud, slipping over cold brutal slabs of rock.

I worried about Cat, descending the wide slippery steps in her heels, but I was the one who lost footing, sliding past her, almost taking her with me as I flew feet first down the slimy stones.

The initial fall knocked my wind out, so I could not release the scream of pain, dread and revulsion welling up in my throat. Cat did it for me. There was nothing else to be done. She could not stop my descent, nor could I. There was nothing to grab onto and the ancient stone slabs angled down in the front from the wear of time. But what footsteps had worn them so, I wondered ridiculously to myself as I tobogganed ever downward. Strange how sometimes the human mind simply shuts out things it doesn't wish to acknowledge, even imminent danger like the injury I would receive when I finally struck bottom. Maybe not so strange. I seemed to have a knack for it. I had been shutting unpleasantness out of my mind for years, ever since I had been eleven and first seen Nicholas transmute to that scaled, hairy serpentine-anthropoid thing and squirm up the bank of the river at the cemetery.

My musing ceased as I hit bottom. The speed I had built was terminated immediately as my body splashed into about three feet of water. I silently praised the Fates—if the water had been stone, my chin would have been permanently skewered by my fragmented hip bones.

I thrashed about in the water until I could stand up. The putrid stench of boggy, long-standing water was all around me. I could hear the scrape and clatter of Cat's heels on the stone steps far above me. I could also hear the sound we had been following, loud enough now to be definable, if not yet identifiable. It was constant now, a sound somewhere between a high chittering of many rodents and the low chuckle of a human being's lascivious mirth. No power in heaven or earth could guess what brand of creatures existed down here—

except possibly Trevor, their keeper or creator. If a cosmology could allow a creature like the Abomination, any and all configurations were possible also.

Cat's footsteps came closer. I peered into the inky blackness but could see nothing.

Eventually the steps were very near. I could hear her breathing, a measured rhythmic sound that spoke of a kind of tense control.

"Steven?" Her whisper echoed like a cannon shot. It told me that the size of the chamber we occupied was enormous.

"Here, Cat," I whispered back. I heard her sharp intake of breath. She had not expected a response. Next I heard the ripple of water as she descended the last few steps and moved to my side. Her hands groped tentatively up my body.

"Are you all right?"

"Wet," I said, "and bruised up pretty good, but nothing broken. What now?"

"Damned if I know," she breathed.

"And damned if you don't," I said.

"I guess we could go on following the sound," she said.

At first I thought she was crazy. The chittering-chuckle surrounded us. But then I listened more closely. Those years of loud guitar playing had taken their toll of my hearing. Her more sensitive ears probably did discern a direction where mine could not.

"You lead," I said. "There may be danger." I was becoming giddy from the tension.

She managed a soft chuckle at my feeble joke. God knows how. Perhaps the strain was warping her mind, too.

Taking my hand, she started off, wading through the brackish water obliquely from the foot of the steps.

The cavern floor beneath the water was smooth, without lumps, bumps or holes, and slime-slippery like the steps. As I bumbled along, she moved with sure, solid steps.

I have no idea how long we walked. We slogged

through the water like dogfaced soldiers in some war-ripped swamp, like Jim Harper must have in Nam. Before the Abomination visited him and made him kill my brother, I thought.

The chittering-chuckle had become directional, even to my ears, and louder. We also seemed to be moving slightly uphill. The water level dropped gradually.

Soon we were out of the water, fighting to maintain footing on the slippery uphill incline.

"I think I see a light ahead," Cat's voice boomed in my ears, though she had whispered. Evidently, her eyes were more sensitive than mine, too.

I had to relinquish the comfort of her hand and drop to a four-legged stance to make forward progress on the slope. I sensed she still moved on, tilted precariously forward on her heels.

Then I could see the light ahead, hardly more than a pitiful relenting of the oppressive darkness at first. It was like awakening in a dark room, opening unwilling eyes that refused to distinguish subtle differences in light and shadow. Slowly, the further we moved up the slope, the light grew. I could make out Cat a few feet before me—her outline at least. I could see no walls or ceiling.

The incline lessened and I could stand again. Slimy moss adhered to my hands that would not wipe off on my clinging wet pants. The light grew and I could see the side terminations of where we walked, about thirty yards, side to side, and got a sense of a big rounded tube. It was as if we moved through a huge pipeline made of native rock.

The pipeline bent, and when we rounded the curve, the light was suddenly intense. The tube opened into a room of phenomenal proportions. I thought of Mammoth Caves, only there were no stalagtites. The walls, ceiling and floor were smooth, as if the rock had been eroded by the secreted acid from some hellish big slug.

The light came from perhaps a million candles, fat and guttering, affixed to the floor and walls by a method I could not discern. I wondered briefly how long it would take a single person to light each of these candles to make them all burn simultaneously. The first would have been long burnt out before the last ones were lit.

My eyes scanned the room as we moved forward. I could make out that the floor was not flat, but had an indent or gully down its center, where we walked, and a trickle of water ran down it, back toward the huge brackish lake we had waded through.

Cat stopped abruptly before me, and I almost ran into her as I studied the gully's width and the trickle of water. I noticed as I stopped behind her that the chittering-chuckle noise that had led us to this place was no longer evident. Only the sound of our breathing and a faint dripping of water falling in a thin stream from some height remained audible.

"What?" I whispered to her, laying my hands on her shoulders. I could feel the tension in her muscles. "What is it?"

Then I looked to where she looked.

Trevor. At the far side of the room, at the end of the gully, he was seated on a throne-like iron chair sculpted with grotesque and gargoyles accompanied by the same obscene ruins that had been on the headboard of the bed of Nicholas.

A trickle of water, coming from an unseeable source in the wall above and behind him, splattered on the floor, making the little stream appear from under his chair, run between his straddling legs, down the gully and into the lake far behind us.

He looked younger, not twenty years older, than the last time I saw him. The beard and glasses were gone, but the white hair, as snowy white as Cat's now, was thick on his head, not thinning as it should have been on a man his age—but then, I had no idea how old he should be. Delilah had spoken of him as an old man when first he met Susan Sorrel, before he made her Susan St. Charles.

He seemed to be sitting there on his throne in his subterranean palace pondering some great thought. But he did not fit the part. He was wearing expensive brushed pigskin bucks that were being ruined by the trickling water, knife-creased flannel slacks, and an Izod shirt with the little alligator on the left breast. I almost laughed at the ludicrous zaniness of it all. Here sat my life-long nemesis—perhaps the man who had broght Evil personified to life to destroy the world—a preppie warlock.

"Who are you?" he grunted, his mouth barely moving.

"What?" I said, my wit spurred by seeing him dressed as if he were waiting to be picked up for a golf date at an exclusive country club. "No prescience? No e.s.p.?"

"What the fuck do you want?" he grunted again. "How did you get here?"

"A long, long trip. It's taken my entire life," Cat breathed. For the first time it struck me that the chrome chain Nicholas had put upon her must be hurting her neck, choking off her air enough to affect her voice.

"What the fuck are you talking about?"

My arm went around her waist, and we moved to within ten feet of where he sat.

"Meet your third child, Trevor . . . or whatever your name is. I doubt it's St. Charles or Trevor. Your dear departed sister Delilah favored St. Charles, but that doesn't mean anything. I'm not convinced she wasn't in on all this from day one. Now that she's dead, it hardly matters. The point is, this is Catherine Charlene. The last time you saw her, she was about two, I think."

"Hmmmph. I remember," he growled sourly, like a senile grandparent being reintroduced to the family's young black sheep. "The failure."

"Failure?" I said. "Oh, yes. Too human, right? Not like the youngest. Not like the payback child, Nicholas, the one who bought you what you wanted."

Mixed emotions crossed his face at the mention of Nicholas—pride mixed with fear, I thought—though he tried to show nothing to us.

"Who are you that you bring my failure back to haunt me?"

I stepped even closer, leaving Cat behind me.

"You mean to say you really don't know me? I thought everyone in this little drama knew me. Apparently, you lost your copy of the script sometime over the last twenty-seven years. I'm Steve Dalton, the idiot in the play, the one written in to bumble through life, enduring the horrors and misfortunes your family group laid out for me, lusting after this woman here," I gestured with an angry thumb toward Cat, "never knowing what to do or what to fear, only to find out after act four that I've been reading from a different script than everyone else. You know me, old man, I'm the Inspector Clouseau in your personal nightmare vision of reality."

"Dalton . . ." he mused. "Just a name. Means nothing to me."

"Oh, come on." I was enraged, seeing him sitting there, Mr. Suburbia in a pre-Inquisition throne in an impossible cavern in the bowels of the earth below a Michigan college town. "There's something really wrong here. Play your part, damn you! This isn't even as good as a B drive-in movie. I have expectations! I've put up with this weird shit from you and your spawn all my life! I have rights here! Where's the drama? Where's the brimstone and fire and demons?"

He stood up. His bulk, which twenty years ago had cowed me, appeared now to be only the fat of an overindulgent man.

"I don't know what the fuck you're on about, young man, but I'd appreciate it if you'd leave me the hell alone. Get out of here. I'm supposed to be meditating."

"What?" I jerked toward him, my fists balled, then checked myself. This would be easy. "No. We won't leave. We're here to kill you."

There was genuine surprise in his eyes.

"Whatever for?"

"Jesus! Jesus Christ!" I cried. "This is unbelievable! You made a pact with the forces of Evil. For money, power, whatever. Your son Nicholas was payment for that pact. He belongs to them. The only way to end his reign of terror on the world is to kill you, thereby ending the pact. Am I right? Man, I guess you didn't

393

read the script at all." I knew I was talking crazily. Hell, this was all crazy.

"Who told you all that?"

"Who . . . ?" I didn't know what to say. He acted like it was all news to him. "Why, your sister, that's who. Your wife. Your son, Nicholas. Everybody. It's what I've been able to piece together over the thirty-eight years of torment I call my life."

"I don't have a sister." And the way he said it, I believed him. I don't know why, but I did. Cat didn't. She had been standing behind me mute, but when he said that, she came up quickly and dug her nails into my arm.

"Don't listen, Steven. It's all a trick! Just do it, get it over! Kill the bastard," she hissed.

"Cat, I can't kill him . . . shit, what if he's just some harmless old kook . . ."

"No! A trick! Do it!" she fairly screamed.

"Cat . . . no . . . I . . ."

Then I heard it. Far off, a thrashing, splashing uproar echoing up the pipeline from the underground lake.

"It's him!" she screamed at me, terror in her eyes, turning to face the sound, teeth clenched, long painted fingernails extended in defensive posture, like tiger claws. "Do it! Kill him! There's no time left! I . . . I'll try to mutate . . ."

I watched her body tremble with the mental and physical effort, but nothing was happening. I turned back to Trevor.

"Listen . . ."

"No," he said, fear glinting in his eyes with the flames from the million candles. "You listen! I'm just an old man." He tried to laugh, but it sounded like a frog croak. "An old kook. Like you said. I don't know her, I don't know you, I don't know anything about any of this . . ."

"No, you called her 'the failure' . . ."

"I was thinking of someone, something else. Please, son! I'm just a crazy old man, I don't want to die."

"Neither do I." The liquid thrashing sound had

stopped. Now there was a slap-thud of heavy naked feet resounding up to us through the pipeline. Nicholas was closer. "Somebody here is a hellish good actor," I said, moving for him.

"It's her, then. Did you ever think of that? Think, son, think! Before you kill me—could it be? Could it be she who is lying? Has been lying to you all these years?"

I looked at her. She was still trying to change, to become some un-Godly creature that might be able to battle her brother, to save my life—or was she? There was a horrible shine of hate in her eyes, but no fear. Could it be? She was like him, not human—or at least, not fully human. Did she want to fight him, want him dead only so she might take his place?

And what of this pathetic old man? How could he be what Delilah and everyone had made him out to be— some cruel, calculating, powerful warlock who made a pact with . . .

He was here. Upon us. The candles glistened reflected diamonds on his wet, slime-coated scales. Still long and lean, mutated for low wind resistance and speed, he began to change for power. Muscles bulged, tripling the depth of his chest, arms lengthened and burgeoned with sinews. Razored claws switchbladed out of sausage-sized powerful fingers. His terrible jaw lengthened, widened, drooled a thick green saliva as huge fangs, twisted tusks thrust up out of the flesh of his mouth. A bony ridge mushroomed up over his slitted yellow eyes to protect them during battle, and he came closer.

"For Christsake, for Jesus Christ sake," Cat shrilled, "kill that fucking bastard! I can't mutate . . . the chains . . . the chains won't let me mutate! Kill the mother-fucking bastard!'"

I looked at her and looked at the Abomination, slowly advancing, savoring the final moment. I looked at the old man I had known as Trevor, trembling. He was as frightened by Nicholas as I was. For a brief instant, all I wanted to do was run. Let the three of them sort it out. I didn't know who to believe, what to think, what to do. But then I never had.

With a fury aimed as much at myself and my wasted, useless, indecisive life as at any power of Evil or fear of death, I struck out. Cat swiveled her head at me, fear instead of anger in her eyes as the blow from my club-like fist landed.

Trevor crumpled, a paper-maché doll, and the Abomination howled as if I had struck him. Then he charged forward. Cat shrieked terror, stretched her arms out and met him. They grappled, in a twisting wild dance of death that I knew wouldn't last long.

I bent over Trevor and smashed his face again with my fist.

The Abomination squealed and dropped Cat. He grabbed at his face, as if my blow had struck him instead of Trevor. Then he dropped his hands from his face, let out a thunderous roar and jumped on her prone form.

My fist slammed into Trevor's face once again. I picked up his head in my hands and bashed it against the rock floor over and over.

"Oh, ye sons and daughters of Satan," he muttered, blood dripping from his lips. "Oh, ye generation of . . . of . . . vipers . . ."

Blood spattered on the rocks from the back of his head, and shot out at me from his nose and mouth. His eyes rolled crazily, but I didn't stop slamming his head on the floor.

"Ye children of the dark . . . ye blas-phe-mers . . ." he wheezed.

The sounds of struggle behind me ceased, but I kept on until I became aware that the only sound other than the trickle of the falling water was the hollow thunk of Trevor's head on the rock floor as I kept on killing him, like a mindless machine.

I stopped. I let his head down slowly. The horror of what I was doing oozed over me like oily slime. I wanted to vomit. I did vomit, and when I looked again more closely at his features, I knew him, then. Even through the ravages of time, I knew him.

I sensed movement beside me. It was Cat, standing

there, looking down. I couldn't look at her, I could only stare at the bloody face between my hands. I sat back, still straddling him. I drew back my hands. I didn't know what to do with them, now that they had killed a living thing.

Trevor's blood-covered eyelids slid back, showing me glazed eyes. His lips parted, and a wheeze of voice sounded through a fresh gout of blood.

"You . . . fool . . . won't end . . . her! Still . . . her . . ."

I watched it happen—as if it were in slow-motion. Cat's foot rose in the air, came down, the stiletto heel of the black gleaming shoe coming down, down, unerringly down, into his left eye, popping the eyeball aside, plunging down, ever down, through the socket and into his brain.

Trevor . . . St. Charles . . . was dead. But most of me was dead at that moment, too.

She got me out of there. I gazed briefly at Nicholas— a pool of pulpy protoplasm on the floor. The trickling, cleansing stream of water lapped at the mass that had been the horror of my life, of hers, of the lives of all the people ever close to me.

Somehow, she found the church where Ronni and Stevie had sought sanctuary. She drove the GTO away from Haines City, away from Michigan, away, away, away.

Epilogue

The old man was right. It wasn't over. It would never be over. I could write down explanations about the underground chambers below his house, how he found them, who made them, what they were used for in the dark past and what will be their use in the future. I could tell of the creatures, still down there, that make the chittering chuckling noise, the billions of them there, below the river. I know all those things now, after months of arcane research, but the knowledge is useless. No other human being would ever believe.

News reports called the carnage in Greenriver the result of some freak atmospheric condition that spawned a killer tornado in September. There are few enough Greenriver residents left to refute it. I know better; Cat, Ronni and Stevie know better; but no other living human does.

The old man was right. It will never be over. It lives in our minds. My agent dropped me, and my publisher dropped me. They say my fiction has become too weird, too steeped in the occult. I couldn't tell them this was not fiction. This was autobiography.

We live in San Francisco now. I used most of my savings to buy us a home in the hills. I also tracked down Jim's bookstore and bought it from his estate. It brings in very little money, but running it occupies my time and mind.

Stevie is finishing high school in the California public school system. She walks with a slight limp. Ronni got her G.E.D. and is going to college at Berkeley. She's studying psychology. Maybe she will give discount rates to family. I hope so. I'd try anything. Because the nightmares are still with me.

Cat dances in one of the less sleazy nightclubs in the Tenderloin district. I don't want to know what goes on behind those gaudily neoned doors. The money she makes keeps us alive. I can't make a living writing anymore, and the bookstore, as I have indicated, barely breaks even.

We are a family unit, the four of us, but the scars run deep, too deep to ever be eradicated. Because of what we know, what we fear, we are different, we are outcastes. It is good that we have each other, for we have no one else in this world.

But the old man was right. Or should I say the Reverend Stoney Miles was right. What I saw in those features, in those last seconds before Cat's stiletto heel thrust into his skull and ended her father's life, was the recognition of an aged but nonetheless identifiable Reverend Stoney Miles. He and B.F. Trevor were indeed the same man, and in both guises, he had warned me of the Abomination. As St. Charles, he found the vessel for the birth of Nicholas. Neither he nor Nicholas ever really understood the role the Abomination was meant to play. Perhaps that is something unknowable to mankind.

Reverend Stoney Miles, I believe, came to be as a reaction to the enormity of St. Charles's crime against humankind. He sought a cleansing of his spirit through evangelism. He spoke out against the Abomination—he meant Nicholas, Cat, Delilah, himself. He could 'see' the future. He probably carried with him in death and knowledge of what Cat is now.

When he chose to become Trevor, he was the evangelist dispirited. He sought to regain favor with the dark force of Evil—drugs, ceremonies, blood sacrifice, the warping of minds to his will and to the will of Evil.

Who was he really? He was all three men—St. Charles, Trevor, the Reverend Stoney Miles. In the end, he was just another man, abandoned by his God. Or Gods. Not a warlock, not even a charlatan magician. Only a man, blessed or cursed with a modicum of psychic power, obsessed with the idea of Evil.

And what of my Cat? What is she, in the final analysis?

She has always been a fantasy woman—never real. She is more the idealized image, the whore-goddess of ancient Babylonion, the Ishtar, the Venus, the Isis, the Mary Magdalene of the twentieth century.

Nicholas used her as lure for his feedings, his damnings of all those countless souls over the years; he used her undeniable sexual attraction. The male victims of Nicholas could not resist her and were oblivious to the danger, her voluptuous charms intoxicating them.

I, too, was drawn in. What cosmic plan linked us, I cannot say. I know only of my obsession, and the suffering that obsession has caused my friends, family, the entire town of Greenriver.

She is my life, my reason for life, and we know our own brand of sad joy. There is beauty in the sky and the sea . . . and the China-blue eyes of Cat, my Cat. We know sad joy and painful comfort in each other arms. But I also know fear. Fear in the night that she, she is . . .

When she comes to me, naked, sensually beautiful, making love to me each night, making me forget, forget in my ecstasy, I believe that all is wonderfully perfect, that . . .

Is she evil? Is she, under the aching beauty that produces lust as a bee does honey, something other than what I have assumed she was all these years? If the chains that to this day bind her are broken, is she Nicholas reborn, the child of Evil's unknown purpose? I think, I pray, the answer is no. I don't know to what God or Gods I pray, but I do pray.

I believe she has the ability to be whatever she choses, just as Nicholas did. Only the chains he placed upon her —knowing finally the truth that she, like him, was a creature of some alien plane of existence—only the chains keep her in check.

And yet, and yet, if the chains should break . . .

Sometimes, in the dark pit of night's belly, I think if I can just make my hands close around her throat, her lovely throat . . . if I can only . . .

I've almost made it, several times, but her lips smile, her lids slide back revealing the eyes, the yellow-slitted goat eyes that only I have seen, and she makes me forget all over again, as she gives the ecstasy that shackles me to my obsession for her love.

It will never be over. If she ever shed those chains . . .

Evil exists in the world, and things supernatural do happen.